MW01088274

FORCE OF CHAOS

DIANA MA

Amulet Books
New York

PUBLISHER'S NOTE: This is a work of fiction. Names, characters, places, and incidents are either the product of the author's imagination or used fictitiously, and any resemblance to actual persons, living or dead, business establishments, events, or locales is entirely coincidental.

Cataloging-in-Publication Data has been applied for and may be obtained from the Library of Congress.

ISBN 978-1-4197-5776-1
eISBN 978-1-64700-452-1

™ & ©2025 SCG Power Rangers LLC and Hasbro.
Power Rangers and all related logos, characters, names, and distinctive likenesses thereof are the exclusive property of SCG Power Rangers LLC. All Rights Reserved.
Used Under Authorization.

Text by Diana Ma
Book design by Becky James and Brann Garvey

Published in 2025 by Amulet Books, an imprint of ABRAMS. All rights reserved. No portion of this book may be reproduced, stored in a retrieval system, or transmitted in any form or by any means, mechanical, electronic, photocopying, recording, or otherwise, without written permission from the publisher.

Printed and bound in the United States

10 9 8 7 6 5 4 3 2 1

Amulet Books® is a registered trademark of Harry N. Abrams, Inc.

ABRAMS The Art of Books
195 Broadway, New York, NY 10007
abramsbooks.com

In memory of Thuy Trang, the original Mighty Morphin Yellow Ranger.
Thank you for being the superhero so many of us needed.

CHAPTER ONE

There is no worse hell than a group project.

Mr. Todd has just announced that our big assignment for junior year History will be a group assignment. I squirm at my desk as twenty pairs of eyes immediately swivel over to me. Hot embarrassment rushes to my face. If alien visitors were observing this scene, they'd think I was popular.

They would be wrong.

This is exactly why I hate group projects. Everyone wants to work with me because they know I'll do the whole thing and won't make them feel bad about it. A hard kernel of anger forms in my stomach, but I ignore it. I've had lots of practice stifling any sign that I might not be as spineless as I seem.

Aimee, one of the school's *actual* popular girls, turns to me and whispers, "Let's be partners."

I resist the urge to ask her if she even knows what time period or region we're studying or my last name or anything at all about me except for the fact that I'll get her an easy A. She probably doesn't. "Sure." Irritation twists in my stomach, but I keep my voice calm. "So, what do you—"

"Whatever you decide is fine!" she trills and whips around so fast that her blond ponytail almost hits me in the face. "Hey Jason," she says to the football captain in the seat in front of her, "I can't wait to see you play in the Homecoming game."

Jason keeps his eyes on Mr. Todd and gives no indication that he heard Aimee. To his credit, Jason takes his classes pretty seriously even though he's practically guaranteed to get into college on a football scholarship.

"Since we've been studying the Bronze Age, your project is a presentation on that time period," Mr. Todd is saying, completely oblivious to the whispered chatter in the class, "but you will need to narrow it down to a specific region. You'll be working in groups of two or three, and I expect your final project to reflect the combined efforts of your group."

Not much chance of that if Aimee is working with me.

Aimee has stopped trying to get Jason's attention for now, but I'm sure she hasn't given up for good. If she spends half as much time on our project as she does in her efforts to win him over, we'll be golden. But I know better.

I sigh inwardly. If our yearbook had a category for "Most Likely to Let You Borrow Stuff and Never Ask for It Back," then I'd be a shoo-in. Do I love that? No, of course not. Everyone thinking I'm a doormat sucks, but it definitely beats being voted "Most Likely to Punch a Kid for Stealing Lunch Money." Yes, that's very specific, and yes, I totally did that, but it was back in kindergarten, and no one remembers that anyway—no one except Zack, that is.

And speaking of my former best friend . . . Zack walks into our first period History class like he doesn't have a care in the world. He was *actually* voted "Most Likely to Get Along with Everyone" *and* "Best Sense of Humor." But if the other kids really knew him, they would have voted him "Most Likely to Hide What He's Really Feeling." A pang hits my heart. I might be the only one who knows about his mom's cancer diagnosis when we were in fifth grade.

"Zoe, Kyle, Sid, what's up?" Zack fist-bumps a few kids on his way in. He has a smile for everyone, including me. "Hey, Trini." I might as well be anyone—certainly not the girl who grew up next door to him and played dress-up with Nai Nai's chest of old clothes so often that she used to say Zack was her grandkid too.

Mr. Todd is frowning. "Zack, if you're done making your entrance, please take a seat. And I'm going to have to mark you as tardy."

"Sorry, Mr. Todd." Zack takes the empty seat next to me. "It won't happen again."

"Okay." His voice softens. Everyone likes Zack, even the teachers. "Just make sure you're on time from now on. It's not like you to be late."

Mr. Todd is right. That *is* unlike Zack. I take a closer look and can just make out dark circles under his eyes. My stomach knots in worry. The last I heard, his mother was in remission from cancer. Has anything changed?

No. I tell myself that I'd know if something happened. We're not best friends anymore, but we *are* next-door neighbors, and our parents still talk.

Mr. Todd gestures to me. "We're just forming groups for a presentation on the Bronze Age. You can work with Trini."

Um . . . *what?* A weird panic rises in my chest. Zack and I used to do group projects together all the time in elementary school, but that was before he made a bunch of new friends in seventh grade and suddenly had no time for me.

Okay, that's not fair. I was making new friends too—well, *one* friend, actually. Billy. But I wouldn't have traded Billy for all of Zack's friends with their too-cool attitudes and hipster pop culture references. They never seemed to understand what funny, outgoing

Zack was doing with me—a shy girl who hardly ever spoke up. At the time, it just seemed easier to let my friendship with him die a natural death.

The rest of the class starts forming groups, and Zack turns to me with a sparkle in his eyes. "The Bronze Age, huh? We can definitely have some fun with that."

So he's going to joke around with me like we're still close? *Calm down, Trini.* It's not like Zack did anything wrong. But I hate that we stopped being friends—not that I ever told him that. And I'm not about to tell him now. "You and I might have radically different ideas about what the Bronze Age is," I say, hiding my chaotic swirl of emotions with a grin. "Or maybe what fun is."

"Oh, I doubt our ideas of fun are that different," he says, returning my smile. "You forget how well I know you, Trini Kwan."

I resist the urge to remind him that it's been a long time since we built forts together and played tag. But he's right—we *did* have fun together. Maybe it's not so terrible that Mr. Todd put us in the same group. We might have grown apart, but Zack will always be the sweet, funny kid who was my first friend. Plus, with Zack in our group, I won't be stuck with all the work now . . .

Oh right. "By the way," I say, "Aimee is working with us too."

He smirks. "Because this is Aimee we're talking about, I'm assuming you're using the word 'working' loosely."

Laughter pops out of me before I can help myself. I glance at Aimee, but she's batting her eyes and flirting with Jason, so it's safe to say she isn't paying attention to us. "Yes, very loosely."

"So it *will* basically just be you and me? Just like old times." His eyes crinkle at the corners. "Count me in."

My mouth twitches in amusement. "But no baking soda and vinegar volcanoes this time."

"That was one project," he says with fake indignation.

"And it would have been completely understandable if we were doing a presentation on Pompeii or something, but if I recall, this was for a fourth-grade book report on *Charlotte's Web*."

"The volcano was obviously a metaphor for how everything erupted in that story."

"Obviously." It feels wonderful joking around with Zack again. Easy and nice, just like old times. "You know that Ms. Martin was convinced that you didn't actually read the book." But I know better. We both cried over the ending. Zack just really wanted to make a volcano.

He's about to reply, but we're both distracted by Aimee standing up and prodding an obviously reluctant Jason out of his seat. Why are they coming over?

"Hey, Trini!" Aimee says brightly as they walk up to us. "Good news. Jason is going to join our group."

Eek. I should have seen that coming. "Um, Zack is already in our group."

"You asked him without checking with me first?" Aimee pouts.

Seriously? It's not my fault she wasn't paying attention when Mr. Todd assigned Zack to work with me. Besides, it's all kinds of hypocritical of her since she invited Jason without asking me.

The old Trini would have had a hard time controlling her inner rage monster. She would've wanted to put the years of martial arts training with Nai Nai to good use. But that's not me anymore.

The Trini I am *now* is easygoing and mild-mannered, and nothing is going to change that—not even self-absorbed girls like Aimee. "Sorry," I say. "Maybe we can check with Mr. Todd if we can have a bigger group."

The pout disappears from Aimee's face, but Jason is looking super uncomfortable.

I couldn't care less about Aimee, but I hate making someone feel left out. "Jason, I'd love it if you joined us." I smile extra brightly at him. "You're always so great in group projects, not that I've ever worked with you, but I kind of assume that because of how good you are at everything." *Yikes—what was that?* My palms grow damp, and my smile slips. It's possible that I went a bit overboard in my attempt to include Jason.

Zack is looking at me like I've just spouted out purple goo instead of actual words—so I'm guessing it *was* too much.

Luckily, Jason is too nice to say anything about my nervous babbling. "Mr. Todd will just give us more work if we're a bigger group," he says.

"Don't worry about it." Aimee crouches down gracefully to sling an arm around me. "We've got a secret weapon. You don't mind a little more work, do you, Trini?"

I try not to be too obvious about easing away from her. I'm seriously tempted to tell her there were dinosaurs in the Bronze Age and make her do her part of the presentation on whatever she's gleaned from the *Jurassic Park* franchise. But then I spot the red flush creeping up Jason's neck. Aimee's cluelessness isn't his fault. "I guess it would be okay."

"Yeah—that's a hard no." Zack crosses his arms, but he's glaring at Jason instead of Aimee. "You can't just stroll on over and demand that Trini do a bunch of extra work. Everyone in this group is going to pull their own weight." Now, he *does* include Aimee in his glare. "And I mean everyone."

Aimee gapes at him, too shocked to pout.

A little part of me is jumping up and down and screaming, *Yes!* But it doesn't seem fair to lump Jason in with Aimee.

Jason meets Zack's glare with one of his own. "Dude, what's your problem? I always do my part." He sighs and throws up his hands. "You know what? Forget it—I didn't want to be in your group anyway."

Whoa. The tension is making my neck prickle with sweat. It's definitely time to step in before this whole situation erupts like Zack's vinegar and baking soda volcano. "I'm really sorry about this, Jason." I give Zack a not-so-subtle nudge. "I'm sure we can work it out. We *all* want you to be in this group."

Zack shoots me an incredulous look, but Jason ignores him. "Don't worry about it, Trini. This isn't your fault." He glowers pointedly at Zack and then stalks off.

Aimee's eyes dart between us and Jason. It's clear she's torn about whether to go after Jason or stay with us and her ever-shrinking hopes of an easy A.

"So, Aimee," Zack says as if nothing had happened, "how are your metal-smithing skills? We should totally make swords for our project." I'm not sure if he really wants to make swords or just wants to get rid of Aimee. It's probably a bit of both.

"Uh." A panicked look comes into her eyes. "I think I'm going to find another group." She practically runs away, calling, "Jason, wait!"

I turn to Zack. "What the hell was that?"

He looks at me in surprise. "I just didn't like how they wanted to mooch off you."

"That was Aimee, not Jason," I say. "Besides, didn't you and Jason use to be friends? You both played football."

"Yeah." His mouth sets. "That was before I quit the team."

I feel a twinge of sympathy. Personally, I think Zack is being a little harsh, but I get where he's coming from. I know how much it hurts to be ditched by a friend.

"It seems like you stood up for Jason pretty fast," he continues. "It figures. He's pretty much the chiseled-jawed teen jock poster boy for the school. Everyone loves him."

My sympathy evaporates. "You're so full of it." I poke him in the chest, hard, and ignore the fact that said chest feels a lot more muscly than I remembered. "I stood up for Jason because you were being a jerk to him."

Zack just shrugs, and I examine him more closely. The Zack I used to be friends with wasn't the type to hold a grudge. Something else must be going on. "How is your mom doing?" I ask abruptly.

His face eases from its grim lines. "She's doing well, actually."

Relief hits me. "Good. I thought that was why you . . . aren't yourself."

"What? You mean charming and lovable?"

Actually, that *is* kind of what I meant, but I'm not about to say it out loud. Besides, I'm mostly wondering why he's suddenly being rude to people and coming to school late. Zack told me once that he's always been hyper aware of how people see a Black kid, so he pays extra attention to small things like being on time and big things like being universally liked. It hurts to think that a nine-year-old kid had all that on his mind, but I do get it.

When I don't respond, he sighs and rubs his face. "You're right. I didn't need to go off on Jason like that. I'm just tired. I've been going to bed late because I had to take a bunch of night shifts and then finish my homework, so it's been kind of hard to get up in the mornings."

The irritation drains out of me. Zack works as a waiter at the only fancy restaurant in Angel Grove. "That sucks."

"Yeah, it does."

My body swells with an emotion I can't name, and before I can stop myself, I reach over and grasp his hand.

His eyes go wide and startled.

Oh hell. I let go of his hand so fast it's like I accidentally touched a hot stove. What did I just do? High schoolers don't just go around holding their platonic friend's hand. *Especially* platonic ex-best friends who haven't spoken much in years.

We just stare at each other, the awkward silence stretching between us. Through the panicked beating of my heart, I hear Aimee giggle and say loudly, "You're so funny, Jason." Poor Jason. It looks like he ended up with Aimee in his group after all.

Zack takes a noticeable gulp. Oh no. He's showing every sign of a guy about to let a crushed-out girl down easy. Not that I like him in that way.

"Trini—" he begins.

"You owe Jason an apology," I blurt out.

He blinks. "What?"

Maybe this wasn't the path I should have started on, but at least Zack isn't looking at me like he's about to break my heart. "It wasn't cool the way you treated him."

His eyes turn stony. "Well, like I said, I didn't like the way *you* were being treated."

"I don't need you to fight my battles," I snap.

"Then why don't you fight them yourself?" Heat comes into his voice. "When we were kids, you wouldn't take crap from anyone. Why am I the only one you stand up to now?"

Probably because he's the only one I trust with the real me. Even after all this time.

My breath catches at that thought. A pang hits me as I realize that I was never okay with how our friendship ended. I've spent the last few years acting like everything was fine because it was easier than acknowledging how hurt I was. But the truth is that Zack was my best friend, and he ditched me like I was nothing. A spark of anger burns in my stomach. I'm sick and tired of pretending I was ever okay with losing him.

The bell rings, making me jump, but Zack is still sitting there, waiting for me to answer.

"I'm not that kid anymore." I glare at him. "We barely even talk now. You don't get to act like you know me!"

"I *do* know you." He stands up and slings his backpack over his shoulder. "The Trini I know is kind and awesomely fierce. I just don't get why you think you need to hide that."

My mouth falls open in shock, but Zack leaves before I can recover my voice. I want to run after him, but what would I even say? Wetness stings my eyes, and I don't know why I'm so upset.

It's not like we're actually friends anymore.

CHAPTER TWO

I block the blow Nai Nai aims at my head out of pure habit, but instead of flowing into an attack of my own, I have to take a few backward steps to recover my footing. My grandmother is only five feet tall, but her tiny frame packs quite the punch.

Nai Nai comes out of her Warrior stance and peers at me in worry. "What's wrong, Xiao Laohu?"

"Little Tiger" is her nickname for me, but I certainly don't feel like one today. "Sorry. I guess I'm distracted." I'll bet there aren't many sixteen-year-olds who apologize to their grandmothers for *not* throwing them to the ground. Then again, most teens also don't have daily martial arts training with their grandmother.

Nai Nai nods and walks over to the patio chairs that are shoved up against the house to give us room to train.

"Let's rest for a minute." Nai Nai takes a seat. "Sit down with me and tell me what's got you so distracted."

I sigh and join her. I have no idea how to explain what happened. All I know is there's been a heaviness in me all day. "I got into a fight with a friend."

"Billy?" It's a safe bet since he's pretty much my only friend.

"No." I shake my head. "Zack."

Her whole face lights up. "I haven't heard you talk about Zack in a long time." One eyebrow rises. "What happened?"

I might as well tell her. It's not like she's forgotten the bouts of crying, ice-cream devouring, and punching of burlap sacks I did in middle school when Zack and I stopped being friends. "We got assigned to a group project together in History. One minute, we were joking around like old times, and the next minute . . . I kind of snapped at him." A pang hits my stomach. To say I have regrets would be an understatement.

"I see," she says sympathetically. "Are you upset about working with Zack?"

"Not exactly," I admit. "I mean, I thought it might be awkward, but it wasn't." Well, not at first anyway. I squirm in my chair as I remember the stunned look on his face when I grabbed his hand. "In a way, that's what made me so mad. Zack seems completely fine with working together because it clearly doesn't matter to him that we're not friends anymore."

"Why don't you tell him how you feel?" Nai Nai suggests.

Eek. I go hot and cold all over. It was bad enough that I forgot the high school rules of engagement when I held my platonic ex-friend's hand. Zack would really freak out if I tried to talk to him about my feelings. I shake my head emphatically. "It seems silly to still be hung up on something that happened so long ago."

"Ignoring the past," she says gently, "won't make the hurt go away."

Except *I'm* not the one ignoring our past. Zack is. "There's nothing Zack and I need to talk about," I say. "We just had a misunderstanding."

She eyes me thoughtfully. "You two are like Chang'e and Hou Yi."

"Uh, come again?"

"The Chinese moon goddess and the Lord Archer," she says as if that should explain everything. "They had a misunderstanding too. Hou Yi received the elixir of immortality from the gods as a reward for shooting down the nine suns threatening humanity, and he thought Chang'e stole the elixir and escaped to the moon with it."

I blink. "Literally none of that makes any sense, and I don't know how that relates to us."

"You and Zack had a misunderstanding, just like Hou Yi and Chang'e. She didn't actually steal the elixir. She was just trying to keep a real thief from stealing it." She pauses. "It's too bad you don't have a heavenly rabbit to intercede."

I'm not going to ask. I'm not going to ask. "Heavenly rabbit?" I ask with a sigh, but come on. How can I *not* want to know?

"Yes, the rabbit stopped Hou Yi from following Chang'e to the moon until he agreed to reconcile with her."

"Look, Nai Nai," I say, "It's not that I don't appreciate this mythological lesson, but sometimes I'd just like some straight-up advice."

"Fine," she says. "You want advice? How about this, then? Go make up with your friend."

My face heats up. "It's not that easy. And Zack isn't my friend anymore."

"But he could be."

I swallow the lump in my throat. What if Zack doesn't want to be friends again? Or worse—if he drops me like he did in middle school? "I don't think that's going to happen."

"I know you were hurt when the two of you stopped being friends," Nai Nai says gently. "The question is whether you're going to let your fear of getting hurt stop you from taking the risk of trying to become close again."

The lump in my throat gets bigger. I absolutely hate when Nai Nai is right.

"The way I see it, you have two choices," she continues. "You can get assigned to a new group or you can stay with Zack and see what happens."

Asking Mr. Todd to assign me to another group would definitely be easier. Then I remember the warm look in Zack's eyes when he was teasing me. It actually felt nice to be talking to him again. Before I yelled at him for thinking that he knew me. But is that really such a bad thing? Is it possible to be friends? More importantly, can I risk getting hurt again?

Nai Nai is waiting for an answer. "I'll stay with Zack," I mumble.

"Good," she says briskly. "Then you need to talk to him." She rises to her feet only to sit back down on the cement ground of the patio, cross-legged. "In the meantime, let's work on breath and meditation."

I groan. "Really? Can't we practice more kicking and blocking?"

Nai Nai smiles. "Wushu isn't just about kicking and blocking. It is also about stillness and focus."

That's almost exactly what she told me eleven years ago when she first started training me. After I got suspended for fighting in kindergarten, the school recommended a socio-emotional support program, but Nai Nai talked my parents into letting her train me in wushu instead.

I sink to the ground and cross my legs. "Stillness and focus. Got it."

And since there's no one I trust as much as my nai nai, I suppose I might as well take her other advice too. I'm going to talk to Zack.

⚡

Swallowing my nerves, I push open the door to L'ange Bosquet. When I went by Zack's house, his mom said he was working at the restaurant tonight. I could have waited until class tomorrow, but the longer I put this off, the more my stomach would hurt. Zack was just trying to stand up for me, and instead of appreciating it . . . I chewed him out. So, I might not have a heavenly rabbit or whatever, but I hope I can fix things on my own.

As soon as I step inside, I immediately feel out of place. The restaurant is filled with snowy white cloth napkins, crystal chandeliers, and a mirrored bar. This place is *fancy*. My hands turn clammy, and I have to wipe them on my worn jeans. I'm definitely not dressed to blend in with the sleek black dresses and suit jackets. It almost seems as if a hush falls over the room as I walk toward the host station, but I tell myself I'm imagining things. Everyone is too busy eating tiny things off big, gleaming plates to pay any attention to me.

The young woman in the crisp white shirt at the host station eyes me doubtfully. "Hello. Welcome to L'ange Bosquet. Do you have a reservation?"

"Um, no." The words squeak out, and I clear my throat. "I'm not here for dinner. I was wondering if I could see Zack Taylor? I'm a friend of his."

She glances around and then leans forward, lowering her voice. "Actually, our boss doesn't like it when friends visit the waitstaff."

My cheeks heat up. I should have thought this through before barging in on Zack at work. "Right, sorry! I don't want to get him in trouble." I start to back away.

She looks at me sympathetically. "Listen, why don't I seat you in Zack's section? He won't get in trouble for waiting on a customer."

I nod, relieved. "That would be great." I don't know why it feels so important to talk to him right now. Maybe it's because this is the closest we've come in four years to becoming friends again, and don't want this chance to slip away. "This is really nice of you, uh . . ."

"Erica," she says. "And don't mention it."

"Thanks, Erica. I'm Trini."

"Well, Trini, let's get you a table." She picks up a leather-bound menu and leads me into the gilded cavern of the restaurant.

Erica seats me at a small table next to a family of three—a middle-aged man in a suit, a woman in a silky jumpsuit, and a girl around my age in a hot pink tank dress. She looks vaguely familiar, and I wonder where I've seen her before. Maybe she's a model or an influencer? Her dress looks as chic as what everyone else is wearing. It's certainly more stylish than my own jeans and black hoodie, but the effect of her clothes is ruined by the fact that she's slouched in her chair with her arms crossed like she'd rather be anywhere but here.

"Your server will be with you in a minute," Erica says with a conspiratorial smile.

"Thanks."

"Waitress!" The irritated shout comes from the man at the next table, waving around an empty bread basket. "We need more bread."

"Your server will be happy to get you more bread," Erica says, sounding unruffled. "I'll let him know." She hands me the menu and bustles off.

"Don't you think you've had enough, Roger?" the woman asks. "The doctor said bread isn't good for your diabetes."

"Prediabetes, Helen. If you're going to micromanage me, then at least get my diagnosis right."

Yikes. Suddenly, the girl's sullen attitude makes a lot more sense. I'd be slumped in my chair too if my parents were sniping at each other like that. For a second, the girl meets my eyes, but then she turns away and starts picking stuff out of her salad.

"Didn't you order that salad without pears?" Helen asks.

"It's okay," she mumbles.

"No, it's not." Roger thumps the table. "A missing waiter and the wrong order. The service here is unacceptable!"

Worry snakes into my body. Zack is not going to have an easy time with that table.

Trying to block out their bickering, I open the heavy menu, but my jaw practically hits the ground when I see the prices printed on the soft cream paper.

"May I recommend iced tea?" Zack appears by my side with an amused twinkle in his eye.

"Finally!" Roger exclaims. "Our bread."

"Of course," Zack says smoothly, depositing the basket he's holding onto their table. "Here you go."

Roger doesn't even thank him. He just snatches up a piece of bread while Helen shakes her head and turns to the girl. "Do you want some, dear?"

Before the girl can respond, Roger says, "So Kimberly can have bread but I can't?"

Zack turns back to me. "How about that iced tea?"

"Thirty dollars for an appetizer? These prices are criminal," I whisper fiercely. They would give both my immigrant Chinese Taiwanese father and Korean Chinese mother a heart attack. Include both my Chinese nai nai and Korean halmeoni—and it would be a quadruple heart attack.

"What do you expect from a restaurant that literally means 'Angel Grove' in French?"

I stare at him. "You can't be serious."

Strains of conversation from the other table float toward me. "The difference is that our daughter is on the gymnastics team," Helen says, "and besides, just look at her."

Zack grins and doesn't seem to notice the tension at the bread table. "Oui."

"Gross. Can we please not talk about my body?" Kimberly says. "Besides, I'm not on the gymnastics team anymore, remember? Angel Grove High doesn't have one."

Oh, so the girl in pink goes to our school. That's why she looks familiar. Come to think of it, I do remember seeing her in the hallways and in the cafeteria, talking and laughing with all the cool kids. For a new girl, she seemed to have gotten popular fast.

Her voice gets louder. "I'm not sure what this dinky little town you've dragged me to *does* have."

Zack finally seems to be tuning into their conversation and turns around. "Hey," he begins, and knowing him, I'm pretty sure he's about to make a joke about Angel Grove and welcome the new girl—but she must think he's about to criticize her for talking smack about our town because a faint flush rises into her face. "If you're done flirting with your girlfriend," she says icily, "can you please bring me a new salad without pears?"

Girlfriend? Is there any chance Zack didn't hear that part? "Wait . . . I'm not . . ." I stammer.

"Taylor!" An older man with a trim mustache comes rushing over. "Are you entertaining your girlfriend instead of waiting tables?"

My stomach drops. *Oh no.* It's painfully obvious that this is the boss Erica warned me about.

"What? No," Zack says.

Kimberly looks horrified, but her father says at once, "The service has been awful! Your waiter brought my daughter the wrong order, and it took forever to get a bread refill."

"Dad!" The flush on her cheeks turns bright red.

Zack's boss says to Roger, "I do apologize, sir."

I need to say something, stand up for Zack somehow, even if it means ordering the thirty-dollar appetizer. In my head, I'm announcing at full volume, *I've never seen this guy in my life!* In reality, it comes out as a small whisper.

"My daughter could have been allergic to pears, and then you'd have a lawsuit on your hands!"

Zack's mouth sets, but his boss turns pale.

Kimberly rolls her eyes. "I'm not allergic to pears. I just don't like them."

"Then why order a pear salad?" Zack mutters under his breath, but unfortunately, his boss hears him.

He turns to Zack. "Taylor, you're fired."

Crap. The breath whooshes out of me. I just got Zack fired.

CHAPTER THREE

'm really, really, really sorry," I say as Zack and I walk out of history together.

"Yeah, I kind of got that when you apologized last night and then every five minutes during class," Zack teases. "And as *I* keep saying, it's not your fault, so don't worry about it. If anything, it's the new girl's fault. I mean, who hates pears so much that they get someone fired?"

Now is not the time to point out that Kimberly probably didn't want to get Zack fired. She did seem pretty appalled about the whole thing. "I wish there was something I could do," I say miserably.

"Well, you could do my part of the History project," he jokes.

"Haha. Very funny." I punch him lightly in the arm. Judging from the surprising lack of other students trying to join us, I suspect Zack has quietly let it be known that the days of taking advantage of me in group projects are over. I have to admit that it's kind of sweet even though I told him I could fight my own battles.

He pretends to wince. "Ow. I can see you're still training with your grandmother."

I look around the crowded hallway to make sure no one heard, but no one seems to be paying attention. Good. I love doing wushu with Nai Nai, but the last thing I need is to be seen as some kind of kung fu Asian stereotype.

Changing the subject, I ask, "Are you going to look for a new job?"

"Yeah." A glum expression flits across his face, but then he smiles. "It's too bad. No other job is going to give me the chance to level up my plate-juggling skills *and* practice my high school French."

I ignore the joke. "What about Ernie? He's always looking for help at the juice bar." Ernie owns the Angel Grove Youth Center, where Zack used to do everything from soccer to running club as a kid, but the most popular part of the center (for the high school students, at least) is definitely the juice bar.

"I don't know. It seems kind of weird to be working at the same place where I used to take all those classes."

"I get it," I say sympathetically. "I don't think there was a sport you didn't play or a fencing class you didn't take."

"So you do know me. I wasn't sure." He grins. "After all, you told the whole restaurant that you had never seen me in your life. It was like you were in a cheesy TV drama."

Damn. He heard me. "Sorry about that."

"Don't be. I like how you stood up for me."

A warm feeling fizzes up in me. "Listen, you were really good at fencing. Maybe Ernie would hire you to teach at the center."

"Nah. Jason has all the fencing and martial classes locked up. It's the juice bar for me."

"Oh, sorry." I dodge a kid barreling down the hallway while texting. "I didn't know Jason taught at the center." Great. Another reason for Zack to dislike Jason. It's weird that Zack gets along with everyone, and now there are *two* people he has a problem with: Jason and Kimberly.

"You should be the one teaching the martial arts classes," Zack says. "You were great when we were kids, and I'm sure you've only gotten better."

"Shh!" My eyes dart around the hallway. It's still crowded since everyone waits until the last possible minute before going to their next classes.

Zack stops in the middle of the hall, making kids eddy around us. "Trini Kwan, are you actually trying to hide . . ." He lowers his voice. ". . . your kick-ass martial arts skills?"

I flush. It's not that I'm embarrassed about doing wushu with Nai Nai. I just don't want anyone to know except for Zack, who's never judged me or made me feel ashamed of anything. "It's bad enough to be the quiet Asian girl," I say at last. "Add martial arts to the mix and I might as well be a walking stereotype."

"Yeah, I get that." Zack would understand. "But don't let what other people think keep you from doing the things you love. I mean, you don't see me giving up hip-hop, do you?"

I laugh. "Maybe there's a dance class you can teach at the center. I don't think Jason is teaching hip-hop."

"I wouldn't put it past him." Zack glances at his phone. Is it just me or did my mention of Jason make his voice go cooler? "I've got to get to French. I might not wait tables at L'Ange Bosquet anymore, but I want to be prepared if we get French tourists at the juice bar or wherever I work next. 'Que voulez-vous boire?' That either means 'What do you want to drink?' or 'What kind of drink are you?' which has a totally different meaning."

"Yeah, I should get to Chemistry too." I pull on my backpack straps uncomfortably. "You know, if we get, um, Chemistry tourists in Angel Grove."

He doesn't even make fun of my cringey attempt at humor. "Au revoir," he says jauntily, sprinting off in the opposite direction. He clearly doesn't feel any of the sudden awkwardness that's gripping me.

I sigh and continue walking to my next class. Why can't things be as uncomplicated as when we were kids?

Abruptly, all thoughts of Zack are driven from my mind at the sight of Billy being shoved into the lockers by the resident asshole school bullies, Bulk and Skull. Hot anger flares up in me as I rush over.

It's easy enough to stick out a foot to "accidentally" trip Bulk. He never pays attention to kids he mows down in his path. "Oh no!" I exclaim as he comes crashing to the floor with a yelp. I hear Skull coming up behind me, and out of the corner of my eye, I see him bending to check on Bulk. Without missing a beat, I whirl around so my backpack smacks him in the face, knocking him down too. "I'm so sorry!"

Skull is holding his head, moaning. He's as skinny as Bulk is big, but I know he's tough in his own way, so maybe I hit him harder than I meant to. Guilt twinges in me, and I'm relieved when he gets up.

Bulk is picking himself off the ground too. "What the hell, Trini?"

"Yeah." Skull rubs the side of his head. "Watch where you're going!"

They both look pissed off. There's no way they think I did that on purpose, but I may have seriously underestimated how mad I would make them. There's a crowd gathering now, and a boy shouts, "Fight, fight!"

A girl says, "Are you kidding me? Just look at how tiny she is. Bulk and Skull will murder her if they fight." Uh, thanks? *I think.* Much as I appreciate the concern, it's not going to come down to a fight. All I have to do is play scared. Bulk and Skull are big bullies, but they're definitely not going to fight me.

I don't take my eyes off the duo, but then I hear the boy reply, "That's Trini Kwan." His voice hardens. "She could go kung fu crazy."

I freeze, and slowly, I turn to look at the boy who spoke. *Carl.* I know him. He's a senior now, but he was a first grader back when I was a kindergartner. My stomach churns. Carl is the boy I beat up in elementary school.

The memory slams into me without warning. I can almost see Carl's terrified face with blood trickling from his nose after I punched him. I had a good reason, or so I thought. Carl was a bully beating up on smaller kids and stealing their lunch money. But when he fell to the ground, all I felt was a raw shame—especially when I looked up from his bloody face to see other elementary school kids staring at me in horror. Then the frightened whispers started.

No. My stomach sickens. I don't want to think about the revulsion on those kids' faces.

Then Billy shoulders through the crowd and stands between me and Bulk and Skull. "Leave Trini alone!"

Crap. I wrench my gaze away from Carl, heart pounding. I have a much bigger problem now. Bulk and Skull might not fight me, but they've never had a problem going for Billy.

"Billy," I whisper, putting my hand on his trembling arm, "let's just get out of here."

"It's okay, Trini," Billy says. "I'm tired of letting them bully everyone."

I'm not actually surprised that he's standing his ground. He has twice the heart and courage of anyone else I know, except for maybe Zack.

"You really think you're going to fight us, Cranston?" Skull sneers.

Bulk smashes a fist into his open palm. "We're going to wipe the floor with your face!"

My mouth goes dry. It's one thing for me to get pushed around, but there's no way I'm going to let Billy take a beating for me. My body tenses, and I roll back my shoulders in preparation. I might have to break out those kick-ass kung fu moves Zack was talking about after all.

But my body just won't flow into one of the fighting stances that come so easily to me when I'm training with Nai Nai.

Carl is chanting, "Fight, fight!" What will he call me if I really *do* fight? *Yellow Peril. Asian Menace. Chink. Slant-eyed bitch.* My chest tightens, and it's suddenly hard to breathe.

Someone else is moving toward us, and the crowd parts. *A teacher?* I really hope so.

"You two—Bulk and Skull," an authoritative voice says. "Stop bothering Trini and Billy." It's not a teacher. It's Jason.

He strides right up to Bulk, puts a big palm on his shoulder, and spins him away from us. Then he glares at Skull, who backs away quickly.

"We weren't doing anything," Skull protests.

"Yeah," Bulk says sullenly. "We were just kidding around."

"Well, it stops now," Jason says calmly. "I don't want to see you anywhere near Trini and Billy again."

"No problem," Skull says anxiously. He might be a bully, but he's quick to stand down in the presence of someone like Jason. "We don't want any trouble. Right, Bulk?"

"Whatever." Bulk rubs his shoulder. "Did you have to grab me so hard? You could have broken something!"

"You're fine," Jason says dismissively. He clearly thinks Bulk is exaggerating, but I know how scarily easy it is to hit someone harder than intended. Luckily, Jason doesn't seem to have done any actual damage, and neither did I.

This time.

My stomach clenches, and I don't look at Carl, but I can still see the kid I sent to the emergency room to get stitches all those years ago.

Bulk and Skull scamper away with their hands raised in surrender. With any luck, Jason's scare tactics will keep them from bothering Billy from now on. And even better—I didn't have to show everyone exactly how well I can take care of myself.

⚡

"Trini! Billy!" a familiar voice calls out, and I turn to see Zack sprinting across the Angel Grove High parking lot. He's not even out of breath when he reaches us. He must be keeping up with his running. "I heard what happened. Are you both okay?"

"Thanks to Jason!" Billy says before I can reply. "He showed up and fought off Bulk and Skull."

That wasn't fighting. But I don't have the heart to say it out loud. Billy has been talking about how great Jason is all day. I think Billy secretly hopes Jason is going to be friends with us now. It's pretty unlikely that the captain of the football team will want to hang out with the school genius and the shy girl, but I'm not going to rain on Billy's parade. I even promised him that I'd go to the Homecoming game with him to see Jason play. "Yes, we're both fine."

Zack knows full well that I was never in danger, but he just says, "Bulk and Skull are such assholes."

Billy nods. "They were so mad even though Trini didn't mean to trip Bulk or and hit Skull in the face with her backpack. It was obviously an accident."

He shakes his head, his expression softening. "You're way too nice, Trini," he says, but he doesn't make it sound like being too nice is a bad thing.

"I'm really not." I look away from him. Billy doesn't know about my wushu training or why Nai Nai had to start teaching me control. How would he feel if he knew I was capable of hurting someone that badly? Maybe he'd think I was like Bulk and Skull, who pick on him all the time. Maybe he wouldn't want to be friends with someone like that.

"Let's just forget about it," I say tightly. In a naked attempt to distract him, I ask, "Are you looking forward to the Homecoming game?"

His eyes light up. "Yeah. And I'm glad Zack is coming with us too. I have to ask, though, is it my imagination, or am I sensing something between you two?"

I laugh, relieved about the change in subject. "It's not like that. Zack and I are just friends." At least, we're starting to become friends again. I think. *I hope.*

Billy smiles. "If you say so."

CHAPTER FOUR

It's obvious that Billy is one hundred percent dead wrong about Zack liking me. For one thing, although Zack is technically sitting with Billy and me in the stands, he's talking to everyone who comes within six feet of him. There are currently no fewer than four girls from our grade who he's chatting with. "I get that the Homecoming Court is a tool of the patriarchy," he's saying now to them, "but what's your take on the dance itself?"

"That depends," Tricia, one of the girls, replies boldly. "Which one of us are you asking to the Homecoming dance?"

He gives her a flirtatious smile. "Why should it be the guy who asks the girl out?"

I grit my teeth hard enough that I might just crack a molar.

"I take back what I said earlier," Billy whispers to me. "Maybe Zack is just a friend."

"You think?" I ask sarcastically. Actually, I'm not sure Zack is even that. A real friend might spend more than five minutes talking to me before flirting with every other girl who walks by. Then again, maybe he's just looking for a distraction. Sympathy creeps over me. It must be tough to be in the stands, waiting for his old teammates, including Jason, to come onto the field.

"Although . . ." Billy continues thoughtfully, "I did notice he hasn't asked anyone else out either."

"Give it up, Billy," I say, louder than I intended to.

Zack turns toward us. "Give up what?"

"Nothing." I catch a glimpse of movement on the field. "Look, the game is starting!"

"That's just the cheerleaders . . . wait a minute." His eyes narrow onto the field.

I look over, stomach knotting. *Oh hell.* Kimberly, the girl from the restaurant, is wearing the red-and-white cheer uniform and doing flawless cartwheels onto the field. She's on the cheer squad, and actually, she's kind of awesome. I remember from the conversation with her parents that she used to do gymnastics. She must have decided being a cheerleader was the next best thing.

"It figures," Zack mutters. He doesn't even seem to notice Tricia and her friends leaving. They must have gotten irritated with his sudden inattention, but I know exactly why he's ignoring them to glare down at the football field.

At the start of freshman year, Zack was briefly on the cheer squad *and* the football team before he was told he couldn't do both. It was no surprise to me that he chose football. He always loved it. And now, of course, he doesn't do *any* sports. Most people seemed to accept that easygoing, fun-loving Zack just decided to move on, but I can tell he misses football. I wonder why he quit, but it's not like I can just come right and ask him. My heart twinges. Of course, there was a time we could talk about anything.

"What's wrong?" Billy asks him now.

Zack points toward the field where Kimberly is doing backflips. "That's the snobby rich girl who got me fired from my job."

I bite my lip to keep from pointing out that he actually hated that job and is much happier to be working at the juice bar for Ernie, who hired him immediately.

"Oh, that's too bad," Billy says. "So, we hate her?"

"We . . . do," I say reluctantly. I just can't shake the feeling that Kimberly felt almost as bad about Zack getting fired as I did.

Zack slings an arm around me. "Trini Kwan, it means a lot to me that you'd actually hate someone for my sake."

I shove him playfully. "Oh no, you don't get to ignore me for the whole game and then act all friendly now that I've joined your vendetta."

He has the grace to blush. "I haven't ignored you for the whole game. It hasn't even started yet."

"It has now," Billy says excitedly as the cheerleaders leave the field.

The student announcer calls out the starting lineup, with Jason first as the team captain. Jason runs out onto the field, not even looking up into the stands as the crowd erupts into cheers. Wow. I have to admire anyone with that kind of intense focus. Nai Nai would totally approve.

I glance over at Zack, who's slumped on his bleacher seat. "You okay?"

"Why wouldn't I be? Snobby girl is a cheerleader and Mr. Perfect Jason is the football captain."

"You don't like Jason?" There's a worried frown on Billy's face.

"What's not to like?" Zack's smile looks completely carefree. "I'm good with Jason."

The frown on Billy's face eases away, but I'm not fooled.

It's killing Zack to pretend that everything is fine and that he doesn't miss doing football or cheer—the things Jason and Kimberly get to do. I desperately want to squeeze his hand, but the last time I acted on a similar urge, I ended up panicking and yelling at him to apologize to Jason.

So, hands to yourself, Trini.

⚡

"Angel Grove is up by fourteen thanks to those two touchdowns Jason threw," Billy says like he's been watching football all his life instead of this being his first-ever game. Then again, a genius like him shouldn't have any trouble picking up on the basic rules.

"Yeah, that about sums it up." Zack stabs a plastic fork into his paper container with unnecessary force.

"I think your cheesy nachos are already dead," I say.

"You can't be too sure." His face lightens up with his first smile since Jason's last touchdown pass. "This one, for example . . ." He picks up a greasy nacho oozing with globs of cheese. "I'm pretty sure it's still got some life in it."

Good. Zack cracking jokes is much better than the unnaturally glum version. "You should just put it out of its misery then."

"As you wish." He pops the nacho into his mouth.

"See? No shrieks of agony," I say smugly. "It was dead."

"Shows what you know. Right before I swallowed it, I heard it whisper, 'My name is Bob.'"

"Bob," I repeat. "You shall be remembered."

Billy shakes his head. "You two are so weird."

I'm about to point out that a junior who studies quantum mechanics has no right to judge, but then shrieks ring through the stadium, making my head jerk up and my pulse kick into overdrive.

Is that . . . a grotesque winged beast with a golden body at the other end of the field? My body goes cold. *What the hell?* That thing just came out of nowhere. "Uh, guys—am I the only one who's seeing a giant gold monster on the football field?" I ask shakily.

"I see it." Zack sounds as shocked as I am. He points into the far stands. "There's something over there too."

"Oh my god." The winged beast is scary enough, but these other creatures look like they came straight from a horror movie. They have vaguely humanlike bodies with arms and legs, but they look like they were made out of clay instead of flesh and skin. Even worse is their featureless, smoothly blank faces.

Billy gasps. "What are those things?"

Aliens? Demons? Science experiments gone wrong? Who knows.

People are noticing them too. Screams come from all around me, and students scramble down from the bleachers to get away from the clay creatures now swarming the far stands. They seem to be looking for something. Or someone.

"We need to get out of here." Zack stands, but others are running down the steps in the aisle and blocking his way out. It's a full-on stampede, and kids are in danger of getting trampled. "Careful!" he calls out to someone who knocked down a shorter boy.

"You're going to hurt him!" I'm on my feet, yelling at the crowd, but Zack has already shoved through the mob and picked up the kid.

Zack makes his way back to Billy and me. "We might be safer up here. Maybe we should wait until the aisle is clear."

I know what he's thinking. Zack could run down the bleachers easily without bothering with the steps, and he knows I can too, but Billy might have trouble.

"Yes." My eyes meet his. "That's a good idea."

Then the gold beast roars so loudly the whole stadium shakes. "Where is your leader? Take me to him or I will destroy you!" He draws an enormous gold sword from a scabbard at his side and begins waving it around.

Um, the gold beast talks? I mean, yes—he talks like his only knowledge of our language comes straight from B movies, but there's no denying that a huge winged giant monster is making clichéd villainous threats on our football field.

The beast suddenly slashes at the stands nearest him with his sword. Fear clutches at my throat as an empty bleacher collapses with a crash. The panicked screams all around me get even louder.

"At least that bleacher was empty," Zack says grimly.

"No, it's not!" Billy's eyes are round in horror as he stares at the collapsed bleacher.

Heart racing, I peer through the dust cloud. *There.* "Two kids are trapped in the rubble." One of the kids is big, and the other is skinny. "I think it's Bulk and Skull," I breathe. Of course it would have to be them. They must have been behind the bleacher when the monster blasted it.

"The clay creatures are headed for them!" Billy says. He's right. The monsters have abandoned their search in the empty stands and are lumbering toward Bulk and Skull as if they sense easy prey.

My gaze swivels to the football team. They're in the perfect position to help Bulk and Skull, but they're all fleeing too—except for one. Only Jason is standing his ground.

"Stay here." Zack sprints down the bleachers and toward the chaos.

Like hell I will. No way am I going to let him face literal monsters on his own. Without a second thought, I'm racing down the bleachers after Zack.

"Wait, Trini!" Behind me, I can dimly hear Billy saying, "Excuse me. Let me through! I need to help my friend." It's not surprising that Billy is following us. He might not be the athletic guy, but he's as brave and loyal as they come.

I leap from the bleachers onto the field, and then I'm dodging kids who are dashing for the exits. A blur of red and white flashes in my peripheral vision. It's one of the cheerleaders, and she's not running away. Kimberly is running *toward* the fight. Astonishment grips me. So not only are we going up against invading alien creatures to save Bulk and Skull . . . but it's going to be Kimberly, Jason, Zack, Billy, and me.

The five of us might be the strangest team-up of all time.

CHAPTER FIVE

Help!" Bulk screams from behind a blockade of broken wood from the destroyed bleachers. "Those monsters are going to kill us!" Skull is lying beneath a beam that has him pinned down. He seems to be saying something, but I'm too far away to hear him.

I try to run faster though my lungs are already burning from sprinting across the football field. There's no way I can reach Bulk and Skull before the clay creatures lumbering toward them suck out their brains or whatever it is that they're going to do. *Faster, Trini.*

Kimberly must push herself harder too since she stays slightly ahead of me. Zack has already reached Jason, and they're standing together, observing the chaos as if deciding what to do.

The gold beast raises his sword in the air, yelling at the fleeing students in a deep, growly voice, "Cowards! Is this not a great arena of warriors?"

We're under attack because some monster thought the football stadium was a warrior arena? The more important question might be why the hell a gold beast is looking for warriors in the first place.

Now that I'm closer, I can see that the beast isn't actually gold. He's wearing golden armor that encases even his wings, making them into sharp weapons, and his face is covered in blue fur, and wait—are those actual fangs?! And red glowing eyes?!

Naturally, the terrified students racing for the exits aren't stopping to answer the scary armored beast, and he turns away from them in obvious disgust. "Putties, do your worst! We need to draw Zordon out."

Putties? Zordon? And then, of course, there's the talking monster himself. I would be wondering about what the hell is happening if my pulse wasn't racing with fear. I hate to imagine what "do your worst" means, especially for Bulk and Skull.

The Putties—those must be the creepy clay monsters—are mere feet away from where Bulk and Skull are pinned down when Jason yells out, "Hey, uglies! Why don't you come pick on someone who can give you a fight?"

"I hope you're not talking to me," Zack quips. "I'm a lot of things, but ugly isn't one of them."

Jason doesn't bother to respond to Zack. He's watching the Putties as they halt their slow march toward Bulk and Skull and turn toward us instead. Chills go through me at the sight of their soulless faces. Their eyes are red like the gold monster's, but flat with no pupils. They have no nose and only a lipless slit for a mouth, and it does not look like they are capable of expression. *Or feeling.*

Kimberly comes up to Jason and Zack, panting from exertion. "What are we doing?" she gasps out. At least she has enough breath to talk. I'm too winded to say anything as I stumble to a halt next to Zack, who's barely breathing hard. No doubt about it—he's definitely keeping up with his running.

"Here's the plan." Jason's gaze doesn't waver from the advancing Putties. "Me, Zack, and new girl—"

"It's Kimberly."

"Whatever," Zack mutters, but too low for anyone but me to hear.

"Okay," Jason says. "The three of us will distract the Putties, but don't fight them."

Good call. I was so focused on the eerie faces that I didn't notice other important features—like the sharpened tips of their fingers and the ropy musculature of their bodies that isn't hidden by clothing.

"They seem pretty slow," Jason says, "so it shouldn't be hard to outrun them. We just need to draw them away from Bulk and Skull. Trini, can you get them out?"

I eye the rubble trapping Bulk and Skull. "Yes." Last summer, Nai Nai put me to work moving heavy rocks, claiming it was part of my training. I called bullshit on that—she just wanted a rock garden, but now I make a mental note to *never* tell Nai Nai how I'm putting all that weight lifting to use.

"I can help Trini," Billy wheezes as he catches up to us.

"Great." Jason gives a decisive nod. "Let's go!"

Making sure we give a wide berth to the Putties, Billy and I run toward the collapsed bleachers.

Behind us, I hear Jason yelling, "Over here!"

"Come get us!" Kimberly calls out.

"So you're called Putties, huh?" That, of course, is Zack. "I would have gone with 'Overgrown Gray Lumps of Eww-iness' or OGLE for short, but I guess Putties works."

How in the world is he able to come up with an acronym while he's facing down scary monsters?

Then I reach the bleachers and tear my attention from Zack and the others. "Are you two okay?"

Skull turns his pale face to me. "I think my leg is broken." He pushes ineffectually at a large beam of wood.

"You'll be fine, buddy," Bulk says breezily.

Easy for him to say. He's not the one with the broken leg.

"It's working," Billy pants as he reaches me. "The others are drawing the Putties away."

I can't help but turn to look for myself. I'm relieved to see that Zack, Kimberly, and Jason are running well ahead of the sharp-fingered Putties lumbering after them. How long will it be before the Putties give up on the others and decide to turn their attention back to the ones trapped under the bleacher? I shudder. *We need to hurry*.

I start lifting away the pile of bleacher fragments. "Help me with this, Billy."

Billy and I clear away the blockade, and so does Bulk from his side. As we work, I realize Bulk probably could have gotten free on his own . . . if he was willing to abandon Skull. My eyes meet his, and Bulk reddens before turning toward Skull. "I can't get this damn thing off of him," he mutters.

"We'll help you get him out," I say gently. Who knew that Bulk had it in him to care more about his friend than his own skin? "Billy, get ready to pull Skull out while Bulk and I lift the beam."

"Are you sure you can lift it, Trini?" Billy eyes the beam pinning Skull down. "It looks heavy."

He's not wrong. If either Bulk or I drop our end of the beam before Billy pulls Skull free, the weight will crush both of his legs. "We just need to lift it up an inch or two and hold it," I say with more confidence than I feel. "It will be fine."

I glance over at the Putties. They're still chasing the others and paying no attention to us, but that might not last for long. One of them nearly catches up to Kimberly, but she puts on a burst of speed and evades its dangerous clutches. Fear slams into my chest. If we don't hurry, the others could get hurt.

I clamber over the rubble and grip one end of the beam, bending my knees to take the weight. Bulk shifts over to take the other end, and Billy hooks his arms under Skull's armpits.

Skull's eyes lock on me, no doubt taking in my small stature. "I don't think this is a good idea."

"We lift on three," I say, ignoring him. "One, two, three." I heave up on my end, and Bulk does the same. My muscles burn in pain, and it feels as if my arms are being pulled out of their sockets, but I don't let go. Billy is pulling at Skull, who's scooting backward.

And then he's free.

The beam crashes to the ground as I let go. I'm shaking, and my whole body feels like stretched taffy. Bulk is rubbing his arms, and his face is red and sweaty. I doubt we could have held it up much longer.

Thank you, Nai Nai, and your desire for a rock garden, I say silently.

Bulk slings one of Skull's arms over his shoulder and helps him limp away, giving the distracted Putties a wide berth and heading toward the stadium exit without so much as a backward glance.

"You're welcome," Billy calls out.

I could swear the back of Skull's neck turns red like he's embarrassed. Bulk keeps trudging along and supporting Skull, but he does give a wave. It doesn't exactly qualify as gratitude but is definitely an improvement over their usual threats to kick Billy's ass.

"We should get out of here too," Billy says.

I nod, but I'm scanning the empty football stadium. Zack, Jason, and Kimberly are still taunting and leading the Putties around in circles. Jason is right; they are slow. One of them even trips and falls as it goes after Zack. Slow and clumsy—even better.

We should be able to escape them. "Yes, let's get the others and go." Then I spot something that chills me.

The gold beast is striding toward our principal, who is cowering under the stage and clutching a megaphone. *Damn.* "Principal Caplan is in trouble!" I shout at the others.

"Didn't he escape already?" Billy looks around, and then pales when he spots him. "I guess he didn't."

As Jason, Zack, and Kimberly turn toward me, I point over to where the beast is looming over our principal. "We have to help him!"

Principal Caplan's toupee has been knocked off, and he looks absolutely terrified, but maybe the megaphone makes him seem like the "leader" the beast is looking for because he's roaring at Principal Caplan, "Tell me where Zordon is, and do not lie to me, Earthling, for I am Goldar, and I will not be trifled with!"

The others run over to us with Zack in the lead. "*Trifled with?* Who says that? This blue winged monkey talks like he's a *Wizard of Oz* extra who wandered into the wrong movie."

"I was just thinking that!" I exclaim.

Jason glares at us both. "Can we focus on more important things, like saving our principal and escaping with our lives?"

I flush, but Zack doesn't seem fazed. He gestures at Goldar. "I say we go with the same plan as before. Distract Goldilocks while Trini and Billy help Principal Caplan escape."

Kimberly tosses her hair out of her sweaty face and says, "Why don't we split up? I can keep the Putties busy while you two draw away Goldar or whatever he's calling himself."

I could really, really get to like this girl.

But Zack grimaces like Kimberly just suggested taking a break to go shopping, and Jason is shaking his head. "Goldar is too fast and strong to take on."

"And let's not forget the fangs and armored wings," Zack adds.

The Putties are closing in on us, and Billy eyes them nervously. "Hey, we really need to decide what we're going to do."

"Alright," Jason says, "we split up and—"

"Crap," I blurt out. I've been keeping one eye on Principal Caplan, and he just slumped over suddenly. Goldar wasn't even doing anything except yelling, "Where is Zordon?" over and over again. "I think Principal Caplan fainted." I don't blame him. In fact, I'm shaking so hard that I can barely stand.

Goldar growls and spins around. And then his fierce red eyes land on us.

"I don't think splitting up is an option anymore," Kimberly says.

She's right. Goldar is stalking toward us and yelling, "Putties, don't let them escape."

A tremor radiates from my belly, but my first instinct is to rush the Putties before they can surround us. I'm not the only one. Jason and Kimberly are tearing away loose planks from the rubble of the bleachers.

"Come on, Trini," Zack calls out before snatching up a plank too. Even Billy grabs one, but I can't move . . . and it's not from fear. Or at least not the totally reasonable fear of being torn to pieces by the sharp-fingered monsters circling us or the fanged beast approaching us.

Of course I'm afraid of *them*, but that's not what keeps me frozen in place. That would be the mind-fogging fear of showing everyone who I am. *Don't be different*, a voice inside my head whispers insistently. *Hide who you are.*

The others face the Putties with their makeshift weapons held out in front of them, and Zack casts me a puzzled look over his shoulder. He knows I should be up there with the rest of them.

Suddenly, there isn't time to decide what to do.

Goldar takes to the air with a gleaming spread of his wings and lands in front of us with an impact that shakes the ground beneath our feet. My mouth goes dry, and Billy gulps visibly. Kimberly, Zack, and Jason tighten their grips on their planks. I'm trembling all the way down to my shoes, and I bet everyone else is too. Goldar towers over us and gnashes his wickedly sharp fangs, his red eyes gleaming and his gold-armored wings twitching with menace.

Up close, Goldar is absolutely terrifying.

Without warning, he throws back his head, and hot gusts of his breath blows over us as he laughs. "Do you children think to stand against my Putty Patrollers and me?"

"That's exactly what we *are* doing," Zack says.

"Shut up, Zack," Jason and Kimberly say at the exact same time.

Hey! Despite the danger we're all in, indignation floods me, but Zack doesn't even glance at Jason and Kimberly. He's looking at Goldar. "What's your name again?" he asks. "Goldar, wasn't it? A bit on the nose in my opinion."

"You speak strangely." Goldar's eyes track him as Zack casually moves away, putting some distance between himself and the rest of us. "What is this talk of noses?"

My heart goes cold. Zack is deliberately provoking Goldar to give the rest of us a chance to escape. *No.* The hell with that.

Zack grins like he's been handed a present all wrapped up in a red bow. "Speaking of noses, yours—nah, actually your nose is fine. But I do have a problem with your—"

"Stop it, Zack." My voice throbs with fear as I cut through whatever ridiculously heroic taunt he was about to lob at Goldar. I don't care if he's trying to save us. I'm not going to run off and abandon him to deal with these monsters on his own. And

I know the only way to stop Zack is to tell him exactly that. "I won't leave you."

Zack doesn't turn around, but from the stiffening of his shoulders, I can tell that he heard me.

"Enough!" Goldar peers around the empty and destroyed stadium, and his gaze comes to rest on us—five frightened teens facing him with nothing more than scavenged boards. The disdain in his red eyes is obvious. "Rita is mistaken," he muses. "Zordon must be looking for his warriors elsewhere. This cannot be his recruiting ground."

Recruiting ground?

We look at each other in confusion. "I understood literally none of that," Kimberly announces.

I would have to agree.

There's a sudden blaze of light that causes me to throw an arm over my eyes. When I uncover them again, I'm blinking at the empty space where the monsters were. Goldar and the Putties seemed to have vanished into thin air.

What *was* that . . . and who the hell is this Zordon?

CHAPTER SIX

Zack turns to me. "Just checking, but I didn't imagine that a blue winged monkey with Play-Doh minions wrecked our football stadium and then disappeared into thin air, right?"

"Not unless we're all hallucinating together." A shiver goes through me as I remember Goldar's fanged grimace when he looked us over.

"Collective hallucinations can occur," Billy says. "It's known as 'folie à deux,' a psychological disorder brought on by shared trauma . . ." He trails off when he notices the rest of us staring at him uncomprehendingly.

Jason points at the shattered bleachers and burnt Astroturf. "We didn't make *that* up." He drops his plank, and everyone else does too. Except me . . . since I didn't actually pick up a weapon.

I gnaw at my lip in guilt, and Zack peers at me questioningly. *Please don't say anything.* He must hear my silent plea because he doesn't.

Kimberly touches the tear in the sleeve of her red-and-white cheerleader sweater. "Oh my god. I think those Putties had *claws*."

"Not exactly," Jason says. "The fingers themselves were sharp." There's a thin scratch on his arm.

It's like the Putties were made to be weapons. I shudder, and my eyes are drawn to Kimberly's torn sweater. She's lucky she didn't get hurt. The Putties might have been slow and clumsy, but they were still deadly. It's starting to hit me how much danger we were all in.

A strange, fuzzy sensation creeps over me. *Oh no.* Am I about to pass out for real?

But Zack is rubbing his stomach, both Kimberly and Jason have a startled expression on their faces, and Billy emits a small moan. So maybe it's not just me. "Hey, does anyone else—" My words are cut off abruptly because I'm not standing in a football field anymore.

I'm standing in a rock cavern lined with computers, blinking lights . . . and is that a huge, blue head floating in a tube of light?

"What the hell is going on?" Kimberly bursts out.

"How did we—Where are we?" Jason's hand twitches like he wishes he had held onto his plank.

"Seriously," Zack mutters. It's not a good sign when Zack is in agreement with Kimberly and Jason about how bad this is.

"Fascinating." Billy looks around like he's on a super-cool field trip and not like he was just mysteriously transported into a weird space-age cavern.

A voice suddenly booms out. "I understand that this must be disorienting for you." Did the floating head just *speak*? Even though I *see* the blue lips move, my brain just won't comprehend it, but then Kimberly shrieks, Zack jumps about a foot into the air, Jason takes a defensive posture, and even Billy looks more startled than scientifically curious.

Yeah, a blue head is speaking to us.

"My name is Zordon," he says calmly like he isn't floating all disembodied in some kind of light tube, "and you have nothing to fear from me."

I gulp, but weirdly, I believe him. Maybe I'd be more afraid if we hadn't already encountered a talking winged monkey with his destructive clay minions.

"Says the guy who's missing pretty much his *entire* body," Zack says.

Kimberly frowns at him. "It might not be a good idea to antagonize the floating head who has the power to move us through space in the blink of an eye."

"Or time," Billy says excitedly. "We might have just time traveled."

"Quiet," Jason orders.

Zack and Kimberly are briefly united in glaring at him, but Billy just looks hurt.

I touch Billy on the shoulder. "Maybe space *and* time," I whisper. "That would be interdimensional travel, right?"

Billy nods, but he doesn't launch into a lecture on the theory of interdimensional travel, so I know he's still stinging from Jason's rebuke. Or maybe he's just as freaked out as I am.

"You are no more than twenty miles from your original location and remain in your same time and dimension," Zordon replies.

"Where exactly are we?" Jason asks.

"Ai-yi-yi! Excellent question."

Startled, I turn to see a metallic creature a little shorter than me bustle up to us. Its head is a gold saucer with a visor of blinking red lights, and it has a red torso and black arms and legs with gold hands and feet.

"You are in the Command Center, a hidden stronghold in the desert outside of Angel Grove," it explains in a high, tinny voice.

Okay—now there's a talking robot. The day could not get weirder.

"This is Alpha 5," Zordon says. "He is a sentient being with artificial intelligence, and he is my faithful companion and assistant."

Billy walks up to Alpha 5 and leans in to look at him more closely. "Fascinating," he murmurs again.

I'm glad that Billy isn't freaking out, which is more than can be said for the rest of us. The others are gaping at Alpha 5 like they can't believe their eyes, and I'm sure I have the same bewildered expression on my face.

"That explains *where* we are," Jason says, "but not why."

"Or why monsters tore up our football stadium looking for you," I add. I haven't forgotten the name Goldar shouted. *Zordon*.

Zordon's head swivels to me, and it's seriously weird to see.

Kimberly nods. "Their leader seemed to think you were recruiting for something."

"Trini's right," Zack says, ignoring Kimberly. "The gold monkey said Angel Grove was your recruiting ground."

"Ah, that would be Goldar, Rita's general." Zordon grimaces.

"Who's Rita?" Billy and I ask at the same time.

"She was the one who sent Goldar after me," Zordon replies. "And as it turns out, Rita is correct. I am recruiting."

"For *what*?" Billy asks.

"Yeah." Zack nods. "Like Alpha 5 said, 'Ai-yi-yi. Excellent question.'"

Wait. If Zordon is recruiting and we've just been beamed into his secret stronghold in the desert, then does that mean . . . ?

Jason's eyes widens as he reaches the same conclusion. "Are *we* being recruited?"

"It took bravery to stand up to Goldar and the Putties," Zordon replies, "especially when you were so ill-equipped to fight them." He smiles at us, and it's weird because he seems almost proud of us. Like he knows us.

"We were watching the whole fight," Alpha 5 breaks in excitedly, "and you all showed great potential."

"I would love to get a look at that surveillance equipment," Billy murmurs, but quietly enough so that I'm the only one who hears him. Kimberly runs a finger across the torn sleeve of her sweater without comment.

A pang hits me. The rest of them are the brave ones. Jason, Zack, and Kimberly risked being injured or even killed by the Putties; Billy is more curious than scared; and they all picked up weapons to defend themselves against Goldar and the Putties. But I don't know what potential I demonstrated. I just stood there, frozen.

"I will answer your question," Zordon says, "but you will need to know something of my own history first. I am a warrior trained in temporal scholarship from the planet Eltar."

"I'm sorry, but . . . *what?*" I blink at him. "Did you just basically say you were a galactic warrior scholar?"

"I wouldn't have put it that way, but I suppose that is accurate."

"We'd get answers more quickly if we didn't interrupt every few seconds," Jason says, shooting me a quelling look.

My face burns, and when Jason looks away, Zack mouths at me, *See? Asshole.*

Zordon's eyes track this interaction, but he doesn't comment on it. "Over ten thousand years ago, my allies and I fought a sorceress named Rita Repulsa who was bent on conquering many planets, including yours."

Ten *thousand* years ago? That was the Stone Age. My mind can't process that we're actually talking to anyone so ancient, and

I can tell Zack definitely wants to comment on the evil sorceress being named Rita *Repulsa*, but with what must be a heroic effort, he refrains.

"It was on Earth where Rita and I had our final confrontation," Zordon continues. "In that battle, she trapped me in a time warp where I am outside of space and time, and that is why I can only communicate by appearing in this energy tube as you see me now. Fortunately, Rita was unable to conquer Earth because I succeeded in sealing her in a secure container orbiting the moon before I was, myself, trapped." His tone is matter of fact, like being imprisoned outside of time and space is no big deal.

I expect Billy to ask about the energy tube or at least mutter, "Fascinating" again, but he just leans forward, drinking in every word.

"Rita has been trapped for ten thousand years," Zordon says, "but I knew that she could escape one day, so I made preparations. Alpha 5 has helped me construct this command center."

"It has been my honor." The lights in Alpha 5's visor blink rapidly, and it's almost as if he's smiling.

"Then the day I had been dreading came," Zordon says gravely. "Mere days ago, Rita's prison arced so close to the moon that the gravitational pull caused the container to crash into the surface. Before I could act, astronauts discovered the prison and accidentally freed her. Rita wasted no time in magically rebuilding her Moon Palace and resuming her operations to create Putties—in order to conquer Earth."

So, to sum up . . . A freaking galactic warrior outside of space and time is trying to stop a freaking galactic sorceress from invading Earth with her monstrous minions.

"Okay, I get that an evil sorceress has just escaped her space dumpster prison," Zack says, "but what I don't get is why Rita Repulsa—and let's put a pin in that name because I have thoughts—"

Impatiently, Kimberly interrupts him. "Why did Rita have her monsters attack us? Why Angel Grove?"

"Because of him." I point at Zordon. "Because he's recruiting." Goldar even said he thought the football stadium was some kind of warrior arena.

"And that brings me back to my original question." Jason stares at Zordon. "What are you recruiting *for*?"

"That is the question, isn't it?" Zordon peers at us, his expression serious.

I have no idea what Zordon is about to tell us, but my body tenses, and I hold my breath.

"I have chosen the five of you to be the new Power Rangers."

CHAPTER SEVEN

*U*h . . . *come again? What the hell are Power Rangers?*

I expect Jason to say something, but he's silent as he pins Zordon with a contemplative gaze. It's exactly how he looked right before he threw that last touchdown or when the Putty zombies were headed toward Bulk and Skull, trapped in the collapsed bleachers.

"That's going to be a hard no for me." Kimberly folds her arms.

Zack shoots her an annoyed look. "Aren't you going to wait to hear what Power Rangers *are* before saying no?"

"I don't care what they are," Kimberly says. "I'm not joining any alien super squad." Before she can say more, Billy breaks in.

"Yeah, about that." He sounds anxious. "This sounds like it might involve fighting, and um, I don't think that's me."

"You have all been chosen for your unique gifts," Zordon says reassuringly. "You, Billy Cranston, have a truly impressive mind, and your scientific gifts would make you a welcome addition to the team, but it must be your choice."

"How do you know my name?" Billy's eyebrows knit together.

"The Command Center has technology that is much more advanced than anything you have seen. As a Power Ranger, you would, of course, have access to everything."

Billy's face smooths out, and he looks around the cave of technological wonder with avid curiosity. It looks like Billy, at least, is tempted.

"None of you will be forced to become a Power Ranger," Zordon says, "but all of you are needed."

I drop my eyes. I don't think Zordon needs a girl who won't fight because she's afraid of what people might think of her.

"It won't work," Jason says, speaking up at last. "Your advanced surveillance tech must not have picked up on the fact that we got our asses kicked today."

Really? For a group of teens with zero experience fighting alien monsters, I think we did pretty well. Sure, we were probably all quaking in our shoes the whole time, but that didn't stop us from giving the Putties the runaround and rescuing Bulk and Skull. Most importantly, no one got killed. I call that a win.

"You did great," Alpha 5 pipes up, "and you didn't even have your Power Coins yet!"

"Indeed." Zordon says. "These five coins are artifacts that can channel an ancient power, giving their bearers abilities beyond mortal capabilities."

"Oh." Kimberly's eyes are wide, and I wonder if she's less sure about refusing Zordon's offer to become a Power Ranger. Too bad my own problems won't be solved by a mystic coin.

"Kimberly Hart," Zordon says, "You are smart and agile, and you can be even more so as a Power Ranger."

Kimberly looks startled and then thoughtful. She's probably used to being valued for her beauty or her money, and I'd bet she's never been chosen for her intelligence or strength before.

"The Power Rangers are the defenders of the universe." Zordon is looking at Zack now.

"That's quite the purpose." Uncharacteristically, Zack doesn't follow up his comment with a joke.

"Zack Taylor, it is not just your athletic ability that would make you a good Power Ranger—but also your bravery and ability to think on your feet."

I think about Zack trying to lead Goldar away from the rest of us. Zordon is right. Beneath that wisecracking facade, Zack has always been the most heroic person I know. He would definitely be drawn to the Power Ranger's mission.

Into the silence, Jason says, "No one should be making any decisions without more information."

"Jason Lee Scott, I saw your capacity for leadership when you fought Goldar and the Putties," Zordon says. "The team won't stand a chance against Rita and her minions without someone who can make the hard calls."

Jason doesn't respond, but he has a strange contemplative expression on his face.

Apparently, Zordon has managed to talk everyone into at least considering the prospect of becoming a Power Ranger . . . except for me.

He says, "The Power Rangers have long stood against the forces of evil. All your abilities are needed to fulfill this team's great purpose." Zordon is looking at *me* now. "Trini Kwan . . ."

"Wait," I say quickly. Does Zordon know about my martial arts training? I avoid looking at Zack—who knows about my wushu. Or at Billy—who *doesn't*. This really isn't how I want Billy to find out that I've been keeping secrets from him. I mean, I don't want him to find out at all, and definitely not from an intergalactic warrior scholar. "I get it. You want all of us," I say to Zordon, hoping he'll leave at that. *Please don't say anything about my abilities.*

A wrinkle forms in Zordon's forehead, but he must see the urgency in my eyes because he merely says, "True. The five of you are uniquely matched."

He pauses, then continues, "Alpha 5, if you would please. Jason has asked for more information. It's time they saw what they're up against."

Relief flutters in my stomach, but it turns to guilt when Billy shoots me a sympathetic smile and Zack looks at me in confusion. Great. Billy feels sorry for me because he thinks I'm the only one who doesn't have any special abilities, and Zack doesn't get why I stopped Zordon from revealing what I can actually do.

"Ai-yi-yi," Alpha 5 says. "Are you sure, Zordon?"

"Yes. Show them." Zordon doesn't so much as glance in my direction, but a lump forms in my throat. Maybe he's starting to wonder if he made the right choice in picking me. Maybe I am the only one who doesn't belong.

With a rapid blinking of lights that seems to indicate anxiety rather than a smile, Alpha 5 goes over to a console of some kind. He pushes a rapid sequence of buttons, and a scene of green fields and rolling hills projects into the space before us. Human-like yellow beings with four arms, round heads, and crab-like pincers for hands are harvesting the fields. They are laughing and talking to each other. Surprisingly, I understand what they are saying.

"A 3D hologram," Billy breathes in wonder, "and it must have a universal translator."

"These are recordings of a few of the planets Rita has conquered," Zordon says somberly. "This is Regda II."

The scene changes suddenly to smoking fields. Regdans are screaming and running for cover while a familiar winged figure in gold armor bellows orders at Putties who are cutting down the Regdans trying to fight them off with farming implements.

Terror seizes me as I watch a Regdan child screaming in the middle of a burnt field while a Putty Patroller slashes at two adults.

"No! Mom. Dad." The child runs over to the fallen parents, and the Putty leaves without a backward glance.

A warm wetness clings to my cheeks, and I realize I'm crying. This is unbearable.

The scene changes again. This time the Regdans are carrying baskets of vegetables, grains, and fruit to a figure in the shadows. Goldar carries a whip that he snaps at any Regdan who stumbles under the weight of the basket or does not move fast enough.

Billy gulps. "Is that Rita in the shadows? Why can't we see her in the hologram?"

"Rita's sorcery obscures her from recording devices, and she can hide her minions too if she chooses," Zordon explains. "In fact, I would guess Rita cast an illusion to make it seem like humans were responsible for tonight's attack. However, her spell wouldn't work on those who actually confronted her minions. That's why it didn't work on the five of you."

None of us speak. We're all riveted by the horror unfolding in front of us. Cities reduced to rubble and dust. And death. So much death.

My chest constricts as I imagine my parents and Nai Nai cut down in front of me by the Putties while I scream my lungs raw, unable to save them.

"Wagnoria, Regda II, Tarmac III, Myrgo," Zordon says heavily. "All planets that have fallen under Rita's desire for conquest."

I wipe my eyes and swallow the ache in my throat. "And now Rita is coming for Earth."

"Yes." Zordon meets my eyes and says gently, "Trini Kwan, this team needs your heart."

I'm not sure what he means by that, but it no longer matters. I have to do everything I can to stop Rita from destroying my home. Looking around, I can see the same determination in everyone else's faces.

"This team needs all of you," Zordon says. "That is why you must all become Power Rangers—to defend your planet."

Jason nods, quick and decisive. "I'm in."

"I am too," Kimberly says, her face fierce and focused.

"Me too." Billy's voice is quiet, but he sounds sure.

Zack nods. "Count me in."

That just leaves me. They all turn to me, and I see doubt in everyone's expression except for Zack's. The others don't know what I'm doing here, and despite Zack's quiet confidence in me—neither do I.

"Come on, Trini," Zack says. "Let's join the Power Rangers—which, by the way, is *not* a sentence I ever thought I'd say."

Out of the corner of my eye, I see a hologram of two squat, blue-furred beings kneeling to a shadowy form and holding out a swaddled child. "Please, spare us," one of them says.

My stomach twinges in pain. I don't know how much more heartache I can bear, and it would only be so much worse if these scenes of destruction and despair were taking place on Earth.

"You can turn it off now," Zordon says to Alpha 5. The android presses a button on his console and the devastating holograms flicker out, although they will haunt my nightmares forever.

I shudder. "I'll do it," I say shakily, although I'm not sure what I'm agreeing to.

"Very well," Zordon says as if he never doubted my decision. Any of our decisions.

We look at each other, and Jason asks the question we're probably all thinking. "What now?"

"Alpha 5, bring out the Power Morphers, please."

"Yes, Zordon." Alpha 5 moves eagerly over to a column of opaque pulsing light next to his console.

"Morphers?" Kimberly asks. "I thought you said we were getting coins."

"The coins are set into the Morphers," Zordon explains. "The advanced technology of the Morphers is designed to channel the power of the coins and allow you to metamorphose and access your Power Ranger abilities."

"Quick question." Zack raises his hand. "What are we metamorphosing *into*, exactly? I don't want to turn into . . . oh, say, a winged blue furry monster."

For once, Jason doesn't give him grief for his jokes. Zack asked the question we were all thinking.

"You won't be changed into anyone or anything," Zordon says reassuringly. "The essence of who you are will stay the same. It's only your abilities that will be enhanced."

I suppose that makes sense . . . as much as *any* of this makes sense, that is.

"Oh, and your Morpher will also create a high-tech suit for you," Zordon continues, "in the color of your coin."

"Like a superhero suit?" I ask, imagining colorful spandex.

Zordon smiles at me. "Exactly." Alpha 5 turns off what must be some kind of energy shield, revealing small objects in five different colors about the size of belt buckles. They're laid out on a square stand. These must be the Morphers. Next to them are wide black belts with an empty slot clearly meant to hold the Morphers. Alpha 5 scoops the Morphers off the stand, attaches each one onto a belt, and brings them over to us.

Zack peers at the colorful assortment in Alpha's hands. "Nice. Both useful and a cool fashion accessory." Then his eyebrows rise. "Why do they have dinosaurs on them?"

I lean forward to look at the five Morphers. Zack is right. Sort of. Stamped on the gold coin in each Morpher is the engraving of a prehistoric creature, although they're not all dinosaurs.

Billy examines the Morphers as well. "Technically, only two of these are dinosaurs."

"The ancient creatures of Earth have much power," Zordon says. "Think of them as an emblem of your individual strength. In fact, we've connected each morphing process to a specific prehistoric emblem. To morph into a Power Ranger, you just need to hold out your Morpher and call out the name of the creature engraved on your coin."

"That definitely won't call attention to us," Zack says sarcastically.

"Eventually, the morphing process will become second nature," Zordon replies, "merely requiring that the coin be on your person. For now, we thought it best to provide . . . what is it that you Earthlings call it? Oh yes—training wheels."

"So do we get to pick?" Kimberly asks.

"Not exactly," he replies.

Jason frowns at the Morphers. "So you'll assign us a coin based on who you think we are?"

"It is the coins that choose—not me." Zordon half smiles. "Each coin has a color associated with the central trait of the coin . . . and of the Ranger. The coin will glow that color when it is in the proximity of the ranger it has the most affinity with."

Alpha 5 walks up to Jason with his handful of Morpher belts, and the coin in the red Morpher begins to glow red. "Jason," Zordon says, "your coin denotes charisma. Your emblem is the Tyrannosaurus Rex, and you will be the Red Ranger."

Alpha 5 hands Jason a belt with the red Power Morpher, and he accepts it without hesitation. "We should start training together as soon as possible," Jason says as he buckles on his Morpher. "We need to function as a team if we're going to stop Rita."

"Spoken like a true leader, Jason," Zordon says. "That is why I have chosen you to lead this team."

"Oh, hell no," Zack says at the same time Kimberly says, "Over my dead body."

Then Zack and Kimberly glare at each other for no reason that I can see except that they don't like to be in agreement about anything.

Zordon ignores Zack's and Kimberly's protests. "My decision is final. Jason Lee Scott will be the leader of the Power Rangers."

Jason exhales heavily. He doesn't seem happy about being named the team leader, but he's not turning Zordon down either.

"You said the coins choose—not you," Kimberly points out.

"True," Zordon says, "but I should have been more precise. Each coin is naturally drawn to a specific ranger, and I have no control over that. However, I am the one who chooses the five rangers *and* the leader of this team."

My heart twinges when I glance at Zack, wondering exactly how upset he is. Honestly, I'm not entirely surprised that Zordon chose Jason to lead us. He's strategic, driven, and as the school football captain, he has the most experience in building a team.

There's just one problem with Zordon's plan: The five of us have never worked together, aren't friends, have absolutely nothing in common, and don't even all *like* each other. So how are we supposed to unite to protect Angel Grove and defeat Rita?

Zack looks like he wants to keep protesting, but Alpha 5 is approaching him, and the coin in the black Morpher is glowing with a smoky light.

Zordon says, "Zack, your coin is associated with creativity. Your emblem is the Mastodon, and you will be the Black Ranger."

Alpha 5 hands Zack his Morpher, which he takes with a grimace. "It figures that I would get this dinosaur," Zack mutters. "*He* gets to be a Tyrannosaurus Rex and I'm a black wooly mammoth."

"The mastodon isn't a dinosaur, but it's still cool," Billy says hesitantly. "And actually, a mastodon and mammoth aren't the same either."

I peer over his shoulder to look at the black Mastodon Morpher and then at Zack. His face is unreadable. How does he feel about being chosen by the black coin? My stomach knots, and I try to catch his eye but he doesn't look at me. My whole body tightens, and I want to say something, but this should be a more private conversation.

Instinctively, I lean forward. All I can do right now is give Zack a distraction. "You'd know that was a Mastodon," I whisper, "if you had been in my group in history when we did the Paleolithic era."

The tension on Zack's face eases. He laughs and whispers back, "Trini, I promise to always be in your group from now on. Starting with this one."

Warmth spreads through my chest, but Alpha 5 has reached Kimberly, so I tear my attention from Zack and focus on the weirdest group project I've ever been assigned.

A coin glows pink in her presence. Zordon says, "Kimberly, your coin is one of intuition. Your emblem is the Pterodactyl, and you are the Pink Ranger." Alpha 5 gives her the pink Morpher.

Okay, is it just me, or does Kimberly being assigned as the Pink Ranger seem a bit . . . gendered? Then again, she was wearing pink at the restaurant. And then there's the way she's eagerly buckling on her Morpher with a smile on her face. She's obviously a fan of pink.

"Is that a dinosaur?" Zack asks me.

Actually, I'm not sure, but Billy overhears and answers for me. "Technically, a Pterodactyl is a prehistoric flying reptile but not a dinosaur . . . oh, blue!" This is in response to a coin glowing blue when Alpha 5 gets to him.

"Billy, you are the Blue Ranger. Your coin is associated with perception, and your emblem is the Triceratops." Zordon doesn't appear to have heard our side conversation about what qualifies as a dinosaur or he might have a lot less faith in his choice of us as Power Rangers.

Billy takes his Morpher from Alpha 5 with a dazed look like he can't believe he gets one. I totally know the feeling.

"Now that's a dinosaur," Zack says, and Billy just nods.

There's only one left, so I already know which ranger I am even before Alpha 5 walks over to me with the last Morpher. My throat grows tight as I stare at the Sabertooth Tiger etched in gold on the remaining Power Coin. Xiao Laohu. *Little Tiger*. It's what my nai nai always calls me. Then the coin glows yellow.

"Trini, your coin is associated with courage, and your emblem is the Sabertooth Tiger." Zordon pauses, and it's as if time has stopped. I am suddenly breathless and lightheaded. Once he speaks those words, there will be no going back. "You are the Yellow Ranger."

That's it then. I swallow hard.

I am the Yellow Ranger.

CHAPTER EIGHT

'm just saying . . ." Zack turns away from the practice ring where Jason and Kimberly seem to be doing more arguing than training. "What's up with you being the Yellow Ranger and me being the Black Ranger?"

"I see your point," I say dryly. I know an intergalactic disembodied head like Zordon can't be expected to be clued into the racial politics of Earth—but *seriously*? Then I remember that Zordon didn't technically choose our colors. The coins did.

"Still," Zack says, his eyes gleaming, "I have to admit that Black Power Ranger has a certain ring to it. I can't say I'm mad about it." He pats the Morpher on his belt. "Good job, coin."

I blink. He not only sounds okay with being the Black Ranger . . . but downright stoked. I wish I could say the same about being the Yellow Ranger. My chest tightens. Yellow peril. Yellow fever. The phrases that associate Asians with the color yellow aren't exactly positive.

"Our coins aren't sentient," Billy says, eying Zack with amusement.

The three of us are sitting in the ringside seats of the Command Center training room watching Jason attempt to give Kimberly a crash course on mixed martial arts. It feels like almost the same setup as last night's football game—minus the football teams, cheerleaders, spectators, and attacking aliens, of course.

"Fine," I say, "but there's also Kimberly being assigned the Pink Ranger. So we can add Earth gender politics to the list of things coins aren't clued into." Billy opens his mouth, and I quickly add, "I know, I know—the coins aren't sentient. But it's a hell of a coincidence."

"True," Zack says. "I could have rocked a Pink Ranger suit, and a Pterodactyl emblem is pretty cool too."

I laugh. "You'd look good in black too."

He grins at me, and my whole body trills. *Weird.* Why am I all giddy suddenly?

Before I can overanalyze it, he says, "You know what? The hell with it. I'm the Black Ranger, and I'm going to own it. Black woolly—I mean black *Mastodon* and all."

"Hell yeah," I say. Zack's excitement is just so darned contagious.

Billy adds, "That's great, Zack!"

Then they both look at me like I'm going to pump my fist in the air and scream "I am the Yellow Ranger!" My smile fades. Nope. Not ready for that.

"I'm glad you're embracing black." I gesture toward Kimberly, who's wearing a hot pink tank top and matching Lycra capri leggings. "Because I don't think Kimberly is giving up the pink." In fact, she's started yelling "Pink power!" as she kicks the sandbag, although I can't tell if that has more to do with annoying Jason than reclaiming pink as a power move. Most likely both. "Kimberly is totally owning the whole 'pink and feminist' vibe."

"Fair enough," Zack concedes. He might not like Kimberly, but he respects feminism.

I sigh to myself. Everyone else seems to be just fine with the colors they got. I guess that means I'm giving all intergalactic disembodied heads and insentient coins a pass on the problematic racialization of Power Ranger identities. Which is not a thought I ever thought I'd have.

Zack bumps my arm. "Admit it, Trini—being a Power Ranger is cool."

Pushing away my doubts, I smile and say, "It is." I mean, it kind of is. So far, the best part of being a Power Ranger is the chance to hang out with Zack like we're friends again. The worst part is definitely the training.

Day one of training is *not* going well.

For one thing, it turns out that Jason is kind of a drill sergeant. He wanted to start training as soon as we all got our Power Coins last night, but the rest of us overrode him and insisted that we needed to get back home so our families wouldn't think that we had been abducted by aliens (even though the official explanation for the attack was "hoodlums in Halloween costumes").

Jason did succeed in getting us all back to the Command Center to begin training, and his first victim . . . um, trainee . . . was Kimberly. He's making her kick a sandbag over and over again while he barks critiques of her form.

Finally, Kimberly stops kicking the bag. "How many of these damn kicks do I have to do?"

"As many as it takes for you to get better." Jason's voice is implacable.

"I cannot believe Zordon made Jason our leader." Zack has mentioned this before. "And I cannot believe rich girl Kimberly is on the team." He's said that already too.

Billy pretends he doesn't hear Zack, so it's up to me to respond. "I know. It's bizarre." I mean it too. I have no idea how it is that the only two people in all of Angel Grove who Zack *doesn't* get along with—happen to also be Power Rangers.

Hesitantly, I add, "Jason does have experience as the captain of the football team. I can see why Zordon chose him to lead us." I mean, besides the fact that Jason is white and male, which is what power looks like on Earth. *Yeah, I'm definitely not going to say that.*

"I can see it too." Zack's voice is hard.

I glance at Billy, but he's still pretending not to hear.

"Face it, Trini," Zack says, "you and I will never be the ones chosen to lead."

Well, I *was* thinking the same thing. My stomach clenches, and I don't respond. What is there to say to that anyway? An uncomfortable silence descends over us.

In the ring, Kimberly grabs a towel from a nearby bench and wipes the sweat from her face. Frowning at the towel, she says, "So much for the claim that this mascara is waterproof." Then she yanks her disheveled hair out of its hair tie and carefully redoes her ponytail. "I'm done, Jason. Torture someone else."

"You won't last long in a fight if you don't train."

She glares at him. "I don't see how kicking a bag a million times is going to help."

I hate to admit it, but Jason has a point. If Kimberly practices often enough, the move will be in her muscle memory—at least that's what Nai Nai tells me. Except for the constant stream of criticism, Jason's teaching methods aren't all that different from Nai Nai's.

"If you weren't so worried about messing up your hair and makeup," he grinds out, "we might actually get somewhere." Okay, Nai Nai would never say *that.*

"I don't need you to tell me how to work hard!" Kimberly tosses her ponytail over one shoulder. "I'm a *gymnast.*"

"So you've said." Jason doesn't sound impressed.

Yikes. "Maybe we should do something," I say worriedly.

Zack leans back. "Nah. Let the two of them figure it out."

But I'm already racing down the stairs to the practice ring. Billy follows me, and so does Zack, who mutters, "It's not like either one of them will listen to us."

"You're doing great, Kimberly," I say as I come up to the padded walls of the ring.

She dredges up a smile. "Thanks."

"You too, Jason," I say. "Uh, you really seem to know what you're doing. Not that I know much about mixed martial arts." Technically, that's true. The only martial art I know is the wushu that Nai Nai has taught me.

Zack makes a gagging sound, and I elbow him.

Jason is looking at me with a quizzical expression.

My stomach sinks. Any minute now, he's going to ask me why I'm here with the rest of them. *Good question.* Kimberly, Jason, and Zack are all athletically gifted, and Billy is, of course, a genius. I'm the only one who doesn't seem to belong.

There's a charged silence, broken when the sliding metal door to the training room opens and Alpha 5 walks in. "When you're all done training, can you please come into the Power Chamber?" Apparently, that's the room that we were first transported into. "Zordon wants to show you something." He turns to Billy. "He is especially interested in your thoughts, Billy Cranston. He thinks you might be able to help us with an issue we're having."

"Sure." Billy's eyes flicker between Alpha 5 and the practice ring like he's torn between his curiosity about the mysterious summons and the need to prove himself in the ring.

"Billy, it's fine if you go with Alpha 5 now," Jason says.

"I haven't had a turn in the ring yet."

Jason shrugs. "I think you'll be better off helping Zordon and Alpha 5 with whatever technological problem they're having."

Billy's face falls. *Ouch.* I squeeze his arm in sympathy, but he barely seems to notice. "I guess I'll go." His shoulders slump as he follows Alpha 5 out.

Jason averts his eyes, and I could swear an expression of guilt flits over his face.

Zack glances at the door as it closes on Billy's retreating back, and his mouth tightens. "I think our training session would go better with less assholery."

To my horror, a laugh bubbles up, but I tamp it down firmly. "You're not helping," I tell him.

Zack's eyes gleam, and I suspect he catches the telltale quiver of my lips as I try not to smile. "But you think I'm funny. Give me that."

Jason glowers at him. "Taylor, into the ring. Now."

"Happy to oblige." Zack starts moving, and I grab his arm.

"We're supposed to be working together, not fighting each other," I remind him. We need to be a team to defeat Rita.

"Don't worry," Jason says to me. "I just want to see what Zack's got. This is all a part of our training."

"It's fine. I'm not going to hurt Jason." Zack strains at my grasp, but I hold on. "Let go, Trini."

I release him, not because I want him to fight Jason, but because I don't want the others to know that I'm strong enough to hold him back. Besides, both Jason and Zack grew up training at Ernie's gym, which has strict rules about the use of martial arts as self-defense only. And Jason is a teacher there, so he's sure to enforce those rules. Zack too, for all his dislike of Jason, doesn't have a vicious bone in his body.

As soon as I let go, Zack hops into the ring.

Kimberly shakes her head before joining me on the sidelines. "Boys," she mutters in disgust. "All they want to do is out-testosterone each other."

She doesn't seem to expect a response, which is good because I don't have one. This is the first time Kimberly and I have actually had a chance to talk with each other, and I have no idea how we're supposed to interact.

In the ring, Zack touches the Morpher on his belt. "What do you say we practice with our new powers?"

My hand sneaks over to my own Morpher. Zack's not the only one curious about the abilities we'd have as Power Rangers.

Jason shakes his head. "Like I said yesterday, it's dangerous to channel our new powers before we're ready. Someone could get hurt. Zordon agreed with me."

"Zordon is thousands of years old," Zack says. "He doesn't even *have* a body. What does he know about training us how to fight Rita's monsters?"

Zack has a point, but Jason frowns. "Can't you take *anything* seriously?"

So far, Jason has implied that Zack is a shallow jokester, Kimberly is a spoiled diva, and Billy is nothing but tech help. If Jason's grand plan as captain is to unite us by turning us all against him—then he's succeeding brilliantly.

Jason lets out a sigh, and that's when I notice the dark circles under his eyes. I can only imagine the stress he's under as the leader of a team of teenagers charged with guarding the entire planet from marauding aliens. Maybe Zack was right about his assholery, but I can't help but feel bad for Jason. After all, he didn't ask to be assigned as our leader.

Kimberly stretches her arms gracefully over her head and makes a face. "As far as I'm concerned, they're welcome to beat each other bloody."

Kimberly's words dredge up my own history with beating somebody bloody. *That's Trini Kwan. She could go kung fu crazy.* I thought Zack was the only one who remembered my elementary school fight. But I was wrong. The kid I beat up clearly did too.

My heart pounds as I remember the malice in Carl's voice as he yelled "Fight! Fight!" Breathlessly, I reach for the calm I felt when Nai Nai first explained the purpose of our lessons. *I am going to teach you control, Xiao Laohu.*

That calm slowly descends on me, but now Kimberly is looking at me with a funny expression on her face. Anxiety licks at me. She was probably watching me get lost in my memories and wondering why I'm acting so weird.

"Hey," she says. "I've seen you before."

My forehead wrinkles. That's not what I was expecting. Of course she's seen me before. "I was at the football stadium yesterday."

"I know *that*. I mean that I know you from something other than fighting aliens." It's generous on her part to include me under the umbrella of "fighting aliens" since I just stood there.

"I remember now!" Then her whole face seems to shut down. "You were at the restaurant. You're Zack's girlfriend."

I shake my head vehemently. "No. I'm definitely *not*. We're just friends."

"I see." Without another word, she turns toward the ring.

Does she think I'm holding a grudge against her too? I want to reassure her, but I don't know what to say—*Hey, my friend hates you, but I don't.* Yeah, probably better not to say anything. Besides, I should be focused on the impending fight.

Zack is putting his hands together and bending at the waist. "If you're going to be a party pooper, let's just spar the old-fashioned way then without Power Morphers or supernatural abilities."

Jason bows too, his face etched in grim lines.

Then, without warning, they clash in a blur of arms and legs. Despite myself, I'm riveted. Jason has the advantage of sheer size and muscle mass, but Zack's lithe body is *fast*. They have different strengths, but they're evenly matched.

Jason slices at Zack with an open-handed blow, which Zack side steps instead of trying to block. He then tries to get under Jason's guard with a strike of his own, but Jason blocks it and aims a kick at Zack. He again spins away, avoiding Jason's attack. Neither one is able to land a blow, and the pattern of Zack evading and Jason blocking continues for a few minutes.

Then Jason sends out a lightning-fast kick that Zack barely avoids by bending backward. He springs back up into a defensive pose.

"I should be learning *those* moves." Kimberly murmurs wistfully.

"You should be training with the Power Morpher," I say without thinking.

Her eyes widen as she turns to me. "What do you mean?"

Damn. I said that out loud. "Zordon told us the Morphers would enhance our abilities," I mumble. "Like you said, you're a gymnast. Instead of training to fight a different way—it would be better to lean into your existing abilities like flips . . . and stuff." Clearly, I'm not sure about what she can do as a gymnast. "I actually think Jason had the right idea starting you off with kicks. You're really flexible, and it shows in how high you can kick. Also, kicks don't rely on upper body strength. You're strong, but no matter how much you train, there's only so much muscle you can build." My voice grows more certain as

I remember the muscular arms and chests of the Putties we encountered. "But think of what you could do if you morphed."

Kimberly glances at the Morpher on her belt and then at the ring where Zack and Jason are still sparring. "So you're saying that I'd be at a disadvantage in a fight up against opponents stronger than me, but . . ."

"The Morpher would give you the strength to level the playing field."

She grins. "I like how you think, Trini."

My face grows hot. It's weird to have someone give me a compliment without expecting me to do all the work on a project. Then again, if the Power Rangers are a group project, then for the very first time in maybe ever—I'm the weakest link.

Abruptly, Kimberly says, "I didn't mean to get Zack fired."

Sympathy flares in me. "I didn't think you did."

Some of the tension seeps out of her face. "It's just that Zack didn't let me apologize, and then he kept making those snide comments, and Jason thinks I'm a rich, spoiled brat too." She throws up her hands. "Maybe I am. I really wanted a fresh start here in Angel Grove but I keep messing up."

I can't imagine why Kimberly, with her stylish clothes and effortless popularity, would need a fresh start, but there's no mistaking the dejected slump of her body. "Listen, I saw you yesterday," I say. "You ran toward the fight because people needed your help. You are *not* a spoiled brat."

Her cheeks grow pink. "Thanks, Trini. We should hang out—I mean outside the Command Center and when we're not fighting aliens."

I blink. Um, what? Kimberly is a cheerleader and I'm a nerd. Why would she want to spend time with me?

"I mean, sure," I say slowly. "Hanging out would be cool." As long as Zack doesn't find out that I'm getting chummy with one of his archenemies after I just started to reconnect with him. A week ago, the thought of Zack having one, much less two, enemies would have been unthinkable. Then again, a week ago, the thought of an intergalactic warrior recruiting us to fight an intergalactic sorceress would have *also* been unthinkable.

Zack and Jason finally break apart, breathing heavily. Neither one has landed a blow; they're too evenly matched. As much as I don't want to see them actually beat each other bloody, I think Zack is right about using the Power Morphers. We can't stop Rita until we learn how to fight as Power Rangers.

But I'm actually kind of glad Jason and Zack aren't using the Morphers, because then they'd have more endurance and we'd be stuck watching them fight all day. Maybe they'll stop now and we can . . . oh, never mind. The two of them have reengaged.

Jason lunges at Zack and finally manages to land a blow that sends him sprawling on the padded floor.

I wince, but Zack just leaps to his feet. "Damn. I was just about to kick your butt, and I mean that literally. My roundhouse kick was inches away from connecting."

"Do you *ever* stop joking?" Jason eyes Zack in irritation.

"Not as long as it keeps bugging you," he says cheerfully.

Come on, Zack. I know he's actually taking all of this seriously, but no one else will see that if he keeps using humor to deflect— not that Jason should be making assumptions.

"So *now* can we use the Power Morphers and fight for real?" Zack asks.

"No. The others aren't ready yet." Jason turns toward us, and I know he means that *I'm* not ready. "Trini, if you're going to be on the team, I'd better train you too. You're up."

My palms grow damp, and I stifle the temptation to run. I tell myself that I can handle kicking a sandbag over and over again. I just have to make sure to give Jason something to critique.

Or . . . I can just show him what I can do. After all, I seriously doubt any of my new team members are going to see me as a racist stereotype at this point.

Then I think of Billy's dejected face when Jason sent him away from the ring. He'll be upset with me if he finds out I've been keeping my fighting skills a secret from my one and only friend. And then there's Kimberly. I let her think I couldn't fight. She might feel I was putting on an act to make a fool out of her. Jason might feel the same.

Okay, letting anyone else but Zack know about my wushu isn't an option. *New plan.* I'll let the others think I'm a fast learner and that Jason is an excellent teacher. Before long, I'll show enough improvement to actually be an asset to the team . . . without anyone feeling betrayed.

Entering the ring through an opening in the low padded walls, I start to walk past Jason and toward the sandbag, but he holds out an arm to stop me. "I want to work on your blocking."

My face flushes in mortification. I get it. Jason doesn't think I'll be much use in a fight, so he's going to limit my lessons to self-defense. Not that I blame him for thinking I can't fight, but how am I supposed to pretend to improve if he won't train me?

"Hey," Zack says, "why don't you let Trini spar and see what she can do?"

Jason glowers at Zack. "That's not funny." Except Zack wasn't joking that time. *He knows I can handle myself. I just don't want anyone* else *to know.*

I shake my head vigorously. "That's okay. I don't want to spar."

"Don't worry," Jason says. "I'll just teach you a few moves to defend yourself." He points at Zack. "Make yourself useful and partner with Trini so I can show her how to block."

For once, Zack doesn't protest. He comes over and stands in front of me. His T-shirt is damp with sweat and clings to his chest, and the heat of his nearness hits me in a way that makes my stomach do a somersault.

I blink. *Focus, Trini.*

"No need to be nervous, Trini," Jason says, totally misunderstanding my breathlessness—not that I understand it myself. "Now bring up your arm like this." He comes over to me and moves my arm to show me a basic block that I first learned when I was five.

"I think she's got it," Zack says dryly.

Jason ignores him. "Trini, when Zack attacks, use that move to block him." Even though Jason is standing right next to me and touching my arm, I don't feel a single flutter at his nearness. But Zack standing two feet away, all lithe and beautiful with that familiar, sweet smile . . . is a different story.

I shake my head, trying to focus.

"Now Zack, I want you to pretend to attack Trini, nice and slow." Jason takes a step back. "I'll be watching to give you pointers. Okay?"

"Okay," I say.

"Okay," Zack says. Then the side of his hand comes at me heavy and fast.

Every instinct screams at me to block and hit back hard, but my arm just won't move. *That's Trini Kwan. She could go kung fu crazy.*

The blow hits me under my eye with a jarring pain that sends sparks flooding my vision.

"Oh *damn*!" Zack's eyes are wide and horror-struck. "I thought you were going to block it. I'm so sorry, Trini!"

"What the hell, Taylor!" Pale with anger, Jason steps in front of me like he thinks Zack is going to hit me again.

Kimberly is running into the ring. "Are you alright, Trini?" In practically the same breath, she says, "I can't believe you hit her, Zack!"

Great. Now Jason and Kimberly think Zack meant to hurt me when we both know full well that I should have blocked that attack easily. The guilt twisting my stomach is worse than the pain of my throbbing face. "I'm fine," I say faintly.

Clearly, no one believes me. Kimberly is examining my face. "I think you're going to have a black eye."

Zack looks absolutely miserable.

A tinny voice cuts through the guilt and tension in the room. "I'm sorry to interrupt your training," Alpha 5 announces, "but Zordon would like to see you all now."

CHAPTER NINE

T he problem with the Zords," Billy explains to us as he gestures at the revolving 3D holograms of what look like robotic dinosaur tanks, "isn't obvious."

I resist commenting that none of this—is obvious. I don't know what the hell a Zord is. But I know Billy. He tends to give explanations without a lot of context, but he'll eventually get around to telling us what he means.

Zordon, floating in his energy tube next to the console where Billy is conducting his lecture, doesn't interrupt.

"I've been over the schematics," Billy continues, "and it all checks out as far as I can tell, although of course my experience with nanotechnology has been mostly theoretical up until this point."

"Nano . . . what?" Jason asks.

I'm nowhere on the same level as Billy, but I took enough AP Physics classes to provide a broad definition. Plus, if Billy tries to explain, no one will have a clue as to what he means. I say, "Nanotechnology is the manipulation of matter at the molecular level."

"Actually, it's quite a bit more complicated than that." Billy launches into a speech that leaves me as confused as everyone else despite my AP Physics. "So . . ." Billy's voice trails off as he takes in our blank faces. "Uh, yeah—what Trini said."

"Okay, fine. Nanotechnology, nanowhatever." Kimberly points at the holograms. "Can someone please explain what *those* are?"

"That's easy." Zack walks around the holograms to get a better look from every angle. "Pterodactyl. Tyrannosaurus Rex. Triceratops. Sabertooth Tiger. And my personal favorite—the Mastodon. I'm guessing these are the Zords?"

"You are correct." Zordon nods in approval. "These vehicles will give you an edge in your fight with Rita's army."

"Where are they now?" Kimberly asks.

"Normally, they're kept at separate hangars around the world," Zordon says, "but right now, they are being stored under this Command Center so we can work on them."

Zack's eyebrows lift. "So you're basically saying that you've got dinosaur vehicles parked in the underground garage."

"They are too powerful to have out in the open," Zordon replies.

"If they're so powerful," Jason says, "then why didn't you show them to us before?"

"Ai-yi-yi." Alpha 5 flutters his hands in agitation. "They are not working."

"We wanted to get them operational before we revealed them to you." Zordon's eyes shift to Billy. "It is my hope that Billy will help us figure out the problem."

"I can try." His voice wavers. "But like I said, I don't have actual experience with nanotechnology. From what I've seen of the Command Center so far, Earth is light-years behind in . . . well, just about everything."

"We can get you caught up," Alpha 5 says excitedly.

Billy doesn't appear to be listening to Alpha 5. He's peering worriedly at me. "Trini, what happened to your eye?"

I probe at my face gingerly. "It was an accident."

Zack winces.

Jason clears his throat. "Zordon, you need to rethink your decision to have Trini and Billy in the field. They're not ready to fight. Trini getting hurt today is nothing compared to what could happen against the Putties."

"And as I said before," Zordon says, "we need them both."

Wait. They had this conversation already?

"Fine. I can see why you need Billy to get the Zords operational, but Trini—"

"Hey!" Zack glares at Jason. "Don't go trying to kick Trini off the team."

"You were the one who hit her in the face!" Jason retorts.

"I'm not defending Zack," Kimberly says, "but this is just as much your fault, Jason."

"How is this my fault?"

My gut wrenches. I don't know what's worse—everyone thinking I'm useless or everyone fighting over me.

"Enough!" Zordon thunders.

My jaw drops. I hadn't really seen the warrior part in the warrior scholar before, but Zordon looks ferocious enough to skewer us all alive. Everyone falls silent.

"Each and every one of you is needed," Zordon says calmly like he hadn't just gone all scary alien on us. "Rita is using her palace on the moon to make Putties," he continues, "and after ten thousand years, the first ones she made were bound to be weak."

Is he saying the Putties that chased us all over the football field were the *weak* version?

Kimberly turns pale, Zack is silent, Billy gasps, and Jason's jaw gets even twitchier . . . so yeah, everyone else has come to the same conclusion.

"Jason." Zordon is watching him closely. "If your team isn't ready, then it is your job as leader to train them until they *are* ready. You're going to need to work as a team to stop Rita."

"I understand," he says shortly.

Billy comes to my side and points to a door. "There's a med bay through that door. I can take you there to get your injury treated, Trini."

I shake my head and instantly regret it when the motion makes my face ache. "I'm good. Really."

"I can take Trini to the med bay." Kimberly examines the contusion under my eye.

"I'll take her," Zack says.

"No, I will," Jason insists.

Wonderful. Not only did I get a totally preventable black eye from my former best friend, but my teammates are about to start a fight over me. Again. "No one needs to take me to the med bay. I can go there myself."

Alpha 5's head swivels to me. "You'll find everything you need to make you comfortable."

"Thanks." I move toward the door that Billy pointed out, but the worry on Zack's face makes me pause. It might help if I make it clear to everyone that I don't blame him for my injury. "You can come if you want, Zack."

"Yes. I do." His face clears, and he hurries to join me. "I really am sorry," he whispers.

"It's my fault." The metal door slides open, and we step through. As soon as the door closes behind us, I say, "I could have blocked you."

"Yeah, about that—why didn't you?"

To avoid answering, I look around the med bay. There are exactly five beds, and they have a complicated console at the head of each one. One wall is lined with metal cabinets and drawers, and another wall has more high-tech consoles along with unfamiliar equipment on the counters. "I just wanted to get an ice pack for my eye. This place looks like it's equipped for brain surgery."

Zack is rummaging around the drawers and opening cabinets. He finally opens what looks like the door to a refrigeration unit and pulls out a purple gel-like square. "I don't know if this is an ice pack, but it is cold. Do you think it's safe to use?"

"If there were anything dangerous in here, I'm sure Alpha 5 would have told us."

Zack walks over to me, but instead of handing it to me, he gently holds the gel pack to my eye. He's right—it is cold. So why is heat suddenly rushing to my cheeks?

Surely, it's not because of the light touch of Zack's fingers on my face as he holds the pack in place. But when his fingers make contact with my skin . . . my pulse jumps like I'm being supercharged.

This close up, I can see the faint stubble on his cheek and the intensity of his gaze on me. "How does that feel?"

"Great," I squeak out, trying to catch my breath.

He frowns and takes away the ice pack . . . and his fingers. "I think it's too cold. Let me find a towel or something to wrap it in."

"No, it's fine." I grab the pack from him and hold it to my face so he doesn't have to touch me and make me feel those strange, confusing sensations again. "I've got it. You can go back to the training room with the others." I'm sure Jason has resumed training by now.

Zack sighs and leans against the metal frame of one of the beds. "I'd rather not be in a room alone with Jason and Kimberly if I can help it."

Great. Our very first day of training together was a bust, and now our team is even more divided than when we started. And the worst part? It's kind of all my fault. I'm the reason Jason and Kimberly are treating Zack like a social pariah.

"Are you feeling better?" Zack asks abruptly.

"I am, actually." It's the truth. The cold has soothed the ache in my face. "The purple gel must have some healing properties."

"Good." He crosses his arms. "Maybe now you can answer my question."

The one about why I didn't block his attack. *Right.* I exhale, trying to loosen the tightness in my chest, but it doesn't help. "Listen, I wish I could go into that training room right now and say, 'Hey, you know what? It turns out that I've been learning martial arts with my grandmother since I was five, so you can all stop blaming Zack for thinking I could take care of myself.' Except . . . then they'll know exactly what I can do."

"Trini, I don't want to be the asshole here," he says carefully, "but I don't understand why that's a bad thing."

Of course he doesn't. Zack wasn't there in middle school when some older kids called me "China Virus" or "Kung Fu Flu." He didn't see the other kids pretend not to hear what happened . . . or me keeping my head down and walking by them. The racist slurs eventually stopped when I refused to react.

But they had no idea what I wanted to do. What I *could* do.

I could have acted out with all the rage burning in my heart and left them bleeding on the ground. But I didn't. That's not what

Nai Nai's lessons were for. She taught me control so I would never hurt anyone again.

Zack doesn't think my skills are a bad thing because he doesn't know how much worse it would be if people knew how dangerous I actually am.

"Trust me," I say, swallowing around the lump in my throat. "It's a bad thing."

"I don't get it."

I know he doesn't. Heat stings the back of my eyes. Maybe it's not fair to blame him for the loss of a friendship we both let go of. But I can't help but think he *would* get it—if he had just been there for me.

CHAPTER TEN

I shake off the dizzy sensation and blink in the bright glare of lights of the Power Chamber. Now that it's been nearly a week, I'm starting to get used to being beamed to and from the Command Center.

"Billy, Zack, and Trini," Alpha 5 says enthusiastically as we step off the transportation pad, "it's good to see you!"

"Jason and Kimberly are already here," Zordon adds.

I wince silently. I'm sure Kimberly is not thrilled about training on her own with Jason, who has somehow gotten even *more* hard-ass since our first day of training.

"Are you on Zord duty again?" Zack asks Billy.

"Yeah." His voice is neutral, and he's already walking toward the lift that will take him directly to the basement where the Zords are kept. Billy doesn't seem thrilled about missing training to work on the Zords, but it's not like training is doing me any good either. It's harder than I thought to pretend that I'm slowly and steadily improving. There's just no way to fake an amateur block with all my years of training.

Zack slings an arm around my shoulders. And . . . cue the tingly sensations. My whole face flushes in embarrassment.

Zack doesn't seem to notice my weird reaction. "I guess it's just you and me against Red and Pink," he says.

Zordon's head swivels over to us. "Actually, I was hoping to have a word with Trini."

My stomach plummets. This is where Zordon tells me he's made a terrible mistake. The yellow coin is supposed to mean courage, and I can't think of anything less brave than hiding my skills. "Um, okay," I mumble.

Zack takes his arm away but squeezes my shoulder in support. "I'd better join the others." He sounds as enthusiastic about training with the Jason and Kimberly as I do about my chat with Zordon—which is not at all. "I don't suppose Billy needs my help?" he asks hopefully.

"Probably not." Zordon eyes Zack with sympathy. "However, the Command Center contains many rooms if you would prefer to train on your own for a little while. Perhaps just until Trini and I finish our talk."

"Yeah, that would be great!" It's clear he's thrilled about the suggestion.

"Alpha 5," Zordon says, "why don't you show Zack to training room 2B?"

"Of course." Alpha 5's lights blink cheerfully as he leads Zack out of the Power Chamber.

Now it's just Zordon and me, and my palms begin to sweat. For someone who didn't even know about Power Rangers existed until last week, I'm feeling pretty freaked out about the potential of incoming rejection. I've never been kicked off a group project before.

"I didn't always want to be a Guardian of Eltar," Zordon says unexpectedly.

I blink. "Excuse me?" This was *not* how I thought the conversation would start.

"The Guardians of Eltar were an elite squad who protected my home planet of Eltar along with the rest of the universe," he explains. "I believe 'intergalactic warrior scholar' is how you put it." His eyes crinkle in amusement. "My point is that when my commander, Zophram, named me to succeed him as the Chief Guardian, I thought he was making a mistake."

I still don't know where he's going with this, but curiosity makes me ask, "Why did you think it was a mistake?"

"Because Zophram's second-in-command was more experienced and a better warrior," he says evenly. I get the feeling he would have shrugged if he still had shoulders. "But Zophram chose me for a reason."

Why was I chosen? The words burn in my throat, but I can't seem to say them, so instead I ask, "Why did he choose you?"

"He told me that he didn't choose me for my skills—but for my devotion to my people. What Zophram told me has stuck with me all these years later." His voice is both grave and gentle. "Trini, your actions speak for you."

A lump forms in my throat. Zordon is obviously trying to be kind, but I can't imagine he ever felt the same inadequacy I feel now. Before I can say this, I notice a sad expression flitting across his face. "What happened to him?" I ask. "Your mentor, I mean."

"Ah." The sorrow deepens in his face. "Zophram was killed when he tried to wield a powerful energy source called the Zeo Crystal."

"Oh. I'm so sorry." My words feel inadequate in the face of what was clearly a great loss.

He smiles a little. "I did not ask for this talk to recount my old grief." He looks at me with understanding. "Trini, if you are questioning why I chose you, the answer is simple. As my own mentor once told me, your actions show me you are worthy to be a Power Ranger."

I understand why he told me his story, but it's just not the same. "I didn't do anything when the Putties attacked—not like the others. I'm nothing special." That might not be strictly true, but if Zordon doesn't know about my wushu training, then I'm not going to tell him.

"My decision to recruit the five of you was not a hasty one made in the heat of the moment," he says calmly. "I did not want great warriors grasping for power and renown. I wanted those who would only agree to being Power Rangers out of a desire to protect others."

I look toward the main console and the globe Alpha 5 used to project images of Rita's conquest. Even now, the memory of that devastation makes my chest tighten. That was when we all agreed to be Power Rangers—after Alpha 5 showed us what would happen to our home if we didn't protect it.

Zordon follows my gaze to the viewing globe. "I have had little to do over the years except watch over Angel Grove as it evolved and grew."

Wait. Zordon has been watching us through his viewing globe. My body tenses. Does that mean he *does* know about my wushu? "In other words," I say, fighting to keep the panic out of my voice, "you've been spying on us."

He shakes his head. "Alpha 5 and I do not look into homes or other private spaces. We only watch public spaces."

I relax a little. That means he hasn't been watching me train with Nai Nai.

"I can learn a lot from what happens in public," he says casually. "Take school hallways, for example. That was quite a remarkable interaction that you, Billy, and Jason had with . . . what were their names again?"

My body tenses right back up again. "Bulk and Skull," I say shortly. "I accidentally tripped Bulk and accidentally bumped into Skull. I don't know what that tells you about me."

He raises an eyebrow. "I might have been referring to how Billy tried to protect you from Bulk and Skull or how Jason stopped them from bothering you and Billy."

I bite my lip. That's not what he was talking about, and we both know it. *Oh hell.* Zordon may or may not know about my wushu training, but he suspects that I'm holding back.

"There's something you should know, Trini." He peers at me intently. "In all those years I was watching Angel Grove, I did not find the one thing I was looking for. Not until recently."

"What was that?" I ask warily.

"Five warriors who the five Power Coins would have an affinity with."

My breath catches. "But I thought . . ." My voice trails off. I assumed Zordon chose us because he needed Power Rangers in a hurry and we just happened to be there.

"I chose the five of you before yesterday's attack by Goldar and the Putties. Of course, I had hoped you would all be somewhat older before you took up the heavy responsibility of being Power Rangers." He sighs. "It would have been nice if you could have all at least graduated from high school. Then Rita escaped her prison, and I could no longer wait." He holds my gaze, and his voice firms. "I know I am right to choose you just as my mentor chose me despite my doubts. You need to trust yourself, Trini. You were the only one the yellow coin would have picked."

I gape at him. Zordon is sounding less like an intergalactic warrior scholar mentor and more like a guidance counselor—if there were a guidance counselor for superhero stuff, which I guess there is. Because Zordon is right here, telling me that it's *not* a mistake that I'm a Power Ranger.

I don't know if I believe him, but this is someone who made a commitment to protect the universe at a great personal cost. When Rita trapped him outside of time and space in their final battle ten thousand years ago, he could have easily given up. But he didn't. Instead, he prepared over the many centuries for this moment—mentoring a bunch of teens to take over for him.

How can I let Zordon down when he's sacrificed so much? I swallow hard. "I think I understand."

"Good," he says with a smile. "Now, I believe you should fetch Zack and rejoin Jason and Kimberly to continue your training." He pauses. "I may have spent a great amount of time observing Angel Grove, but there is still much about human teens that I do not understand."

"Are you asking me to explain what's going on between Zack, Jason, and Kimberly?" *Oh, wow.* Where do I even start? Come to think of it . . . I'm not actually sure *I* get what's going on. I know Zack is mad at Kimberly for getting him fired, but his grudge against Jason is harder to understand.

"I'm afraid it won't do any good," Zordon says. "Despite my years surveying Angel Grove, I'm out of my element here."

Is it my imagination or does his head *shudder*? I guess it makes sense that the warrior scholar Guardian of Eltar doesn't have experience dealing with human teenagers.

"But maybe you could do something about the, er, tensions in the team?" he asks hopefully.

"Like Zack said," I say dryly, "Are you sure I can't help Billy with the Zords?" That might be an easier task.

"I have complete faith in you, Trini Kwan," Zordon says with a twinkle in his eyes.

I don't exactly share his confidence, but Zordon is right about one thing: We need to work together as a team to beat Rita. And maybe I *do* know where to start.

I press the button on the panel to open the door to training room 2B before I can change my mind. The door slides open to reveal Zack running through tires. "Looking good!" I call out.

He finishes the tires and waves me over. "Want to join me?"

"No thanks." I eye the tires on the ground skeptically. "I have to say, that does not look fun. I'm lucky my nai nai never came across this training technique." Actually, I'm surprised that a woman who made me move rocks didn't add tire running to my training regimen.

"It's kind of awesome." He grins. "I haven't done this since I was on the football team."

Well, I'm not going to get a better opening than that to figure out what he's got against Jason. "So, speaking of the football team . . ."

Zack visibly tenses, and I almost chicken out and offer to tire race him or something. Then I remember Zordon saying, *I have complete faith in you, Trini Kwan.*

But maybe I won't lead with, *Hey Zack, why are you holding a giant grudge against the captain of the football team?* Carefully, I say, "Every time I talk to you, I get the sense that you miss football. And cheerleading too."

"Nah. I just miss the uniforms." He laughs, but it sounds strained. "Gotta love the shiny tracksuit of the cheer squad and the spiffy shoulder pads of the football team. I wanted to play in the tracksuit after I dropped cheer for football, but Coach vetoed that idea."

Despite the lightness of his tone, I catch the small twist of his mouth. "You miss football," I say with certainty.

"Maybe I just got bored and moved on," he says.

Suddenly, I remember one time when we were nine, Zack claimed he was too old for dress-up and dance parties, but I knew damn well that he loved nothing more. Back then, it was easy to call him on his bullshit, and that's just what I did. The nine-year-old Zack caved at once and put on a cape and a tiara. Then he spun me around the room until we were both breathless with giggles.

I don't think it will be that easy now. It's been a long time since then. But this past week has shown me that neither of us have changed as much as I thought we had. He's still Zack and I'm still Trini.

"You don't have to pretend with me," I say softly.

He opens his mouth, and I just know a flippant comment or a joke is coming, so I say, "I should have been clearer." I glare at him. "Don't you dare pretend with me, Zack Taylor."

His mouth twitches up. "I remember that look. You used to give me that death glare when I'd do something jerky like announcing that I didn't like dance parties anymore."

"I was just remembering that!" I can't help but grin. This is how it used to be—reading each other's minds and telling each other exactly what we're thinking.

"I miss the dance parties," Zack says. "And okay, I miss football. I miss your death glare too." His smile disappears, and he looks dead serious for once. "I miss you."

A lump forms in my chest. If I'm demanding that he be honest with me, then I have to do the same. "I miss you too."

I don't want to ruin this moment, but Zack still hasn't answered my question. I take a deep breath. "So why did you quit football?"

His shoulder's slump. "Well, you know about my mom's cancer."

Fear swirls in my stomach. His mother was diagnosed when we were in elementary school, but she was successfully treated and has been in remission since then. As far as I know. "Did it come back?" I ask with a hitch in my voice.

"No, nothing like that," he assures me. He glances at the tires on the floor. "But we had a lot of medical bills, and my parents were pretty worried. I figured I could get a job and help out."

"Oh Zack." It's just like him to quit football so he could help his family. Tears clog my throat, but I tamp them down to focus on what he's telling me.

"My parents wouldn't have let me quit if they knew I was doing it for them, so I pretended I was bored with football." He looks up at me. "I didn't tell anyone the real reason I gave it up. I mean, I would have if anyone had asked."

"But no one did." *Not Jason. Not even me.* I take a step forward and hug him, and he hugs me back just as tightly. I am finally holding my old friend the way I should have all these years when he was dealing with his family's money problems on his own. "Let's be friends again," I whisper into his chest.

I can feel his answering smile against my shoulder. He steps back and looks at me. "Okay. I'm in." He holds out his hand. "Pinkie swear?"

I laugh and hook my pinkie around his. "I, Trini Kwan, solemnly swear to be friends with Zack Taylor." I pause and add, "Again, still, and always."

"Ooh. That's good."

"I know," I say smugly.

"Alright. My turn." He clears his throat. "I, Zack Taylor, solemnly swear to be friends with Trini Kwan." He looks at me with absolute seriousness like he really is making me an unbreakable vow. "Again, still, and always."

CHAPTER
ELEVEN

That bad, huh?" Billy asks sympathetically as he sips chocolate milk across from me at our school cafeteria table.

"Worse." Just the thought of yesterday's training makes me want to plunk my head down into my tray of fish sticks and Tater Tots. My talk with Zack was the only bright spot, but things went downhill fast when we rejoined Jason and Kimberly to train. "Jason told Kimberly she wasn't trying hard enough, so then Kimberly told Jason that *he* wasn't trying hard enough to be a human being, and Zack made a joke about . . . turning into human pumpkins at midnight, maybe? I don't know—you had to be there, I guess." It's safe to say that day five of training did not go any better than day one, although no one got a black eye, so that's an improvement.

"I guess I should be glad I wasn't there." Billy's expression turns inward. "Although I didn't have any luck with the Zords either."

I glance around the cafeteria, but the lunchtime crowd is too loud for anyone to overhear him. Plus, Billy and I are sitting at a table by ourselves as we always do. I kind of hoped Zack would join us, but he's sitting with the drama kids today. He tends to table-hop and doesn't have a regular group, although I notice that he's avoiding the cheer table now that Kimberly has joined them. It's also been a while since he sat with the football team, and that's probably because of Jason.

I give myself a mental shake. I need to stop thinking about Zack and focus on Billy. "You'll get the Zords up and running," I say confidently. "You're the guy who audits graduate-level university science classes for fun."

"This is different." He picks up one of his Tater Tots and then lets it drop listlessly back onto his tray. "I've only read about science like this. I've never seen it in practice. *No one* on Earth has. I don't know why the Zords aren't working, much less how to fix them."

I reach over and clasp his hand. "If anyone can, it's you."

"That's what Zordon said." Billy doesn't sound happy about our alien mentor's vote of confidence. "He's counting on me to get the Zords operational. It's the only reason I'm on this team."

"That's not true," I say automatically, but I mean it. "You could have run for the exits when Goldar and the Putties attacked, but you didn't."

"I couldn't just leave you!"

"That's what I mean." I smile and squeeze his hand before letting go. "You have the biggest heart, Billy."

"Thanks, Trini. You're a good friend." He pauses. "You're also the only one on the team who gets me, and I kind of mean that literally. When I talk, everyone else just hears technobabble."

This is not the time to tell him that I only understood about one word in three when he was explaining the science behind the Zords. "The team might not understand everything you say, but no one doubts how necessary you are."

"But I can't fight like the others can." His gaze drifts to my face, where the faint outline of my black eye is still visible despite the miraculous purple gel pack. "Sorry," he mutters guiltily, no doubt remembering that I supposedly can't fight either.

I stiffen with my own guilt, and I don't know what to say in response. Would he still think I'm a good friend if he found out I've been lying to him all this time? My face burns with shame, and I duck my head.

The crackling of the cafeteria speakers interrupts the silence between us. "Attention students!" Principal Caplan's voice comes through the speakers. "I have the great pleasure of announcing your Homecoming Court."

"I wonder if Jason will be on the court," Billy says.

I raise my eyebrows, relieved to have a change in topics. "Billy Cranston, do not tell me that you voted in the Homecoming Court election. I thought you didn't care about this stuff."

He turns pink as Principal Caplan announces, "This year's nominees for Homecoming Queen are Veronica Clark, Angela Grey, and Kimberly Hart."

Cheers from the cheerleaders take over the cafeteria, and I clap for Kimberly too. I glance over to see her reaction, and to my surprise, she's looking at me too. She gives me a sheepish smile, which I return with a wide grin. I hope making it onto the Homecoming Court will help with the fresh start Kimberly thinks she needs.

"Didn't you vote?" Billy has to raise his voice to be heard over the applause.

"Nope." I don't have much interest in the popularity contest of who gets to be on the Homecoming Court, but I am happy for Kimberly.

A loud voice that I easily identify as Aimee's says, "I can't believe Kimberly made the Homecoming Court! She hasn't even been here a whole semester."

I follow the sound and find Aimee pouting at the next table. She must be furious that she didn't make it onto the court, especially since Jason is a shoo-in to be nominated for Homecoming King.

"And this year's nominees for Homecoming King are . . ." The cafeteria falls silent to listen to Principal Caplan's announcement. "Richard Curtis, Jason Lee Scott, and Zachary Taylor."

Delight fills me, and I turn toward the drama kids, who are all hugging Zack. His eyes find mine, a sheepish smile on his face that's almost identical to Kimberly's.

"Good for Zack!" I exclaim.

"Jason is on the court too," Billy reminds me.

"Oh right!" Belatedly, I glance at the loud football table, where Jason is receiving congratulatory whacks on the back that would knock over a lesser person. "That's cool." I can't actually imagine that responsible, focused Jason would care much about this.

"Well folks, these six students are the nominees for Homecoming Court," Principal Caplan booms. "Don't forget to vote for your Homecoming King and Queen, who will be crowned at the Homecoming dance on Saturday."

Billy's forehead wrinkles. "Who are you going to vote for? Jason or Zack?"

"Neither." I dip my fish stick in ketchup and take a bite. "I'm sitting this election out."

"That's a good idea," he agrees, "but it looks like Jason is already campaigning."

I turn around to see what Billy is talking about, and sure enough, Jason is approaching the drama table. But he doesn't talk to the other students. Instead, he has a short conversation with Zack. Without taking my eyes off them, I mutter, "What the hell is going on?"

"I have no idea," Billy replies. "The *Zords* are easier to figure out than whatever this is."

Zack is getting reluctantly to his feet and following Jason to the cheerleaders' table. *Oh.* "I think Jason is trying to get Zack and Kimberly to call a truce." I turn back around to face Billy because they probably don't need an audience.

"That would be great," Billy says.

"It won't be easy," I say. "Zack and Kimberly were at each other's throats at yesterday's training session." At Billy's alarmed look, I add, "Figuratively speaking, of course. Jason isn't letting any of us spar." Not after my black eye. I wince, but not because my eye hurts. It's my fault that Jason is playing it safe.

"I understand why Jason wanted to be careful." Billy looks at me sympathetically.

"*Careful* won't help us get ready to fight Putties," I say before I can stop myself. "Jason won't even let us morph. The only thing Zack and Kimberly agree on is that we should be training in our Power Ranger forms." I'm about to say that I agree too, but then Billy's eyes suddenly widen as he looks over my shoulder.

I turn to see Jason, Zack, and Kimberly approaching our table. From the frowns on everyone's faces, it does *not* look like Jason was on a peacemaking mission, or maybe it just failed spectacularly. Zack sits down next to me, Kimberly on my other side, and Jason takes the seat next to Billy. "We need to talk," Jason says.

"You'd better not tell us we have to train after school," Kimberly says. "I have cheer practice."

"And I have a shift at the juice bar." Zack snags a Tater Tot off my tray and pops it into his mouth. "And can we have a rule about no Power Ranger meetings at lunch? I didn't get to finish my fish sticks."

I give him a playful shove. "Hey. Hands off my tots."

"Payback for all those cafeteria fries you stole from me when we were kids." He winks at me.

"And I have football practice after school," Jason says, ignoring our banter. "We'll train tonight like we planned, but there's something else I want to talk to you about. I have an idea for how we can come together as a team."

Zack groans. "If it's paintball or sumo wrestling—"

"Which is problematic appropriation of Japanese culture," I add.

"Right." Zack nods. "Cultural appropriation is a big no. That's why I'm vetoing sumo wrestling, and I'm vetoing paintball because it's just so clichéd." He sneaks another Tater Tot off my plate, and I let him have it because he backed me up on sumo wrestling.

"It's not a rope course, is it?" Billy asks anxiously. "My parents sent me to a camp that had one of those and it didn't go so well."

"And no trust falls," Kimberly declares. "I hate falling backward while someone else is supposed to catch you."

"Trust issues, much?" Zack murmurs sarcastically. "That's a shocker."

I'm glad he says it quietly enough so that no one but me hears him. But yeah, I get the feeling that Kimberly *does* have trust issues.

Jason sighs. "No nothing like that. We're going to the Homecoming dance together as a team-building exercise."

It could have been worse. I wasn't planning to go to the dance, but it's better than any of the other guesses about Jason's team-building plan.

"I retract my paintball veto," Zack says.

Does he already have a date to the dance? My stomach cramps as I remember him flirting with the girls at the football game.

"That's not going to work for me." Kimberly frowns. "I already have a date."

"It's nonnegotiable." Jason is already getting to his feet. "We're all going to the Homecoming dance together."

⚡

"Let me see if I have this right." Mom is beaming at me as I shrug on a jacket. "You're going shopping. For a dress. With a new friend. For the Homecoming dance." She says the sentence in chunks like she can't quite believe any of the things she's uttering.

"That's wonderful, Trini!" My dad's voice sounds a little sleepy over the speaker on Mom's phone. I think it's early in the morning in Taiwan, where he's at a medical conference.

Dad was born and raised in Taipei, so he identifies as Taiwanese. Nai Nai still identifies as Chinese even though she spent most of her childhood in Taiwan and raised Dad there. Even more confusing? Mom spent more time in China than either Dad or Nai Nai because her parents emigrated there from South Korea, but Mom identifies as Korean. That's why the "What are you?" question always throws me. To understand who I am, you'd have to understand a complex history of war, colonialism, and Western imperialism.

"I cannot believe you called Dad long distance and then put him on speakerphone for this. It's just a dance." Defensively, I add, "And it's not like I don't have friends."

"Of course. I know you have fun doing science experiments and watching movies with Billy. I just think it's nice that you're trying new things." Mom can't seem to stop smiling.

Nai Nai, on the other hand, is frowning at me. "How did you say you got that black eye again, Trini?"

"Um, I tripped and fell." I hate lying, but it's not like I can tell them that Zack accidentally hit me when we were training as an elite fighting squad to battle invading aliens.

Nai Nai frowns even harder. She knows how unlikely it is that I'd trip and fall. She trained me too well for that.

Luckily, I see Kimberly's car pull up out the window before I can get even more tangled up in lies. "Gotta go! Bye!" I slip on my shoes and practically run out the door.

Kimberly smiles when I hop into the passenger seat. "You seem excited about our trip to the mall."

"I am." Surprisingly, it's true.

"Thanks for coming with me. I really want to get a new dress."

I sneak a look at her, chic as always in a black jumpsuit with a thin pink belt. I would have thought someone as fashionable as Kimberly would have a Homecoming dress by now, especially since she has a date. "You don't have a dress yet?"

"I did." She glances at me with a conspiratorial smile. "But it's not pink."

Oh. It seems like both Zack and Kimberly have fully embraced their black and pink Power Ranger colors. I wish I could embrace mine too. But every time I think about it, my stomach twists in knots. Firmly, I push away these thoughts. I'm not going to ruin this outing with my doubts about being the Yellow Ranger. "Are you sure it's okay to skip your cheerleading practice to go shopping?" I ask.

"Sure." She pulls away from the curb smoothly. "Veronica and Angela are ditching too. They both already had dresses, but now that they're on the Homecoming court, they decided to step up their game."

"So why aren't you shopping with them?" I blurt out. My face flushes.

"I wanted to go shopping with *you.*"

Really? Fortunately, I don't say it out loud.

She glances over and laughs at my expression. "I want to get to know you better, Trini Kwan."

"Me too." I smile. "It will help with team building." I grimace inside. Why did I say that? Now Kimberly will think I'm only hanging out with her because I have to, which isn't true at all.

She drives for a moment without responding, and I hold my breath. This is why I don't have more than one friend—two if I count Zack.

Abruptly, Kimberly says, "I don't give a damn what Jason told us to do. I'm hanging out with you because you're funny, kind, and interesting, and because I *want* to."

I let out my breath, and relief spreads through me. Maybe I didn't blow it with Kimberly after all. "I think you're cool too." I really don't want to ruin things, but I want to be fair to Jason. "I know Jason is hard on us all, but he's just as hard on himself. I think he's feeling the pressure of getting us ready for when Rita attacks again."

"You're probably right." She doesn't sound convinced.

I know I'm right. But being ready is more than training and getting strong. We have to be a team, and that means it's not enough for me to get along with my teammates. I'm going to have to help my teammates get along with each other.

⚡

"Sorry, but no." Kimberly shakes her head. "No offense, Trini, but that dress does nothing for you."

I look in the mirror of the changing room we're sharing. The dress I'm wearing is pale blue with lots of ruffles . . . and Kimberly is right. The color washes me out, the skirt just sort of balloons around me like I'm wearing an upside-down umbrella, the tulle ruffles are scratchy, and the bodice has some kind of boning that's cutting off my circulation. "How can a dress be both this ugly *and* uncomfortable?"

She laughs. "It is kind of amazing."

"It's horrendous," I say cheerfully and then glance at Kimberly. "You, on the other hand, look gorgeous." To be honest, I tried on the upside-down umbrella dress because the dress Kimberly chose also had a short tulle skirt, minus the extraneous ruffle. Hers is hot pink, not powder blue, and she looks like a punk fairy princess— and she's totally rocking it.

"Wait here," she says, jumping to her feet and dashing out of the dressing room.

It's not like I'm going to leave in this ruffled abomination. By the time I wrestle it off, Kimberly has returned with a marigold yellow slip dress with spaghetti straps. "It's perfect for the nineties theme of the Homecoming dance."

"Yellow? A bit obvious, don't you think?" I ask as I take it from her.

"Lean into it, Trini." She grins. "We're freaking Power Rangers."

The dress is shimmery bright and feels silky in my hands, and it can't be worse than the other one. "Okay, I'll give it a try." It's easy to slide over my head, and the smooth fabric clings softly to my figure. Although the dress reaches down to mid-calf, there's a thigh-high slit that allows for ease of movement . . . and creates a slinky sexiness. It fits like a dream, and the vibrant color makes me look like I'm glowing.

"Wow, Trini," Kimberly breathes. "You look stunning."

"Yeah?" I twist around to see the back in the mirror, and there are thin crisscrossing straps across the open back that add an elegant touch.

"Definitely. Anyone who sees you in that dress will go wild over you."

For some reason, Zack pops into my head, and my face burns.

"Ooh." Her mouth curves into a mischievous smile. "Okay, spill. What's making you blush so hard?"

"I don't know what you mean." I take off the dress and put my leggings and oversize sweatshirt back on.

"Come on, Trini. I can keep a secret." Then a shadow crosses her face. "Actually, it's fine. Never mind."

Confusion makes me pause in putting the dress back on its hanger. Why is she acting weird all of a sudden? "There's really nothing to tell."

"Even if there were something," she says hollowly, "maybe you shouldn't trust me with it."

Whoa. What is this about? Then I remember what she said about wanting a new beginning. "Why wouldn't I trust you?" I ask softly.

"Let's just say I didn't leave my old high school under ideal circumstances." Kimberly turns her back to me and shimmies out of her dress. She doesn't face me again until she's dressed in her regular clothes. "I was hoping Angel Grove would be different, but I didn't get off to a great start."

"You mean the . . . incident with Zack."

"If by incident you mean that I was the asshole who got him fired—then yeah." There's genuine regret in her voice.

"I realize you'll have to take my word for it," I say, "but Zack is actually pretty chill. He'd understand if you just explained."

"I've *tried*." Kimberly snatches up a clothes hanger. "Apparently, I'm really good at burning bridges and total crap at apologizing."

Okay, I'm not going to push it now, but these two need to resolve things, and not just for the sake of the team. If Kimberly is going to be my new friend and Zack is going to be my old-friend-turned-current-friend—then they're going to have to get along.

"Listen, I know you messed up." I'm not just talking about accidentally getting Zack fired, but also whatever she's not telling me about her old high school. "But we all mess up sometimes." I'm thinking of how I hid my skills in our fight against the Putties. "I'm not holding it against you. Angel Grove *can* be different for you." Before I can second-guess myself, I add, "And I think we could be friends."

"Friends." Kimberly smiles, and a faint pink tinges her cheeks. "Yeah, that would be nice."

CHAPTER
TWELVE

Kimberly is going to be late," I say as I walk up to the entrance of the high school gym. "She's having dinner with her date before coming to the dance."

Jason frowns. "I made it very clear that we were meeting at the entrance of the gym at eight sharp."

"No one shows up to a high school dance right at the start," Billy grumbles. It's surprising that he's complaining about Jason ordering us all around . . . and even more surprising that Zack isn't.

Zack is staring at me, strangely speechless.

"Do I have something on my face?" Unlike Kimberly, I didn't have a dinner date, but I did scarf down noodles with my family right before coming here.

"Uh, no." He blinks at me like he's coming out of a trance. "Sorry, I was just thinking about something else."

He's probably regretting breaking a date to be in Jason's team-building exercise. Zack looks awesome in dark jeans with a vintage-style tuxedo jacket, and he certainly didn't get dressed up for all of us.

"You look nice, Trini," Billy says.

"Thanks. You do too." Like Jason, Billy is wearing a plain black suit, and they both look handsome, though not as downright devastating as Zack. "You all look great." I smile and hook my arm through Billy's. "Shall we go in?"

We enter the gym, decorated in maroon, gold, and teal streamers and bouquets of balloons in the same colors. A gigantic sign says "Angel Grove Homecoming Dance" in sparkly glitter, but it seems a little sad considering that the vast space is nearly empty except for a few faculty chaperones and a handful of freshmen who apparently didn't realize it wasn't cool to show up at a school dance on time.

"Excuse me for a moment," Billy says to us over his shoulder as he makes a beeline for our AP Physics teacher. "Mr. Barts! Can I talk to you?"

Mr. Barts has that slightly panicked expression he always gets when he's talking to Billy. Even a science teacher with a graduate degree in physics is intimidated by Billy's scientific knowledge.

"Hey," Jason protests, but Billy is already out of earshot, or maybe he's just pretending not to hear him.

"Who thought going to Homecoming dance together would bring us together as a team?" Zack stage whispers to me. "Oh right. It was Jason."

"We're supposed to stay together." Jason starts to go after Billy, but then Aimee comes out of nowhere and plants herself in front of him.

"Well hello there, Jason!" she says. Why is Aimee here at the start of the dance with no date or even her usual crowd of friends in sight? She does her signature pout. "When you said you were getting here at eight, you didn't mention that you were bringing a group."

Ah. Now it all makes sense. Aimee was lying in wait.

Jason turns bright red. "Uh, hi, Aimee." He's probably wondering if he accidentally gave her the impression that they were supposed to be on a date. I doubt he did, but Aimee isn't above manipulating him into one. Sympathy flashes through me.

"So, Aimee," he manages to say, "we didn't actually . . ."

". . . come together as a group," Zack finishes smoothly. *What is he doing?* He knows full well the whole point was to build our connection as a team. "In fact," he adds, "Trini and I were just going to get some punch." He takes my arm, pulling me away and ignoring the stormy expression in Jason's eyes. "Enjoy your night!" Zack calls out.

"Leaving Jason in Aimee's clutches was cold, even for you, Zack Taylor." I shake my head, but it's hard to be mad at him when he's still holding my arm, leaving a trail of electric currents on my bare skin.

"Jason will survive." He smiles at me. "Besides, Homecoming is more fun this way."

He's right. Zack looks smoking hot in his vintage tux, I'm wearing a seriously slinky dress, and we're at Homecoming dance together. It's almost as if *we* are on a date. I know that's not what he means, but I smile back at him. "It is more fun," I agree.

On our way to get the punch, we pass Billy, who still has Mr. Barts pinned in a corner. "So *theoretically*, it's possible to har-ness energy from prehistoric matter to power completely *hypothet-ical* vehicles? Just curious to hear your thoughts on this."

"I have no idea," Mr. Barts says desperately.

Zack's eyes light up in amusement. "Billy is talking about Zords, right?"

"Oh, definitely," I say. "Poor Mr. Barts. This is worse than when Billy tried to get him to help with his project on genome sequencing."

Zack's mouth twitches. "I'll take your word for it." We reach the punch table, and he pours us both a glass, handing me mine with a flourish.

I accept it and then peer over his shoulder. "More people are here now." Delight fills my voice. "Kimberly and her date just came in." Not only is she wearing the pink dress but also a matching shade of lipstick, strappy heels, and even a little pink clutch purse. "She looks amazing!"

Zack doesn't even glance at the door. "I like that dress."

My forehead wrinkles. "You're not looking at Kimberly's dress."

"I meant yours."

Oh. "Thanks." My tongue feels all knotted up, and I can barely get the simple word out. To hide my sudden awkwardness, I take a big swallow of my punch and instantly regret it when the syrupy sweetness assaults my taste buds. "That is foul." I set my glass on a tray table for discarded drinks.

He takes a smaller sip and grimaces. "I think this might actually be made of toadstool and eye of newt." He puts down his glass too. "Okay, what time-honored school dance tradition should we try next? Selfies with cheesy props?" He points toward the DIY photo booth where students are posing in oversize glasses and feathered boas with a glittery curtain as a backdrop. "Or, and I realize it's unorthodox—we could actually dance." He gestures to the empty dance floor.

I laugh, thinking he's joking. "No one else is dancing."

He grins. "Well, we're going to have to change that. Come on."

I shrug and follow him as he makes his way to a group of students gathered against the wall. I don't recognize any of them, so maybe they're freshmen or sophomores. Zack doesn't appear to know them either, but that doesn't stop him from bouncing up to the group with a wide smile. "Hey, having a good night?"

They eye him warily, and one kid replies, "I guess so."

"Well, how would you all like to be self-aware ironic trendsetters? Or maybe just confident in your geekiness? Who knows and who cares? Let's dance!" He waves down another pack of kids who drift closer, pulled in by Zack's infectious energy. "You too! You look like brave souls." Before I know it, he's leading at least a dozen kids to the dance floor, and more are starting to join.

"You're like some teen pied piper," I whisper to him.

"Teen pied piper in a killer tux." He winks at me. "Don't forget that part."

I laugh as he pulls me onto the floor with the rest of the crowd, and we all start bopping to a Spice Girls song. I remember the dance parties Zack and I used to have and the cheesy moves we used to think were so cool.

"Remember this, Zack?" I do a little wiggle and pretend to go underwater.

He groans but mirrors me. "There. Happy now?"

"Nope," I say cheerfully. "You know what I'm about to say."

"No, Trini! Don't say it."

"Dance. Off."

"You're on." His eyes gleam. "Remember that you left me no choice." He starts to moonwalk because he knows I could never do that, and he looks so funny moonwalking to the Spice Girls that I double over with laughter and can't even try to mimic him.

"You win," I gasp. I should go say hello to Kimberly but I'm having too much fun.

Then the song fades out, and Principal Caplan's voice booms out. "Attention, please!" Everyone turns to find him standing on the small stage before us with a microphone in his hand and toupee neatly perched on his head. He looks fully recovered from being terrorized by Goldar. "I hope you're having fun, students!"

"Well, we were," Zack says to me.

"It is time to crown the Homecoming King and Queen," Principal Caplan announces. "Will the Homecoming Court come to the stage?"

I see Kimberly wave goodbye to her date and Jason pry himself from Aimee to go to the stage, but Zack doesn't move from my side. "Aren't you going up there?" I ask.

"Nah. I abdicated, or whatever it's called when you decline a chance at the throne."

"I'm not sure it's that kind of royal court." I raise an eyebrow. "And I didn't know you could abdicate. I'm surprised Principal Caplan didn't give you a lecture about civic responsibility and decades-old tradition."

"Well, he did, actually." He smiles. "But he changed his mind when I said that I would campaign on the platform that the Homecoming Court is a heteronormative institution that should be done away with. So it turns out that you *can* abdicate the throne."

Most people would assume Zack gave up his spot on the Homecoming court to be funny, but I know better. He has a serious side and isn't afraid to stand up for what he believes.

Everything inside of me goes gooey. "I love that you did that."

"I know you do." His eyes are intent on me.

For a moment, the chatter and noise of the decorated gym fade away, and it's as if Zack and I are in our own little bubble. My breath hitches.

Slowly, it registers that people are clapping. I glance at the stage and see that Jason and Kimberly are sitting in the two thrones and wearing gold foil crowns. Principal Caplan must have just announced that they've been elected Homecoming King and Queen. Belatedly, I start clapping too, and so does Zack. He doesn't seem annoyed by their victory.

Jason and Kimberly, on the other hand . . . don't look happy. Jason is scowling, and Kimberly is deliberately twisting in her chair so her back is to him.

The music starts again, and the sweetly angsty strains from another nineties song fill the gym. "They're really leaning into the theme," I say. "I don't know this one."

"It's No Doubt's 'Don't Speak.'" He laughs at my raised eyebrows. "I may not know genome sequencing, but I do know my nineties power ballads."

"You are a complex man with many layers, Zack Taylor."

"True."

Around us, couples are pairing up. It's a slow dance.

"Shall we?" He holds out his hand to me.

My pulse racing, I take his hand, and he pulls me close. I inhale a shaky breath and rest my head against his chest. His heart quickens under my cheek, and my bare skin feels like it's being scorched from his light touch on my back. In fact, my whole body is burning up as we sway in time to the music, and I'm suddenly having trouble breathing. *What is happening?* This is Zack, my friend since I was a little kid. Why is my nervous system going haywire just because we're slow dancing together?

A scream breaks through my daze, sending my heart into overdrive. "It's that gang in zombie costumes!" somebody shouts.

Putties? Now?

Zack and I break apart, and I frantically scan the gym. All around us, people are shrieking and running as Putties tear apart tables and chairs with their claws. Red punch and shattered glass are flying everywhere. It's only a matter of time before the Putties turn their attention from furniture to people and someone gets hurt.

"Where is Zordon?" Goldar bursts through the gym doors, his golden wings gleaming under the strobe lights. "No one leaves until you bring him to me!"

Putties are blocking every exit, and panicked students and chaperones are huddled in fear as far from the Putties as they can get—which isn't that far. Oh damn. *We're trapped.*

Then another thought makes my throat seize up in fear. Our team is nowhere near ready to fight them.

CHAPTER THIRTEEN

Jason and Kimberly are leaping down from the stage and running toward us. "We have to get everyone out," Jason says.

"Obviously," Zack says, his voice curt.

"That's the plan—get everyone out?" Kimberly asks sarcastically. "It's a good thing you're our leader."

"It's the Putties," Billy says, running up to us.

"We gathered," Jason says dryly.

I want to scream at them. This is not the time to be fighting with each other. "We need to morph." It bursts out of me without conscious thought.

Everyone stares at me, and my face grows hot.

"No," Jason says decisively. "It's too dangerous."

Kimberly folds her arms. "I know I'll be able to fight better in the suit." Yikes. I'm the one who told her that.

"True," Billy says slowly. "Theoretically, we'll all be stronger that way."

"Stop holding us back, Jason," Zack says roughly. "Let's morph."

Jason's face reddens, and I hold my breath. No. This is all wrong. Ganging up on our team leader is *not* what I meant by working together.

A scream rips out, and I look over to see two Putties closing in on a teacher. Horror hits me in the gut. The Putties are rounding up the chaperones.

Aimee and a few of her friends run up to us. "We can't get out! Jason, what do we do?" Aimee asks in a high-pitched voice.

Good question, and it's one he's going to have to answer fast because it's chaos around us with kids screaming and adults being taken captive.

For a fleeting moment, the agony of indecision flashes over Jason's face, but then it's gone. "Find cover and hide," he says to Aimee and her friends.

"What—" Aimee begins to ask, but her friends are already dashing off to take Jason's advice, so she breaks off and runs after them. "Wait for me!"

Jason turns back to us. "Fine," he says in a driven voice. "We'll morph, but don't blame me if it goes sideways."

I suspect Jason won't need any help in taking the blame if things go wrong. He's good at doing that all by himself. It's a feeling I can identify all too well with.

"We can use the photo booth." Kimberly points to the sequined curtain that people were using as a backdrop for their selfies.

"This isn't the time to take pictures," Jason snaps.

Kimberly rolls her eyes, and I say hastily, "She means we can go there to hide our morphing from everybody."

"Oh. Right." Jason has the grace to blush.

Thankfully, everyone stops bickering, and we dash toward the photo booth. We must look like we're just running away with the others because the Putties don't pay any attention to us. They're busy rounding up the frightened chaperones and herding them toward Goldar, who has flown up to the stage and is now sitting on one of the thrones reserved for the Homecoming King and Queen. Is Goldar planning to interrogate them for information about Zordon, or does he have more deadly plans for the chaperones? Fear yanks at my stomach.

We skid to a stop at the photo booth, and as soon as we duck behind the sparkling curtain, doubt seizes me. Morphing was my idea. What if it goes horribly wrong?

Jason is removing his Morpher from the belt under his suit jacket, and Billy is doing the same. Jason pauses. "Maybe I should have checked before, but does everyone have their Morphers?"

"Yup." Zack takes his from the inner pocket of his tux.

Kimberly snaps open her pink purse and removes hers. "I've got mine too."

I clutch the fabric of my slinky skirt. "Can the boys turn around for a minute, please?"

Zack lifts an eyebrow but turns around without comment, and Jason and Billy do the same.

As soon as their backs are to me, I lift my skirt and remove the Morpher from the garter belt around my right thigh—the one that's not revealed by the slit in my skirt.

"Now why didn't I think to carry my Morpher like that?" Kimberly asks.

I smile. "Because your skirt is too short." I slide my Morpher free and let my skirt fall back in place. "Okay, you can turn around now."

"Please tell me you picked that dress with this in mind," Kimberly says.

"I'm not telling." The truth is that I've *always* wanted to hide a dagger in a garter belt, and a Morpher is the next best thing. Nai Nai has a set of wicked daggers that she only lets me use on stuffed burlap sacks, and she would never let me take them out of the house, which is totally fine, but it does ruin my fantasy.

"Lalala—I'm not hearing this." The tips of Billy's ears are red.

Zack doesn't say a word, but his eyes are wide.

"Can we get on with this?" Jason mutters.

I clutch my Morpher with shaking hands. "I'm ready."

"I'll go first," Jason says, "then Zack, Kimberly, Billy, and Trini. Got it?"

We all nod. Zack smiles. "Go, go Power Rangers."

As usual, Jason ignores him. He lifts up his Morpher. "Tyrannosaurus Rex!"

There's a brief flash of light, and then suddenly, the Red Ranger is standing there in a form-fitting red suit made of some kind of fluid material, complete with a red helmet and visor that covers his entire head.

Before I can do more than gasp, Zack is lifting his Morpher. "Mastodon!" In another flash of light, Zack has become the Black Ranger. *Damn.* He looks good in that suit. It clings to his muscled frame in a way that makes me want to reach out and—I make myself keep my hands at my sides.

Kimberly lifts her Morpher. "Pterodactyl!" She's the Pink Ranger.

"Triceratops!" Billy calls out. He's the Blue Ranger.

Now it's my turn. I take a deep breath and lift my Morpher. "Sabertooth Tiger!"

A strange feeling sweeps over me, like every cell in my body is floating free, and my head is filled with a dizzy swarm of light, making it impossible to see anything. I gulp and try to get my bearings. Where am I? Then my vision clears, and I'm relieved to find myself still in the gym, behind a shimmery makeshift curtain with the other rangers. Except I don't feel like myself anymore.

Power pulses through me, like I could snap the snack table next to us in half without even trying. Fear twists in my chest as the image of Carl bloody on the floor in front of me flashes through my vision. In this suit, I could be more in danger of losing control than ever.

I jump when a tinny voice speaks into my ear. "Jason, Zack, Kimberly, Billy, Trini! My computer readouts tell me that you have all morphed into your Power Ranger forms!" It's Alpha 5.

"What the hell?" My heartbeat slowly returns to normal. "Alpha 5, how are you in my head?"

"I took the liberty of opening up a channel so I could talk to you and so you can communicate with each other," he says.

I reach up to my ear and feel a hard, rounded material. Right. The helmet. That must be how Alpha 5 is talking to us.

"We're at the Homecoming dance, and Goldar and the Putties are attacking," Jason says. His voice sounds deeper than usual, and I wonder if the helmet is disguising his voice. "We're going to stop them."

"Good luck, Rangers," Alpha 5 says.

Jason doesn't waste any more time talking to Alpha 5. "Zack and Kimberly, clear that exit of Putties." He points to a small side door. "Trini and Billy, get everyone through that door. I'll lure Goldar away from the chaperones."

So basically, Billy and I are crowd control.

Zack turns to me, and I shake my head at him before he argues for me to take a more active role. He gives a micro shrug. "So how do we feel about 'Go, go Power Rangers!' as our official motto?"

"We're not a cheer squad." Kimberly is probably rolling her eyes underneath her pink helmet.

"Let's go—" Jason breaks off. "I mean, let's begin . . . whatever. Kick ass."

We leap out from behind the curtain and into action. Jason dashes over to the stage, calling out, "Hey, Goldie!"

"He definitely needs better taunts," Zack comments before running after Kimberly toward the Putties guarding the side exit.

Billy is already herding a group of students toward the door.

I turn to the nearest group, which happens to be Aimee and her friends, crouched behind an overturned punch table. "Get close to that exit!" I point to the door. "Once it's clear, run out of here!"

Aimee's eyes go round. "Who . . . are you?" she stammers.

"Putties, attack!" Goldar roars from his throne on the stage.

My attention snaps to Jason facing off with a dozen Putties blocking his path to Goldar, who looms over our chaperones huddled on the floor of the stage. *He can't fight them all by himself.* The Putties come after him, less lumbering and not as slow as I remember them. They have him surrounded, and he'll have no choice but to fight.

Then Jason does a flying kick that is truly a thing of beauty . . . except he completely misses any of the Putties he was aiming for. I can sense his frustration as he clumsily barrels his way free of the Putty barricade. This is not good. Jason is in retreat and wasn't able to lure Goldar off the stage and away from the chaperones. Why is it that we're doing worse than we did when we faced off against Goldar and the Putties the first time? We were completely on our own that time too.

Unfamiliar strength surges through me, and my hands clench. I don't want to be herding people to safety—I want to be fighting. But I also don't want anyone to get hurt because I can't control myself or my new abilities.

I turn back to Aimee and her friends. "I'm a Power Ranger."

"A what?" Another girl asks.

"Never mind," I say quickly. "I have to get other students ready to escape. You know what to do?"

"That exit doesn't look safe." Aimee sounds scared.

I whirl around to see Zack and Kimberly fighting Putties at the door where Jason has now joined them. Kimberly jumps up, but the suit gives her so much power that she sails over the heads of several Putties. I hate being right about this, but she really should have been training in the suit all along. Zack manages to land a punch on a Putty, knocking it down, but it just gets right back up again. My heart rises into my throat.

Is it my imagination . . . or are the Putties stronger?

I try to exhale through my worry for my teammates. I can't help them right now. I have a job to do. "Be ready to run," I repeat to Aimee and her friends before dashing over to a big group of kids who are inexplicably lying face down on the floor in the middle of the dance floor. What kind of emergency do they think this is—a fire drill? Although, to be fair—*none* of our school drills have covered alien invasion.

"Get up," I say. "You all need to get closer to that exit." I point without looking. If I see how Zack, Kimberly, and Jason are doing, I'm not going to be able to focus. "The other Power Rangers are fighting off the Putties, so that's your way out."

The kids stare at me in bewilderment, but some of them are getting up.

"Putties?"

"Power Rangers?"

"Who are you?"

I sigh. "The gray zombies with Freddy Krueger fingers are called Putties, the color-coordinated superheroes fighting them are

Power Rangers, and I am the Yellow Ranger." I haul the last couple of kids to their feet, and even in the urgency of this moment, I'm stunned by how easy it is—how *strong* I am. "Get closer to the exit but stay clear of the fighting until I give the signal."

I'm relieved that they do as I tell them without further questions.

Billy runs up to me, and I note that he's not panting. "Okay. Everyone is primed to escape once the others get rid of the Putties."

"Everyone except for the chaperones," I say grimly.

Billy's blue-helmeted head turns to the corner where Goldar is still guarding the adults. "Mr. Barts is over there too." He takes a step toward them.

Jason's voice comes through my helmet. "Get the students out first. We'll worry about the teachers later."

"We can't just abandon them," Zack says.

"We don't have a choice," Jason snaps.

My stomach clenches. They're both right. Our teachers are in danger, and there's nothing we can do about it.

"Can we have less talking and more fighting, please?" Kimberly complains. "I don't know if you noticed, but these Putties are stronger than they were last time."

"And faster," Jason adds.

So it *wasn't* my imagination.

Billy and I turn to the side door. Kimberly, Zack, and Jason are barely holding their own and making what looks like zero progress in clearing the exit of Putties. They have to do better than that if we're going to get the other students out.

"We need to help them," Billy and I say at the same time.

"No." Jason sounds breathless, and it's weird to hear him in my helmet and see him in the distance trying to punch Putties at the same time. "Round up the students and get them together in a pack. They'll have a better chance of pushing through the Putties that way."

"They'll also have a better chance of trampling each other." The thought makes me shudder.

"And isn't our goal to get rid of the Putties guarding the exit?" Billy asks.

"Working on it," Zack says just as a Putty kicks him so hard that he falls to the ground. He leaps back up again before the worry in my throat blossoms into full-blown panic. "Dammit," he swears. "We should have trained in our suits."

"Seriously guys." Kimberly leaps toward a Putty, managing not to overshoot her mark this time. Unfortunately, the blow she aims at its head doesn't connect. "Less talking."

I should be there with them. I don't care what Jason told us to do—rounding up the students isn't going to do a damn thing if they don't have a safe way out. I need to help clear the Putties from the exit.

But before I can move, commotion at the main entrance draws everyone's attention.

"That's enough." An imposing woman in a horned headdress and a gown with a black armored bodice sweeps into the gym. "Putties, to me." To underscore her command, she lifts her jeweled scepter in an imperious movement.

My jaw drops. This can only be Rita Repulsa.

The Putties swarm over to her, and Jason yells, "Now's our chance. Get everyone out."

He's right. "Go!" I frantically motion the students toward the entrance, and Billy helps me control the stampede, picking up students who fall and making sure no one gets trampled.

"Stay," Rita says over her shoulder to the Putties like they are nothing more than overgrown dogs. Then she strides over to us.

Heart pounding, I turn my back to the fleeing students and face Rita. If she wants to stop them from escaping then she's going to have to go through me. I barely have time to think this before the other Power Rangers are by my side.

Goldar flies over to land at Rita's feet, halting her progress. "My empress."

Now might be a good time to get the chaperones out, but there's no telling what Goldar will do if they try to escape.

Goldar kneels before Rita. "These puny humans have refused to tell me where Zordon is, but fear not. I will peel the skin from their miserable bodies, and then they will talk readily enough."

Principal Caplan slumps over in a faint again, and another teacher moans in fear.

My stomach knots in dread. Can we stop Goldar before he tortures our teachers for information they don't have?

Rita laughs. "No need, Goldar. I have what I came here to find out." She steps past him and examines us closely.

Cold prickles my neck. The silver horns of her headdress are banded with black and gold metal, and they glitter under the disco ball. Her lips are painted a blood red, and her eyes are dark like mine. Zordon didn't tell us Rita seemed so human. Or that she looks Asian . . . like me.

"So," Rita says scornfully, "you five are Zordon's new Power Rangers. Pathetic."

From the corner of my eye, I'm relieved to see Ms. Appleby, my English teacher, herding the other chaperones toward the unguarded side exit. One of the other teachers is supporting Principal Caplan, who has come back to consciousness.

"Just give us a little time," Jason says evenly. He must have noticed the chaperones sneaking away too, but he doesn't turn around. He knows we have to keep Rita and Goldar distracted long enough to let them escape.

"You know what's pathetic?" Zack asks. "A sorceress bent on world domination trashing a high school Homecoming dance with Play-Doh soldiers led by an overgrown *Solid Gold* dancer." In an aside to Jason, he says, "*That's* how you do taunts—work with the existing material. You can't just throw in a random 'Hey, Goldie' and call it good."

I'm sure Jason is glaring behind his opaque visor, but he doesn't respond to Zack's "Heckling the Villain 101" lesson.

"I hate to say it," Kimberly says, "but he does have a point." She turns to Rita. "Why are you bothering with football games and high school dances?"

"It doesn't seem like the most efficient method for world domination," Billy agrees.

They're not wrong. An uneasy feeling worms its way through me.

"Empress." Goldar rises to his feet and spreads his sharp gold wings. "Let me tear apart these upstart Rangers for you."

She ignores him. "I have a message I want you to take to Zordon." Abruptly, she raises her scepter, and the jewel set inside the gold crescent of the scepter glows blood red. A red energy beam shoots out and blasts the stage where Goldar was holding the chaperones. "Tell him that I will destroy what is most dear to him."

My stomach wrenches as I stare at the wreckage of the thrones and the wood slivers. If our teachers were still there, they would be dead by now.

"I'll let you in on a secret." Rita's eyes glitter with malice as she leans toward us. "I don't care about conquering your backward planet. What I *do* care about is making Zordon suffer. He had the entire universe to pick from, but this miserable little town is where he's chosen to recruit his warriors, so I think he will suffer when I destroy it . . . along with his precious Power Rangers, of course."

My breath whooshes out of me. Rita is going to destroy Angel Grove.

"You're not going to find us so easy to defeat," Jason says grimly.

She laughs. "Oh, don't worry. I'm not going to destroy you right now. There would be no fun in that. This was a test." She snaps her fingers at Goldar. "And you have failed, Power Rangers."

She sweeps majestically out the door with Goldar and the Putties in her wake.

"What the hell was that?" Kimberly asks.

No one answers her, not even Zack. We're probably all trying to figure out the same thing. The rampaging space army is gone, but I don't mistake it for a victory. My body feels heavy. We should have been working together as a team, but instead, all we've done is show Rita just how defenseless Angel Grove is.

Like Rita said—we've failed.

CHAPTER
FOURTEEN

There was nothing more you could have done," Zordon says after Alpha 5 teleports us back to the Command Center. His voice is somber. "Rita was able to improve her Putty Patrollers much more quickly than anticipated."

Actually, there was a lot more *I* could have done. I tug at the skirt of my dress, which isn't even wrinkled from being in Power Ranger form. We've all morphed back and are in our fancy Homecoming clothes again.

Jason loosens the collar of his dress shirt. "And then there's the fact that Rita is specifically targeting Angel Grove."

"Because of Zordon." The words come out of me before I can stop myself, but it's true. Rita is targeting my home because of her vendetta against Zordon.

"Trini is right," Zack says. "Why is Rita so furious at you? Is it because you trapped her in a space dumpster for ten thousand years?"

Zordon closes his eyes and doesn't respond right away. Finally, he opens them and looks at us. "Rita isn't used to losing," he says. "She's conquered many planets in order to strip them of their natural resources, and she will do the same to Earth unless we stop her."

"Except that's not her plan this time." My chin lifts. "She told us herself—she doesn't want Earth. She wants to destroy Angel Grove piece by piece to draw out your suffering."

"What's so special about Angel Grove anyway?" Kimberly is watching Zordon narrowly. "This is where you built your Command Center to wait for Rita's return, and this is where you recruited us."

I'm wondering the same thing. *Why Angel Grove?*

"Yeah," Jason says slowly. "You explained why you picked us, but not why you picked Angel Grove." He glances at Billy. "I understand Billy—he's exceptional anywhere, but the rest of us . . ." His voice trails off, but we all know what he means.

Other than Billy, we're not that special, although we might be the best Angel Grove has to offer. There are better gymnasts than Kimberly, better leaders than Jason, better athletes than Zack, and definitely better martial artists than me. But Zordon never even mentioned my martial arts.

Billy flushes. "I'm not *that* exceptional."

"We did the calculations." The lights in Alpha 5's visor blink rapidly. "You five were the best candidates."

I remember then what Zordon told me. *I have had little to do over the years except watch over Angel Grove as it evolved and grew.* "We were the best candidates . . . in Angel Grove," I say abruptly.

Everyone turns to me in surprise, but Zordon says, "You are right, Trini. I wanted the Rangers to be from Angel Grove."

Zack's forehead scrunches up. "Why?"

Zordon takes a deep breath. "I wanted warriors who will fiercely protect this town I love." A soft expression comes over his face.

"You love Angel Grove?" Kimberly asks in surprise.

I'm surprised too. It had never occurred to me that an alien mentor—who had lived for thousands of years and traveled across multiple galaxies—could actually care for my home.

"Yes," he says simply. "When I was first a Guardian of Eltar, I fought Rita's forces and protected planets from her because it was my moral obligation. But I was never in one place for long, and I was so busy fighting that I seldom got to know the planets' inhabitants I was protecting."

Billy gapes at Zordon like he's having trouble processing this. "So what changed?"

Zordon pauses before responding. "It was my mentor Zophram who advised me to get to know one town on every planet Rita sought to conquer . . . so I would always understand what I was fighting for."

I think of the grief in his voice as he named the planets that had fallen to Rita's conquests. Wagnoria, Regda II, Tarmac III, Myrgo. My heart twinges. There must have been a town on each of those planets that Zordon had loved.

"Your home is not an insignificant and abstract town on a planet I am duty-bound to protect," Zordon continues. "For me, Angel Grove *is* Earth."

An unexpected swell of emotion fills my chest. That's why Zordon chose us. As he said, he wanted Power Rangers who loved Angel Grove enough to protect it with everything we have.

Jason glowers at Zordon. "Does Rita know about how you get invested in a town on every planet you defend against her?"

"I believe so." Zordon's expression turns grim. "It would grieve me greatly to see Angel Grove destroyed."

There's fear in the faces of my teammates, and it doesn't make me feel better that they think we're doomed too.

Zordon peers at us. "You must not underestimate yourselves," he says. "It isn't just your abilities that make you Power Rangers. You were all chosen for a reason, and it might not be what you think it is."

"It seems obvious to me," Zack says bitterly. "We were in the right place and the right time."

Zordon shakes his head. "No, Zack. You all chose to stay and help others when Goldar and the Putties attacked the football stadium. It is not your abilities but your *choices* that matter in the end."

That was basically what I told Kimberly. What does it mean, then, that I've chosen to keep hiding my abilities?

"That's a nice sentiment, but the truth is that we need to be better." Jason shoves his hands in his pockets. "We have to train harder. I'm not about to lead my teammates into a fight they're not ready for."

"I think," Zordon says carefully, "that it might be time to tell you about the Megazord."

Megazord? What the hell is that?

It's so quiet that you could hear a pin drop in the Power Chambers.

"I'm sorry," Kimberly says, "but did you just say Megazord?"

"As in one big-ass Zord?" Zack asks.

"More like five Zords in one," Billy replies, making it obvious that he's in on this whole Megazord thing.

"This will help you understand." Alpha 5 hits a button on the console, and the holograms of the five Zords shift together into one . . . well, big-ass Zord. But this one doesn't look like a prehistoric creature. It looks like a sci-fi mech warrior.

A muscle twitches in Jason's jaw as he stares at the hologram of the Megazord.

"It will take all five Zords to form the Megazord," Zordon says. "Jason, if your team isn't ready, then it is your job as leader to train them until they *are* ready. You're going to need the Megazord to stop Rita."

"I understand," he says shortly.

"I still have to get the individual Zords working first," Billy reminds Zordon.

"You will," I say.

Zordon smiles. "I share Trini's faith."

"The rest of us can get in some training tonight," Jason says.

"Are you kidding?" Kimberly takes her phone out of her clutch. "I have fifty million worried texts from friends, including *my date*, who I abandoned to morph and fight Putties."

I totally see her point. Everyone at the dance who would check up on me are right here in this room, but Kimberly must be dying to make sure her friends are okay and reassure everyone that she's fine too. Zack and Jason probably have a bunch of worried texts they need to answer, and although Jason is clearly too focused on getting us into fighting shape to bother with anything else, I'm surprised Zack isn't checking his phone like Kimberly is.

"Yeah, I'm going to pass on training too," Zack says. "You know, since we actually fought Putties in our Power Ranger forms tonight."

"And we got our asses kicked!" Jason says.

"Agree to disagree." Zack waves an airy hand.

"Just because you were too busy cracking jokes to notice how badly we did doesn't make it less true." Jason turns to Kimberly, who's texting on her phone. "Oh, I'm sorry—are we interrupting your social life?"

"Who's making the jokes now?" Zack asks.

"Stop!" I gulp when everyone *does* stop. My voice drops to a whisper. "We have to stop fighting."

"Maybe you should *start* fighting, Trini." Zack's eyes are serious. He's not even trying to pass it off as a joke.

"Not funny, Zack." Kimberly stops texting and puts a protective arm around my shoulders.

"Trini is right," Zordon says calmly. "You cannot forget who your real enemy is. I have faith that you will all do whatever you need to defeat Rita."

I don't have the heart to tell him that his faith is misplaced . . . because I suspect the one thing we must do to defeat Rita is the most impossible.

We have to learn how to work together as a team.

⚡

I meet up with Zack outside the training room without taking the time to change out of my slinky dress and heels. Zack is still wearing his vintage tux and raises an eyebrow when he sees how I'm dressed. "So you're not going to train either? Good. Let's go tell Jason."

"Kimberly beat you to it," I say. "She already announced that she was going home, so I didn't bother to change . . ." I shrug because Jason won't continue with training if it's just me.

"Were you *actually* going to train?" Zack gestures to the metal door of the training room. "Because if you were, then I'll get changed right now and meet you back here in ten minutes."

My stomach tightens. I can't risk it. "No."

His face drops. "Well, let's get on with it then. Someone has to tell our fearless leader that he's the only one staying tonight." He doesn't sound happy about the thought of disappointing Jason, but I know Zack would rather face a hundred Putties than let Jason know his opinion actually mattered to him.

"Zack," I say impulsively, but he's already pushing the button on the wall console.

The door of the training room slides open to reveal Jason stacking mats in his sweats. No one else is in sight.

"Oh, darn." Fake regret drips from Zack's voice. "Kimberly bailed?"

Jason looks up. "We'll start early tomorrow. Alpha 5 will beam us all here at eight A.M. sharp, so be ready."

"Got it." Zack is already backing away. "Well, let's go get beamed back home, Trini."

But I'm looking at Jason, who's now picking up towels scattered around the training room. There's a tiny slump to his broad shoulders. "Go ahead," I tell Zack. "I'll help Jason clean up."

Zack's eyes dart between Jason and me, and his jaw sets for a second before he shrugs. "Fine by me." He leaves without another word.

"You can go home too," Jason says, turning his attention to dropping towels into a hamper. "I can finish this on my own."

Without responding, I walk into the training room and pick up a spray bottle. "What still needs to be cleaned?"

He sighs. "I guess you can spray off the exercise equipment over there. I'll wipe while you spray."

The weight machine, ellipticals, and treadmills are all recognizable, so Zordon and Alpha 5 must have outfitted the room with standard Earth equipment. That makes sense since they meant to recruit human Power Rangers.

We spray and wipe for a few minutes before I speak up. "You've got to stop pushing people away, Jason."

"You're still here, aren't you?"

He probably wouldn't appreciate knowing that I stayed behind because he seemed like he could use a friend. "Well, I'm stubborn." I smile at him. "I'm not going to let you get rid of me."

He uses his towel to scrub aggressively at the already gleaming handles of a treadmill. "I'm not trying to turn everyone against me. I just have to get us all ready if we're going to stand a chance in this fight."

"But you don't have to do it alone. We're supposed to be a team," I remind him. "In fact, we need to be a team to defeat Rita."

"I know." His voice sounds hollow. "And I know I'm supposed to be the leader, but . . ." He stops scrubbing the treadmill. "I don't actually *want* to be. Who would want that kind of responsibility?"

"Oh." I almost tell him that he's doing a great job as a leader, but the truth is that he's kind of doing a crummy job right now. I remember what Zordon said. *It is not your abilities but your* choices *that matter*. Jason could be a great leader, but he has to make better choices. Maybe now isn't the right time to tell him that. Instead, I say, "Do you want to talk about it?"

He nods but doesn't look at me. "I don't mean that I'm afraid of responsibility." He still doesn't meet my eyes. "I just have enough already."

"Oh?" I keep my voice neutral, hoping he'll tell me more but sensing that he doesn't want to be pushed.

"Did you know that my family runs Angel Grove Hardware?" he asks abruptly.

"No, I didn't," I say carefully. "Do you work there?" Maybe that's what he means by responsibility.

But he's shaking his head. "I used to, but my parents won't let me anymore. They want me to focus on my grades and football. No one in my family has ever gone to college. They want me to be the first."

I'm starting to understand. "That sounds like a big responsibility."

"Yeah." He sighs. "It's bad enough that my parents are pressuring me to get perfect grades *and* a football scholarship, but now

I'm supposed to be leading a team of teenagers in an intergalactic war. It's a lot."

"It *is* a lot." Sympathy wells up in me. "I don't blame you for not wanting to lead the team."

"I might not want to be the leader." He finally glances at me. "But I won't let you down. If I'm going to be leading the Power Rangers, I'll make sure the team is prepared."

"I get it." I hesitate. I want to leave it at that, but I can't keep trying to fix everyone's relationship with Jason. He's got to do it himself. "You know that what you're doing isn't working, right?"

"I noticed," he says bleakly.

"Zack and Kimberly are trying their best, and it would help if you noticed *that*," I say. "Billy isn't just the tech support of this team either. If you let him, he can fight too."

He eyes me thoughtfully. "What about you, Trini?"

"Me?" I squeak. "What about me?"

"Never mind. You just told me I have to do better, and you're right, so maybe I shouldn't ask why you're on this team . . . oh damn. Sorry." He reddens.

My pulse races dangerously. I knew he was thinking it, but that doesn't make it easier to hear. I set down the spray bottle. "It's okay. I'm kind of wondering the same thing."

"Zordon thinks you belong here," he says encouragingly, and I'm touched that he's trying to make me feel better.

"Zordon is an interdimensional being who's been hanging out in a time warp for ten thousand years." I attempt a smile. "I'm not sure how qualified he is to pick a team of human super soldiers." And I'm still not sure about his claim that the coins individually choose us.

Jason sighs. "He's the one who decided I should be the leader, so you might have a point."

"No." I straighten up. "Zordon was right to choose you. You just have to stop being the leader you think we all need and figure out how to fix your relationship with your team."

He's silent for a moment like he's thinking over my words. "I want to," he says at last. "I just don't know how."

"Maybe you could talk to everyone and listen to what they have to say." But even as I'm saying it, I know it's not that easy.

"I screwed this all up," he mumbles. "I don't blame them, but no one is going to give me a second chance. Except for you." He meets my eyes. "I don't know how to get the others to talk to me."

I put my hand on his arm. "You can try."

"Yeah, I guess I can." He clears his throat and starts gathering up the towels. "I think we're done here." He dumps the towels in the hamper. "We should both go home. We have an early training tomorrow."

I'm tempted to tell him that scheduling a training for eight in the morning the day after a normal Homecoming dance would be the kind of asshole move I'm talking about. But an early morning training after a Homecoming dance spent fighting Putties? That's going to earn him undying resentment from the rest of the team. Still, I know that Jason will probably be getting the training room set up way earlier than eight, so I bite my tongue. As hard as he is on everyone else—he's way harder on himself. "Good night, Jason."

He smiles, although it seems strained. "What? No last words of advice?"

"Give yourself a break, Jason," I say gently. "That's the only advice I have."

Maybe it's advice I should take myself. Even though I didn't actually do any fighting tonight, it's after midnight and I'm exhausted. Plus, my feet are throbbing in the strappy gold heels I'm not used to wearing. I can't wait to go home, take off my Homecoming finery, and crawl into bed. What we all need is a fresh start.

Tomorrow will be better. It *has* to be.

CHAPTER FIFTEEN

Something hits me at my ankles as I walk through my front door, and I'm tucking and rolling on the floor and coming to my feet in a defensive stance with my pulse going wild in panic. *A trip wire.*

"So," a voice says from the shadows, "you haven't forgotten all I've taught you."

"Nai Nai!" I relax out of my defensive stance. "What the hell?"

"Shh. Don't wake your mom up. She's still sleeping." Nai Nai turns on the lights and walks over to the door to roll up the thin, nearly invisible fishing line that she strung across the entrance. Then she closes the door gently.

I stare at her in utter confusion. "Do you want to explain why you decided to set up a booby trap for me in the middle of the night?"

Without answering, Nai Nai peers at me closely. "Not a scratch on you," she announces, "and good form in recovering from the trip wire even in three-inch heels. I taught you well. You didn't get that black eye from accidentally falling, Trini."

Is that what this is about? I touch my healed eye and wince, but not from pain. I don't want to keep lying to Nai Nai, but it's not like I can tell her that I'm secretly a Power Ranger.

She waits, and when I don't say anything, she sighs. "You're not going to tell me what's really happening, are you?"

"I'm sorry," I say miserably, "but I can't."

Nai Nai puts the rolled-up fishing wire in a drawer and then sits down on the living room couch. "Come here, Xiao Laohu."

But I don't feel like her Little Tiger right now. I feel like a confused fledgling who doesn't know where I'm going. I sit next to her and swallow hard. I want to tell her that I'm not involved in anything dangerous or scary, but that would be another lie. "I promise it's nothing morally wrong."

"Of course it isn't." She takes my hand in hers. "This is you, Trini. You would never be involved in anything wrong."

Her faith in me both eases my heart and makes it heavier. How can she trust me when I won't confide in her?

"Just tell me one thing," she says.

I hope she's not going to ask me again how I got my black eye, because there's no way I'm going to tell her that Zack hit me. Then again, she wouldn't believe me, and she'd be right. Zack would have never thrown a punch that he thought I couldn't block. "I'll try."

"What is making you so sad?" Her eyes are filled with sympathy.

That's . . . a harder question to answer than I thought it would be. "I don't think I'm sad," I say slowly. "Not exactly. It's more that I'm worried." Scared to death would be more accurate.

"About what?" She gives my hand a squeeze.

"Well, a bunch of us were assigned . . . uh, a group project." I suppose being part of a superpowered squad given a mission to save the world from a galactic sorceress is *technically* a group project.

"The history project you and Zack were assigned to do?"

"Uh, no," I say. "I mean, yes, Zack is in the group, but it's a different project." *Way* different.

"And it's important?" she asks.

"Very." My hands clench in my lap. "Actually, it's super-high-stakes, world-ending important." She probably thinks I'm being all teenagery dramatic, but I only *wish* I was exaggerating.

Nai Nai pulls a throw blanket off the back of the couch and wraps it around me. "You must be cold in that dress."

I smile. "So trip wire in the doorway is fine, but you're worried about me getting cold?"

"Oh, I knew you could handle the trip wire." She waves an airy hand. "I was just proving a point."

Right—the point being that I lied to her. The smile slips from my face.

"So what's the problem?" she asks.

I burrow deeper into the soft blanket. It's true that my strappy dress wasn't great at keeping me warm, and this blanket is heavenly. "My group isn't getting along."

"It seems like the solution is obvious, then."

"It is?" I certainly don't see it. Hope swells in my chest.

"You, my Xiao Laohu, just need to help them get along."

That hope pops like a balloon. Grumpily, I pull the blanket tighter around me. "I've been trying. It's not that easy."

"Why not?"

"I tried talking to them but it didn't do any good." My voice rises in frustration. "They just won't talk to each other, and it's not like I can make them."

"Hm." She pats my knee. "Do you know what is so special about the tiger?"

No, but I'm sure she's going to tell me.

Nai Nai does not disappoint. "The tiger is crafty and patient, gifted with a shrewdness and cunning that allows it to do what others cannot."

I eye her suspiciously. "Are you seriously advising me to be *sneaky*?"

"You said it was important for your group to get along." She smiles serenely. "So it seems to me that you know what you have to do."

I blink. *Wait* . . . can it be that simple?

⚡

"I cannot believe Jason changed the time of our training to seven," Zack grumbles blearily as we walk down the hall of the Command Center.

Guilt twinges in me for lying to Zack, but I tell myself that it's for the greater good. These two need to have a heart-to-heart. "Well, you know Jason."

"Yeah, I do." His voice is grim.

I gulp. Maybe telling Zack that Jason wanted to meet an hour earlier wasn't the best way to facilitate a truce between them. *I have regrets.* As we approach the metal door of the training room, I say, "Please don't be mad, Zack."

His face scrunches up. "Mad about what?"

"Jason doesn't know we're coming," I say quickly, and hit the button to open the door. "I lied about the change in time."

Zack gapes at me as the door slides open to reveal Jason doing bicep curls.

He stops at once when he sees us and sets down his dumbbells. "What are you two doing here so early?"

Before I lose my nerve, I pull Zack into the training room with me. "You two need to talk."

"Oh no." Zack digs in his heels. "I don't know what you're doing, Trini, but I want no part of this."

I lean toward him. "You told me you wanted me to fight," I say, keeping my voice low. "This is me fighting for my team."

"I meant you should power up and kick some space invader ass, not . . ." He makes a gesture toward Jason. ". . . whatever this is."

"I don't know what's going on either, but I'm not getting involved." Jason picks up his dumbbells and resumes his curls.

"See?" Zack takes a step backward. "He doesn't want to talk."

"That's because he doesn't know why you're mad at him." I raise my voice so Jason can hear me, and there's an infinitesimal pause in his bicep curls.

"My problem with Jason isn't exactly a mystery." Unfortunately, Zack is also talking louder. "He's a—"

I interrupt quickly. "I mean the *real* reason."

Jason sets down his weights again. "What do you mean?"

"Trust me," I say to Zack. "Please."

He sighs. "Are you sure you don't want me to fight back-to-back with you against Putties instead? Because I'd trust you with that."

"I know. This is harder."

"It is," he agrees, but he lets me lead him over to Jason, who's watching us warily.

"Jason," I say, "you said you wanted to fix things. Here's your chance."

"I said that?" Jason asks at the same time Zack asks "You said that?" They glare at each other.

My stomach drops. *This is not going well.* "Okay, let's start over . . . no, actually, let's go back." Their feud didn't start with the Power Rangers. It started with a hurt that's been festering for a long time. "Zack, tell Jason how you felt when you had to quit football." Panic flits over Zack's face, and I know he's tempted to deflect, so I add, "No jokes. Just *talk* to him."

Zack glances at me. "Trust you, huh?"

"Please." I'm not sure if he *should* trust me, but I don't know what else to do. My heart thumps against my ribs. I just hope I don't make things worse.

"Fine." He takes a breath. "Jason, I hated quitting football. And I hated it even more when you didn't even seem to care. You were supposed to be my friend."

The hurt in Zack's eyes makes me ache, but I'm glad he finally got that off his chest.

Jason's jaw drops open. "You didn't want to quit the football team?"

"Why the hell would I *want* to quit? It was just that my mom was sick and—" His voice gets tight, and he gestures toward me. "Trini can tell you the rest."

I get it. Some things are too hard to talk about. "Zack's mom had cancer," I say softly. "She's in remission now, but he quit all his sports to work after school to help pay off the medical bills."

"Oh man. I didn't know." Jason sounds stunned. "I thought—" He stops abruptly.

"Thought what?" Zack's tone isn't accusatory. He just sounds tired.

"You were always joking around," Jason says carefully, "so it never occurred to me that the team mattered to you. But I was clearly wrong." He clears his throat. "For what it's worth, I miss having you on the team."

"You do?" Zack sounds surprised.

"Yeah, you're a damn good running back. Plus, it's a lot less fun without you."

And then they're hugging and slapping each other on the back.

Wait. Is *that* all it took to get them to make up? No heartfelt apologies or long explanations needed?

Boys. I don't understand them, but sometimes, they can be pretty great.

Jason pulls away. "I'm sorry, Zack. I was a shitty friend."

"To be fair, it wasn't like I told you what was going on," Zack admits. "I'm sorry too."

There we go—apologies all around. Things are going to be just fine between Zack and Jason.

Jason turns to me. "Thanks, Trini."

"No problem." I blush. "Sorry I told Zack that you changed the training time."

He smiles. "It's okay, but you don't need to drag Kimberly or Billy here for a fake early session. I'll talk to them and fix things on my own."

"Deal." I smile back at him. It looks like we're on track to finally being a team.

"Good luck with Kimberly." Zack is frowning. "She's not interested in anything but getting people fired from their jobs over pears in her salad."

Damn. So close.

"That's oddly specific," Jason says doubtfully.

Zack shrugs. "I guess you can try talking to her."

"I will. First, I'm going to find Billy," Jason says, moving toward the door. "I think he's already here, tinkering with the Zords." Now that Jason's started, it doesn't seem like anything is going to deter him from making up with the team.

Zack, on the other hand—is going to need some help.

As the door closes on Jason, Zack turns to me. "Thanks, Trini." He bumps my arm. "But no more tricking me into early morning training sessions, okay?"

I nod sheepishly. My next plan doesn't involve a fake training time, but he *really* isn't going to like it. "Are you working this afternoon?"

"Real subtle change of topics," he says teasingly. "Yeah, I'll be at the juice bar later." He smiles. "Unlike my manager at L'ange Bosquet, Ernie has no problem with friends visiting while I'm working. Want to come by?"

I smile back at him, hiding my sneaky thoughts. "I'd love to."

CHAPTER SIXTEEN

Y ou're going to love this place," I promise Kimberly as we walk toward the Angel Grove Youth Center. "Ernie, the guy who owns it, is big on making sure teens have a safe place to hang out, so when he opened the gym in the nineties, he included a juice bar."

"That sounds great." Kimberly bounces a little as she walks. "Does it have any gymnastics equipment?"

"Maybe, but it's pretty basic. I think there might be a balance beam."

"That's okay. Jason asked Alpha 5 to order some high-end gymnastics equipment for the Command Center training room." Her eyes are shining.

Jason pulled Kimberly aside for a talk this morning, and the upshot was that she showed him what she could do in gymnastics, and they're working together on adapting her training to take advantage of her existing skills. She also trained in her Power Ranger form today, and she was incredible. It's safe to say that she and Jason are good now.

"How does that work?" I shift the straps of my backpack. "I can just imagine Alpha 5 ordering online and typing in 'Command Center, Middle of the Desert' for the shipping address."

She laughs. "I didn't ask. But they're able to literally teleport us back and forth between the Command Center and Angel Grove, so I'm sure getting a bunch of equipment won't be a problem."

"Good point." Everything is starting to come together. Zack and Kimberly are no longer fighting with our team leader, and Jason also followed through on his promise to talk to Billy, so they're on good terms too. *Three down. One to go.* A pang hits my conscience. Zack might have forgiven me for ambushing him with Jason, but he is really not going to be happy about me showing up with Kimberly.

Covering up my guilty thoughts with a bright smile, I stop in front of the Youth Center. "Here we are." I'm trying to remember why I thought it was a good idea to get Zack and Kimberly to talk here. Oh, right—I felt it would be awkward with the rest of the team around, but maybe this is worse.

Too late to turn back now. Pushing away my doubts, I open the door to reveal rows of ellipticals and treadmills, which are mostly in use.

Ernie looks up from the desk at the entrance of the gym. "Hey, Trini. I haven't seen you in a while!" He smiles at Kimberly. "And I see you brought a friend."

"Hi, Ernie," I say. "This is Kimberly."

Ernie and Kimberly exchange hellos, and then Ernie says, "If you're looking for—"

"Juice," I say quickly before Ernie can mention Zack. I'm half-convinced Kimberly will storm right out if she knows we're here to talk to him. "We're looking for juice." I grab her hand and pull her away. "Thanks, Ernie," I call out, ignoring his puzzled expression.

"It's just around the corner," I say to Kimberly.

"You must really want juice." She sounds amused. For now at least.

"Yeah, I guess I do." My forehead is damp with anxiety by the time we round the corner and enter the juice bar area where a few teens are hanging out at Formica tables.

Kimberly stops dead in her tracks when she sees Zack with his back to us, stocking a refrigerator behind the counter. "You knew he was working here, didn't you." Her voice is flat, and she doesn't ask it like a question.

"You said you felt bad about getting Zack fired," I remind her. "Here's your chance to tell him that."

She doesn't answer, but she lets me steer her up to the bar. I take a breath and say, "Hi, Zack."

He turns around with a smile, but it dies as soon as he sees who I'm with. "This is where I draw the line, Trini." He's glaring . . . but not at Kimberly. My oldest friend is glaring at me.

Oh hell. My stomach goes all shaky. It's possible I miscalculated how mad Zack would get.

"If he's going to be like this, then we should just go," Kimberly says to me.

This is only getting worse. Is it possible Alpha 5 has a time machine stashed away at the Command Center? If so, I know what I'd use it for.

Zack's glare transfers from me to Kimberly, and I'm not sure if that's any better. "Did you come here to get me fired from *another* job?"

"We just want to talk." I'm amazed to find that my voice is steady. "When can you take a break?"

"Zack, why don't you take a break now?" Ernie says from behind us. "Go talk to your friends. I can cover for you."

For a minute, I think Zack is going to protest, but he says, "Thanks, Ernie. I guess I will talk to my *friends*."

I doubt Ernie heard the sarcastic emphasis on "friends," but I wince. This isn't going to be easy.

Zack waves us toward a table that's a little out of the way, and we all sit around it like we're about to commence peace treaty talks—which I guess we are. And I happen to be figuratively and literally caught between the two of them.

I nudge Kimberly. "I think there's something you wanted to say to Zack."

"Right." She examines her hot pink fingernails like she's bored and just wants to get this over with, but one foot is doing a nervous little tap dance on the floor. "I'm sorry about the whole salad misunderstanding."

"That's all you have to say?" His voice is incredulous, and I don't blame him.

I sigh. He has no idea how much Kimberly really cares about making things right between them. "Zack," I say, "Kimberly is genuinely sorry."

She doesn't contradict me, but she's going back to staring at her fingernails like they contain the secret of the universe, so she's not exactly making a great case for her level of sincerity.

"Fine. I accept your apology," he says stiffly, and it couldn't be more obvious that he's only doing this for me, which is under-scored when he turns to me and asks, "Happy?" He misses the flash of hurt that crosses Kimberly's face.

"See?" Kimberly stands up. "This is a waste of time."

Damn. My stomach sinks. Somehow, I've managed to make things *worse* between them. "Listen—"

The sharp sound of shattering glass comes from the front of the gym, making my heart stop cold. *No.* People are screaming and running down the hall to hide in the gym's many exercise rooms. *Oh hell.* Those are definitely the sounds of Putties wreaking havoc.

The three of us leap to our feet, but before we can do anything to stop him, Ernie runs to the front of the gym, yelling, "Hey, what's going on?"

We all grab our Morphers and do a quick check to make sure no one is in sight, but everyone has fled, leaving the juice bar area to us.

Zack has his Morpher out first. "Mastodon." A quick flash of light, and he's the Black Ranger.

Then Kimberly. "Pterodactyl." She's the Pink Ranger.

I pull my Morpher out from my backpack and hold it up. "Sabertooth Tiger." This time, the metamorphosis into the Yellow Ranger is less jarring. Also less surprising is Alpha 5's voice coming through the speakers in my helmet.

"Oh good," he says. "You three have morphed. I've already tele-ported Jason and Billy to the school where Rita's army is attacking. I'll teleport you there too."

"Negative," Zack says. "They're here at Ernie's too."

"Besides," Kimberly adds, "the school isn't open on Sundays, so there's no one else there right now."

"Unlike the gym, which is full of people," I say, my voice twist-ing in fear.

"Ai-yi-yi." Alpha 5 says. Then he falls silent.

The three of us run toward the front of the gym where, dis-turbingly, I no longer hear Ernie yelling.

We stop dead in our tracks when we see the devastation that awaits us. The place is crawling with Putties, and Ernie is wild-eyed and shaking as he stares at the wreckage of exercise equipment lying on the shattered glass of his windows. "My gym," he moans.

"Trini," Kimberly says, "get Ernie to safety. Zack and I will get rid of the Putties."

"But you're outnumbered," I protest. There are at least twenty Putties currently tearing apart the gym.

I expect Zack to try and convince me to join in the fight, but he just leaps for the Putties with Kimberly by his side. I guess I've succeeded in convincing him I'm useless after all.

Swallowing hard, I steer Ernie to the hall that leads to the exercise rooms. "Tell everyone to stay hidden."

He seems to come out of his haze. "Right." He takes a few steps down the hall before turning and saying, "Thank you." Then he's running away.

Ernie shouldn't be thanking me. I'm the only Power Ranger who isn't doing anything of use, but I don't have time for self-pity.

I whirl around to see Zack trying to block more Putties from pouring through the broken window while Kimberly tries to keep some Putties from wrecking the few pieces of exercise equipment left standing. My skin goes clammy with worry. *They aren't working together.*

Even as I think this, the Putties coming through the window rush Zack with a sudden flurry of slashing claws. "Zack!" I scream, but it's too late. They have him pinned. Desperate fear pulses through me, but I can't move. Showing Kimberly I can fight now will mean I have to explain to everyone why I didn't earlier.

Kimberly looks up at my scream, and her helmeted head whips around to Zack. In one smooth motion, she throws off an attacking Putty and dashes over to help Zack. At her approach, some of the Putties turn away from him. My stomach clenches when I see that he's no longer trying to block Putties from coming through the window and simply trying to fight his way to freedom. But Kimberly does a flying kick that takes down a couple of Putties, and hope rises in me. It seems like my teammates might succeed in driving them off.

Then, without warning, the Putties rush Kimberly as if they were one fierce sharp-fingered deadly mass. Shock sends ice into my whole body.

"No!" Zack cries out as they pick Kimberly up and throw her across the room.

I'm running toward her, thinking I can catch her, break her fall—but she crashes to the floor and stays in a motionless heap. I fall to my knees by her side, fumbling to find a pulse. Then I remember we're being monitored by the Command Center. "Alpha 5," I yell. "What are Kimberly's vitals?"

His tinny voice comes through my helmet. "Her blood pressure is—"

"No. Dammit." My chest tightens in dread. "Is she alive? Is she okay?"

"Yes. Kimberly is unconscious with a mild concussion, which can be treated at the Command Center."

Relief fills me, and I'm about to ask Alpha 5 to beam her there, but then Zack's voice comes through the speakers. "Teleport her to the Command Center."

I start to ask Zack how he is doing, but then I look up and the words freeze in my throat. The Putties are clawing and pressing in on him, redoubling their efforts to take him down. Cold, sweaty rage seizes me.

Enough is enough. It's time for me to get into this fight.

CHAPTER SEVENTEEN

Adrenaline, fear, and anger pumps through me as I launch myself toward the Putties attacking Zack. I leap up into the split kick Nai Nai first taught me when I was five, but I have *never* jumped so high or kicked with so much force, and the Putties on either side of me go flying. *Whoa.* I mean, yes—our world is in danger, and I need to help save it, but how did I not realize how *kick-ass* being a Power Ranger would be?

Zack punches his way through the Putties to reach my side. "About time." I can practically hear his grin.

I'm already spinning to grab another Putty, tossing it aside like it's nothing but a sack of feathers. "Well, I couldn't let you have all the fun."

"Now that's the Trini Kwan I know." He moves so we're back-to-back, and I hear the thud of his feet and fists as he guards my back. Determination fills me. No Putty is getting through me to Zack.

I use my suit-protected arm to block a Putty lunging at me with sharp fingers extended and kick it away. It's really unfair that they basically have built-in knives. "You know what we need?"

"What's that?" Zack huffs like he's out of breath, but I don't glance over my shoulder. I trust him to have my back.

"Some sharp weapons of our own." Maybe I can use Nai Nai's daggers on more than burlap sacks.

"Ooooh!" Zack draws out the word. "Have I ever mentioned that I love the way you think?"

I blush and am glad he can't see it. I punch an advancing Putty in the stomach, but it doesn't seem to feel pain, not even when I throw it in the path of another Putty. They both go down without a single whimper.

Alpha 5's voice comes over my helmet speaker. "Zordon requests that you put a pin in it."

Put a pin in it?

"Not the right context, Alpha 5," Zack says. "We'll work on that later."

"Zachary Taylor, have you been teaching Alpha 5 Earth slang?" I demand.

"Clearly, I haven't been successful," he says, "but let's focus on the problem in front of us. Want to dance?"

"You and I have wildly different ideas of what 'focusing on the problem in front of us' means." I leap up and kick another Putty.

"I should clarify," he says. "I mean *swing* dance."

Ah. When we were little, Zack and I both thought swing dance meant his dad swinging us around in a circle until we were dizzy.

I smile. "I would love to dance with you, Zack."

We reach for each other's hands, and then Zack is swinging me around in a wide arc so I can kick out—*hard*. My feet connect with satisfying *thunks*, and soon Putties are sailing through the air. Exhilaration floods me. *Oh, much better.*

"Woo-hoo!" Zack yells, and I know just how he feels.

He sets me down, and we take defensive positions again, but the Putties aren't coming at us. They're turning toward the broken window and walking through the empty frame.

"Did we actually win?" Zack asks.

"I kind of think we did." Even to my own ears, I sound startled.

"Nice job, Rangers." Alpha 5 says through the speakers in my helmet. "Please prepare to be teleported to the Command Center."

The wobbly, unsettling feeling of being yanked through space shoots through me, and then I'm standing in the Command Center's Power Chamber in my normal clothes. Relief makes my knees go wobbly to see Kimberly with a purple gel pack pressed to her forehead. She's standing in front of the computer console where Alpha 5 is working on something. Zordon is missing from his energy tube, so I guess even interdimensional beings take breaks.

"Kimberly!" I rush over and hug her. "I'm so glad you're okay."

She hugs me back. "I'm glad you're okay too." Then she steps away and looks between Zack and me. "But how were you able to stop the Putties?"

He opens his mouth to answer, but I say quickly, "Zack was incredible, and the Putties just sort of retreated." All true . . . although it's far from the whole truth.

Zack gives me a pointed look, but if I tell everyone about my abilities now, then I'll have to explain why I didn't for so long. Why I lied to Billy all these years. Why I stood by and did nothing when Kimberly was under attack. She got hurt because of me. I can't stand them knowing how I betrayed them all.

"Really?" Kimberly sounds suspicious, and my stomach knots. She knows I'm keeping something from her.

"Really." Guilt flutters into my throat.

Kimberly places the gel pack in an empty spot on the console behind her. Stiffly, she says, "I'm sorry I couldn't help."

"Are you kidding?" Zack asks. *Oh no.* He's going to continue the argument that the Putties interrupted. Then he grins. "If you hadn't come to my rescue when the Putties had me pinned in a corner, I would have been toast. You only got knocked out because you were trying to help me. I guess what I'm trying to say is—thanks, Kimberly."

A smile spreads over my face. This is a *very* good sign.

"Oh." Her eyes go wide. "I really am sorry I got you fired." It comes out rapid-fire fast, but I can tell it's sincere.

And this time, so can Zack. "You know," he says, "I kind of hated working there anyway."

"I can imagine," Kimberly replies without missing a beat. "The customers are probably snobby jerks."

"They're not the only ones," he says sheepishly. "I was kind of a jerk too. Look, I'm sorry I said you were a spoiled rich girl." He holds out his hand. "Let's start over. I'm Zachary Taylor—Zack to my friends, so that's what you should call me. Welcome to Angel Grove, home of Putty attacks and subpar cuisine."

Then they're shaking hands and smiling. *Yes!* That is officially all my teammates on good terms.

Alpha 5 looks up from the computer console. "I am teleporting Jason and Billy back."

Damn. How could I have forgotten them? While we were fending off Putties at the gym, Jason and Billy were fighting Putties at the school. My whole body tenses up.

There's a beam of multicolored light, and then Jason and Billy are standing in front of us. Jason's mouth is set, and Billy's entire body droops. It's obvious that their battle didn't go well. At least they're both standing, and since no one else was at the school on a Sunday, that means no one else got hurt either.

"Where's Zordon?" Jason asks.

"Apologies." Alpha 5 doesn't look up from the controls at his consoles. "I'm having a little trouble getting Zordon to appear."

Billy walks over the console with a slight limp in his step, and worry creeps into me.

"Did you get injured, Billy?"

"It's nothing." He doesn't even glance at me. To Alpha 5, he says, "Have you tried to adjust for multidimensional fluctuations of the Morphin Grid?"

Morphin Grid? That's new.

"Why don't you try?" Alpha 5 shifts over to let Billy take his place in front of the console.

Even though I'm still anxious about Billy's limp, it's clear that he's handling the advanced science of the Command Center just fine.

Billy inputs something, and Zordon's head appears suddenly in the plasma tube.

"Good work!" Alpha 5 claps his hands.

Zordon peers at us. "It seems like I've missed a lot."

I look around, taking in the purpling bruise on Kimberly's forehead, the tight lines around Jason's mouth, Zack's sweaty face, and Billy's hunched shoulders. I don't know how I look, but I can feel the exhaustion weighing down my bones. We might be getting along better as a team, but our problems are far from over.

"We were beaten," Jason says. "Again."

"Actually," Kimberly says, "Zack was able to drive off the Putties from the gym."

"Zack and Kimberly both did," I say quickly, ignoring the disquieted look Zack throws at me.

"What about you, Trini?" Jason asks with quiet disappointment in his voice. And I don't think I'm imagining Kimberly avoiding my eyes. They're not aware of my fighting abilities, but they know I have the suit. It's obvious they don't understand why I couldn't even try to help.

"Oh. I . . ." My tongue gets tangled, and I find I can't speak. *Me? I used the wushu skills I've been keeping from most of you to kick Putty ass. But not in time to keep Kimberly from getting hurt.* Nope. I can't say that.

Billy glares at Jason. "I was no help either, so maybe neither of us belong on the battlefield."

Great. Billy is standing up to Jason for my sake. My stomach knots. If it ever comes out that I've been hiding my martial arts skills, it's my best friend who will feel the most blindsided.

Jason flushes, but before he can reply, Zordon cuts in. "As I have said before, you are all needed." His eyes linger on me, and I bite my lip nervously.

Kimberly squeezes my arm. "It's okay, Trini," she whispers, making me feel even worse.

Zack stays uncharacteristically silent, but I can feel his gaze boring into my skull. I can't bear to see the judgment on his face, so I don't look at him.

"Actually, you did fine, Billy," Jason says bracingly. "You're obviously needed in the Command Center *and* the battlefield."

Unlike me, who's not needed *anywhere*. Well, at least Jason is taking my advice to stop treating Billy like he's tech support. Then I peer more closely at my best friend, who doesn't seem cheered up by Jason's words. *Weird.* Something is up with Billy.

Before I can ask him what's wrong, Alpha 5 speaks. "Zack, was my use of the term 'Put a pin in it' erroneous?"

"Huh?" Zack looks confused. "Sorry, Alpha 5, but what are you talking about?"

It takes me a moment to remember the context, but when I do, my heart beats faster. "I think Alpha 5 is talking about our conversation about weapons."

"Yes. You said I had gotten the expression wrong, Zack." The lights in Alpha 5's visor blink rapidly. "Yet, according to my research, 'Put a pin in it' does indeed mean that we should remember to come back to the discussion at a later time."

"As a matter of fact," Zordon says, "I believe that 'later time' has come."

"Okay, I'll be the one to ask." Kimberly sighs. "What are we talking about?"

Good. I'm not the only one who's tired of Zordon giving us information in little dribbles. I mean, he probably doesn't want to overwhelm us, and his initial reveal that we've been chosen as Power Rangers to fight an alien sorceress . . . okay, never mind. I guess I understand why Zordon is pacing himself.

"I mean that it is time to talk about weaponry," he says.

I blink. Unlike the other stuff Zordon withheld—weapons are something we needed *much* earlier.

"Weapons?" There's an unaccustomed edge to Billy's voice. "And do these weapons need to be fixed too?"

My worry for him grows. I've been so wrapped up in my own problems that I missed how much my friend is struggling.

"These weapons are already functional," Zordon reassures Billy. He pauses and then says gently, "Don't worry, Billy. As I said before, you are making more progress on the Zords than Alpha 5 and I ever could on our own."

A little of the anxiety eases from Billy's face. *Oh good.* Zordon, at least, has noticed that Billy needs support.

"So, back to the weapons. Why is this the first time we're hearing about them?" Jason's eyes narrow on Zordon.

"Weapons would have been helpful to know about." Kimberly picks up the gel pack and holds it to her forehead again.

"Agreed." Zack turns to Alpha 5. "Sorry I questioned your grasp of Earthling idioms, but for future reference, when we're getting pummeled by Putties, weapons are always a discussion for *now*."

"I agree too," Billy says.

Apparently, all that we need to unite the team is the idea of weapons. And we don't even know what these weapons are. "Me too," I say, but I'm distracted. *Why* hasn't Zordon hasn't told us about them?

"Noted." Lights whir again in Alpha 5's visor.

"With these weapons, you will become even more dangerous," Zordon says.

"Yeah, kind of the point," Zack says.

But I know what Zordon means. My stomach clenches. Nai Nai gave me the same speech when she let me hold her twin daggers for the first time. *Fighting with weapons requires a calm mind and heart. To wield these daggers rashly or in anger could result in great danger—to both you and others.*

Jason glances at me. "We'll be careful, even when we're just training." He doesn't mention Zack accidentally giving me a black eye like he might have before the two of them made up, but I squirm internally.

"Got it." Zack sounds subdued. He doesn't look at me.

Kimberly removes her gel pack from her head and nods gingerly.

"For what it's worth, I'll be careful too," Billy says.

I take a breath. *Weapons.* As the saying goes—be careful of what you wish for. "I will too." I was the one who wanted weapons in the first place, but nervousness still twinges in my stomach. What I can do with my bare hands is dangerous enough, but it will be nothing compared to what I can do with a weapon.

"Very well, then." Zordon does not repeat his warnings. "Morph into your Power Ranger forms. It is time to receive your weapons."

This time, none of us fumble or hesitate. We all morph as if we've been doing it all our lives. Even me, with all my doubts and worries.

"Now what?" Jason asks from behind his red helmet.

"Simple," Zordon replies. "In your Ranger state, each of you has access to Morphin Grid energy. You are capable of drawing upon that energy to form a weapon unique to each of you."

I tell myself the swirling excitement in my belly is from my desire to defeat Rita, but to be honest—energy weapons sound pretty damn cool.

"That's it?" Zack asks. "We just think of a . . ." There's a flash of light, and then he's holding a black and gold battle axe by its handle. "Whoa."

Jason reaches out his hand, and a sword with a red handle forms in his hand. "That will work."

"Fascinating," Billy says, and then he's holding a blue double-edged lance. "Uh . . . am I supposed to use this?"

Another flash of light results in Kimberly holding a pink bow. "I don't know how to use mine either," she says, although her voice is bright with curiosity.

"You will all learn. As a warrior of Eltar, I have trained with each of these weapons and have created training holograms." Zordon's head turns to me. "Trini, I believe you have not yet formed your weapon."

"Right." I reach out my hand like Jason did, but nothing happens. Worry pierces me, and I let my hand fall back to my side. But then I remember my training with Nai Nai, and a tingling feeling rushes into my palms. Even before they take shape, I know what my weapons will be. Twin daggers.

"Those are awesome!" Kimberly says.

Zack whistles. "Elegant and deadly. Those are very you, Trini."

"I wish." I smile, even though he can't see my expression behind the faceplate of my helmet, and then I heft the yellow gold and silver daggers in my hand. They're not quite as slim and light as my nai nai's daggers, but I have no doubt I can get used to them. I'm already starting to get a feel for the smooth hilt of the dagger in my hand and can imagine the thrusts and blocks I can do with these. They seem like an extension of my body. *Yes.* These are *very* me.

I look around at my teammates. Everyone is examining their weapons while Zordon gives us an introduction to each one.

For the first time, I feel like I might belong on this team.

CHAPTER EIGHTEEN

o you want to talk about it?" I face Billy from across the console, where he's busying himself with some clearly complicated calculations. The rest of the team is in the training room, but Alpha 5 has a hologram of them projected into the Power Chamber so Zordon can observe and give them instructions on how to use their weapons.

"There's nothing to talk about." His grimace is visible because we've both morphed back into our normal, non-powered forms.

"Okay, then why aren't you in the training room, learning how to use that new lance of yours?"

He looks up from the console. "Why aren't *you* there, learning how to use your twin daggers?"

It's definitely not the time to tell him that I don't need the practice because I've been training with my nai nai's daggers since I was ten. Instead, I lean across the console. "I stayed behind to talk to you. We've been friends long enough that I know when there's something bothering you. So talk to me, Billy."

He sighs and stops fiddling with the console. "There's nothing wrong with the Zords that I can see."

"That's good news, isn't it?"

"It would be if they were working," he says glumly. "The problem is that I have no idea why they aren't."

I examine the dark circles under his eyes, and worry spreads through me. "You're putting too much pressure on yourself."

"The thing is . . ."

"Go on," I prompt.

"This is *all* I can do," he says in a rush. "This is why I was chosen to be a Power Ranger. I can't fight like the others can. If I can't get the Zords working, then what good am I to the team?"

Sympathy rises in me. Yeah, I can relate.

Off to the side, Alpha 5 claps his hands. "Well done, Kimberly!"

Billy and I turn to a hologram of Kimberly using her bow to shoot one pink arrow after another into the bull's-eye of a target while Zack and Jason spar off to the side with their own weapons.

"Very nice," Zordon says. "The Power Bow is an elegantly complex weapon, and you're a natural at it, Kimberly. You should also know that your bow has a nearly endless supply of energy arrows." His eyes track the hologram. "So don't worry about running out."

"Got it," Kimberly says without pausing her steady stream of arrows. Even with her faceplate hiding her expression, I can sense her pride in Zordon's praise.

"Zack, excellent footwork, but don't be afraid to use your Power Axe," Zordon says. "You won't hurt Jason in his morphed form. Jason, the same with your Power Sword. You are doing well, but keep in mind that you can use the sword for more than blocking."

"Uh, Zordon," Jason says, "I kind of stabbed the stuffing out of that dummy with my sword. Are you sure I should stop holding back?"

"I'm not going to just stand here and let you stab me," Zack jokes. "I'm no dummy."

"Indeed," Zordon says with a smile before his voice turns serious. "And neither are those Putties. They won't be holding back, so you shouldn't either."

Zack and Jason both nod and resume their sparring alongside Kimberly's archery practice. The others are getting really good under Zordon's mentorship. *I should be with them.*

A pang hits me, but I firmly tamp down the guilt surging through me. Supporting my best friend is more important right now. I turn back to Billy. "Listen, I get it," I say, "but trust me, you're definitely necessary to the team."

"You don't understand," he says. "It's different for you."

My mouth goes dry. Has he found out about my martial arts skills? Is he going to hate me now?

Then he says, "You're friends with all of us. I've never had that."

I frown in confusion. "You and I have been friends since middle school." Since seventh grade Science, to be exact. We were partners on a science ecosystem project, and even though Billy was fully capable of pretty much building a graduate-level terrarium on his own, he treated me as an equal partner and made me a part of every decision. We've been friends ever since.

"But you're my only friend." His shoulders hunch. "I've never had a group of friends before, and I guess I'm having trouble figuring out how I fit in."

Oh. I think I understand now. Joking with Zack, hanging out with Kimberly, and even cleaning up the training room with Jason—Billy doesn't have those relationships with the rest of the team. "You know," I say, "there might be a different way you can approach the problem of the Zords." A plan is taking shape in my head. "Remember how we became friends?"

He raises an eyebrow. "I'm not sure if I'm following you."

"You included me in our science project even though you could have done it on your own. Well, this time, you can't do it on your own, so maybe you should explain your problem with the Zords to us."

"This is a little different." He pauses, and I can tell he's trying to figure out how to be tactful. "This isn't exactly like a seventh-grade terrarium project."

"I know that," I say dryly. I wave a hand toward the hologram. "But you're not the only one who doesn't know how to fit in. The rest of us don't know how *we* fit into what you're doing. So explain it to us."

He looks thoughtful. "I suppose it couldn't hurt."

"Great." I turn to the hologram of our other teammates. "Sorry to interrupt your weapons training, but would you mind coming back to the Power Chamber? Billy would like to tell us more about the Zords."

⚡

"So, as you can see," Billy says, pointing to the holographic schematics of the Zords projected into the middle of the Command Center. "I have run every diagnostic, taking into account every possible and *impossible* reason for why the Zords aren't working, and I can find no explanation."

I have no idea how he distinguishes between the possible and impossible reasons he listed for us, and judging from the glazed looks in everyone's eyes, no one else understood any more than I did.

Billy peers at us, and his face visibly droops.

My stomach twinges in worry. Maybe asking Billy to include us in his process wasn't the best idea. "Thank you for explaining the . . ." I grope for the words to describe what I gleaned from his lecture. ". . . symbiotic relationship between us and the Zords." I think that's right, and Billy doesn't correct me. Then again, he might just be too despondent about the failure of my big plan to connect with our other teammates.

"Your diagnostics were very thorough, and more than Alpha 5 and I could do on our own," Zordon reassures Billy, who doesn't seem cheered by the praise.

"Uh-huh." Zack sounds sympathetic, but also confused. "I'm sure you did all you could, Billy."

"Maybe it would help if we could see the actual Zords?" Kimberly asks tentatively.

"Yeah." Jason gestures at the rapidly scrolling equations and graphs next to the 3D blueprints of the Zords. "I mean, this is . . . interesting, but it would be cool to see the real thing."

"That can certainly be arranged," Zordon says. "Alpha 5?"

"Yes." Alpha 5 busies himself at the computer console. "I could teleport you there, but I think it's simplest for you to take the turbo lift to the lower level of the Command Center where we are keeping the Zords."

Billy brightens. "They are pretty spectacular. I can show them to you."

Cheering Billy up with a group field trip to see his giant toys in person wasn't exactly part of my team-building plan, but I'll take it. Besides, my inner geek is screaming in excitement at the chance to see the Zords up close.

"The lift is ready," Alpha 5 proclaims.

We all follow Billy into the lift and cluster into the metal-enclosed space that is just large enough for us all.

"Prepare to descend," Alpha 5 announces over the lift's speakers.

With a sudden whoosh, the lift starts moving downward, and my stomach turns queasy. I actually think I prefer the disorientation I get from being teleported to the terror of falling through many layers of earth.

"It's fast," Kimberly comments. Her expression is neutral, so it's hard to tell what she thinks about the speed at which we're plummeting.

"It's *very* fast." Jason sounds just as neutral as Kimberly.

Zack grins. "Zords and a built-in amusement park ride. The Command Center is just the best."

"I looked up the schematics of the turbo lift," Billy says, "and it runs at approximately forty-five miles per hour." The lift glides to a smooth stop, and he glances at his watch. "Our descent lasted just under a minute, so we are roughly three quarters of a mile underground."

Zack stops smiling. "I don't love that."

"I'm with you," Jason says as the doors to the lift open. "Hanging out under a mile of rock and dirt isn't my idea of fun."

I have no problem with being underground, but if we were a mile *above* ground? I would be hyperventilating and squeezing my eyes shut. That's how much I hate heights.

Then I step out of the lift with the others, and all thoughts of heights flee my head.

Oh my. There they are—pink Pterodactyl, red Tyrannosaurus Rex, blue Triceratops, black Mastodon, and, of course, my yellow Sabertooth Tiger.

No one told me that the Zords were so beautiful.

I walk up to the tiger and reverently touch the clawed metal foot, which is almost as tall as I am. Everyone else is walking to their own Zords as well.

"Each Zord is approximately forty-one meters tall," Billy explains. "That's about one hundred and thirty-five feet, and they weigh around five hundred and seventy tons."

"Got it." Zack peers up at his Mastodon. "So it would really hurt if one stepped on your foot."

"How do we get inside?" Kimberly asks eagerly.

"There's a hatch on top of each head, but that's not how we get in," Billy replies.

Oh good. I was so not looking forward to climbing a ladder up roughly thirteen stories.

Jason peers thoughtfully at his towering Tyrannosaurus Rex Zord. "Can Alpha 5 teleport us into them?"

"Yes . . . and no." Billy pats the treads on a huge wheel of his Triceratops. "There is a cockpit inside each Zord, and we can be teleported there. But operating the Zords is not as simple as Alpha 5 teleporting us into the cockpit."

I resist the urge to point out that two weeks ago, none of us had any idea that the Command Center, Zords, or any of this existed, and now Billy is talking about teleportation being *simple*.

"As I explained, it's actually a fascinating symbiotic relation-ship—" Billy catches himself, no doubt remembering how he lost us all with his earlier lecture. "Basically, when the Zords are oper-ational, we'll be able to merge with them on a molecular level."

"That's the nanotechnology part Billy told us about," I say, but judging from my teammates' confused faces, I'm not sure that my clarification helped.

"So." Jason has a disquieted look on his face as he glances at his Tyrannosaurus Rex. "We *become* the Zord?"

Zack groans. "I don't remember anyone saying I had to morph into a Mastodon when we signed up to become Power Rangers."

"No, no! It's not morphing." Billy pauses. "Although the Zords do draw on the same energy of the Morphin Grid."

"Right," I say quickly. Billy had spent a large chunk of his lecture going over the fact that the Morphin Grid is a multidimensional power source, and I don't think anyone wants a repeat of that. "So we don't become the Zords, but we *do* merge with them." I think back to the part of his lecture that I *did* understand. *Symbiotic relationships.* "Is this some kind of psychic link?"

"Actually . . ." He blinks. "Yes."

Okay, now we're getting somewhere. But my satisfaction fades when I glimpse the frown on Jason's face.

He shakes his head like he's trying to clear it. "Can you tell us more about the controls inside the cockpit? Do you have a manual or something on how to drive these things?"

"There are no controls, no manual," Billy says. "That's what I've been trying to say."

Judging from the bemused look on Jason's face, he still has no idea what Billy is trying to say. "We need to link psychically with the Zords to operate them," I summarize.

"Not just with the Zords," Billy says. "We all have to be connected through the Morphin Grid to form the Megazord." He raps the wheel of his Triceratops. "But all this is moot if I can't get the individual Zords operational."

"Don't worry, Razorbeak." Kimberly pats the wing of her Pterodactyl. "Billy will get you working again."

"*Razorbeak?*" Jason's eyebrows rise. "You've named your Zord?"

"I'm just trying it out," she says airily.

Zack leans against the leg of his Mastodon. "I'm thinking of Stompy for mine. Or maybe Wooly."

"A bit on the nose, don't you think?" I ask dryly.

"You're right. Rover, it is."

"They're not *pets*." Billy runs his hand through his hair. "And they're not sentient. They're battle vehicles."

"Rover is offended," Zack says.

I run my hand over the smooth metal of my Sabertooth Tiger Zord again. They might not be sentient, but Billy did say that we operate them through a psychic link. "What if you go about this a different way?"

Billy's eyes lock onto me. "What do you mean?"

"Well, you said you couldn't find anything wrong with the Zords," I say slowly, "so what if the problem isn't with *them*?"

His mouth drops open, and he just stares at me.

"Hey." Kimberly waves a hand in front of Billy's eyes. "What's going on in there? Talk to us."

"Trini, what did you do to our resident genius?" Zack asks.

"Billy," Jason says, "are you okay?"

"He's fine." I've seen Billy this way before—like when he realized we could create mechanized tectonic plates for our seventh-grade terrarium. "This is just how he gets when he's having a brainstorm."

"You're right, Trini." Billy turns to the others, his eyes shining. "All of *us* are the key to getting the Zords operational."

CHAPTER NINETEEN

You are cleared for the Zord activation trial," Alpha 5 tells us over the cool communication devices we wear on our wrists that Billy made for us. "Our scans do not pick up any other human activity."

I have no doubt that Alpha 5 is right. There's nothing but sand and more sand in the area outside the Command Center where he's teleported us and our Zords.

"What are we supposed to do again?" Jason asks.

"If we do the same thing we do to take our Power Ranger forms," Billy replies, "then we should be able to merge with our Zords. *Theoretically*, we just hold up our Morphers and say the name of the prehistoric creature on our coin, but this time, we think about forming a connection with our Zords."

Zack opens his mouth, and I just know what he's about to say.

"Nope." I shake my head. "Not Rover. Or Wooly. Or Stompy."

"You take the fun out of everything, Trini." But his smile contradicts his words. Heat flushes my face and for a moment, I can't breathe. Luckily, Zack's attention is back on his Zord, so he didn't notice me getting all flustered over nothing.

I shake my head. I'm supposed to be preparing giant dinosaur mechs for a battle against an invading space sorceress, not drooling over my childhood best friend.

"So that's pretty much it," Billy says. "It's simple."

"If I had a dollar for every time you said something was simple," Zack remarks, "I could quit my job at the juice bar."

"And I was planning to take you up on the offer of the friends and family discount," Kimberly says.

"Anytime," he says. "Juice discount for all my world-saving, Putty-destroying friends."

Friends. It makes me glad to see Zack and Kimberly getting along, and I'm not the only one. Kimberly is beaming at us all, way happier than a juice discount would justify.

"Let's save the juice for after we beat Rita." Jason doesn't sound irritated like he used to whenever Zack would make jokes.

I smile. It's clear that we're more connected and a much stronger team than when we started.

"We might have to wait. It will take a while before Ernie is able to repair the gym from the Putty damage." This time, Zack's voice is grave, and I can tell he feels responsible.

Kimberly's gaze turns inward, and the smile slips from her face. I have no idea what she's thinking, but then her words from when we went dress shopping pop into my head. *Let's just say I didn't leave my old high school under ideal circumstances.* I respect her privacy, but I can't help but wonder what happened at her last school.

Anxiety worms into me. We might be more connected now, but there are still things that are unresolved—Kimberly's secrets, Billy's self-doubt, Jason's fear of failure, Zack's guilt—then there's my own special brand of insecurity. Between the five of us, that's some seriously intense stuff, and it could affect the psychic link that Billy says we need to get the Zords working. My stomach tightens. Can we overcome all that in order to merge with our Zords?

Jason looks toward Billy. "Should we have Alpha 5 teleport us into the cockpits first?"

"Well, theoretically, once we merge with our Zords, the power of our psychic link should automatically teleport us inside."

"And if I had a dollar for every time you said *theoretically*," Zack says, "I'd have enough to buy my own juice bar."

I reach over and squeeze his arm because I recognize where the jokes are coming from—the same nervousness that is winding me into a tightly coiled spring.

"Hey," I say, "we've got this."

Zack flashes me a smile, and it might be my imagination, but I think some of the tension eases from his body. "You should go first, Jason." There's no hint of bitterness in his voice, but I remember what he said to me after Jason was chosen to be our leader.

Face it, Trini. You and I will never be the ones chosen to lead. I see it now. A pang hits me. Zack would be just as good a leader as Jason, but Zack wasn't the one who was chosen.

"I guess someone needs to do it." Jason unbuckles his Morpher and holds it up. "Tyrannosaurus Rex." He morphs into the Red Ranger . . . but he remains on the ground with the rest of us. The Zord next to him remains motionless.

Damn. I was really hoping it would work.

"Damn." Billy echoes my thoughts, and I stare at him in surprise because he never swears.

I have to help him see that this is just a small bump in the road, and that he *can* succeed. He needs to remember that he's solved impossible problems before. "Billy," I say, "What do you do when your hypothesis doesn't work?"

"Adjust the variables and try again." His face clears. "Jason, you're more connected to the Morphin Grid in your Power Ranger form. It should be easier for you to merge with your Zord now that you're the Red Ranger. Try again."

Jason holds out his Morpher again, then repeats, "Tyrannosaurus Rex."

Nothing happens.

"It didn't work." Jason's voice is emotionless, giving no hint of how he feels about his failure, but my heart wrenches in sympathy. I know it must be eating him up inside.

"It's okay," I say gently. "It's not all on you, Jason."

He nods. "I'll keep that in mind." He doesn't say anything else, but I hope he's remembering our conversation in the training room.

Zack glances at me. Before I can ask him what he's thinking, Billy interrupts me.

"Trini is right," Billy says glumly. "It's not all on Jason. We *all* have to be able to merge with our Zords to form the Megazord. And if Jason can't do it, then I don't know how the rest of us can." He doesn't finish the rest of that thought—that we have to form the Megazord to beat Rita. But he doesn't have to say it because we're all thinking it.

"At least we'll have a place to start if one of us can merge with a Zord," Jason says decisively. "Someone else should try."

"It shouldn't be me," Kimberly says, her voice hollow and faint.

I have no idea what memories are haunting her, but it doesn't matter. My chin lifts and I take a step closer to her. I might not know what secrets she's keeping, but I know what kind of person she is. "Of course it should be you." I put my arm around Kimberly and give her a squeeze. "It should be *all* of us."

She winds her arm around my waist and hugs me back, but she sounds puzzled. "What do you mean?"

"We're a team," I say, releasing her and looking at everyone, "so we should do this together."

"Actually," Billy says, his eyes brightening, "that might just work. The connection between all of us might be the extra power we need to merge with our Zords."

"All right." Life comes back into Jason's voice. "Let's do this all at once as a team."

My hands are clammy as I take my Morpher from my sling bag and hold it out in front of me as everyone else retrieves theirs.

"Ready?" Jason asks.

"It's Morphin time!" Zack says cheerfully.

I roll my eyes, but I'm glad that he's trying to lighten the mood. He understands that we need this. "Seriously?"

"What?" he asks. "Kimberly can try out 'Razorbeak' as a pet name for her Pterodactyl battle mech, but I can't try out a team catchphrase?"

"Fair point," Kimberly says.

"As team captain, I'm going to have to veto 'It's Morphin time.'" There's a faint smile in Jason's voice.

"I like 'Go, go Power Rangers' better," Billy says.

"I'll keep at it," Zack promises, "but don't worry. I won't let us go into battle against the Putties without a kick-ass catchphrase."

"Obviously, that is our biggest problem," I say, trying to keep my lips from twitching up into a smile. "The lack of a kick-ass catchphrase."

Jason clears his throat pointedly. "Can you all just morph already so I'm not the only one standing here in space spandex?"

Zack has a gleam in his eyes, and I say hastily, "I'm nixing any catchphrase with 'space spandex' in it."

"No. Fun. Trini." Zack enunciates each word.

"Let's just say I know you too well," I say. And I know what he's doing—giving us a lighthearted moment to bond together. Billy said we need to feel connected with each other to merge with our individual Zord. If this works, it's in large part because of Zack. "Sabertooth Tiger!" I call out, and I morph into my Yellow Ranger form.

Zack, Kimberly, and Billy morph too.

"Okay," Jason says, "We'll try to merge with our Zords at the same time on the count of three." He takes an audible breath. "Three. Two. One. *Go.*"

My hand is shaky as I hold up my Morpher. "Sabertooth Tiger," I say as everyone else says the name of their own Zord. There are flashes of light around me . . . and then nothing.

I look around to find that I am still standing in the desert next to my Zord.

Alone.

But where is everyone else? I stare in shock at my lifeless Sabertooth Tiger as, all around me, mechanical prehistoric beasts are roaring to life with gleaming eyes and loud thumps—Pterodactyl, Mastodon, Triceratops, Tyrannosaurus Rex. But my own Sabertooth Tiger is immobile in all its yellow and gold glory.

Slowly, it starts to sink in, and my heart feels like it's been dropped into an abyss.

I am the only one who didn't merge with my Zord.

CHAPTER TWENTY

I throw myself onto my living room couch. *What the hell happened back there?* I hurl a pillow across the room, where it bounces harmlessly off a wall, and then I bury my face into another pillow to muffle the sound in case I start screaming out my frustrations. Alpha 5 already confirmed that my house was empty before he teleported me back, but I don't need the neighbors to think I'm being murdered in my own home.

A knock on the door jolts me from my grim thoughts. Did Nai Nai forget her key again? With a sigh, I pad to the door and open it, but it's not Nai Nai.

It's Zack.

"Hey." He gives me a small smile. "I thought maybe you would want to talk."

"Sure." My voice sounds unenthusiastic even to my own ears. It's not that I don't want to talk to him, but I'm less than thrilled for him to see me at such a low point. I hold the door open. Mom would be horrified that I don't offer him something to drink and eat, but I just can't summon the energy. Listlessly, I shuffle back to the couch and plop down.

Zack toes off his shoes and comes over to sit next to me. "So what happened out there?"

"Beats me."

"Do you want me to tell you what *I* think?"

I eye him narrowly. "Can I stop you?"

"Nope." He eyes me sympathetically. "So here's the thing—I think you've been so busy helping us all get along and figure out who we are that you've lost sight of who *you* are."

I stare at him. "That's ridiculous."

"Do you have a better explanation?"

"Yeah." I close my eyes and see Carl, that elementary school bully, wiping a trickle of blood from his face and staring at me with fear in his eyes. None of the others know what it's like to lose control like that. Or to train nearly all my life so it never happens again. Then I see Kimberly lying on the ground, cold and still. No matter what I do or don't do, I'm a danger to someone.

My eyes open and lock onto Zack. "Face it, Zack. I'm no good to the team."

"Bullshit." He leaps to his feet and starts pacing. "You're the reason I'm getting along with both Kimberly and Jason, and you got Jason to ease up on his hardcore drill sergeant routine. Plus, Billy wouldn't have figured out the Zord problem without your help."

"Don't you see?" My voice is stiff. "I *am* the Zord problem." My heart twinges. Deep down inside, I know why I couldn't merge with my Sabertooth Tiger. It's because I don't belong on the team. "The rest of you were able to merge with yours, but I couldn't do it."

"You will." There is absolute confidence in his voice, and I don't have the heart to tell him that it's misplaced. "And until you figure out the whole Zord activation thing," he says, "there's still your martial arts skills. You know—the real reason we were able to drive the Putties away from the Youth Center." It obviously doesn't sit well with him to take sole credit for that victory.

I squirm uncomfortably on the couch. All I can think about is that moment when the Putties were swarming Zack. Kimberly didn't hesitate, but I did. With all my wushu training, I couldn't even help my oldest friend when he most needed me. And Kimberly got hurt because of it.

Zack gives me an exasperated look when I don't respond. "Why don't you just tell the others what you can do?"

"No!" It comes out more forcefully than I intended. "And you can't tell them either." I don't want the others to know I've been lying to them. It's obvious that I should have listened to Zack and come clean at the start, but it's too late now.

"Why not?" The frustration in his voice is clear. "I don't understand why you have to hide who you are."

I shake my head. "You don't know who I am. Not anymore." *I am a girl afraid of her own power.*

"Trini." He swallows hard. "It's me, Zack. I've known you since we were little. We played dress-up and had dance parties as kids. Your grandmother let me train with you. Of course I know you."

But Zack hadn't been there in middle school when kids teased me about the hum bao and marinated tea eggs that Nai Nai packed me for lunch. He wasn't there when I was tripped in the halls or when kids pulled their eyes into a slant to mock me. He didn't know how badly I wanted to *hurt* the kids who hurt me or how scared I was of what I could do. I'm *still* scared of myself. After so many years of holding back, I don't know how to fight when it matters.

But Zack doesn't know that because he wasn't there. And that was the worst part—I didn't have my best friend at my side to help me through any of it.

"You don't get to say that you know me." Sudden anger surges through me, and I stand up from the couch to face him. "We haven't been friends since the start of middle school. Remember?"

"I know that we haven't been as close for a while." A wary expression passes over his face. "But I like to think we're still friends. Especially now."

Bitterness stabs into me. "And what if we hadn't been chosen for the same superhero team? Would you have just kept on ignoring me for the rest of high school?"

"Whoa." He holds up his hands. "We're talking about why you won't come clean to the team about your martial arts skills. This isn't about two kids who drifted apart in middle school."

Of course it isn't. Not for him at least. After all, it was Zack who moved on when I didn't. "Maybe it didn't matter to *you* that we weren't friends anymore. You were the one who suddenly didn't have time for me." The words just come tumbling out. "You were the one who dropped me for cooler friends."

"What are you even talking about?" He looks genuinely confused. "Yeah, I was hanging out with other kids, but you were becoming friends with Billy too."

"That's different." Yes, Billy was my friend, but he would have wanted to be friends with Zack too. The problem was that neither of us was cool enough for Zack's new friends. And if that wasn't bad enough—I was starting to get the impression that I wasn't cool enough for *Zack* either.

"How was it different?" he demands.

"Billy never made anyone feel like they didn't belong!" I blurt out. It's like the things I could never say, or even *think,* have congealed into a hot mass in my chest. But now all those stifled words are blazing out of me. "Billy never made you feel like you didn't matter—not like your new friends did with me."

A flush steals over his face, and he opens his mouth to speak, but I'm on a roll now and won't be stopped. "I haven't forgotten what your friends used to say. 'Hey Zack, why do you hang out with *Trini Kwan* all the time?'" I say my name the way they did, with mocking disbelief. "And you didn't say, 'Because she's my *friend.*'" I pause, my breathless rage turning into sadness. "You never said anything. You just ditched me."

Zack goes still and is silent for a long moment. I bite my lip when I realize my chin is starting to quiver, and I blink rapidly to prevent tears from falling. He finally speaks. "Okay, I messed up," he says somberly. "I'm sorry, Trini."

I messed up too. I should have told you how I felt. But I can't push the words past my constricted throat. I've been holding my grief at losing our friendship for so long that I don't know what to say now that it's out in the open.

When I don't speak, his eyes flash. "To be fair, you seemed just fine with not being friends anymore. How was I supposed to know what you were feeling? And it was *four* years ago. If you really wanted to stay friends, you could have put me in a headlock or something until I admitted I was being a jerk."

My head spins, trying to process his words. "I was *hurt*, Zack." My voice rises in disbelief. "Are you really saying I should have kicked your ass in middle school?"

"Why not?" Then he smacks his forehead. "Oh wait. I forgot. Trini Kwan stopped fighting for anything she wants."

Heat rushes into my face. "Better than fighting with everyone because you're holding ridiculous grudges." Which is epically unfair because Zack doesn't hold irrational grudges, and he had good reason for being mad at both Kimberly and Jason. But he has no reason to be mad at *me* . . . except that I'm not the girl he thinks I am.

"What is that supposed to mean?" He glares at me.

I glare right back. "You think you know me," I say, "but like I said—you don't. And you don't get to be pissed off because I'm not who you think I am."

"You're right," he shoots back. "I don't know you anymore. The Trini *I* knew stood up for everyone, including herself. And yeah, I was an asshole for dropping you for new friends. But they weren't 'cooler.' No one is cooler than you. I wish I saw that then, and I wish you could see that *now*."

My eyes burn with tears that I refuse to let him see. "And I wish you would stop trying to make me someone I'm not."

"I just don't understand why you'll stand up for anyone *except* yourself." His face hardens. "But you're fooling yourself if you think you don't fight anymore. The difference is that the person you're fighting now is yourself."

"Actually," I spit out, "the person I'm fighting is *you* at the moment." I don't let myself wonder why I'm not afraid to let Zack see my anger, why he's the only one I trust to see me . . . or if he might be right. "Get out."

"Fine! I'm leaving." He begins to stalk toward the door, but he fires one last parting shot over his shoulder. "If you're so afraid to let the others in, then maybe you should get off the team."

My heart stops. He can't possibly mean that.

I stare at his retreating back and have to clap a hand over my mouth to stop a sob from escaping. Maybe he's right.

Maybe I should quit the Power Rangers.

Alpha 5's voice comes through our wrist coms, making me jump. "Zack and Trini, come in."

Zack stops a few feet from the door and turns around. Our eyes meet, and my body tenses. "We're here," I say into my wrist com after clearing my throat. My voice sounds shaky to my own ears.

"Putties are attacking downtown Angel Grove." Alpha 5's voice is grim. "It's bad. I'm teleporting all the Power Rangers there immediately."

CHAPTER TWENTY-ONE

The thick smoke almost obscures the damage. Almost. My breath catches to see overturned cars, burning buildings, and people running and screaming as dozens of Putties swarm the streets, destroying parked cars and storefronts.

"Oh my god," Kimberly says next to me.

We've all been teleported into the plaza in front of the town hall, but for a moment, none of us move.

Then Jason says, "Weapons, everyone."

That, I can do. I concentrate on my twin daggers, and they form, slim and deadly, in my hands. Everyone else has manifested their weapons too.

Jason points to the town hall. "Kimberly, get on top of that roof and shoot down as many Putties as you can. Billy and Trini, clear the area and put out the fires. Zack, you and I need to stop the Putties from destroying the stores."

I remember then that Jason's family runs Angel Grove Hardware, and a sick feeling hits my stomach.

"Jason," Alpha 5's voice says, "should I teleport the Zords to you?"

"Negative." He uses his sword to point to the wreckage of the main street. "If we use the Zords, we'll just destroy what's left of Angel Grove."

"That's okay." Zack hefts his axe. "I'm happy to take on the Putties without the Zords."

"Me too." Kimberly grips her bow and runs toward the town hall.

"Let's go, then." Jason and Zack race toward the Putties on the street, weapons extended.

I should go with them. Am I making the right decision in hiding my ability to fight?

Billy turns toward me. "I'm not sure what my lance or your daggers can do against fire, but I have an idea of how to put it out."

"Good." I look at the people fleeing from the Putties. They seem to be clearing out just fine without any help from me. Then I glance at the flames flickering over the buildings, and my heart starts thumping. Did everyone get out?

I think fast. "Alpha 5, is there anyone left in those burning buildings?"

"I'm reading two life signs in one of the buildings," Alpha 5 replies promptly. "Follow the red dot."

A blinking red dot appears in my visor. "Are our suits fireproof?"

"They can withstand up to twelve hundred degrees Celsius," the android replies.

I look toward Billy, and he says, "Yes, they're fireproof. More or less, anyway."

I'm not going to dwell on the "more or less" part. "I'll get people out while you work on extinguishing the fires." Billy nods, and I take a deep breath. "I'm going in." I let my Power Daggers dissipate and race down the street toward the burning building marked by the red dot.

It's not until I'm right in front of the charred brick exterior that I realize which store this is. The neon sign is cracked and burnt, but I can still make out the words "Angel Grove Hardware." *Oh hell.* It's Jason's family store. Flames are licking at the building, and thick smoke spirals out of the broken front window.

"Help!" a voice screams from inside.

I go cold all over, and without thinking, I leap through the broken window. The sight that greets me is straight out of a nightmare. Flames surround a burly man trying in vain to lift a case of metal shelves that have toppled over. He turns at my approach and doesn't even blink at my Power Ranger suit. "Please help. My daughter is trapped."

I see her then—a little girl pinned by the case. My breath whooshes out of me.

"Dad, help!" she sobs.

Fear pumps through me as I dash through the circle of flames and lift up the metal case in one easy movement, thanks to my Ranger powers. I toss it aside and scoop up the girl, who clings to me. "Hang on. It's going to be okay."

"Thank you," the father says, but then he starts choking on the smoke and has to cover his mouth with his arm.

My stomach sinks as soon as I realize that my suit might be fireproof, but their clothing isn't. I can't get the girl and her father out the way I came in. "Alpha 5, I need to talk to Billy."

"Opening a channel now," Alpha 5 says promptly.

"Billy," I say urgently, "Have you figured out a way to put out the fires yet?"

"Yes," he replies, "but I need to run a trial test—"

"There's no time," I interrupt. "I'm in Angel Grove Hardware, and I need you to put out this fire *now*."

The little girl in my arm starts coughing, her eyes watering. My own throat tightens even though my helmet is filtering out the smoke.

"Is that a *kid* I hear?" Billy sounds horrified.

"Yes." I lift the neck of her shirt to cover her mouth and nose. "Hurry."

"On it." The channel goes dead.

"Go." The father forces out the words through gasps for breath. "Take her with you."

I take a shaky breath as I stare at the flames growing taller and taller around us. It would be risky to take the girl through that, but we'll all be dead if we stay much longer. "Not yet," I say at last. I have to give Billy a chance.

A prickle of sweat starts in the middle of my back. Even with my fireproof suit, I'm starting to feel the heat. I have to go now if I'm going to have any chance of saving the trembling girl in my arms. I look at the father and meet his eyes, barely visible over the neck of his shirt he's using to cover the lower part of his face.

"Go," he whispers.

My gut clenches. I have no choice. I have to abandon this man to his death.

Then a cascade of water descends on us.

Relief spreads through me as I hug the girl to my chest. The father is sputtering under the deluge, but the flames are being doused.

Billy's voice asks anxiously, "Are you all okay?"

"Yes." My voice quivers. "You did it Billy."

Still clutching the girl, I grab the father's arm and steer him out of the smoking store. I help him through the broken window, careful to avoid the shards of glass still in the frame.

When we emerge, I find Billy standing next to the fire hydrant a block away. He has rigged some kind of force field to funnel water from the hydrant directly to the fires.

But then I take in the rest of my surroundings and my stomach drops.

Half the town hall has been reduced to rubble as the Putties continue to swarm the town hall, trying to get to Kimberly. She's shooting arrow after arrow at them from the part of the roof that's still left, but they just keep coming. More Putties are tearing up chunks of the street itself and flinging them at Zack and Jason, who have taken defensive positions back-to-back and using their weapons to fend off the attack. All around us, people are screaming and running or hiding.

Heart in my throat, I hand the girl to her father. "I have to help my friends."

I barely hear his stuttered thanks as he runs away with his daughter clutched firmly in his arms. Taking a deep breath, I form my twin daggers.

Before I get more than a few feet toward them, I hear Jason's urgent voice over my headset. "We need to get them away before they destroy all of Angel Grove."

"Is it time for Zords now?" Alpha 5 asks.

"No," Zack says, swinging his axe in a wide sweep that takes down a few Putties.

I expect Jason to echo Zack, but he doesn't. Instead, Jason glances at his family's destroyed store—the one I'm standing in front of. My body twists in regret. I wish I could have saved it.

"Maybe we rethink the Zords," Jason says fiercely as he stabs an attacking Putty through the chest with his sword.

"Wait." Panic whirls in me. I get that Jason wants revenge, but I'm also pretty sure he'll regret unleashing the Zords on the densely populated downtown. The streets are now clogged with honking cars trying to get out, people fleeing on foot, and others hiding behind overturned cars and rubble. "If we use the Zords, we'll wreck what's left of Angel Grove."

"I think that ship has sailed." Jason's voice is cold with anger.

Zack leaps up and kicks down a Putty. He doesn't acknowledge my comment like he would have before our argument, and I know it's ridiculous to care about the rift between us when our town is being decimated—but I feel like all the Putties have just hit me at once in the solar plexus.

"Billy, any ideas?" Zack asks without even turning his head toward me.

There's a pause, and then Billy says, "I'm thinking."

"I have an idea." Kimberly sounds breathless, but she doesn't pause her stream of arrows. "What if I use my Pterodactyl to draw the Putties into the desert? My Zord is airborne, so it won't do any damage on the ground like your Zords will."

"Do it, Kimberly," Jason says decisively, and my body weakens in relief. "Go toward the desert. The rest of us will follow and form our Zords once we're in the clear."

Damn. My relief fades. I forgot that I was the only one who hasn't merged with my Zord yet.

Alpha 5's voice says, "Teleporting Pterodactyl Zord to your location now, Kimberly."

The Zord forms in the air next to Kimberly on the roof, and I don't even see her lift up her Morpher or call out "Pterodactyl" before she disappears in a flash of pink light. Awe fills me. *Go Kimberly!*

The Pterodactyl Zord hovers in the air for a split second before shooting off a few beams of . . . are those *pink* lasers? They strike down a couple Putties and blast the ground hard enough to make it shake. All the Putties turn toward the Zord, recognizing it as the biggest threat.

"You've got their attention, Kimberly," Jason says, "but no more lasers." I'm glad Jason has put aside his anger and is focused on trying to minimize the damage to Angel Grove.

"Okay, I'm headed for the desert." Kimberly's Zord flies off slowly enough for the Putties to follow, and they do.

I watch the Putties closely. They're *much* faster and stronger now, and there are a lot more of them too. If they keep improving like this, they'll soon be unstoppable. I shiver.

"Everyone, follow the Putties." Jason is already running after them. "Make sure to keep them heading out of town."

Zord or no Zord, I can't let my team go without me. I join the others in pursuit of the Putties. Is it my imagination, or does Zack shift over to put Billy between us?

"Yeehaw," Zack yells, swinging his axe. "Get along little Putties!"

"And keep your distance," Jason adds. "We want them to head out of town but not like we're trying to herd them."

"Even though we are," Zack says.

"Right." Jason confirms, "but subtly so we don't spook them."

No one replies. We're all saving our breath for the grueling race over torn-up streets. Even with my superpowers, I feel the burn in my lungs and calves. And we have a long way to go before we're out of town and in the clear.

Several miles later, Billy says, panting, "I'm not sure the Putties are making independent decisions."

He has a point. The Putties are all following Kimberly's Zord without seeming to notice that the rest of us are trailing after them.

We haven't had to do any herding at all. But if they're not acting on their own, then who's giving the orders?

I spare a glance up into the sky. "Where is the big, bad Goldie anyway?" It's a genuine worry, but I'm also kind of hoping Zack will tease me about my lack of originality in name-calling. He doesn't reply.

"Good question." Jason glances up too, like he expects Goldar to drop suddenly out of thin air. He returns his gaze to the ground and weaves around an overturned car. "Let's concentrate on the Putties for now. We can worry about Goldar later."

And Rita. I haven't forgotten about her either, but Jason is right. We need to focus on getting the Putties away from Angel Grove before they can do any more damage.

⚡

"How's this?" Kimberly asks as her Pterodactyl slows down. There's nothing in sight but desert sand, rock formations, straggly trees . . . and dozens of Putties.

"Alpha 5?" Jason wheezes out, sounding as exhausted as I feel. We must have run thirty miles or so at a speed that's not humanly possible.

"Scanners indicate that you are in the clear," Alpha 5 pronounces.

"Thank god." Even Zack, with all his running practice, is audibly out of breath as he slows to a halt.

Jason pulls up too. "Okay. We make our stand here."

Billy doesn't say anything, just stops dead in his tracks and bends over.

I stop beside him and gulp in deep lungfuls of air. I hope none of us barf into our helmets from sheer superhuman exertion.

"Teleporting Zords to your location," Alpha 5 says.

Seconds later, we're standing next to our Zords. I touch the smooth metal foot of my Sabertooth Tiger as anxiety snakes through me. What if I fail again?

"Merge with your Zords!" Jason calls out. Like Kimberly, he doesn't hold out his Morpher or call out the name of his Tyrannosaurus Rex. There's a flash of red light, and his Zord shakes the ground as it wades into the army of Putties.

Billy is next to disappear in a flash of blue light, and his Triceratops joins Jason's Zord in charging at the Putties. He didn't speak or hold out his Morpher either.

That just leaves Zack and me, facing each other. My jaw is stiff with tension. "You're all getting good at this."

"You could merge with your Zord too." He touches the Morpher at his belt. "If you'd just stop hiding." His hand falls away from his Morpher, and then he's gone in a flash of black light.

Zack's Mastodon joins the fight, and I'm the only one left on the ground now.

My throat tightens as I try to channel whatever power the others used to merge with their Zords, but nothing happens. *I can't do this.* But I have to try. Fingers slippery with sweat, I fumble with the Morpher at my belt and hold it up, the hard contours digging into my palm. "Sabertooth Tiger!"

Again, nothing happens. A heavy feeling sits on my chest.

Zack was right. I don't belong on this team.

"Trini, watch out!" Billy's voice calls out. His Triceratops Zord is heading straight for me.

Heart pounding, I leap aside as his Zord swerves. Why the hell is Billy charging toward me? Then his Zord turns around and shoots energy blasts at the Putties behind me that I didn't notice when I was trying to merge with my Zord.

"Trini, get out of the way," Jason snaps.

Shame washes over me as I duck behind a rock formation. *Fantastic.* Not only am I useless—I'm also a liability.

A whirlwind of yellow flames forms from behind the line of Putties. "What the hell is that?" Kimberly asks as her Pterodactyl Zord swoops and shoots down a few Putties in her path.

My heart stops. *Good question.* But I don't think we're going to like the answer.

The flames coalesce into Rita with Goldar at her side. Her laugh rings out. "Excellent. I have you right where I want you."

She raises her scepter, and all around us, hundreds of gray blobs rise from the ground and form into Putties.

Icy fear pours over me. *It was a trap all along.*

CHAPTER TWENTY-TWO

I clutch the edges of the rock formation I'm hiding behind . . . and watch in helpless terror.

The Putties are swarming the Zords on the ground, using their sharp fingers to claw their way up. Even though they're so much smaller than the Zords, the sheer number of them turns them into a shifting mass. Zack's Mastodon kicks away a few, but he can't get to the ones already climbing up the legs of the Zord. "Tricky little critters," he mutters. "I don't love that there are a lot more of them now."

"And they're too small for us to fight effectively," Billy says. The frustration in his voice comes through my helmet loud and clear. He tries to use his Zord to spear the Putties but misses. "Or we're too big." He's right. The Putties are small enough that they can avoid his deadly Triceratops horns.

"Keep moving so they can't get traction." Jason's Tyrannosaurus Rex swings its tail, sweeping aside several Putties leaping at him. "Kimberly, take out as many Putties as you can. They can't get to you while you're in the air."

"Got it." She blasts a few Putties running toward Billy's Triceratops.

"Thanks, Kimberly," Billy says.

Goldar laughs, hefting his gold sword. "Why don't you come after me, little pink bird?"

"With pleasure," she says cheerily. Lasers blasting, her Pterodactyl heads toward Goldar. Unfortunately, his armor seems to absorb the damage without noticeable effect.

"Wait!" Jason and I call out at the same time. Goldar goading Kimberly into attacking him can't mean anything good.

But her Pterodactyl is already veering perilously close to Goldar, and he slashes at her wing with his sword, sending the Zord spinning.

"Kimberly!" I scream.

"I'm okay," she gasps, straightening her Zord in midair.

"I'm coming to you, Kimberly," Zack says, but as he reaches her, the Putties swarming his Mastodon tear at its knee joints with their knifelike fingers—making his Zord stumble.

"Zack." This time I whisper it. I can't keep hiding my abilities. But what use will I be against the Putties unless I merge with my Zord? Frozen in indecision, I stay put.

"Billy," Jason says, "Be careful. There are Putties to your right." His Tyrannosaurus Rex stomps on a Putty, but more keep coming.

"I see them." Billy's Triceratops digs in its heels, but the Putties keep slamming into him and climbing up, toward the view window that shields Billy. His voice catches. "There are so many."

"At least Goldar isn't using his sword anymore," Kimberly says bleakly. "He nearly took out my Zord with it."

She's right. I peer out from behind my rock formation at Goldar, where he's standing next to Rita, sword slung casually over one shoulder. Then my gaze swivels toward the swarm of Putties continuing to climb up Zack's, Billy's, and Jason's Zords. "They're trying to get to your cockpits."

"Yeah." Zack sounds pissed. "That's exactly what they're doing."

Kimberly's Pterodactyl circles overhead. "I can't shoot the Putties. They're all over you, and I'll risk hitting your Zords if I try to blast them off."

"I might be close enough to aim a bit better." Billy's Triceratops shoots its tail cannons, dislodging a couple of Putties off Zack's Zord, but more immediately take their place.

Billy lets out his breath. "You remember when I said we're too big? Well maybe I was wrong," he says. "They wouldn't be able to scale us if we were even *bigger*. We need the Megazord."

"Trini," Jason says grimly, "if you're going to merge with your Zord, *now* would be a really good time."

No pressure. Doubt knots my gut. Even though it's probably futile, I hold up my Morpher and shout out, "Sabertooth Tiger!" And again—it doesn't work. I feel like I can't breathe. "Sabertooth Tiger! Dammit, come on! Sabertooth Tiger!" Again, nothing. I'm still here, alone and powerless.

"I'm sorry." Tears of frustration sting my eyes as I replace the Morpher onto my belt. "I just can't do it."

Jason inhales audibly. "You should get out of here, then."

I shrink against the rock formation. Of course. I'm useless to my team, so I might as well run and hide.

"I could teleport all of you to safety," Alpha 5 says, his robotic voice revealing nothing of what he might be thinking.

Jason's reply is slow. "Not yet," he says at last. "I want to find out what Rita is up to." His Tyrannosaurus Rex is half-covered in pale gray Putties. "But I don't want Rita to get her hands on our Zords."

There's a flash of red light, and Jason is standing on the ground, next to his suddenly motionless Tyrannosaurus Rex. "Everyone, unmerge with your Zords." He's running toward

Zack and Billy, who are now standing next to their own Zords. A second later, Kimberly is on the ground too.

"Alpha 5, teleport our Zords back to the Command Center," Jason calls out, "and Trini too."

"No." I straighten from my crouching position behind the rock formation. "I'm not leaving." I might not be of much help to my team, but I'll be damned before I abandon them. I sprint toward the others, dodging Putties as I go.

"Teleporting the Zords now," Alpha 5 says.

"Wait a second," Billy calls out suddenly, but it's too late. The Zords shimmer in bright light and then disappear. "Oh no!"

"Ai-yi-yi-yi-yi," Alpha 5 cxclaims. "I see what you mean, Billy."

What now? I push through the Putties, who seem to have no interest in stopping me from reaching the others. They want us all together—trapped by an army of Putties.

"What's wrong?" Jason asks.

Billy sighs heavily. "I realized too late that teleporting the Zords back and forth from the Command Center would take too much power. Alpha 5 won't be able to teleport us back any time soon."

"That is correct," Alpha 5 confirms.

This is not good.

Zack echoes my thoughts. "Oh hell."

I shove the last Putty aside to get to the others, and Kimberly grips my hand as I join them. Billy pats me awkwardly on the shoulder, and I'm relieved that they, at least, aren't holding my inability to merge with my Zord against me. Even Jason gives me a short nod. But Zack doesn't even look at me. My stomach plummets. He thinks this is my fault, and he's not wrong.

I'm the reason we couldn't form the Megazord. And now we have no way to escape Rita.

And speaking of her . . . Rita is moving toward us with Goldar trailing her. The Putties part to make way for her. "Well, well," she says with a sharp smile. "Here we are again."

"What do you want?" Jason replies calmly like Alpha 5 hadn't just told him that we have no way out.

Rita doesn't answer. Instead, she drags her scepter on the ground as she walks over to where I'm standing. "Yellow Ranger." Her voice is thoughtful. "I didn't see you on the battlefield."

My mouth turns dry. Where exactly is she going with this?

"This one is weak." From behind her, Goldar grins menacingly at me. "Shall I kill her for you, Empress?"

Fear surges through me, but before I can react, Kimberly pushes me behind her, Billy steps in front of me, and both Zack and Jason draw their power weapons.

"Interesting," Rita muses. "I wonder what's so special about this one that you are all so willing to die for her."

"No!" Frantically, I try to push past the human wall Kimberly and Billy have formed in front of me. I can't let them get hurt trying to protect me.

Billy gives way in surprise, but Kimberly doesn't budge. "Stay back," she orders, trying to shove me behind her.

Quick as a cat, I duck under Kimberly's arm to face Rita. "There's nothing special about me."

"That's not true," Zack says fiercely as he grips his axe. "You'll have to go through us to get to her." My heart jumps to hear the emotion in his voice, but this is *not* the time to show that he still cares about me.

"It will be my pleasure to go through you, human," Goldar hisses.

"Not yet, my faithful warrior," Rita murmurs, holding her scepter between Goldar and the rest of us. "But don't worry. You will have your chance to prove yourself."

"How are you supposed to prove yourself with that big-ass sword and an army of Putties at your back?" Jason eyes the Putties surrounding us. "It hardly seems like a fair fight."

"What gave you the impression that I care about fairness?" Rita asks in amusement.

"Actually . . ." Jason turns to Goldar. "I was talking to *him*."

What the hell is Jason doing?

Then I notice Billy, standing still and muttering softly the way he does when he's trying to figure out complex calculations. I'll just bet the inside of his faceplate is lit up with numbers and formulas. My breath catches. Billy is trying to figure out how long it will take for Alpha 5 to transport us out of here. And Jason is trying to buy us all time.

Rita's eyes narrow in obvious displeasure. "Goldar is my minion. You will address *me*, Red Ranger."

Jason ignores her. "What do you say we go one on one . . . um, Goldie?" In an aside to Zack, he adds, "I know it's unoriginal name-calling."

"But points for effectiveness," Zack says as Goldar drops his sword to the ground.

"Very well!" Goldar roars. "I accept your challenge, Earthling."

"Need I remind you," Rita says with deceptive softness, "that I am still in charge here?"

My blood chills. I recognize the rage blazing through the sorceress. It's what I felt before I hit that boy in elementary school. That ability to hurt someone is what I fight every day to hide. *Be careful, Jason*. I don't know if he understands that he's playing with fire.

Goldar bows his head, although his eyes are still glowing red. "Forgive me, Empress."

"Let this be a lesson." Rita turns to Kimberly and me without acknowledging Goldar. "I was born into a world much like yours many thousands of years ago." Conversationally, she says, "Do you know why I call myself Rita Repulsa?"

"Wait." Zack sounds disbelieving. "You call *yourself* that? I thought it was a nickname Zordon gave you."

Her face hardens, and I gulp. *Big mistake.* He clearly hit a nerve in bringing up Zordon.

"Zordon," she spits out, "had nothing to do with naming me. I *chose* my name. Repulsa." She fans out her fingers with their blood-red nails and gestures down the length of her armored dress. "People will always be afraid of a dangerous woman they can't control."

Her words strike a strange chord in me. Again, I'm remembering the circle of classmates staring at me after I knocked Carl down. Then the names I've been called over the years. *Ching Chong Trini Kwan. Kung Fu Flu.* An ache stabs into me because the last thing I expected was to feel a connection with Rita.

"What is that supposed to mean?" Kimberly sounds calm, but I can feel her trembling next to me.

"It means she hasn't always been the one in charge," I breathe. Come to think of it, Zordon hasn't told us *nearly* enough about Rita's past. It might be a good idea to find out more.

"Very good, Yellow Ranger." Rita smiles. "But I confess—I still don't see why Zordon chose a girl useless in a fight to be one of his precious Power Rangers."

Rita's words hit me like a blow to the heart. *She's right. I don't belong here.*

"It's not like Zordon to be swayed by sentiment." Her gaze is intent on me. "Perhaps he has a soft spot for you, little Ranger. Perhaps it would hurt him to lose you."

Next to me, Kimberly grips my arm, Jason visibly tenses up, and Zack's breath hisses out of him. Even Billy seems to snap out of his calculations. His lance flashes into his hands. I feel a surge of power in my palms as if my daggers are struggling to take form The agony of guilt stabs into me. I want to stop hiding my abilities, but I can't seem to make myself do it. Like Rita, I know the risk of being a dangerous woman.

"Look at you all." Rita's voice drips with disdain. "So eager to protect her. I was like you once." Her black eyes flash. "And it made me weak."

I'm jarred from my own turmoil of emotions. What does she mean by that?

Before anyone can comment, she says, "Don't worry. It is not your pathetic Yellow Ranger that I want." She raises her scepter and brings it to the ground in a sharp movement. The Putties surrounding us begin to form straight lines, facing away from us . . . and toward Angel Grove. My chest constricts with fear.

"You have exactly seven days to bring me Zordon," Rita says coldly. "If you fail, I will unleash Goldar and my Putty army on your home again." The skirt of her armored dress sweeps the dusty ground as she whirls away. "And next time—there will be nothing left."

⚡

"Rangers, are you alright?" Alpha 5 asks.

It might be my imagination, but his robotic voice sounds concerned as he surveys our sweaty, disheveled appearance now that we're out of our ranger suits. I can't speak for anyone else, but I am exhausted. Rita's threat to destroy our home has drained me of everything I have.

"Damage report, please," Jason says shortly.

"Your Zords were only slightly damaged, and we will be able to fix—"

"I meant Angel Grove," Jason interrupts.

"Ah." Alpha 5 hesitates. "That is more complicated."

Zordon's head forms in the blue column of light. "The important thing is that all of you are unharmed."

"Not good enough." Zack wipes sweat off his forehead. "We need to know what happened to our town."

Kimberly nods. "And our families."

"And everyone," Billy adds.

I couldn't agree more, but my heart twists at the thought of seeing the destruction we left in our wake—the home we failed to save.

"Very well," Zordon says somberly.

A 3D projection of blasted streets and smoked-out buildings fills the space in front of us. Firefighters are sifting through rubble, and paramedics are bandaging up townspeople and lifting stretchers into the back of emergency vehicles.

My gut clenches. People were hurt because of our failure to stop Rita.

Another hologram of a newscast in progress pops up next to the first one. There's a blurry image of Rita holding her scepter. She must not have been bothering to use her camera-masking magic at that moment. The caption says, *Dragon Lady Vandalizes Angel Grove.*

All the air in my lungs whooshes out, and Zack mutters, "Holy racism, Batman."

I don't respond. I'm thinking of Rita with her blood-red lips and nails, gesturing down the length of her armored dress. *She knew.* Rita fully understood that she would be viewed as a Dragon

Lady. But unlike me, she's not afraid of being someone else's nightmare.

"Not even Rita can escape an Asian stereotype." The words slip out of me.

"Technically, Rita isn't Asian." Billy gives me an anxious glance, and I know he's trying to help, but it's really, really *not* helping.

"Since Rita is from outer space," Kimberly adds. *Still not helping.* She takes one look at my face, and whatever she sees there makes her redden. "Never mind. Sorry."

"Me too," Billy mumbles, and I feel a tiny bit better.

"Shh," Jason says, watching the newscast as Rita's picture is replaced with a close-up of the male news anchor.

The anchor says, "And now we go to our reporter Brenda, who is live at the scene."

The video cuts to a reporter standing next to the smoking ruins. "Witnesses say that a gang of costumed arsonists is responsible for the destruction you see here."

"Is there a connection between the arson and the gang that crashed the Homecoming dance?" the news anchor asks.

"Quite possibly," the reporter replies. "Both gangs were wearing similar costumes."

Kimberly snorts. "They can't possibly think *humans* did that."

"It's Rita's illusion spell that leads people to believe that this destruction is human-made," Zordon reminds us.

Alpha 5 stops the hologram of the reporter, leaving only the image of destruction.

Next time, it will be worse. Rita's words reverberate through me. *Next time—there will be nothing left.*

"Rita wanted you, Zordon." Jason isn't looking at Zordon. He's staring at the charred storefront of his family's store. "She swore to destroy Angel Grove if we didn't bring you to her in seven days."

"I am aware." Nothing in Zordon's voice hints at his feelings about this.

"We're not actually considering giving up Zordon, are we?" Kimberly demands.

"That's going to be difficult," Zack says dryly. "Seeing that he's a floating head." At Kimberly's glare, he holds up his hands. "Hey, I'm not saying we should give up Zordon. After all, he's *our* floating head."

"More accurately," Billy says, "Zordon is trapped in an inter-dimensional pocket outside of time and space and doesn't have a corporeal form."

My stomach sinks. "In other words, even if we wanted to, we can't bring Zordon to Rita." And that means we have no way of stopping Rita.

"I'm afraid that is correct, Trini," Zordon says heavily. "Rita never knew her last spell against me succeeded in trapping me in a time warp, so she does not know she is asking for an impossible task."

"It doesn't matter." Jason turns away from the holographic projection of our damaged town. "Whether or not we can give Zordon to Rita isn't important. We need to focus on how to defeat her."

Everyone is suddenly looking at me . . . and I know exactly what they're thinking. A swirling tension forms behind my eyes. "I'm the reason we can't form the Megazord," I whisper. And we can't beat Rita without the Megazord.

"Trini," Billy says carefully, "you were the one who helped me see how important the psychic connection is to activate the Zords."

Zack turns to me at that, but he doesn't say anything, which is good because I'm about two seconds from melting down in screaming frustration.

"Is there something blocking you from merging with your Zord?" Kimberly's eyes are anxious as she reaches out to me, and even more so when I shrug off her hand.

"I don't know." I back away from them, stopping only when I realize I've moved into the edge of the 3D hologram and that scenes of Angel Grove's destruction are being projected onto my body. "Can someone please turn that off?"

Without comment, Alpha 5 touches a button, and Angel Grove disappears. Icy fear spreads through me. That's how easily Rita can wipe my home off the face of the planet.

"Trini, this is important," Jason says, like I don't *know* that. "If you could just try—"

"I have been trying!" My hands are clenched, and I force myself to relax them. I start one of the breathing exercises Nai Nai makes me practice. If I'm not careful, I will lose all the control she's taught me in the last eleven years.

"Your team needs you to try again," Zordon says, and I could swear there's disappointment in his eyes.

Breathe in the air that sustains you. Everything in me is coiled tightly. *Breathe into the spaces that need to open.* It doesn't help. All I want to do is run or throw a punch. *Breathe out the fear and anger.* Desperation rises in me. Nothing is working.

"Trini," Zack says, just my name. But it doesn't help. Nothing can.

"No," I manage to force out. I'm responding to Zordon, but I'm aware of Zack watching me with that heavy, inscrutable gaze. "What my team needs is someone else."

"Trini, don't." Zack's eyes flash with emotion.

"Don't what?" Billy asks in confusion.

"What's going on?" Kimberly asks me.

"You heard Zordon," Jason says. "We need you to work with us."

I don't respond to any of them as I lock eyes with Zack. I haven't forgotten what he said to me at the end of our devastating fight. *If you're so afraid to let the others in, then maybe you should get off the team.*

With fumbling fingers, I unclasp my yellow Morpher with the power coin shining in the center and toss it toward Zack. I think he'll catch it, but he doesn't even reach out. The metal ringing of the Morpher hitting the ground sounds like a death knell.

No one moves a muscle as I take in a shaky breath. "I quit."

CHAPTER TWENTY-THREE

I burst into my house with a roaring headache and a ball of fiery emotion under my breastbone. This time, the living room isn't empty. Nai Nai sits on the couch, balancing a wooden staff across her lap.

"I'm not in the mood to train," I snap.

"Yes, I can see that." She peers at me. "It's a good thing I didn't put another trip wire in the doorway. In the state you're in, you might not have caught yourself this time."

"And what state is that?"

If she hears the dangerous edge in my voice, she doesn't seem troubled by it. "You, my Xiao Laohu, seem ready to fight."

But that's exactly the problem. I'm not her *Little Tiger* who's ready to fight, or at least—I'm not ready to fight for my team. That's why I don't deserve to be a Power Ranger. "You couldn't be more wrong," I say tightly.

Nai Nai sets the staff on the ground and pats the space next to her on the couch. "Then it's time that you explain."

I sit down, but my throat clogs up. How can I explain that I just quit a supernatural team charged with protecting Earth against a space sorceress? The simple answer is that I can't, but I still need to give her some excuse for my bad mood. "I got into the worst fight ever with Zack." Oops. That's not what I meant to say. It sounds too much like the truth.

She nods. "And what did you fight about?"

"I quit that group project we're supposed to do . . . and he got mad."

"Hm." Nai Nai leans back and peers at me. "That doesn't sound like either of you."

I squirm on the couch next to her. "Well, it was a *hard* group project."

"I suppose it was important if Zack was upset about you quitting."

"You could say that." I mean, if she counts saving Angel Grove from utter destruction as important—then, yeah.

"So why did you quit?" she asks evenly.

Because I let my team down. I swallow past the dryness in my mouth. "Like I said—it was hard."

"Xiao Laohu," she says tenderly, "you don't quit something because it's hard."

"You don't understand!" I burst out, and I should stop there—but I don't.

I'm tired of keeping secrets.

It all comes out. Zordon, the Power Rangers, hiding my wushu skills from everyone but Zack, being the Yellow Ranger with the twin daggers that I desperately want . . . and *don't* want to use. My failure to merge with my yellow Sabertooth Tiger Zord, Rita creating an army of Putties in her Moon Palace, and her threat to destroy Angel Grove if we don't give up Zordon.

And through my breathless, rapid-fire explanation, Nai Nai just sits on the couch next to me, listening intently as if I'm simply recounting one of the old Chinese myths she's always telling me.

"And that's why I quit," I finish miserably. "Because I can't be the Yellow Ranger my team needs."

"Then don't be that Yellow Ranger." Nai Nai places her hands on mine. "Be the Yellow Ranger you *are*."

Okay, I'm glad Nai Nai isn't freaking out about me being a Power Ranger (and our town facing imminent destruction)—but *what the hell?*

"I'm not sure you're getting it, Nai Nai. This isn't some metaphor for my high school project or anything. What I'm telling you is real."

"A sorceress named Rita Repulsa is going to destroy Angel Grove if you don't bring her the intergalactic warrior named Zordon, who's trapped in a time warp, and you need to merge with your Sabertooth Tiger so your team can form the Megazord to stop Rita. Did I get that right?"

"Actually . . . that about sums it up." I should have known my nai nai, who tells me fairy tales and legends as if they're real, would have no trouble believing all this.

My forehead furrows. "I'm the only one who hasn't been able to merge with my Zord. It's obvious that I'm not meant to be the Yellow Ranger."

"Why not?" she asks. "The only thing stopping you is your refusal to embrace who you are."

My breath stops. That's what Zack said.

"You are not just the Yellow Ranger." Nai Nai squeezes my hands. "You are my Xiao Laohu. That makes you a Yellow Ranger with a Chinese heritage and a tiger mythology of your own."

The warm steadiness of her hands on mine is the only thing stopping me from leaping off the couch and out the door. "They called Rita a Dragon Lady on the news," I whisper. "That's how they'll see me in my yellow costume and twin daggers."

"Dragons," she points out, "are revered in Chinese culture and important to our stories. Like tigers are. And the color yellow is a symbol of power from the heavens. What does it matter if they see you as powerful?" Her voice goes low and fierce. "You *are* powerful. And dangerous. Let them be afraid."

I snatch my hands away from her. Carl flashes through my head. "You were the one who taught me to hide my strength," I whisper.

"No. I trained you so that *you* would be in charge of your power." There's both love and sadness in her voice. "I never meant to teach you to hide your strength."

"What did you mean to teach me, then?" Anger rises in my chest. "Wasn't that the point of all those breathing lessons—to learn control so I would never hurt another person?" *Carl bleeding on the ground.* "So no one would ever fear me again?" *The other children staring at me with wide, frightened eyes.*

She's silent for a moment. At last, she says, "Yes, I wanted you to learn control, but I forgot to teach you the right moment to *use* your strength." She lets out a long breath. "Then again, maybe that is something you must learn for yourself."

I think of Kimberly being thrown across the room by Putties, landing lifelessly on the floor while I watched. She survived—but it doesn't change the fact that I entered the fight too late that time. Whether I fight or not—someone gets hurt. "I don't know how," I whisper.

"You've been so afraid of being a stereotype," Nai Nai says gently, "that you've rejected your own culture and your own strength."

My body clenches. "So how do I stop being afraid?"

"It is the simplest and hardest thing to do."

Oh, great. "That's what you told me about breathing." I didn't know what she meant at first, but eleven years of breathing practice later—I totally get it. It's incredibly hard to do something so simple with full attention and care.

She nods. "Exactly. It is both intuitive and intentional."

But she still hasn't told me how to be unafraid. "Intuitive and intentional to do *what*?"

"To be yourself, of course."

"What if . . ." I swallow hard and stop. I remember how Rita faced us in the desert, her smile a wicked red curve on her exultant face. In that moment, watching her—I understood her. She reveled in her power over us, and deep down inside, I wanted to be that fearless too. I wanted to be her. No. I knew I *could* be her. "What if who I really am . . . isn't someone who I want to be?"

Nai Nai just watches me with her dark, calm eyes, waiting for me to tell her more.

Reluctantly, I confess what I haven't been able to say out loud. "Rita isn't afraid of her own strength, and she hurts people. What if I'm like her? I don't want to hurt anyone." *Not again.*

"You won't." Nai Na says. "Rita has lost her way, but the path she has traveled will not be the one that you choose."

I blink. "Nai Nai? Why are you talking about a conquering space sorcerer like you know her?"

"Of course I don't know her." She pauses. "But maybe I know *of* her."

I almost topple off the couch. "You're going to have to explain."

"Do you remember when I told you the story of Chang'e?"

It takes me a moment, but then I remember. "You mean the Chinese moon goddess?" My voice is incredulous, but Nai Nai just smiles.

"So you do pay attention to my stories," she says. "Didn't you say Rita had a palace on the moon? Chang'e fled to the moon after stealing the elixir of life from her husband, the Lord Archer. Who's to say that Chang'e hasn't been nursing a grudge for her banishment all this time? Just like this Rita."

Wait . . . no way is Rita some version of the Chinese moon goddess. Besides, Zordon said Rita had been trapped in a space dumpster for ten thousand years until her prison crashed into the moon recently, freeing her. It was back in the *freaking Stone Age* when Zordon imprisoned Rita. It's not like she was languishing in her Moon Palace all that time, serving as inspiration to prehistoric humans for their moon goddess myths. "Unless Chang'e also wore an armored dress with a horned headdress and carried a scepter with a glowing red jewel—I'm pretty sure she and Rita are *not* the same person."

"I believe I have an illustration of her somewhere." Nai Nai rises from the couch and goes to the bookshelf in the corner of the living room. She usually tells me stories from memory without consulting a book, so it takes a while before she pulls out a dusty tome and brings it back to the couch.

I glance at the cover as she sits down. It's a colorful collection of Chinese fairy tales. I'm finding it hard to believe that there's a picture of an evil conquering sorceress in a children's book.

Nai Nai flips through the pages and stops on an illustration of a woman in a flowy white robe and a multicolored sash. She has long, black hair and is floating up toward the moon while a man with a bow is watching her ascend, out of his reach. Her features are delicately beautiful, and she extends one slender, graceful hand up to the moon and the other one back to the Earth she is escaping.

Rita has her own beauty, but I see nothing of her clever sharpness or terrifying power in this depiction of Chang'e. Yet, there is *something* in the artist's rendering of Chang'e's expression that reminds me of Rita's pain and fury.

I put a shaky finger on the picture. "When was the Chang'e story first told?"

"Let's see . . . I believe it was during the Zhou dynasty."

Thanks to my history project on the Bronze Age, I know that the Zhou dynasty was about three thousand years ago. My breath catches. Rita was trapped in a space dumpster for *ten* thousand years, not *three*. Or at least that's what Zordon told us.

"You have no need to be afraid." Nai Nai smooths a strand of my hair and tucks it behind my ear. "The moon goddess's fate is not yours. And neither is Rita's, whether or not she is Chang'e."

I push down the dread spiraling through me. "Oh good," I say sarcastically. "I'm relieved that I'm not going to end up stranded on the moon with a heavenly rabbit . . . because yes, I totally pay attention to your stories, and no, I still don't know what the heavenly rabbit does."

"The rabbit makes the elixir of immortality with a mortar and pestle," she explains, as if *of course* that's what a heavenly rabbit does. "But the rabbit doesn't have much to do with the story of the moon goddess. The heart of the story is the rift between Chang'e and her husband, Hou Yi."

That's when I remember when she last told me the story of Chang'e.

Nai Nai said I was like Chang'e and Zack was like the heavenly archer—unable to reconcile because of a misunderstanding. Well, this time, it's one *hell* of a misunderstanding.

"Can I borrow this book?" I ask hesitantly. "I think I need to read Chang'e's story."

"Of course." She places it in my lap. "But I do not think you will find what you are looking for in a book."

A heaviness settles in my stomach. She's right, of course. What I'm looking for is back at the Command Center. "I totally messed up everything, and I don't know if my friends will forgive me." My voice goes small. "What do I do now?"

"Do you know why I call you Xiao Laohu?" she asks, which is such a typical Nai Nai response that I can't help but sigh.

"Of course I do." She's only been telling me this all my life. "It was your mother's nickname for you, and her mother's before that. It's what the women of our family have always been called."

"That's right. Your ancestors will always be here with you," Nai Nai says tenderly, "but we cannot tell you what to do. You, my Xiao Laohu, must find your own path."

I squeeze my eyes shut, but there's no more denying the truth. I open my eyes and square my shoulders. I might be able to hide who I am from others—but I can't keep hiding from myself. Tomorrow morning, I will go back to the Command Center and face my fate. I glance at the book in my lap.

And while I'm at it, maybe I need to find out why Rita shows up in Chinese mythology first told three thousand years ago.

CHAPTER TWENTY-FOUR

I face the sliding metal door of the training room and take a deep breath.

"Would you like me to go in with you?" Alpha 5 asks. He hasn't said much since I used Billy's wrist com to beam me into the Command Center.

I was tempted to confront Zordon about Rita and the moon goddess stories right away, but frankly—I have bigger things on my mind.

I shake my head. "I think I have to do this on my own."

He turns and walks away, calling out over his shoulder, "Good luck then, Trini."

Drawing all my courage into my shaking body, I push the button to open the door.

At the sight of me, my entire team stops what they were doing. Kimberly, who was mid-kick, comes to both feet. Billy lets go of the sandbag he was holding for her. Zack and Jason stop sparring with each other, sharing a look before silently leaving the ring to walk over to me.

Oh damn. My stomach knots in terror. I have no idea what I'm supposed to say to them. *Hey, you know when I quit, leaving you without a way to form the Megazord? Well, just kidding! I'm back.* Yeah—no. Maybe I don't lead with that.

"I'm sorry," I say instead. "I shouldn't have left."

I can't look at Zack directly, but I see him stiffen out of the corner of my eye.

"Oh good." Billy's face lightens with relief. "I'm glad you're back."

"Me too," Kimberly says.

But Jason is shaking his head, and my heart drops. "What makes you think you're ready this time?" He folds his arms across his chest. "I'm sorry, Trini, but I can't let you rejoin the team."

It feels like I've been punched in the gut, but honestly—what did I expect? I abandoned my team, and I can't expect them to welcome me back with open arms.

"It wouldn't be fair to you or everyone else." Jason's voice softens. "Either you'll get hurt or one of us will get hurt trying to protect you."

Kimberly's face falls, but she doesn't speak up, and neither does Billy. They both think Jason is right.

My body tenses. How do I show them that I *am* ready to be a Power Ranger?

"What if Trini can prove herself?" Zack asks suddenly.

I swivel toward him, scared to hope. Is Zack still on my side? My heart rises to see the determination on his face as he looks back at me. *Yes.*

"I don't know what you mean, Zack." Jason frowns in confusion.

"One-on-one combat," I say before I lose my nerve. "If I win, I'm back on the team."

Billy's mouth falls open, and Kimberly's eyes widen.

Jason peers at both Zack and me doubtfully. "I don't know if you remember, Trini, but the last time you and Zack were in the ring together, he gave you a black eye."

"Not Zack," I say. Jason will never believe that Zack isn't pulling his punches. He'll think the same of Kimberly and Billy too. There's only one way to convince him I have what it takes to be the Yellow Ranger again. I point directly at Jason. "You."

"Me?" Shock washes over his face. "You can't be serious."

"Dead serious." I exhale and gather my courage. "Like I said, if I win against you, then I'm back on the team. Deal?"

"No way." The shock on Jason's face is giving way to stubborn refusal.

"Why not?" Zack asks calmly.

"Zack," Kimberly whispers, but loudly enough to hear, "Trini could get hurt."

"I'm not sure it's a good idea," Billy adds worriedly.

"She'll be fine." The casually confident way Zack says it warms my heart. To Jason, he says, "Trini might not have been able to merge with her Zord, but she's earned the right to prove herself."

"She did help free Bulk and Skull when they were trapped," Billy adds, "and she saved that kid and her father from a burning building."

"None of that was fighting, though." Kimberly bites her lip. "Sorry, Trini. No offense."

"None taken." She's making a valid point, and it's not like I can blame her.

"I agree with Kimberly," Jason says. He pauses and adds, "My dad told me that someone in a yellow costume saved two customers that he didn't know were still in the store. Thank you for that," he says soberly, "but my decision stands. If you can't fight or merge with your Zord, then you're a liability the team can't afford."

I still don't know if I can merge with my Zord, but I *do* know I can fight. I meet Jason's eyes. "If you're worried about my ability to fight, then there's only one way to find out if I can." I nod toward the ring.

He sighs. "Fine, but don't hold it against me if you get another black eye."

I smile. "Deal."

Zack sings out, "And don't hold it against Trini if she gives *you* a black eye, Jason."

Jason just snorts in response, but that's okay. He'll see what I can do soon enough. *And everyone will see that I've been lying to them.* My stomach twists. Will they hate me once they find out? And even if I prove I can fight, what if they still don't want me back on the team?

"I don't like this at all," Kimberly mumbles.

"Me neither," Billy agrees.

Well, it's too late to turn back now. My back tenses up as Jason and I enter the ring with the others lining up to watch.

"No suits and no weapons," Jason says as he faces me.

"Fine by me." I would definitely be holding back if I had the power of the twin daggers at my fingertips.

Zack leans against the wall of the ring on the spectator side. "You've got this, Trini."

"Go easy on her," Kimberly says anxiously.

"I wasn't serious about the black eye, Trini," Jason says. "Don't worry. I'll be careful." He obviously doesn't think I'm a threat.

And his dismissal lights a fire in me. *You* are *powerful. And dangerous. Let them be afraid.* Nai Nai's words come back to me, dispelling my doubts. "Oh, you should be careful, Jason." I smile and take a defensive stance, legs wide and hands up and ready to strike. "Very careful."

"Good form." He sounds surprised.

"I know."

"Are you two going to fight or just exchange pleasantries all day?" Zack grumbles. "Come on, Trini."

But it's Jason who moves first, coming at me slowly and giving me plenty of time to sidestep or block him.

Instead, I drop to the floor, avoiding his outstretched arms, and then I sweep his legs from under him. He falls with a grunt of astonishment, but then he leaps to his feet at the same time I rise and flow into a flying kick that knocks him off balance, although he does keep his feet this time.

"Alright, Trini!" Zack calls out. A flutter goes through me to hear the pride in his voice, but I don't turn around. Billy and Kimberly are, presumably, too shocked to react.

"You were telegraphing your intentions," I say to Jason, aiming lightning-fast blows at him that keep him too occupied to go on the offensive. "You should keep your opponent guessing."

He just growls and then lunges at me. I sidestep it easily and use his own momentum to shove him to the floor. "Saw that coming too. You're relying too much on your brute strength."

Jason comes to his feet again. "Is this a fight or a lesson?"

I smile. "Both." I close in and hook a foot around his knee, but he aims a fist at me, and we're both suddenly blocking and striking in a blur of quick movements. Yes! At last, Jason isn't pulling his punches, but I don't have the breath to comment. I'm too busy trying not to get my ass kicked. Literally.

Jason jumps into a roundhouse kick that I barely avoid by bending backward and kicking upward at him with one hand balanced on the floor behind me—this would be a great move for Kimberly with her gymnastic ability, and I hope she's watching closely.

Unfortunately, he doesn't go down, and I don't spring up quickly enough before he knocks me off balance with a glancing blow. I stagger backward, but when he comes at me swinging, I'm able to sidestep and aim a strike at his back. "Telegraphing again," I grunt.

He responds by suddenly flipping me onto the mat. Damn. I roll quickly away and kick out at him as he tries to pin me. If he gets me in any kind of lock, I'm done for. There's no denying that superior strength is an advantage. *But I'm faster.* I leap to my feet before he does and kick at his knees. I miss connecting, but just barely, and then I'm fighting off a flurry of renewed punches.

"Be careful, Trini," Billy calls out, but he sounds subdued as if he realizes that I don't need the warning.

Jason stops abruptly, dropping his arms to his side. "This fight is over."

Tension pulses through me, and I keep my hands up, ready to block or strike. "No," I pant. "I haven't won yet."

"I think it's safe to say it's a tie."

"Give me ten more minutes and I can break the tie." Of course it's pure bravado. Jason and I are pretty evenly matched. "I need to win to get back on the team. Those are the terms."

"Not necessary."

I stiffen. Maybe Jason never had any intention of letting me back on the team.

"You lied to us, Trini," he says with a sigh, "but you can fight, and we need you. As far as I'm concerned, you're a Power Ranger again."

My eyebrows rise. Jason's clearly not happy about it . . . but does this mean I'm on the team again?

"I'm not so sure." Kimberly announces.

Shame twists in my stomach. Now she knows I could have stopped the Putties that came after her. "I'm sorry, Kimberly."

She marches into the ring, followed by Zack and Billy, who seems unhappy. Zack's expression is unreadable.

I should have known it wouldn't be that easy to get back on the team. Not that single-handed combat with a star football player and trained martial artist who outweighs me by about a hundred pounds is exactly *easy*.

Billy speaks first. "I didn't know you could do all that, Trini."

"My nai nai taught me." I'm not sure what else to say.

"We've been friends since middle school." His eyes look hurt. "Why didn't you ever tell me?"

"I don't know," I stammer. "I guess I didn't want people to think I was weird."

The wounded expression in Billy's face doesn't go away, and I can tell my explanation isn't enough for Kimberly or Jason either. I'm going to have to do better. I have to tell them exactly who I am.

I take a deep breath. "Billy, you know that guy Carl—the one who said I could go 'kung fu crazy' when he was egging on Bulk and Skull to fight me?"

Kimberly gasps, and Jason's eyes widen.

Zack's mouth sets. "Racist *and* ableist," he mutters.

"Yeah, I remember." Confusion mixes with the hurt on Billy's face.

"Carl was scared of me." My throat locks up, but I make myself say the rest. "Because I beat him up when I was in kindergarten."

"For being a first-grade bully and stealing kids' lunch money," Zack interjects.

"That doesn't matter," I say, but I keep my gaze on Billy. "When I saw Bulk and Skull shoving you around, I wanted to hurt them.

I could have hurt them. Then everyone would know why Carl said—"

I'm interrupted by Billy tackling me in a big hug. "I would never think those things of you," he says fiercely. "And you're not weird. I mean, except in a good way, like when you campaigned to save the frogs from being dissected in middle school."

"Even though it threatened our joint Science grade?"

"Well." He lets go of me and shrugs. "You also stood up for me when I told Mr. Webb that his calculations were wrong, and he knocked both our grades down for that." He's definitely smiling now. "So I guess we're even."

I smile back in relief. "I'll back you up anytime." I realize now that Billy and I have too many years of friendship to let one secret ruin things between us—but the same isn't true of Kimberly.

Her face is stony as she stares at me. "None of that changes the fact that you lied to us about your abilities."

My stomach wrenches. She has every right to be angry. I let her get hurt by the Putties because I was hiding a secret.

But she says, "You didn't trust us."

I gape at her. *That's* why she's so angry?

Then I remember her standing next to her Zord as we were trying to decide who should try first to merge first. *It shouldn't be me.* Kimberly has always been afraid that she's not to be trusted.

"I do." I take a step forward and place my hand on hers. "I trust all of you. It was myself who I didn't trust." I have a feeling Kimberly will understand that.

Kimberly is silent for a moment, her eyes searching my face, and I hold my breath. At last, a tremulous smile breaks over her face. "I guess I don't want to be the only girl on the team."

I let out my breath in a grateful rush as we clutch each other's hands.

"It's settled, then," Jason says with satisfaction. "We're all in favor of Trini being on the team again."

"Yes." Billy reaches over to squeeze my shoulder.

I'm so glad that Billy, Jason, and Kimberly have forgiven me for my secrets, but Zack still hasn't said anything. And he's the only one I *didn't* lie to.

My chest clenches as I turn toward him. He's looking back at me with an unreadable expression on his face. It was his idea to let me prove myself, so there's no good reason for being this worried about his reaction. "What about you, Zack?"

"Me?" He smiles, but it doesn't quite reach his eyes. "Why would I object to such a kick-ass teammate?" he asks lightly.

My stomach drops. Maybe no one else can tell, but I know that he's using humor to cover up something. Sure, he helped me become a Power Ranger again, but I did yell at him about trying to make me into something I'm not. A pang hits me. How are we going to recover from our big fight?

"Fantastic!" Jason doesn't seem to notice Zack's lukewarm reaction as he gathers up Billy, Kimberly, and me in a group hug like we just won the football championship with a miraculous touchdown. "Nothing can beat us now!"

I steal another look at Zack's inscrutable face. *I wish I could be so sure.*

CHAPTER TWENTY-FIVE

Dammit!" I close my eyes and drop my forehead against the smooth metal of my Sabertooth Tiger Zord. "It's still not working." I lift my head to face Billy wearily. "I don't think I'm going to be able to merge with my Zord."

Billy and I have been in the garage under the Command Center for an hour, and my Zord hasn't so much as twitched. He looks up from the handheld device that Alpha 5 gave him. "Give it some time."

"We don't have time." Frustration fills my voice. Of the seven days Rita gave us to bring her Zordon, only five are left, and Jason is insisting we all attend school as usual even though we're facing the destruction of Angel Grove. I doubt any of us were able to pay attention in class today—not even Billy.

Billy nods reluctantly. "I'll let Zordon know that we need a plan to stop Rita without the Megazord."

Guilt twinges in me. "I'm sorry."

"Don't be." Wryly, he adds, "At least you can fight."

"So can you." I peer at him closely. "In fact, why are you here with me? You should be in the training room with the others."

"It won't do me any good. I can't fight like they can." He glances at me. "Or like you."

"You don't need to fight like anyone else." I pause because I don't want to sound like I'm criticizing Jason, but I really think half of Billy's problem is the way Jason is teaching him. Billy has always been a quick study, and I bet he'd be a natural at figuring out his opponents' weaknesses and adapting to exploit them. Trained right—he'd be lethal. "Look, Jason is a good teacher, but he hasn't been working with your strengths. I could help you if you want. The Command Center does have more than one training room."

His eyes light up. "Do you think it would do any good?"

"Definitely." I pat the foot of my Zord. "And it would be a better use of our time than trying to merge with my Zord."

"Well, if you really think so, I guess it couldn't hurt."

"Come on." I cast one last wistful glance at the gleaming yellow of my Sabertooth Tiger before I turn away. I might not be able to merge with my Zord, but I can at least help Billy. "Let's go train to be Power Rangers."

⚡

I was right. Billy is *stunningly* good at this. He's learning to anticipate my moves before I make them, and even though his technique needs work, I can see he'll be a formidable warrior in no time.

"Let's call it a day," I pant, sweat pouring down my back.

"Are you sure? I can keep going." He's bouncing on the balls of his feet and adjusting the band that keeps his glasses secure.

"We've been at this for over an hour," I point out. "Besides, you're already good enough to take down Bulk and Skull if they come at you again."

He stops fiddling with his glasses. "You didn't accidentally trip Bulk and Skull that time, did you? That was on purpose."

Flushing, I say, "They had it coming."

"But you still didn't really hurt them." He looks at me earnestly like he wants me to understand something. "You don't have to be afraid of what you can do."

"I know."

"Zack says you're still afraid of hurting people."

"He did, did he?" I grab a towel and start wiping my face more vigorously than I need to. I've been trying to talk to Zack, but he keeps putting me off in a way that he's never done before.

"Is there . . ." Billy hesitates. "I mean, are things okay with you and Zack?"

No. Definitely not okay. Not even close. "Sure." I stalk over to the hamper and fling my towel in. "It's all fine."

"Because I wonder if that might be why you can't merge with your Zord," Billy says doggedly. "You know how I said the merging process relies on our connection with each other? Well, maybe—"

"I get it, Billy," I grind out. This isn't the first time I've wondered if my unresolved tension with Zack is the reason I haven't been successful yet, but I really, really don't want to talk about it.

Alpha 5's voice comes over invisible speakers. "Billy and Trini, will you please join the others in the Power Chamber? Zordon would like to speak with you."

"On our way." Grateful for the distraction, I move toward the door. "I guess Zordon is ready to share his plan to defeat Rita."

"That was fast." Billy falls into step next to me. "He hasn't had much time to come up with a new plan."

Guilt worms into me. Whatever Zordon's new plan is—it won't include the Megazord. We leave the training room together, and I'm glad Billy doesn't bring up the Megazord again as we walk to the Power Chamber in silence.

When we reach our destination, we find the others already there, waiting for us.

Jason raises his eyebrows as we come in. "You look like you were training." It doesn't exactly take great powers of deduction given that Billy is in sweats and I'm in leggings and a tank top. "I thought you were both trying to get Trini to merge with her Zord."

"It didn't work," I say shortly, glancing at Zack, who won't meet my eyes.

Kimberly looks sympathetic. "I'm sorry, Trini."

"That is why I've called you all here." There's a grave expression on Zordon's face. "We need a new plan to deal with Rita, and we only have five days. If there's one thing I can be sure of," he says, "it's that Rita will follow through on her threat to destroy Angel Grove."

"You sound like you know her," Zack comments.

That's what I said to Nai Nai. And then she told me the story of Chang'e. My eyes narrow on Zordon. "Actually, there's something I've been meaning to ask you."

Alpha 5 glances up from the computer console but busies himself again with whatever calculations he's occupied with. I wonder what Alpha 5 is thinking. He's been Zordon's confidant for thousands of years. I'll bet there's not a lot he doesn't know.

Zordon's head turns to me. "Yes, Trini?"

"It's something my nai nai said—that's 'grandmother' in Mandarin Chinese."

"I'm aware of what 'nai nai' means." Zordon's voice is dry.

"Universal translator," Billy whispers to me.

"Got it." I pause. I'm not sure how to subtly ask if Rita is actually an ancient goddess who stole the elixir of immortality and ascended to the moon, so I just come out with it. "My nai nai thinks Rita might be the inspiration for Chang'e, the Chinese moon goddess."

"Interesting theory." Nothing in Zordon's face gives any clue to what he's thinking.

"Interesting or not—we have a town to save," Jason says impatiently. "Do we really have time to stand around and talk about old folktales?"

"If Trini brought it up," Zack says neutrally, "then it's important."

The weight in my chest lightens a bit. Zack still isn't looking at me, but it feels like he's on my side.

"I'd like to hear more about this . . . um, moon goddess," Kimberly says.

Billy blinks rapidly like his scientific brain is having trouble wrapping itself around the idea of a legend being relevant to our current dilemma. His face clears as he glances at me. "Like Zack said, if Trini thinks it's important, then it's important."

A thoughtful expression comes into Jason's eyes. "Okay, let's hear what you're thinking, Trini."

I wouldn't have blamed them for being skeptical. It is kind of far-fetched to think that an ancient myth could have anything to do with Rita, and it's even more far-fetched to think that Rita can actually be Chang'e. *So maybe I shouldn't push it.*

Zordon is watching me intently, and I remember the fury in Rita's eyes when she spoke of him. Then I think of Nai Nai telling me how Chang'e fled to the moon to escape the Lord Archer. Maybe no one will believe me—but I'm tired of staying quiet and burying my secrets deep in that silence.

"Zordon," I say, "according to you, Rita has been trapped in orbit around the moon for the past ten thousand years. Right?"

Is it my imagination or does Zordon's face stiffen? "What is your point, Trini?"

"The thing is," I say, "The story of Chang'e originated in the Zhou dynasty."

Jason, Kimberly, and Billy stare at me blankly, but Zack's eyes widen. My former best friend might not be talking to me, but at least he's keeping up with his research for our history project on the Bronze Age. He knows the Zhou dynasty started roughly three thousand years ago.

Zordon's face goes still, and that's when I know I'm right—the secret of Rita's rage against Zordon is hidden in the old tale of Chang'e.

Zack meets my eyes at last. "That shouldn't be possible."

"I know." I'm relieved that he's taking me seriously, but then again, he always has.

"Anyone want to tell me what's going on?" Kimberly asks with a frown.

Jasno shrugs. "I don't have a clue."

"Me neither," Billy admits.

"The Zhou dynasty was three thousand years ago," I say. "Not ten thousand."

"Oh." Billy's voice is startled.

Turning to Zordon, Kimberly says, "You said that the first time she's stepped foot on Earth in ten thousand years was when she trashed the Homecoming dance."

"Zordon didn't actually say that," Alpha 5 pipes up suddenly.

"But I did imply it," Zordon says heavily.

Jason folds his arms across his chest. "Explain."

"Trini is right," Zordon says. "Rita did break out of her prison three thousand years ago, long enough to try to conquer Earth again during the Zhou dynasty . . . when she fell in love with a human and had a daughter."

My mouth drops open. "Sorry, but *what?*"

"I don't understand," Billy says. "What does this have to do with why Rita is attacking Angel Grove now?

"Or why she's demanding your head on a platter," Zack adds.

A sudden memory rises to the surface of my brain. *Look at you all. So eager to protect her. I was like you once. And it made me weak.* I was so focused on my shame of being the useless team member that I didn't even think about who Rita was once so eager to protect.

"What happened to Rita's daughter?" I ask softly.

Zordon exhales. "I'm not proud of what I did."

Kimberly looks pale. "What, exactly, did you do?"

"You must understand," Zordon says, "Rita would have raised her daughter to be a conqueror . . . much as Rita herself was raised. She intended to subjugate the people of your world under her daughter's rule."

Dread swells in my body. I don't know what's coming, but I'm starting to understand why Rita is so bent upon revenge against Zordon.

"You killed her daughter?" Billy's voice is filled with horror.

"Zordon would never kill an infant!" Alpha 5 says indignantly.

"True, Alpha 5." Zordon's face is grave. "But I'm not certain that what I did is much better."

I think back to my interactions with Rita. There was so much fury in her—the kind that must have come from pain. She truly believed it was love that made her weak.

The illustration of Chang'e pops into my head—the moon goddess looking back toward the earthbound husband after taking the elixir of immortality. I read the book Nai Nai let me borrow, so I know at least one version of Chang'e's story. The Lord Archer never forgave his wife for what he saw as her dangerous ambition. But the story didn't say how Chang'e felt about her husband's distrust. *A misunderstanding*, Nai Nai called it. Nai Nai also said that Zack and I reminded her of Chang'e and Hou Yi.

Before I can help myself, I glance at Zack.

He's looking at me too, and our eyes lock. For a moment, it feels like all the air has been sucked from the chamber and there is no one but the two of us and the heavy weight of regrets between us.

If it's true that Zack and I are like the mythical couple, then I'm sure both Chang'e and Hou Yi felt betrayed by the other.

I wrench my gaze from Zack and back to Zordon. "You said Rita fell in love with a human." I swallow. "Who did she fall in love with?"

"A hero of your world." Zordon pauses. "And my friend."

There's no use asking what happened to him. It was three thousand years ago, after all. Rita's mortal lover is long dead, but judging from the sorrow in Zordon's eyes—not forgotten.

I don't have the heart to touch that old pain. Instead, I say, "It wouldn't have been easy to trap Rita again once she escaped her prison."

"It wasn't." Zordon watches me warily.

Foreboding tightens my chest. "You would have needed a very strong lure."

"The baby," Kimberly breathes.

"Yes." Zordon's face droops as if weighed down by guilt. "I used her daughter to trap her, and Rita believes that I killed her."

"But you *didn't*," Alpha 5 points out sharply.

"No," Zordon says, "but I made Rita believe her child was dead. If Rita had escaped again, she wouldn't have rested until she found her daughter. It would have been a heavy fate for the child to be molded in her mother's image . . . as Rita herself was raised in her father's image."

Chills feather over me. Rita did not strike me as a woman willing to be molded in anyone's image. I cannot imagine that she remained under her father's control for longer than she could help it.

"So now," Jason says, eyeing Zordon, "Rita won't rest until she's had her revenge against *you*."

"Better me than the child," he replies sadly. "I could not fail her daughter as I failed Rita herself."

I gape at him. *Uh, what?*

"Many thousands of years ago," Zordon continues, "I swore to protect Lady Fienna and her infant daughter from her vicious husband, but I failed them both." He clears his throat of emotion. "Rita's father killed his wife and raised his daughter into the heartless and dangerous woman who now threatens your home."

"Not exactly heartless," Zack says dryly, "if you were able to trap her with her daughter."

Sorrow fills Zordon's face. "True."

"So now we have to fight off an avenging sorceress because she thinks you killed her daughter," Kimberly says coldly.

"How are we supposed to trust you now?" Billy asks. Of us all, he's probably spent the most time with Zordon. Naturally, he would feel the most wounded.

Jason faces off with our mentor. "That's a good question."

"It is," Zordon says sadly. "Your anger and mistrust is completely justified. All I can say is that I made a mistake and am deeply sorry for it."

That I can understand. I turn to the others. "It's true. Zordon made a mistake," I say, "but he's also made huge sacrifices to do what he thought was right." I stare at Zordon in his blue tube, trapped in a time warp and denied a physical body because of his choice to defend Earth. "I, for one, will be damned before I give him up to Rita."

Zack gives a short nod. "Agreed."

"Yeah. Me too," Kimberly says.

"I might not understand what you did," Billy says, "but I'm not going to let Rita have you without a fight either."

"What they said," Jason adds.

Zordon blinks like he's holding back a great swell of emotion. "Thank you, Rangers. That means a great deal to me."

Jason clears his throat. "We still need to figure out how to stop Rita."

"Yes," Alpha 5 says hastily. "Zordon and I have formulated a few possible defensive plans for when Rita attacks."

"Defensive?" I ask. Surely, we're not just going to wait around for Rita to attack.

"Without the Megazord," Zordon says, sounding like he's recovered his usual calm, "I feel these are our best options."

I drop my gaze. Of course. I can't merge with my Zord, so that means no Megazord.

"We still have the other Zords," Billy points out.

"No Zords," Jason says shortly. "They'll tear apart Angel Grove."

"I understand," Zordon says, "but you don't stand a chance against Rita without the Zords."

"I don't like it either," Kimberly says, "but I think Zordon is right."

"There's got to be another way." Zack's fists are balled up at his side.

Memories of Jason's burned-out store and the shattered glass of the Youth Center are seared in my brain. Angel Grove is just starting to fix the damage of the last attack, but there's a long way to go. There's no way to win if we wage this battle of Zords against Putties in our home. Now that I know how deep Rita's anger runs, I know that she'll lay waste to Angel Grove to punish Zordon—and us for protecting him. My heart twists painfully. Whether or not we use the Zords, Angel Grove is doomed.

I think of the picture of Chang'e in Nai Nai's book of fairy tales. The illustrator captured the moon goddess's sadness, but there must have been anger too—Chang'e was driven out of her home by her husband's distrust. In my mind's eye, I see Chang'e rising into the air, her white robe and colorful sash trailing behind her as she leaves her earthbound husband.

My breath suddenly stops, and my mouth falls open. *Oh*.

"Trini," Zack says, "you have an idea." He doesn't ask it as a question. That's how well he knows me.

A spurt of excitement straightens my spine. "What if," I say slowly, "there *is* another way?"

Zordon's head turns to me. "What are you thinking, Trini Kwan?"

I'm thinking that an intergalactic warrior scholar must have a means of space travel. "We need to take the fight to Rita." Everyone is looking at me, but I don't feel self-conscious or worried about what they think anymore. I know we all want the same thing—to protect our home.

"To the desert?" Alpha 5 asks.

"No." There is steel in my voice when I say, "To the moon."

CHAPTER TWENTY-SIX

"Going to the moon is a good plan," Billy says as he ducks a blow from Jason. He's been repeating variations on this theme for the past two days.

"You don't have to convince me." I jump up, grab a bar on the ceiling, and flip myself so I'm facing downward. Then I push off from the ceiling and dive at Jason, hitting him hard enough that he falls to the floor. Billy designed this training room to imitate conditions on the moon. Technically, metal bars set into the walls and ceiling aren't a part of the lunar environment, but they were part of the original design of the room, and I'm glad Billy kept them.

Bouncing upright on my toes, I can't help but grin. Oh yes. This is a *great* plan.

Kimberly flips backward out of Zack's reach, grabs a bar to lift up, and kicks him in the chest, sending him tumbling in midair. *Damn.* The moon's surface gravity really gives Kimberly the chance to show off her gymnastic skills.

"Argh!" Zack tries to regain his balance. "I can't tell what's up or down."

"I can fix that," Billy says. "Computer, switch to Earth conditions."

Caught off guard, Zack stumbles and falls. Kimberly and I find our footing with relative ease, but Jason was already jumping up and is now clinging awkwardly to a bar on the ceiling.

Jason lets go of the bar and lands hard on the cushioned floor of the training room. "I hate moon gravity."

"A little more warning would be nice, Billy." Zack gets to his feet and morphs out of his suit, and I can see that he's smiling. Despite his complaints, he's having fun.

"You know I programmed the training room computer to recognize all our voice commands, right?" Billy morphs out of his suit too. "You could change the conditions to whatever you want. For example, zero-g would be interesting."

"Yes!" Kimberly claps her hands.

"Yes, please!" Excitement runs through me as I imagine what we could do in zero-G.

"Why not?" Zack says.

"No!" Jason morphs out of his suit and exhales. "It doesn't matter if it's zero-G or moon gravity. I'm just not getting the hang of this."

"You're getting better." I morph out of my suit to smile at Jason, and Zack gives me an indecipherable look, his own smile fading.

I suck in my breath. It feels like Zack just poured ice water all over me. He's been distant or flat-out avoiding me ever since I rejoined the team, and it kind of feels like middle school all over again. My gut clenches. *No.* This time will be different. I'm not going to stand silently by while our friendship implodes. We both said some pretty awful things to each other, but like Nai Nai keeps telling me: Ignoring the past won't make the hurt go away.

"I might be getting better, but it's not good enough," Jason says. His expression turns contemplative, and he taps his fingers on his thigh for a moment. At last, he refocuses on us like he's come to a decision. "We're going to need a recon team to scope out Rita's compound on the moon. According to Zordon, Rita is churning out Putties there, so we have to cut off her army at its source. But we need to know what to expect."

Kimberly morphs out of her suit. "Works for me."

"Quick question." Zack raises his hand like he's in class. "Have we figured out how we're going to get to the moon yet? I'm assuming we can't just teleport there."

Jason gestures toward Billy. "Billy just gave me his latest report before we came into training. He can explain the situation better than I can."

"Right." Billy looks startled but pleased that Jason is deferring to him. "Zack, you're correct that it's too far for us to teleport."

"So, does Zordon have a spaceship stored in the closet of the Command Center or something?" he asks.

"Actually," Billy says, "he sort of does."

Kimberly's eyes light up. "Please say you're not kidding."

"It's complicated." Billy glances at me, and then away again. "The Zords are equipped for space travel, but they're meant to travel through space in the Megazord form."

My stomach drops. *Not the Megazord again.* I hunch my shoulders as my teammates carefully don't look at me.

"So we still don't have a way to get to the moon?" Kimberly keeps her voice even, but I see the disappointment flit over her face.

"There is one option," Billy says. "Most of our Zords can't fly through space on their own, but your Pterodactyl can, Kimberly. It's faster than any Earth tech and can get us to the moon in just an hour or two."

She starts to smile, and I hate to burst her bubble, but I don't know how we're all going to fit into her Zord. While I'm trying to think of how to say this tactfully, Zack asks, "So we're all going to cram into the cockpit of Kimerly's Pterodactyl? And what about the other Zords?"

Kimberly's face falls, but Billy says, "I might have a solution. Alpha 5 and I are constructing a trailer for the other Zords that the Pterodactyl can tow." He looks at Jason. "In the meantime, the Pterodactyl's cockpit can hold one other person in addition to Kimberly."

Jason nods. "That brings me back to the recon mission. Two people are enough to do recon. Kimberly, are you willing to go?"

"Fly my Zord in space and find a way to sabotage a Putty-making factory?" She grins. "I'm so in."

"It's a good thing you're great at navigating moon gravity," Jason says, "but I'm not. I was planning on going with you, but for the mission to have the best chance at succeeding, your partner should be just as good at navigating moon gravity."

Wait. Does that mean what I think it does?

Jason turns to me. "Trini, you're the best choice to go with Kimberly. Will you do it?"

A shiver of anxiety goes down my back. I don't want to let them down . . . or Kimberly to get hurt again. But I also don't want to keep failing the people I care about because I'm too afraid to act. Like Jason said, we have to find out what we're up against. "Yes. I'm in too."

"Be careful." Zack says it to both me and Kimberly, and I must be imagining that his gaze lingers on me.

"I will," I say softly.

Kimberly grabs my arm and squeezes it. "When do we leave?" She sounds way more excited about this mission than she did about being chosen as Homecoming Queen.

"We only have three days left before Rita attacks," Billy says even though we're all keeping track as closely as he is. "I've already made all the calculations I need on the Pterodactyl for the trailer system, so I can work on that while you're gone."

"You can leave whenever you want, then," Jason says to us.

Kimberly and I look at each other, and I see the same resolve on her face that is tingling through my spine. "No time like the present," she says.

I sneak a glance at Zack and glimpse worry creasing his face. I desperately want to pin him down and make him talk to me—but it's going to have to wait.

I turn away and face Kimberly. "I'm ready too."

⚡

The surface of the moon is oddly beautiful.

I suck in air from the oxygen tank attached to my suit and look around at the coldly pale rock formations and magnificent craters.

"We're a few miles away from where Billy calculated the Moon Palace is." Kimberly takes a graceful leap over the rocky lunar terrain, her pink suit flashing brightly against the gray environment.

"You know, if the point is to remain incognito, maybe bright pink and yellow space suits weren't the way to go." I take a running leap after her, marveling at how quickly I move due to the lack of air resistance here.

"Billy said he couldn't change the color," she says, keeping up with the jump-running we're doing.

What he actually said was more complicated. Something about symbiosis, Morphing Grid, nanotech—but yeah, it boiled down to not being able to change the color of our suits.

"Honestly, I think our suits are a lot less noticeable than a big-ass pink Pterodactyl." There's a grin in her voice as she points to the Zord still visible in the distance.

"Point taken."

We bound over the rocky ground, and I have to say that I *love* running on the moon. At this rate, we should be able to cover the miles to the Moon Palace in no time.

"You know," Kimberly says abruptly, "I never told you why I had to leave my old school."

Where did *that* come from? It was obvious she had been holding something back, but I didn't expect a spy mission on the moon would be when she decided to confide in me. Then again, we're going into a dangerous situation where we have to trust each other. Maybe there's no better time to clear the air. I'm not sure what's on her mind, but I do know what it's like to have secrets burning in your chest. "Do you want to tell me about it?"

Kimberly doesn't say anything at first, and I wonder if I misjudged, but then she says, "I got suspended for bullying."

My jaw drops, and I'm glad she can't see my expression through my faceplate. I'm not sure what I expected, but it wasn't that. Keeping pace with her, I turn over possible responses in my head. *Did you really do it? Were you framed? Was it a hypnotic trance?* I associate bullying with guys like Bulk and Skull—not Kimberly.

She takes a longer leap to pull ahead of me, but I kick off from the ground hard so it feels like I'm flying through the air to catch up with her. As gently as possible, I ask, "What happened?"

Kimberly glances at me, her faceplate obscuring her face. "I got involved with a group of girls, and I thought they were so cool. I just wanted them to like me, so I went along with a lot of things they did. Like posting mean comments on social media." She speaks so quietly that I have to strain to hear her. "You know—the things that girls say to each other to make them feel bad about themselves."

I *do* know. My stomach twists, and I don't ask questions because I can imagine, all too well, the shaming comments that can cut a girl to the bone. What girl doesn't know? But I also know the things that pit one girl against another and turn them into each other's enemies.

Kimberly has never—not once—been my enemy. She's my friend.

"That's not who you are anymore," I say with confidence.

"You don't know that." Her voice thickens. "One of the girls we were bullying? She was my ex–best friend."

Oh hell. No wonder Kimberly was worried about my reaction, but it doesn't shake my faith in her. She may have done awful things, but she's still the girl who fought Putties by my side.

"We were only suspended for a few days," she says without looking at me, "but my parents were embarrassed by the whole thing. My mom never wanted to live in LA anyway, so we all moved here, and now my parents are fighting all the time. I mean, I guess they were fighting before too, but I can't help but think it's my fault."

"I'm sure the problems between your parents are not your fault." I think about how they bickered at the restaurant. Those two clearly have issues that have nothing to do with Kimberly.

"Maybe," she replies, "but what I did to my friend was definitely my fault. I told my parents I didn't want to move, but secretly, I was relieved." Her voice breaks. "I just couldn't face her again."

"I get that." I think about how guilty I felt after she got hurt in the Putty attack in the gym. It was one of the reasons I quit the team.

Her smooth running gait falters. "I hoped Angel Grove would be a fresh start."

I don't think it would help to repeat what Nai Nai told me after I quit—that you can't outrun your problems. I'm pretty sure Kimberly knows that already. We're literally running to a space sorceress's compound that's churning out deadly Putties, so it's safe to say that Kimberly is done running *away* from her problems.

"If becoming a Power Ranger to save your new home isn't a fresh start," I say, "then I don't know what is."

"You may be right." Her voice sounds a little lighter as she slows down to what passes as a walk in the lower gravitational pull of the moon.

I match her pace. "Anyway, I don't judge you for your past," I say. "I mean, look at my past. I beat up a kid in kindergarten. And then I hid my martial arts skills from all of you because I was afraid of what I could do."

Kimberly chuckles. "I forgave you for that already."

"Then you can forgive yourself too." A small weight eases from me. Maybe I should take my own advice and stop judging myself for *my* past. "What matters is that you've always had my back, so I'll always have—"

A sudden movement behind Kimberly catches my eye, and before I have time to think consciously, I'm pushing her out of harm's way and leaping up to stab an attacking Putty with the dagger that instantly manifested into my grip. The other dagger forms too, and I whirl to block the sharp fingers of another Putty, burying my other dagger in its chest. Two pink arrows, in rapid succession, fly past me, downing the Putties coming at me.

Then it's over. Four Putties are on the ground, and they don't seem like they're going to get up again. Heart pounding, I scan the area but don't see any more.

Kimberly and I look at each other, and relief pours through me. "See?" I grin. "We have each other's backs. Just like I said."

She laughs. "I didn't think you were going to prove it so literally."

"Neither did I." I'm still smiling, and it's not just because we put down four Putties in a few seconds. I was there for my teammate when she needed me, and this time, she didn't get hurt.

Kimberly adjusts her grip on her bow. "I don't know about you, but I *really* like fighting with weapons."

"Totally agree." I balance the daggers in my hand and use one to point in the direction the Putties came from. "I think we're getting close."

She nods, and we proceed at a slower pace, keeping our weapons drawn.

Before long, we approach the lip of a crater. Without a word to each other, we hop toward a large, rocky outcropping near the edge and crouch behind it. I retract my energy daggers to free up my hands so I can grip one of the rocks as an anchor, and Kimberly does the same. With the low gravity of the moon, we have a tendency to bob up and down like yellow and pink balloons, and that would definitely attract attention.

"Ready to see what we're up against?" I ask.

"Let's do it."

Keeping low, we pull ourselves toward the edge of the crater, kind of like we're rock climbing horizontally.

"Holy crap," Kimberly says suddenly, but I don't respond.

All the breath whooshes out of me at the sight of what lies in the crater. There's a massive fortress made of dark lunar rock with four lopsided turrets on each side and a giant orb of blue energy crowning the tall central tower. This can only be Rita's Moon Palace—where she is creating Putties. But it's not the palace itself that is causing horror to rise into my throat.

"Is that . . ." Kimberly's voice trails off as she points.

"Yes." I watch as the gray tide of Putties pour out of the open stone doors of the Moon Palace to assemble in straight rows. "That's Rita's army of Putties."

And there are *thousands* of them.

CHAPTER TWENTY-SEVEN

O kay, it could be worse." Jason whacks the whiteboard for emphasis. He was drawing while Kimberly and I were reporting back, and now he has a rough sketch of the Moon Palace on the board, with black rows representing the Putties.

I spare a moment to wonder where Jason was able to find something as old school as a whiteboard in the high-tech Command Center, but mostly I'm wondering what Jason thinks would be worse than thousands of Putties with a Moon Palace churning more of them out by the minute.

"I don't see how," Zack says dryly. "Unless there were big eyeball monsters or something that you forgot to mention?" He directs the question to Kimberly, but I'm tired of his "pretend Trini is invisible" act. It took us four years to become friends again, and this time I'm not going to lose him without a fight.

"Oh, didn't we tell you about the twenty-foot purple monster made of eyeballs?" I ask sweetly. Billy gives me an alarmed look, and I say quickly, "I'm kidding."

I glance at Zack, and there's no reaction. Not even a twitch of his mouth. *That does it.* I have to make him talk to me.

"The good news," Zordon says, interrupting my thoughts, "is that there is a limit to how many Putties Rita can make."

Billy snaps his fingers. "The blue orb."

Huh? We all stare at him as he goes over to Alpha 5 and points at something on the bank of computer screens. "Alpha 5, can you give me the energy readings at these coordinates over the past week?"

"Of course, Billy."

"Trini, Kimberly—you described a ball of blue energy, right?" Billy asks.

"Yeah," she says. "It was glowing."

I'm starting to get it. "Wait . . . are you implying that the blue orb is powering whatever mechanism Rita is using to create the Putties?"

"Yes," Billy says excitedly. "Or rather, it *was* providing the energy to create the Putties. According to these energy readings, it's very sporadic. Rita must need to recharge it."

"Very good, Billy," Zordon says.

"How long does it take to recharge?" Jason asks, taking a blue marker from his bucket of markers and coloring in the orb on the white board.

"About forty-eight hours," Alpha 5 replies.

"Then that's our window," Jason says. "We need to strike before she can make more Putties."

It's also about how long we have left of the time Rita gave us to deliver Zordon to her.

"Billy, how's the Zord trailer coming?" Jason asks.

"It will be ready in time." Billy sounds confident, but from where I'm standing, I can see that he has his fingers crossed behind his back. Firmly, I tamp down my worry. If Billy says he can get it done in time, then he will.

"We're still outnumbered," Zack points out. "By a lot."

"When I last had a body," Zordon says thoughtfully, "I faced situations when my team was outnumbered."

Judging from my teammates' expressions, I'm not the only one thrown by the casual way Zordon mentioned once having a body. We've all gotten so used to his presence as a floating head that it's hard to remember he wasn't always this way.

"The trick," Zordon continues, "is to fight the battle you can win—not the one your enemy wants you to fight."

"What?" Kimberly nudges Billy. "Did you understand any of that?"

"Nope." Billy scratches his head. "Battle strategy isn't my thing. I'm more of a science guy."

"Trini understands," Zordon says, jolting me out of my contemplation of the disastrous fallout in the feud between Zordon and Rita.

"Er . . . sorry," I say sheepishly. "What are we talking about?"

"You, Trini," Zordon says, "understood that the battle Rita wanted you to fight was on Earth. But the battle you can win is on the moon."

"Oh." I blush, not sure of what to say.

Jason beams at me. "Okay, let's make a game plan for a fight we can win."

I blush even harder, and Zack glances at me before scrunching his body deeper into his hoodie.

I wish I knew what was going on in his head. A heavy mass sits in my chest. We still haven't talked about our big fight, and I've been wanting to tell him that he was right. I *was* afraid of letting the team see me for who I am. There never seemed to be a good moment to have that conversation, and this certainly isn't the time, but we are *way* overdue for a heart-to-heart.

Fortunately, Jason doesn't seem to notice the weirdness between us. He turns his attention to the white board and whips out a bunch of colorful markers in very recognizable colors.

"We need a strong defense," he mutters. "Maybe a Four-One Formation." Jason scribbles and draws for a few minutes, mumbling things like "scatter," "bursts," and "lookie" before stepping away and gesturing to the colorful diagram on the board. "And that," he says proudly, "is our new game plan." His face falls when he takes in our faces. Everyone except Zack looks as confused as I feel, and even Zack is frowning.

"What exactly are we looking at?" Billy asks.

"Is this an Earthling way of developing a battle strategy?" Zordon asks.

Kimberly shakes her head. "Only if you're a football player."

Oh. That would explain why only Jason and Zack seem to understand the circles, X's, and arrows.

Still frowning, Zack steps up to the board and traces the arrow drawn from the yellow X to the blue orb.

My eyes widen. Is the yellow X supposed to be *me*? I tilt my head and take in the whole diagram with new eyes. "Jason, are you suggesting that the team draws the Putties away from the Moon Palace with their Zords while I sabotage the energy source?" It's actually not a bad plan.

Jason's eyes light up. "Yes! That's exactly it."

"Won't it be dangerous?" An alarmed expression crosses Billy's face.

"She won't have a Zord to protect her!" Kimberly protests. She bites her lip and glances at me.

It's true that I won't have a Zord, but I'll have my daggers and a lifetime of training. "I can do it."

Alpha 5 looks up from the computer console. "Unfortunately, the power source will most likely be force-field protected."

"True," Zordon says. "Trini, if you do this, you'll have to go through the Moon Palace itself to sabotage the power source."

"I don't suppose there's a clearly marked off switch," I say with an attempt at humor.

"No," Zordon says, taking me literally, "but there's probably a control center much like we have in the Power Chambers." His head swivels to Alpha 5. "Do we have any schematics of the Moon Palace?"

"Negative," Alpha 5 replies.

"I can figure out a way to pinpoint the most likely location of the control center based on energy output." Based on the stressed-out look in Billy's eyes, he has just mentally added that task to his already daunting to-do list, which includes "designing a Zord trailer for space."

"I'll have to train you all in a system so I can call the plays in the field," Jason says.

"Right," Zack says. "Like they're going to memorize plays like 'Green Right X Shift to Viper Right Three-Eighty-Two X Stick Lookie' before we all blast off for the moon."

Come again?

Kimberly shakes her head. "That's way too complicated, and we only have two days. It would be easier to structure our plays like a cheerleading routine."

"Not exactly easier," Zack interjects, and I remember that he's done both football and cheer. "But Kimberly has a point. How about a simplified call system with the structure of a cheer routine and flexibility of football plays? We could plan out a number of set plays to practice like a routine and come up with a few simple calls."

"I like it," Jason says thoughtfully.

Zack peers at the whiteboard again. "Can I make another suggestion?"

"Be my guest." He holds out the markers to Zack.

Zack takes the black marker and draws a new arrow from my yellow X to the door of the Moon Palace and then draws another arrow from the black X—also to the Moon Palace.

What is he doing? The muscles down my back clench in wariness.

Zack steps back from the board. "I say we double-team the defense here." He looks at Jason instead of me. "We don't need that many Zords to draw the Putties away. The mission to sabotage Rita's Putty-making capabilities will stand a better chance of succeeding if there's two of us."

"That's a good point," Jason says.

"Do I get a say in this?" I ask sarcastically. Zack's modification does make sense, but it would be nice if they weren't making plans as if I wasn't even here.

Jason starts guiltily. "Sorry. Is this okay with you, Trini?"

I eye Zack, who's studiously doodling in the corner of the whiteboard and not meeting my gaze. It makes sense to have a partner, and he can't keep avoiding me if we're working together. "Actually . . . yeah."

"Shouldn't it be me?" Kimberly asks. "No offense, Zack, but Trini and I can both navigate moon gravity better, and we've already fought Putties together so we know we make a good team." So do Zack and I, but Kimberly was unconscious at the time, so she can be forgiven for not knowing how well we fight together.

Jason shakes his head. "We're going to need your Pterodactyl to draw the Putties away, Kimberly."

"Oh, right," she says.

"I'm not as good as you or Trini in moon gravity," Zack says, angling his body so we can't see what he's drawing, "but I can manage."

"It's settled, then," Jason says.

"Except for one not-so-small thing." Zack steps away from the board, revealing a stick figure with wings and a horned head. "Goldar."

"Oh yeah. I actually did remember him." Jason points at the black question mark in the corner, opposite of Zack's stick-figure Goldar. He reddens. "I didn't have a gold marker. Or your . . . um, artistic imagination."

Zack smiles. "You're welcome."

"We didn't see Goldar on our scouting excursion," Kimberly offers. "Maybe he won't be around."

"Let's hope Rita keeps him locked up in her dungeon between Earth invasions," Zack comments.

"Goldar is not the only problem you have to worry about." Zordon sighs heavily. "I'm afraid that destroying Rita's power source will not be enough. She will still have the Putties she already made and Goldar, her fierce and loyal general."

Billy looks from the board to Zordon. "What would happen to Goldar and the Putties without Rita?"

"Goldar would be left without direction or motivation to conquer your planet, and the Putties would lose the animating force that is Rita's sorcery."

That seems clear enough. I eye Zordon. "You're saying we have to capture Rita."

"I'm afraid so."

Everyone stares at Zordon.

Zack's eyebrows shoot straight up. "You want us to infiltrate a Moon Palace, avoid Goldar's notice, sabotage a blue orb thing—and put Rita back in her space dumpster?"

"Zordon is right," I say to Zack.

He looks at me, apparently too shocked to keep pretending I'm invisible.

This is our chance, not only to make sure our mission succeeds, but to clear the air between us. "And if we're going to pull this off . . ." I let my words trail off and grin fiercely at Zack "Then we have to train with each other."

CHAPTER TWENTY-EIGHT

L ook, spaghetti arms," I call out as I break Zack's hold and bring my knee up to kick out at him. "This is my dance space."

"You missed." I can tell he's smiling even though we're wearing our suits with the helmets. "But points for the *Dirty Dancing* reference." He leaps into the air and dives down at me, feet first.

Instead of dodging his attack, I jump up to meet him. "This is your dance space," I say, striking a blow to the chest before he spins away. "I don't go into yours; you don't go into mine." I come down to the floor, bouncing a little in the lunar gravity programmed into the training room.

We've been training ever since school let out a few hours ago, and it feels as if things are back to normal between us. I mean, we're full-on fighting each other with superhero powers and cracking jokes about Baby and Johnny's epic dance rehearsal—but for us, that's as normal as it gets.

"You know those lines don't really work." He lands as lightly as I did and kicks out at me. I block him and try to flip him down to the mat, but he just bounces up again. Damn lunar gravity. "Considering we're *definitely* in each other's physical space," he adds.

My cheeks heat up, and I falter in my attempt to get under his guard. Did Zack just get flirty with me?

"Oh hell." Zack morphs out of his suit, and his face is somber. "Sorry, Trini. I crossed a line that I shouldn't have."

Huh? I can understand him being embarrassed by an unintentionally flirty comment, but why does he look like he just accidentally killed my pet goldfish or something? I morph out of my suit too. "It's not a big deal," I say because it really isn't.

He doesn't seem to hear me. "I know you don't think of me like that . . . I mean, not like you do Jason."

"What does Jason have to do with anything?" Confusion crests over me.

"Well." He blinks sheepishly at me. "Don't you like him?"

I almost burst into laughter at the absurdity of his question, but his serious expression stops me. Wait . . . is *that* what the weird awkwardness over the past week was all about?

No, it can't be. Our problems run a lot deeper than some misunderstanding about Jason.

My confusion is starting to turn to indignation. "We need to talk," I say abruptly.

He eyes me warily. "Okay . . ."

I take a deep breath. I don't want to talk about the fight, but Nai Nai is right that it's the only way to heal the past. "Are you still mad at me for quitting the team?"

"What? No!" Zack gapes at me, but then his mouth firms. "We do need to talk."

"I've been trying!" I fling up my hands in frustration. "But you kept making jokes and avoiding me. This is the first time we've been alone since our argument—" My voice dies in my throat because there might be another reason why Zack has been acting this way. I force myself to go on despite the nerves twisting up my insides. "Do you think I'm a coward?"

He glares at me like he really *is* mad. "Don't be ridiculous. I never thought, not for one moment, that you were a coward. Like

I said, you're the bravest person I know . . . when it comes to fighting for others." His face softens. "I just wanted you to see that *you* are worth fighting for too."

"Oh." My body is filling up with something light and inexpressible. "Then why were you being so . . ."

"Assholey?" he suggests, a glint in his eye.

"That's not how I would put it." I'm starting to smile. "Mostly because 'assholey' isn't actually a word."

"The reason I was being assholey . . ." He pauses to add, "Yes, 'assholey' might not be an actual word, but it *legit* describes how I was acting."

"No argument there."

"When we fought—" Zack swallows audibly. "I said some pretty harsh things. I just wanted you to be who you are—brave, brilliant, wonderful *you*. But I pushed you too hard," he says ruefully. "I thought I'd blown it for good with you, and I was so relieved when you came back to the team. I didn't want to ruin everything again."

A swell of emotion rises into my throat. "I said some harsh things too," I admit. "It's not true that you don't know who I am anymore."

"But it *is* true that I abandoned you in middle school," he says guiltily, "when you needed me to be a friend."

Yes, but it's time that I let go of the past. "You're here now, fighting by my side," I say thickly, "and it's going to take more than an argument to ruin our friendship." I brush away the tears in my eyes. "After all, we did make a pinkie swear to be friends. Again, still, and always."

There's a sheen in Zack's eyes too. "I will never underestimate the power of a pinkie swear again," he says solemnly.

For one breathless moment, we just stare at each other. Then a flush steals over Zack's face. "Uh, as your friend, I should tell you that Jason is a great guy."

"Not this again," I mutter. Jason isn't the one who has been living rent-free in my head. Unlike a certain infuriating guy with a Mastodon Zord. I glower at Zack, and he takes a step back at whatever he sees on my face.

"You don't have to say anything," he says earnestly, "but I noticed how you keep standing up for Jason, and I'm sure he likes you too. He knows how incredible you are."

My heart is doing triple flips to hear Zack say I'm incredible, but . . . the context is all wrong.

"He just needs a little time to make a move," Zack continues.

I stare at him in shock. I don't want *Jason* to make a move.

"Um, you're kind of just standing there, not saying anything." He peers at me anxiously. "Are you okay?" All of a sudden, it occurs to me what our big argument was really about. *Trini Kwan stopped fighting for anything she wants.*

And Zack was right.

Then a thought hits me with the force of a thunderclap, stunning me with its surety. What I want is . . . Zack.

But I haven't forgotten what else he said. *If you really wanted to stay friends, you could have put me in a headlock or something until I admitted I was being a jerk.*

Except that I don't want to just stay friends anymore. My chest tightens. I don't want to mess it up now that things are finally normal between us, but is normal what I want with Zack . . . or do I want more?

Zack's eyes darken as he stares at me, and a muscle jumps in his jaw. My fingers suddenly itch to reach out and trace his tense jawline until his face softens. I'm desperate to feel the faint stubble over his skin against my fingertips.

So . . . I guess I want more. Definitely more.

And I'm starting to think I'm not the only one. Of course, I could also be completely mistaken in thinking that Zack staring at me with his face all intensely broody means he shares my feelings. Maybe it's just indigestion from cafeteria Tater Tots. My head starts to whirl like it does when I'm too high up on a ladder or an amusement park ride.

But maybe it's time to fight for what I want—and damn the consequences.

"Computer," I say, "switch to Earth gravity."

"Trini, what are you doing?" Alarm creeps into his eyes as the gravity in the room increases and we both become more rooted to the ground.

"I'm putting you in a headlock so you'll listen to reason," I say calmly. Without further warning, I rush at him, but he quickly puts up his hand and blocks me before I can get a grip on his head.

"Okay, I get it!" he says, sidestepping me. "You don't want to talk about Jason."

"This has nothing to do with Jason." I angle for a leg sweep. "*You* were the one who suggested that I put you in a headlock when you're being a jerk."

"Hey!" Indignation pulls him out of his defensive stance.

Now. I slip under his guard, and for a breathless moment, we're right up against each other. I can feel the heat of his body through my thin tank top and hear the frantic thud of his heart. *Oh hell.* What was I supposed to be doing?

"Trini," he murmurs, swallowing hard.

I don't know if he moves first or if I do—but his head lowers as I lift my face up to his. I wrap my hand around the back of his neck, and he cups my chin with a gentle hand at odds with the hunger of his mouth as it descends upon mine.

And then we're kissing at long last.

A wave of desire bursts through me as I kiss my sweet, wonderful Zack. My body goes liquid with the heat flooding me, and I finally understand what it means to go weak in the knees. In fact, mine are buckling from under me, but Zack is holding me tightly to his chest, and I know he'd never let me fall.

It seems like an eternity later when I pull away from him, my breath all tangled up in my chest and my cheeks flushed with emotion.

Zack takes a step backward, a dazed expression on his face.

"So just to be clear," he says, "you're not interested in Jason?"

"I'm not," I say firmly. "And he's not interested in me either."

"In that case, there's something you should know." He looks at me tenderly. "Trini, I am head-over-heels crushed out on you."

My whole body is bubbling with joy. "For the record . . ." I flush. "I, uh, like you." That's a weak-ass way to say that I full-on explode with sparkly glitter and fireworks when I'm with him, but my tongue is thick with unaccustomed emotions.

But he's grinning like he knows what I mean and feels the same way. "It took you long enough."

I arch an eyebrow at him. "To do what?"

"To put me in a headlock and make me listen to reason."

"Technically, I didn't actually put you in a headlock." I take a step toward him.

His eyes gleam. "Maybe we should practice, then."

I laugh. "I'm not sure this is what Jason meant when he agreed to let us to train together."

"You know," Zack says as he pulls me back toward him. "I'm suddenly finding that I don't give a damn what anyone else thinks."

"I see your point," I murmur as I curl into his chest.

There are a million things I need to be focusing on, and kissing my former best probably shouldn't even make the top one hundred. But being with Zack is a powerful pull that I can't resist . . . and don't want to. It feels so *right*.

⚡

"Zack and Trini," Alpha 5's voice comes over the speakers of the training room. "I'm reading sustained elevated heart rate and high heat expenditure."

We jump apart guiltily.

"Your level of movement does not justify the unusual read-outs," he continues. "What is your current condition?"

"We're fine," I say hastily.

"Just trying out a new . . . training method," Zack adds.

I shove my arm over my mouth to stifle giggles.

"Very well," Alpha 5 says. "Perhaps the others would be interested in this new training. Billy wants to talk to everyone, and they're all coming to you now."

I remove my arm and exchange a wide-eyed look with Zack. "Thanks for the heads up, Alpha 5."

"No problem," the android says cheerfully.

"Good thing Alpha 5 gave us a warning." Zack is smoothing down his shirt and running his fingers through his hair.

"Stop it," I hiss, keeping an eye on the door. "They'll know something is up."

He peers down at his shirt and then glances at me. "You're sure we don't seem a bit . . . rumpled?"

I resist the urge to straighten my own tank top. "We're supposed to be training," I point out. "It will look more suspicious if we're *not* hot and sweaty." I flush. "You know what I mean."

"Hell yeah, I do." His eyes darken in a way that does super fluttery things to my stomach.

Throwing caution to the wind, I start leaning toward him at the same time he does . . . and then the door slides open and our team comes charging in.

I snap back from Zack and swivel to the door in utter panic. "Hi!" I call out in an overly bright tone. "How's it going?"

"We were just training hard," Zack says quickly. "I mean, not hard. Enthusiastically. No, not that either."

What are you even doing? I mouth at him, but I'm fighting a smile. Zack, nervous-babbling, is just so darned cute.

"I mean yes, we were training," he concludes weakly. He throws me a look of utter panic, but there's no way we're going to recover from that.

Billy smirks at us. "It's about time."

"I knew it." Kimberly's eyes are bright. "You could practically see the sparks flying between you two."

"Uh." Jason looks at us all in confusion. "What's going on?"

Zack and I exchange looks, and he shrugs sheepishly. I reach out to hold his hand. "Zack and I are . . ." Oh, oops. We were so busy making out that we somehow skipped over the conversation of what we are.

"Dating," Zack says, squeezing my hand. "Even if we haven't had an actual date yet—despite my best efforts."

I gape at him. "What do you mean?"

"Haven't you noticed? I've been trying to ask you on a date forever."

What? The Homecoming game was Zack's attempt to ask me out on a *date*? Oh, actually—duh, of course it was. A giddy feeling envelops me.

Jason clears his throat. "May I remind you that we do have a space sorceress to stop."

I blush. "Right."

"Of course." Zack doesn't let go of my hand.

"On the plus side, I guess this means you're working well together." A grin spreads over Jason's face, and he comes over and claps us both on the back like we just won a football game. "Also—I love this for you guys."

Billy catches my eye. "I told you Zack was interested," he says smugly.

I'm about to respond when I suddenly remember Alpha 5 telling us that Billy wanted to talk to us all. "Billy," I say with rising excitement. "Did you build the Zord trailer?"

"I did." His face splits into a smile. "I just ran the final diagnostics. It will work."

I beam at him. "I knew you could do it."

"Way to go, Billy!" Zack pumps a fist in the air.

Kimberly hugs him, and Jason goes up to Billy and whacks *him* on the back. I guess we should expect that with a football captain as our leader.

I look at Billy and remember his theory that my tension with Zack is what's keeping me from merging with my Zord. Well, I've definitely resolved *that*. "Actually, do you all mind if I try merging with my Sabertooth Tiger one more time before we use the Zord trailer?"

"Great idea!" Jason says, and I step back hastily before he can clap me on the back again.

"Alright," Zack says, giving my hand a squeeze. "Let's give it a try."

⚡

I breathe out a sign of frustration and stare at my inert Saber-tooth Tiger in the underground garage. Damn. I thought for sure it would work this time. Why can't I do this?

Zack puts his arm around me. "It's okay, Trini."

"We still have the Zord trailer," Billy reassures me.

"We can still get to the moon," Kimberly says. "It will be fine."

Jason looks disappointed, but he musters up a smile. "You tried your best, Trini, and like Kimberly said, we can still get to the moon."

"Does that mean we're going now?" Kimberly asks.

"Yeah, I suppose so." Billy stifles a yawn.

"No." Jason glances at Billy. "Rita gave us seven days, and our time doesn't run out until tomorrow evening. We'll leave first thing in the morning."

"Why wait?" Billy asks. "I mean, the trailer is ready."

My eyes narrow. "When was the last time you slept, Billy?"

"Slept?" He looks like he doesn't remember what the word means.

That's what I thought.

"We could all use a good night's sleep," Zack says. "Tomorrow isn't going to be easy."

"Zack's right." Jason puts his hand on Billy's shoulder. "We're going to need everyone at full strength tomorrow."

Billy blinks like he hadn't expected to be included in the fighting part. A small smile forms on his face.

That's right, Billy Cranston. You're the badass who built us a Zord trailer, and you're going to kick ass tomorrow too. I'm frustrated that I still can't merge with my Zord, but I'm so proud of Billy that I could burst.

"Let's all go home and have dinner with our families," Jason says. He doesn't add, *because this might be our last chance.*

But in the silence that falls over the training room, we all hear those unsaid words. I'm sure we're all thinking of our loved ones— the reason why we're fighting.

Tomorrow, we go to war to save our home.

CHAPTER
TWENTY-NINE

Who wants pizza?" Dad calls out from the front door. He just got back from Taiwan yesterday. Dad struggles to balance the boxes while toeing off his shoes, and I rush over to take them from him.

"Smells great." I breathe in the hot cheesy goodness. "Thanks, Dad."

Mom comes into the living room. "I understand we're supporting the businesses reopening after that horrible fire," she says, "but Trini was going to make dinner tonight."

I flush as Dad turns to me. "Trini requested pizza," he says.

Mom gives me a puzzled look. "I thought you were going to make black-bean sauce noodles for dinner."

"I did," I say. "It's all ready."

"She asked *me* for green onion pancakes," Nai Nai says as she walks into the living room. "I just finished making them."

I duck my head in embarrassment. "Um, it all sounds good." I might have gone a little overboard in planning what might be my last meal on Earth.

Dad ruffles my hair. "She's just hungry, and no wonder with all that wushu training you do with her, Ma."

Nai Na looks at me sharply. "True."

"Pizza, noodles, and pancakes," Mom says cheerfully. "Works for me." She takes the boxes from me. "Since you and Nai Nai did all the cooking, why don't I go set the table?"

"I'll help," Dad says. "All I did was go downtown and pick up pizza. I have to say, the repairs on those vandalized buildings are going quickly. Angel Grove is almost back to normal."

An ache stabs into me. If we don't stop Rita, Angel Grove will be completely destroyed in her next attack. "No more take-out for a while," I say firmly. "In fact, there's no need to go downtown at all tomorrow." Downtown is where Rita is most likely to attack.

"I think we'll have plenty of leftovers," Mom says dryly before going into the kitchen with Dad.

That leaves me alone with Nai Nai.

"What's going on, Trini?" she asks softly.

I swallow a lump in my throat. "Can you keep Mom and Dad home tomorrow?" I ask without answering her. I don't know how bad or how widespread Rita's rampage will get, but I'll feel better if my family stays here.

"Trini—" she begins, but I interrupt her.

"Can we not talk about it? I just want to spend time with all of you." I look around the living room full of family photos. "Please." I need a moment of normalcy before we head off to the moon. Like Zordon said, it's important to remember what we're fighting for.

Nai Nai is silent for a moment, and then she nods. "Come eat," she says tenderly. "I have a feeling you'll need to keep up your energy."

She puts her arm around my shoulders, and I lean into her. *This.* This is what I'm fighting for.

⚡

We land in the same shadowed part of the moon as we did last time, except now, Kimberly and I have brought a trailer full of

Zords with us. Since the individual Zords are all designed for space travel and Kimberly's Pterodactyl is equipped to power the entire Megazord across space, the trailer ended up being pretty simple. It's just a big, flat metal bed with clamps to hold the Zords in place.

And on that trailer is my inert Sabertooth Tiger, the only Zord that doesn't have a pilot. The others insisted we bring it so I can hunker in there if things go horribly wrong. My heart twists, but I push away my feelings of shame to focus on the mission at hand.

"Incoming solar winds," Billy comments from his Triceratops. His voice comes through loud and clear on the speakers in the Pterodactyl's cockpit that Kimberly and I are sharing.

"Should we wait it out?" Jason asks from his Tyrannosaurus Rex.

"We could be here all day if we try to wait out a solar storm," Billy says dryly. "They're unpredictable, and they occur all the time on the moon."

"I don't remember any solar storms from our scouting trip," Kimberly says. "Do you, Trini?"

I shake my head. I read up on solar storms when we first planned to confront Rita on her own turf. As far as I can tell, they're made up of high winds and an onslaught of chemicals. "We'd definitely know if we had encountered any."

"So," Zack says from his Mastodon. "The suits will protect us, even in the storm, right?"

"They should, theoretically," Billy replies, "but it's hard to run definitive tests."

"Now you tell us," Zack mutters.

"Trini, you and Zack are the ones who will be out there." Kimberly fidgets in the pilot seat of the Pterodactyl and turns to me in the smaller seat next to her. "The rest of us will be in our Zords."

"I'm sure it will be fine," Zack says.

"The radiation levels out there are a much bigger concern than the solar winds," Billy says in what he probably imagines is a reassuring tone.

"That's so not helpful." Kimberly grimaces.

"How is it not helpful to—"

"I got it, Billy," Zack says quickly. "Thanks."

"Any sign of Putties nearby, Billy?" Jason asks.

"Negative. We're about five miles from the Moon Palace and shouldn't encounter Putties this far out." He hesitates. "Then again, the charged particles from the solar storm make it hard to say for sure."

I peer out of the eyes of the Pterodactyl but don't see anything but swirling grayness. It really doesn't help that the Putties are the same dull gray color as the lunar surface.

"Good enough." Jason sounds like he's come to a decision. "Rangers, suit up."

"Ooh, 'Rangers, suit up,' that's not bad," Zack says, "But my vote is still for 'Go, go Power Rangers!' with 'It's Morphin' time!' a close second."

"I'll keep that in mind the next time we're invading the moon," Jason replies with a smile in his voice.

Instinctively, I reach for the power surging within me and morph into my Yellow Ranger state. It's kind of unbelievable how natural morphing now feels to me. Like the others, I don't need the Morpher anymore. Instead, I'm wearing my coin on a chain around my neck, nestled against my heart. Next to me, Kimberly morphs into the Pink Ranger.

"We all know the plan?" Jason's voice is now coming through the speakers in my helmet.

I touch my helmet and envision the little X's and O's on the whiteboard. "The rest of you draw the Putties away, and then Zack and I will sneak into the Moon Palace and put the Putty-making factory out of commission."

"And capture Rita, if you can," Billy adds.

"Piece of cake," Zack says breezily.

"Right." I ignore the swoop in my stomach. Capturing Rita has always been the fuzziest part of the plan.

"Rita is a secondary objective," Jason reminds us, "no matter what Zordon says." It's pretty impressive that Jason has come so far as a leader. He's not just taking Zordon's directives and goals as his own—he's working with us to decide what's best for the team. "Zack and Trini, you know what to do."

Yeah, I do. I just really, really wish it didn't involve heights.

"I'll fly as low as I can," Kimberly whispers to me. "And slowly too."

"Thanks." I try not to sound as queasy as I feel.

She pops open the door of the cockpit for me, and I climb out gingerly, pushing against the wind that threatens to suck me over the edge. Unfortunately, I make the mistake of looking down, and a sick, dizzy feeling shoots through me. My head goes light, and my knees turn rubbery. How did I not realize how tall the Zord was? *Oh hell.* I did not think this through. Kimberly isn't even *flying* the damn Pterodactyl yet and I'm already about to pass out.

There's a flash of black light, and Zack appears next to me on the metal back of the Zord. Billy did explain that the act of merging and unmerging with the Zords gives rangers a bit of teleportation power, but I'm not in any state to appreciate this scientific miracle. I'm too busy hyperventilating into my helmet.

Zack grips my arm. "Breathe, Trini." *I can't.* "Come on." His voice is calm and confident. "I know you can do this."

Breathe in through the nose. Expand your chest. Nai Nai's lessons take over, and I draw in a steady breath at last.

"There you go." Zack crouches down with me and wraps my fingers around the handles Billy has installed for this purpose. "Now, we're just going to hold on, and then when we get close enough to the Moon Palace, Kimberly's going to let us off." He doesn't elaborate how we're going to get off this monstrous bird, but there's really only one way: We're going to have to jump off.

My breathing quickens at the thought, but I just nod and grip the handles hard.

"Are you okay, Trini?" Billy asks anxiously. "I totally forgot you were afraid of heights."

"I'm fine." With Zack by my side, I can almost believe that.

"You're doing great," Jason says reassuringly even though he's probably thinking, *Why the hell didn't anyone tell me Trini was afraid of heights?*

"Sorry," I say, kicking myself for assuming the suit's powers or the urgency of our mission would be stronger than my lifelong phobia. "I didn't think it was going to be a problem."

"Um," Billy breaks in. "I'm getting some strange readings."

My body clenches. I *really* don't like being so high up with a surprise on the way.

"Strange how?" Jason asks sharply.

"I don't know." Billy's voice rises. "Trini and Zack, do you see anything out there?"

"I can't see anything in this damn storm," Zack says.

I peer out through the gray shifting sands. Is that a shadow moving over the ground? "Actually . . ." My stomach slithers in fear. "I think I *do* see something."

"What is it?" Kimberly asks.

A shadow. No, *more* than one. Even with the fine dust blowing over my visor—I can see them. My blood freezes.

"Putties," I breathe.

"Great. Just what we need—a Putty welcome party." Zack peers through the storm.

"How the hell did they know we'd be here?" There's a thread of panic in Jason's words, which is weird because he doesn't panic. This is really bad.

Guilt slams into me. It was my idea to attack Rita on the moon, so if this goes sideways, it won't be Jason's fault. It will be mine.

"No reason to worry yet." Jason's voice sounds calm again. "We've been training for different scenarios, and this is one of them. We're better prepared than the last time we encountered them."

"I have a reading on the Putties now, and they're coming in fast." There's a thump like Billy just hit his dashboard in frustration. "They'll be here in minutes."

"How many?" Zack asks, scanning the gray masses in the distance.

"I'd say at least a hundred," Billy replies.

"But no one saw us on our scouting mission!" Kimberly bursts out.

My throat constricts. Maybe we weren't as careful as we thought. Or more likely, Rita has a magic surveillance system. Yeah, we probably should have anticipated that.

"Never mind," Jason says. "Billy, release our Zords."

"On it." Billy sounds somber. He must be feeling bad about not detecting the Putties sooner. There's a loud clanking as the metal clamps holding the Zords to the bed of the trailer are released.

If only I could merge with my own Zord, we would stand a better chance in this fight. My stomach swirls with doubt.

"Trini." Zack looks down at me where I'm still crouching on the back of Kimberly's Zord. "Now is probably not the time, but I wanted to say—"

That gets through to me. "Don't you dare apologize, Zack Taylor."

"Noted." His voice is amused. "I was just going to say that you look super hot in that yellow suit."

"Damn right." Warmth flares through me. Zack saw that I was spiraling in guilt and understood exactly how to distract me from my thoughts.

I know what I have to do.

Heart pounding in fear, I let go of the handles and stand up, bracing myself against the sand whipping all around us. "Zack, you need to merge with your Zord." I refuse to look down.

"You'll be on your own." The amusement is gone from his voice.

A gleam of gold flashes across the sky, and Billy yells, "It's Goldar!"

Damn. I remember Goldar launching himself into the air with one stroke of his powerful wings and using his deadly magical sword to strike Kimberly's Pterodactyl hard enough to do serious damage.

Someone has to take out Goldar before he has a chance to use his sword on the Zords.

"Get to your Zord, Zack." A stream of power runs down my arms, but it's not time to form my daggers yet. "Kimberly, get me as close to Goldar as you can."

"What?" she exclaims at the same time Zack says, "Damn."

"Are you out of your mind?" Billy asks, but Jason cuts across him.

"Do it." Jason knows we stand a better chance if we don't have to worry about Goldar coming after our Zords.

And as the only one without a Zord—I'm the one who has to stop him. "I won't be on my own, Zack," I say, "but you have your part to do, and I have mine."

"Be careful." Zack inhales audibly. Then, in a flash of light, he's gone. His Mastodon paws the bed of the trailer and jumps off to join Billy's Triceratops and Jason's Tyrannosaurus Rex.

My breath flutters in my chest like a trapped moth as I crouch down again and grab the handles. "I'm ready when you are, Kimberly."

That's when Goldar lands with a mighty thud among the gray masses closing in on us. "Putties, attack!" he roars.

"Offensive Formation Dinosaur Stomp!" Jason yells. "Kimberly and Trini, break off. The rest—attack!"

"Here we go," Kimberly says as the Pterodactyl lifts off.

My stomach plummets. *Oh crap, oh crap, oh crap.* I cling to the handles, my hands growing sweaty in the gloves of my suit. At this speed, the wind buffets me even harder, threatening my footing. But I'll be damned if I fail my team again. I grit my teeth and concentrate on crouching down on the slippery metal back of the Zord. We race toward Goldar, and I notice that he's holding his sword loosely at his side and casually surveying the battle from the ground. *Good.*

Billy's Triceratops and Jason's Tyrannosaurus Rex are stomping through Putties as they flank Zack's Mastodon, spearing Putties on its tusk and flinging them aside. The Dinosaur Stomp routine is definitely a winner.

Suddenly, the Pterodactyl is right over Goldar, but he's raising his sword, which blazes like a dozen red suns. He's aiming it right at Zack's Zord. Any second now, he'll launch himself up into the air and attack. Oh, *hell* no. Taking one more fortifying breath, I release my death grip on the handles.

And then I leap straight off the Pterodactyl's back into the swirling gray storm.

CHAPTER
THIRTY

Shooting toward the gold of his armor like an arrow seeking its mark, I slam into Goldar with both feet.

Goldar didn't even see me coming. "I will crush you, human pustule!" he yells as he falls to the ground.

I leap to the side as Goldar springs to his feet, but before he can swing his sword at me, I make my own move, forming my power daggers. He brings up one gauntleted arm to block the dagger I thrust at his throat, but that's not my true target.

As one dagger rings against the metal gauntlet, I plunge the other dagger into the glowing blade of his sword, feeling the jarring impact of the strike all the way to my shoulder. The sword breaks apart in a shower of sparks and smoke, and the force of the explosion throws me several feet backward. I was not expecting the sword to *burst* like that.

I come down on my feet and stab my daggers into the ground to stop myself from skidding. A fierce exultation fills me. *Take that, Goldar.*

"Nice!" Zack yells. "I'm going to call that play the Sword Buster Routine."

Goldar throws the hilt of his ruined sword at me with a frustrated roar, but I backflip away to avoid being hit. Elation fills me. I can't believe that actually worked.

"Empress," Goldar calls out, raising his hands to the dark swirling sky. "Send me your aid!"

Aid? My belly goes cold.

"That does not sound good," Kimberly says as her Zord blasts Putties with pink lasers. "I'm guessing we can plan on more Putties?"

"It will take them a while to get from the Moon Palace," Billy says, bringing his Zord into a protective position between me and Goldar. "According to my calculations, the Putties can run point two miles a minute—"

Kimberly interrupts him. "How long until they get here?"

"Roughly fifteen minutes." Billy swings his tail cannon around to casually pick off the few Putties trying to climb his Triceratops. His aim has definitely improved.

"Then we need to mop these guys up fast." Zack stomps more Putties while Kimberly shoots the ones Zack misses. Her aim has improved too.

Goldar launches into the air and tries to fly over Billy's Triceratops to get to me, but Billy whips up his tail cannons and fires at Goldar.

He is forced to retreat back to the ground by Billy's blasts. "How dare you attack the mighty Goldar! My mistress will see you suffer for this affront."

I jump-kick a few Putties coming at me. There are only a few dozen Putties left standing, but who knows how many more are coming? "Billy, how fast can the Zords go?" I refuse to glance at my Sabertooth Tiger still on the space trailer as I stab another attacking Putty in the chest with a dagger.

"The ground ones can move at point two five miles a minute, but they're much slower than the Pterodactyl."

"Still faster than the Putties," Zack says, still stomping Putties. "I see what you're getting at, Trini."

"Me too," Jason says as his Zord charges through the remaining Putties. "Okay, new plan. Trini, hop aboard Billy's Zord. We'll evade the incoming Putties and circle back to the Moon Palace, taking it while it's undefended. Kimberly, guard our retreat but rejoin us before the Putty reinforcements get here. Your main job is to keep Goldar too distracted to follow us."

"With pleasure." She swoops down on a swordless Goldar, who leaps aside from her lasers. This could actually work. My hopes lift as I run through the blasting wind to Billy's Triceratops.

And then the solar storm stops suddenly.

Or, more accurately, the sand and pebbles are all sucked into one whirling funnel of gray next to Goldar. *What the hell?*

Kimberly swears as her Pterodactyl gets caught on the edge of the tornado and spins out of control.

"Kimberly!" I scream, heart in my throat. I'm not the only one yelling. Everyone else is too, but I'm too focused on the pink Zord in the sky to make out what the others are saying.

"I'm okay," Kimberly says breathlessly as her Pterodactyl straightens out, "but what just happened?"

"Good question," Jason says grimly. "Billy, I don't suppose that's a typical solar storm?"

"No, definitely not."

"Trini," Zack says urgently, "you need to get into Billy's Zord now."

"Right." I'm already sprinting toward the Triceratops. I didn't need Billy to tell me that's an unnatural solar storm, and I definitely don't want to be out in it.

Then the cyclone dissipates in an eruption of yellow flames, revealing Rita with her scepter in one hand and a wicked smile on her face.

Next to her, Goldar stands tall, his red eyes alight with exultation. "Now you will all know what it is to suffer."

Oh hell. My stomach sinks as I remember how Rita used her scepter to conjure Putties from the ground. The remaining Putties fall back and form a line behind Rita and Goldar.

"I guess we don't have those fifteen minutes before we have to fight more Putties," Zack says wryly.

"No one panic," Jason says steadily. "Remember our training. We'll go with the Alpha routine. Kimberly, take point. The rest of us will fall behind her in Defensive Triangle Formation."

"Got it." Her Pterodactyl flies over to hover before Rita.

"But what about Trini?" Billy protests.

That's right. Defensive Triangle Formation involves the ground Zords facing outward to guard each other's backs against Putties. I won't be able to get to Billy's Triceratops in time.

"I can handle myself." I grip the hilts of my daggers and move aside to give the Zords room for the Defensive Triangle Formation—but not so far that I can't help. It won't be like last time when I cower in fear while the others fight. Jason's Tyrannosaurus Rex faces Rita while Zack's Mastodon and Billy's Triceratops form a triangle behind him to guard all sides.

"Pity." Rita takes a step toward Jason's Zord, ignoring Kimberly above her. "It seems you did not take me up on my generous offer to trade Zordon for your pathetic town and your little lives."

"Should I blast her?" Kimberly mutters over the comms. "I'm right here."

"No," I say, eyeing Rita's scepter. "She's too dangerous."

"I agree," Jason says. "Don't attract her attention, Kimberly, and watch out for that scepter."

The scepter. What if I can get to it before Rita can summon her Putties?

Jason's voice booms out of the Tyrannosaurus Rex. "We're not going to let you destroy Angel Grove, Rita."

"It won't be up to you, Red Ranger." Then her gaze slides to me. "What have we here? One of these things is not like the others," she purrs. "Lost your Zord, Yellow Ranger?"

My body tenses. I hoped to stay unnoticed. A dozen fiery retorts rise to my lips but I bite them all back. I have to convince her I'm insignificant. "I suppose so." My eyes burn as I wrench my gaze from her scepter.

"This one destroyed my sword." Goldar glares at me. *Damn that winged monkey.*

"Hey, how do you get your Zord to talk, Jason?" Zack asks. "I'm working on some insults for Goldar involving moon and gold cheese, and they would be awesome coming out of the mouth of a giant Mastodon."

"Psychic connection," Billy reminds him. He's getting really good at boiling down complicated scientific explanations.

"Zack," I whisper, "can you insult Rita instead?"

"Why would you want Zack to insult Rita?" Billy asks.

"Hell," Zack says flatly, understanding exactly what I'm planning. "You're going after the scepter, aren't you?"

"You know it." I keep my voice low. Rita can't hear the others in their Zords unless they deliberately broadcast, but she'll be able to hear me if I speak above a whisper.

"So, you destroyed Goldar's sword." Rita's eyes rest on me with more interest than I'd like. "Not so weak after all, are you, little Yellow Ranger?"

I reply, my voice loud, "I think my friend here has something to say to you."

"We don't have a routine or any calls for this play," Jason protests.

"Jason!" Kimberly exclaims in exasperation.

"Sorry," he says sheepishly. "Zack, insult the space sorceress so Trini can steal her scepter."

"On it." Zack's Mastodon breaks formation and turns toward Rita.

I have no doubt that he's got this. Zack is the funniest person I know. Also the sweetest, most generous, and hottest, but maybe this isn't the right time to be thinking of that.

Rita ignores the Mastodon like she ignores the Pterodactyl hovering overhead. Her eyes are fixed on me. "I know what your friends can do, but I'd like to see what *you* can do."

"Distraction," Zack mumbles. "Okay, here goes." His voice comes out of his Zord. "Hey Rita, how many Putties does it take to screw in a light bulb?"

Okay . . . maybe my confidence was misplaced.

Rita's turns to the Mastodon, her face scrunched up in puzzlement. "What?"

"You tell me—you're the Putty baker."

Kimberly flat-out groans. "Come on, Zack. You can do better than that."

Zack doesn't respond to her. "Knock knock," his Zord voice says cheerfully. "Don't they have knock-knock jokes on the moon, Rita? Here's how they go. I say 'Knock knock,' and then *you* say, 'Who's there?'"

I'm starting to see what Zack is doing. He isn't trying to crack good jokes. He's just trying to get Rita's attention—and it's working. She isn't looking at me anymore, and neither is Goldar. They're both staring at the giant mastodon telling knock-knock jokes.

I start edging toward Rita. Zack knows the trick to a good distraction isn't to be funny—it's to be *distracting*.

"Enough!" Rita gives herself a little shake. "It is time to end this little chat, as odd as it has been."

I freeze and assess the distance between us. Even with my suit's power and the lack of gravity, it's still too far for me to leap and take her by surprise. Frustration shoots into me. I was *so* close.

"It was a good try, Trini." Jason sighs. "Zack, get back into the Defensive Triangle Formation. Everyone, prepare for Putties."

"Will do," Zack says dejectedly. His Mastodon falls back into position.

"Remember," Rita says, "I gave you the chance to avoid this fate." She raises her scepter, the red jewel on top glowing brightly.

Even though I know it's useless, I run toward her and take a flying leap and land at least ten feet short of her. Goldar bares his teeth threateningly at me, but instead of attacking me, he turns toward Rita and kneels.

Before I can wonder what's going on, Rita points her scepter at *him*. The jewel releases a bright glare of red light as she exclaims, "Arise, my great warrior!"

Warrior? As in singular? And why are there no gray blobs rising from the ground like last time? Confusion and dread sit like a weight in my stomach.

And then Goldar begins to grow.

Oh, *hell* no.

CHAPTER
THIRTY-ONE

Please tell me it's my imagination," Kimberly says shakily, "but is Goldar getting bigger?"

Damn. Kimberly sees it too. There goes my theory that I'm hallucinating.

"It's not your imagination," Jason says glumly.

Goldar springs up from his kneeling position, and his armored wings flare out, twice the span they originally were—and he's still growing. "Nothing will stop me," he roars at us, "until I crush you in the name of my empress!"

"A little long for a catchphrase," Zack comments, "but it does have a certain flare." Despite his casual bravado, I can tell that he's scared too.

"Rita must have used a lot of power to create so much mass," Billy murmurs.

It's true that she's leaning heavily on her scepter, and her red lips are at odds with her pale face. This is my chance to get to her while she's vulnerable, but then I glance at Goldar at her side, and icy fear sweeps through me. The Zords are now dwarfed by Goldar, who is now the size of a tall building. We don't stand a chance against something that big. Even more frightening is Rita. Despite her clear exhaustion, vengeance burns in her eyes as she stands in front of the towering chaotic power she is about to unleash on us.

I have to do something—at least try. Maybe Goldar is so big that he won't notice me sneaking up on him, and then I can . . . do what exactly? Climb into one of his red glowing eyes and annoy him?

To hell with it—I'll figure it out as I go. "I have to get closer," I say.

"Absolutely not!"

"No effing way!"

"Nope!"

"Not going to happen!"

They all speak at once, so I'm not entirely sure who said what, but the overall message is clear. "Okay! I got it. I won't attack the enchantress and the giant gold monster on my own."

"Good," Zack says tersely. "Jason, we don't have a routine for Goldar-on-steroids that I forgot about, do we?"

Jason just grunts in response. "Billy, how long will it take us to all get back on the space trailer and take off?"

"Too long," Billy says shortly.

"Right," Jason says like he knew that would be the answer. "Kimberly, pick up Trini and get out of here."

"I'll get Trini," Kimberly says, "but I'm not leaving."

"I'm not going anywhere either." My throat closes as I glance up at Kimberly's Pterodactyl, still circling. She's the only one who can escape. I should encourage her to leave, but it's obvious she feels the same way I do. Neither of us will abandon this team.

"Trini," Zack says, a catch in his voice. "I don't want to watch you die."

I shudder as my eyes turn to his Mastodon. I don't want to watch him die either, but it's better than leaving him. "There's not enough time for Kimberly to get me anyway."

"We'll give you the time," Billy says resolutely. "We can cover your escape."

"Go," says Jason. "Both of you."

"No." I stare up at Goldar looming over us. *We won't survive this.* Out loud, I say, "We'll stand together."

Then Goldar stops growing, and my heart beats in wild fear. His red eyes sweep over us in malignant triumph, but he stays towering behind Rita as if he's a monstrous attack dog waiting for her command.

"Believe it or not," Rita says somberly, "I take no joy in your destruction. It was Zordon's death that I craved. Not yours."

"That's small consolation," I say bitterly.

"I imagine it is." Rita raises her scepter, and her yellow flames are weaker and dimmer than before. Behind her, the remaining Putties melt into the ground, but I barely notice. They're nothing to the threat of Goldar. "Be that as it may, I have no desire to watch you all die in the name of that pathetic so-called warrior."

I gape at her. "Does that mean you're going to let us go?"

"No," Rita says, almost regretfully. "It means that I'm not going to stay and watch." She looks up at her gigantic general. "Goldar, you may attack."

Then she disappears into her flickering fire, and chills feather over my body.

"At last!" With a ferocious cry, Goldar gives one thunderous flap of his deadly wings and shoots up into the sky. Kimberly flits away and barely evades being swatted like a fly.

I swallow hard. *That was close.*

Kimberly circles back toward me. "Trini, I'm going to try to pick you up."

"Watch out," I yell, heart pounding, as Goldar streaks toward her.

"Damn!" She pulls up, flips her Pterodactyl around like she's doing a gymnastics move, and zooms away. "He's fast."

"I've got this," Zack says. His Mastodon charges at Goldar just as he starts to take to the sky after Kimberly's Pterodactyl again. They meet in a loud clash of tusks and gold armor, but then Goldar punches down at the Mastodon with one armored fist that lands with a sound like thunder.

My mouth goes dry with fear.

"Crap." Zack sounds shaken. "My control panel just flared out for a second. That's not a good sign, is it?"

"No." Billy doesn't elaborate, which isn't a good sign either.

"Disengage, Zack," Jason orders.

Zack's Mastodon breaks away from Goldar and retreats to the side of the Tyrannosaurus Rex. "Goldar isn't just bigger," he says soberly.

"He's faster and stronger too," I finish for Zack, despair spreading through me.

"Break formation!" Jason yells. "Dodgeball Routine."

That's not a routine we came up with, but no one asks questions. We all know what he means—we're out of plays, and now we have only one goal. My belly trembles with fear. *Try not to die.*

"On my way to you, Trini," Zack says. The three ground Zords break from the triangle formation, and Zack heads toward me.

"Okay." I retract my daggers and balance on the balls of my feet, ready to spring onto the Mastodon and climb up to the cockpit as fast as I can. My fear of heights can just be damned.

Then Goldar lands between us with an impact that makes the ground rumble. It takes all my training to keep my footing, and even Zack's Mastodon stumbles. My hands grow slippery with sweat, and I really want to form my daggers and stab that overgrown monkey right in his smug face. Unfortunately, a dagger will feel like a mere bee sting at his current size.

"You all want to protect this weak little Yellow Ranger so badly," Goldar sneers, turning away from me to face the others. "What makes her so special?"

"She's our friend." That comes from Kimberly's Zord as she swoops down and takes a position right over Zack's Zord. "So hands off."

"She's one of us." Billy's Triceratops lumbers next to Zack and lowers its horned head as if ready to charge. "We won't let you hurt her."

A lump forms in my throat.

"She's not weak." Zack's voice is firm. "She is the strongest person I know."

If I'm strong, it's because of his belief in me. Tears sting the back of my eyes. I can't let him down. I can't let any of them down. I inhale a lungful of air, and something hard shifts across my chest. The Power Coin. My breath stops, and I hardly dare to hope.

"She's a Power Ranger." Jason's Tyrannosaurus Rex takes its place next to Billy. "Offensive Line Formation, everyone."

His words hit me like a blow to the solar plexus. *Offensive* line formation.

My team isn't just protecting me; they're going to fight for me.

"Fine," Goldar snarls without a backward look at me. "Then you will all die."

Not if I can help it. I whirl toward my Sabertooth Tiger with its tall metal body and ferocious swordlike teeth. My fears and doubts kept me from merging with my Zord before, and I can't deny that I'm definitely still afraid. But if I don't try, my friends will die. Billy keeps saying it's a matter of psychic connection. I try to imagine myself inside the cockpit of my Zord . . . but just like every other time, nothing happens.

My heart fills with bitterest disappointment.

"Zack and I will flank," Jason says quickly, "while Billy and Kimberly charge straight on. Attack!" he yells, and they all move toward Goldar.

With a sneer, Goldar extends his deadly wings to knock aside Jason and Zack on either side of him. Then he seizes the Triceratops with both clawed hands, ignoring the pink lasers Kimberly is shooting at him, and throws Billy's Zord at the Pterodactyl. Both Zords go crashing in the distance.

Shock washes over me even as the Triceratops stumbles to its knees and the Pterodactyl flutters its wings. But the Triceratops doesn't make it all the way to its feet, and the Pterodactyl doesn't fly back up.

"I'm okay," Billy says shakily, "but I think I'm down."

"Me too." Kimberly sounds furious.

Goldar laughs. "Your little dinosaur vehicles are so easily overpowered!"

Icy fear floods my veins. He's toying with us. Goldar could finish us off at any time, but he's going to draw out the battle for his own amusement.

"Jason," Zack says urgently, "your Zord is faster than mine." He follows it up with a bunch of rapid-fire football terminology that causes Jason to audibly hiss out his breath. Before I can process what's happening, Zack's Mastodon is leaping at Goldar while Jason's Tyrannosaurus Rex gallops toward me.

No! My body goes still, and everything narrows into the moment the Mastodon slams into Goldar's armored chest. Zack's play becomes suddenly, painfully clear—he's sacrificing himself to give Jason a chance to save me.

Goldar staggers back as the Mastodon bounces off him and back to the ground, but with a flap of his wings, Goldar regains his balance. He throws back his head and roars . . . but not with anger. To my horror, I realize he's laughing. "Is that all you have?" he demands. "I thought Zordon's legendary Power Rangers would be harder to beat."

My mind goes white hot with anger. There's no hesitation in me as I take a flying leap at the Tyrannosaurus Rex approaching me. Hitching a ride on a dinosaur is the best way to get to Zack. I was aiming for the Zord's shoulder, but I fall a little short and end up clinging to its stubby arm. My gloved fingers frantically scrabble at the smooth metal, and my stomach churns with terror as I start to slide.

Then the fingers of my gloves suddenly flare with light, and then they're sticking to the slippery metal of the Zord. Gratitude for interstellar tech flows over me as I start to climb. "Jason, we have to help Zack."

"I'm not sure if we can." But Jason is already turning in a swift move that has me clinging to his Zord's side for dear life.

Move, Trini, I tell myself sternly. Breathlessly, I keep climbing, my gloves sticking and peeling exactly as I need them to. As soon as I pull myself up to the Zord's shoulder, I turn to the battle between Goldar and Zack with my heart in my throat.

Almost lazily, Goldar pulls back his leg and kicks Zack's Zord like it's nothing more than an annoying dog to him. It crashes down next to Billy's and Kimberly's Zords and twitches as if in pain.

I gasp. "Zack!"

"I'm fine." He sounds anything but fine.

"Hold on, Trini," Jason says grimly, suddenly swerving to change directions. My boots glow as they cement me to his Zord's shoulder, but that doesn't stop the rush of dizzy terror in my head. Then he's racing toward the others with me perched on his shoulder in a crouch. He comes to a screeching halt next to our friends in a heap of downed Zords. "We'll make our final stand together."

He doesn't mention that the two of us are the only ones left standing, and I don't count. Not without my Zord.

Goldar peers at us, his face grotesquely contorted with delight. "Look at you, humbled in your defeat," he says as he passes a cluster of tall, jagged gray boulders.

Then he picks up the boulder in mid-stride and throws it.

Oh hell. The boulder is coming right at us. My stomach shudders, and I have just enough time to peel my boots off Jason's Zord and jump before the boulder collides into the chest of the Tyrannosaurus Rex. I land on the ground and then immediately leap aside and take cover behind Zack's fallen Mastodon. Jason's Zord staggers against the boulders that Goldar is pummeling him with. Horror seizes my body. Jason won't last long under the onslaught.

Then the Tyrannosaurus Rex comes crashing down in a thunderous collision with the ground, gray dust rising into the air in thick, sooty plumes. From behind the leg of the Mastodon, I stare at the Zord's dented red body, my pulse thumping in disbelief.

"Dammit," Jason curses. "I'm out now too."

I don't say what I'm thinking, and neither does anyone else—that it wouldn't have mattered anyway. One Zord couldn't have beaten Goldar.

"At least we're together," Kimberly says. "Any plays left, Jason?" Her tone makes it plain that she already knows the answer.

"Sorry." Jason's voice is heavy with defeat.

Everything in me aches. All Kimberly ever wanted was to be a good friend, and all Jason ever wanted was to be a good leader. Kimberly cares more about us than her image or popularity, and Jason has learned that being a leader isn't about being in charge—it's about putting the team before himself. I wish I could tell them that they're more than they ever wanted to be. My eyes fill with tears as I think of Billy rushing over the football field to help the two bullies who had tormented him throughout high school. His desire to help was stronger than his anger or fear, and I want to tell him how he's always inspired me. And then there's Zack. I love how seriously he takes all of us. I hope he knows how much that means to me. How much *he* means to me.

"I just want to say . . ." Billy clears his throat. "It has been an honor to be on this team with you." It should have sounded sappy, but it doesn't. Not coming from Billy.

"Yes," Zack says gravely, "it has been an honor."

Tears burn down my face. I realize this might be the last chance I get to tell any of them how I feel. There's no time to say everything, but this will have to be enough. "Hey, everyone." My chest swells with the raw hurt of emotion. "I love you all."

"Same." Kimberly sounds like she's fighting back tears.

"Me too," Jason echoes.

"Exactly what I was thinking," Billy says.

"Yeah." In a choked voice, Zack says, "I love you. All of you."

My throat closes. I'm standing next to a bunch of wrecked Zords, certain that I belong to this team more than I've ever belonged to anything—and I feel sliced apart because this will be the last time we're all together.

I can't let that happen. Desperate love rushes into me.

I have to try one more time.

"I am tired of this game." Goldar is striding over to us, his every step making the barren lunar ground quake. "It is time to end it. Time to end *you*, little Rangers."

Fear and doubt twist through me. He'll kill us all if I can't do this. I glance over at the bright yellow gleam of my Zord, still stationary on the space trailer, and then back at my friends' damaged, banged-up Zords. Goldar is getting closer, his red eyes glittering with malice.

My fingers stiff with terror, I place my hand where the coin rests heavy against my chest. Against my heart. *Come on, Sabertooth Tiger Zord.*

Something deep inside me stirs. *A connection.* Nai Nai said that I had to stop trying to mold myself into what others expect and tap into the connection with my own culture and heritage. My tiger is how I fight for my friends, but it's not the giant metal tiger Zord I need. I need the one that has been inside of me all along.

I can almost hear the whisper of my nai nai's voice in my ear. *Xiao Laohu.* That is who I am. My grandmother's Little Tiger, just as she was her own mother's Little Tiger. I am the tiger descended from a long line of women that stretches back for generations to arrive here, in this moment—with these four people I love. *That* is the tiger I am.

I feel a jolt of power, and there's a bright flash of yellow light that makes me close my eyes. When I open them again . . . I am sitting inside a cockpit with a loud purring sound in my ears and in my own chest.

I am the Yellow Sabertooth Tiger.

CHAPTER THIRTY-TWO

No freaking way! Shock ripples through me as I stare around at the gleaming lights and metal walls inside my Zord. It's like the cockpit of Zimberly's Pterodactyl, except this one is *mine*. Fierce pride rushes through me. I feel like I'm in the beating heart of a tiger. No—I *am* the tiger. Courageous and powerful. I stretch out an experimental hand, and my paw moves at the same time. Okay, this is really happening.

Goldar pauses in his march our direction, and his head swivels toward me as if the movement caught his attention.

"Trini, where did you go?" Zack's voice is panicked.

"Um, I think I merged with my Sabertooth Tiger." I still can't quite believe it.

There is a moment of stunned silence, and then Billy yells, "Megazord!"

"Yes!" Jason shouts.

"Yay! Way to go, Trini!" Kimberly cheers.

"Go Go Trini!" Zack echoes.

Out of the corner of my Zord eye, I see Goldar give himself a small shake and turn back to the others. I need to grab his attention fast, so I give a twitch of my tail.

He stops again. "So, the little Yellow Ranger has her Zord."

I see you have found your path, Xiao Laohu, I imagine my nai nai saying fondly. Yes, I am the Little Tiger. But now I can be big—with all my friends.

"No matter." Goldar changes direction and begins to stride toward me. "I prefer to fight you this way."

Oops. I didn't expect to get that much of his attention. "Hey, everyone, can we figure out the Megazord situation? I really don't want to go one-on-one with Goldar."

"Copy that." Zack's Zord struggles to rise but falls down again.

"Billy," Jason says urgently, "how do we form the Megazord again?"

"Psychic connection," he replies promptly.

Um . . . okay. "I think we already knew that." My Zord body tenses as Goldar smiles at me in a truly terrifying way, fangs on full display.

"You are the Ranger who destroyed my sword," Goldar says. "I hope you will give me a better challenge than your friends did."

I gulp, and my Zord shifts restlessly on the bed of the trailer.

"We're going to need a little more instruction, Billy," Kimberly says, desperation in her voice.

"I don't know what else to say," he replies frantically. "Didn't you say my explanations were too detailed and scientific? Well, I *really* don't have time to go into it now."

"Something between 'psychic connection' and a two-hour nanotech lecture would be nice," Zack says. "That blue monkey is going after Trini!"

All their Zords are now writhing on the ground, straining futilely to get to me. Even though they can't help, an aching love for my friends pulses through my body. I feel it then—the same thrum of energy that binds me to my tiger.

"Actually," I say, "maybe Billy has already told us all we need." Goldar is almost to me, and I crouch down, feeling the power gather in my hind legs. I'll bet I can jump a *lot* higher in my Zord than I could on my own legs, suit-powered or not.

"What do you mean?" Jason asks, an anxious note leaking through the stoic calm he's clearly trying to maintain.

"We've been training for this," I say, thinking of the hours we spent practicing routines and plays. "We can do this."

"Forming the Megazord isn't as easy as doing the Pyramid Routine!" Kimberly says.

"Why not?" Billy asks practically.

"I'm in," Zack says. "Go Go Friend Pyramid Routine!"

I couldn't have said it better myself. My tail flicks in readiness. "I just need to get to you all."

Goldar is nearing, and I can smell his rage and triumph. I envision tackling him like a play out of Jason's football book. But that's not what I have to do.

I launch myself up in the air toward Goldar . . . and leap over his head. Then I'm flat out racing to my friends as Goldar bellows behind me. I can feel the rumble of his footsteps as he gives chase, but at least he's not flying after me.

"Focus on *our* connection!" I call out breathlessly, my muscles straining with the effort of outrunning Goldar. There is no separation between my human body and the body of my Sabertooth Tiger—and that's the connection I have to make with my friends. "We're a team. That's all we need!"

There's a powerful jerk in my stomach as I slide to a stop next to my friends, and my Zord begins to elongate upward, my tiger head forming the powerful right foot of a collective being that stirs in the deep recesses of my subconscious.

It's as if I have always known exactly what the Megazord will look like—and my part in it.

Goldar grinds to a halt in clear shock. "What is this?" His gauntleted gold hand pulls back in a fist.

But he's too late.

Our connection is beyond Goldar's comprehension, and my team knows what to do without any further discussion.

Next to me, Billy's Zord is transforming in the same way as mine, his Triceratops head becoming the left foot and its body the left leg. Jason's Zord is forming the torso, Zack's Zord wraps around the back, forming arms with the Mastodon's head as the left hand, and Kimberly's Zord attaches to the back to give the Megazord flight. A head arises from the neck, but it is not the Tyrannosaurus Rex's head. It is the head of a helmed and horned warrior that represents us all.

There is a flash of red, black, pink, blue, and yellow light—and I am no longer in my Sabertooth Tiger Zord.

I am a part of the Megazord and in the head's cockpit with my friends. Disbelief shoots through me. *We actually did it.*

And then there's an eruption of voices.

"Way to go, Trini!" Zack pumps his fist in the air from the seat behind me.

"I can't believe we actually formed the Megazord!" Billy says from next to Zack.

"Alright!" Jason yells from the seat next to mine.

"Friendship Pyramid Routine rocks!" Kimberly bounces in her seat on the other side of Jason.

"Maybe we could just call it the Megazord Routine," I suggest with a grin.

"Whatever we call it," Jason says, "we still need to fight Goldar."

On cue, Goldar exclaims, "Your robot is no match for my empress's sorcery!" Then the Megazord is rocked by a fist slamming into its chest.

Pain explodes in me, and I gasp from the staggering blow to my own heart. Right. *Psychic connection.* It feels as if my vision, as well as the rest of me, is divided in two—separate but also connected to the Megazord. Part of me sits in the cockpit with the others, but part of me can see Goldar, roughly the same size as we are, pulling back his fist for another attack. Pulse racing, I brace myself.

"Zack, block!" Jason yells. "Billy, step up! Trini, kick!"

Oh. *Yes!* I will never criticize Jason for telegraphing his moves ever again.

Zack brings up the left arm to block, Billy moves the left leg to shift us into position—and I kick Goldar right in his gold-armored crotch.

Goldar howls, staggering back, and fierce satisfaction fills me. If the students at Angel Grove High could see me now, they wouldn't think I was so meek and mild-mannered.

With a powerful beat of his wings, Goldar shoots straight upward. "I will crush you for this affront!" He clearly intends to drop down on us.

"Kimberly," Jason calls out, but she's already taking us up in a rush of speed.

"Literally already on it," she says as we fly up and crash into Goldar in a tangle of wings, dinosaur heads, and angry screams on Goldar's part.

Jason wastes no time in shifting into quarterback mode, calling out a flurry of moves. I understand now why Zordon made him the leader, and it's not because he's faster or stronger or smarter than the rest of us—because he isn't. And it's not because he's white, straight, and male, either. Any one of us could have been the team leader, but the rest of us have other necessary roles.

Jason is the only one who can pull back and let us fight just like he must have done a hundred times before when he let the ball fly and trusted his teammates to catch it and take it down the field. When we trained, he was always the unmoving base of the pyramid or the one who pulled back and watched how we functioned, coordinating our moves. So he's not the one who has the arms to punch or the legs to kick or the wings to fly. He's here to support us all, and that's the lesson he learned as our leader.

Our movements flow together in beautiful, synchronous motions, blocking, kicking, punching, swiveling, and tumbling in midair. Goldar is forced into a defensive position, trying to pull away with ever more frantic beats of his wings, too battered to shout out insults.

And as we fight, I am somehow not afraid. I suppose all it took was being part of a Megazord to get me over my fear of heights. We flip away from Goldar's desperate lunge, and Billy and I kick out in unison, landing a blow square in Goldar's chest. He's thrown backward but recovers his balance with a frenzied flap of his wings.

"This isn't over!" Goldar is panting as he says it, and there is a bloody gash across his face and deep dents from my fangs, Zack's tusks, Billy's horns, and Kimberly's wings all over his armored body. It might not be over yet, but it will be soon, and he knows it. Abruptly, Goldar turns and flies away.

"Follow him!" Jason says.

Kimberly gives us a burst of speed. "He's not moving very fast. Should we catch up and finish this fight?"

"He's heading to the Moon Palace," Billy says.

"Back to Rita." My body tenses as I think of what else she might conjure up with her scepter.

"Can she make Goldar even bigger?" Zack asks.

Eek. I didn't even think about a bigger Goldar.

"I doubt it," Billy replies. "It's basically the first law of thermodynamics, which is what Einstein's law of conservation of mass and energy is based on."

"What?" Jason asks.

"E equals MC squared," Billy says, like that explains everything.

Maybe I should help out. "Rita needs energy to make stuff, and her battery has probably run out."

"Ah, got it," Jason replies.

"Isn't that what *I* just said?" Billy asks.

"I'll bet Goldar doesn't know that Rita is too drained to help him," Zack says gleefully. "He doesn't exactly seem like he has a degree in physics."

"You don't need a degree in physics to understand E equals MC squared," Billy mutters.

"So do I catch up with Goldar or not?" Kimberly asks.

"Let's hang back a bit," Jason says thoughtfully. "We can follow him to Rita."

My stomach tightens as I think of the pity in Rita's eyes as she left us to Goldar's untender mercies. I'm not sure she's as weakened as everyone thinks she is, but I have nothing to back up that hunch. It's just a feeling. "I thought you said capturing Rita was a secondary goal, Jason."

"It is," he replies, "but we still need to knock out the Moon Palace's generator or whatever it is that gives her the power to make Putties."

Jason has a point. I stare out at Goldar ahead of us, laboriously beating his wings as he slowly flies back to Rita. His empress might not have the magic to make him stronger, but Goldar will have a battalion of Putties to command at the Moon Palace. My mouth sets. "Billy, do you have a lock on the location of the off switch for that blue orb on top of the Moon Palace yet?"

"Sort of." Billy hesitates. "As far as I can tell, the highest concentration of power isn't actually in the orb. It's *under* the Moon Palace. Actually, my readings are showing unbelievable levels of power under the palace."

Zack groans. "So we have to tunnel down to take out the power source?"

"I'm not even sure if it's possible to destroy something that strong," Billy replies. "The good news is that it doesn't seem like Rita can access the power source directly. I'll bet she's using something to focus the energy—kind of like how we used our Morphers to focus the Power Coins before we could access them directly."

I touch the Sabertooth Tiger coin I wear on a chain over my heart. "So we have to destroy Rita's . . . Morpher?"

"Basically."

"No problem," Kimberly says. "We'll just fly over and smash the blue orb."

"Rita wouldn't leave something as powerful as a Morpher so exposed," Jason says glumly.

"Unfortunately, Jason is correct." Billy rubs the side of his faceplate like he's forgotten he's wearing a helmet. He's probably lost in the streams of data and numbers whizzing before his eyes. "I've analyzed the energy schematics, and I don't think the device Rita is using to access the power source is stationary. Actually, I don't think it's the blue orb after all."

"It's the scepter," I say with a dawning realization as I remember the red lightning streaming out of Rita's scepter to make Goldar grow to monstrous proportions.

"Exactly," Billy says.

There's a moment of stunned silence, and then Jason says, "Okay, if we find Rita, we find the scepter." He sighs. "Finding Rita is no longer a secondary objective."

So we're back to the original plan. I glance back at Zack. "It looks like you and I are sneaking into the Moon Palace."

"It's not how I imagined our first date going, but I'll take it," Zack says, and I can't help the thrill jolting through me. Then his voice turns serious. "Billy, can you track the scepter?"

"I should be able to, but I'll need to get closer to pinpoint the exact location."

"Actually, Billy . . ." Zack says, "you *are* closer."

"We all are," Kimberly says.

Below us looms the starkly gray Moon Palace with its leaning towers and spinning blue orb, and in front of it are *thousands* of Putties.

My muscles tighten with momentary fear, but I remind myself that this battle is different. I'm not holding back on using my powers anymore, and I'm fighting in tandem with my team.

And—together, we're one huge-ass Megazord.

"Now!" Jason yells. "Tackle Goldar." There's a kick of adrenaline in my body as Kimberly gives us a surge of power, and we lunge at Goldar.

"No!" Goldar bellows, swiveling in the sky to face us. "You will not defeat me."

But Zack is already closing our Megazord's arms around him, pinning his gold wings to his side.

Billy and I wrap our Megazord's legs around Goldar's thrashing body. Then I glance at the ground below us with my Megazord vision, but this time, it's not the fear of heights that makes my breath catch. "Those Putties are gathered pretty close together."

"We could take out most of them if we go fast enough to create an impact crater. We need to hit the ground *there*," Billy says excitedly, and because we're all connected, I can feel, in my very muscles, exactly where Billy means.

I'm amazed to find myself filled with unreasonable exhilaration at the thought of dropping from thousands of feet up in the sky, especially with Goldar twisting in our grasp and screaming, "You will all die painful, excruciating deaths!"

"I think it's time for the Putty Crush Routine," Kimberly calls out.

"Can we hurry?" Zack grunts. "Goldar is pretty squirmy, and his wings are still sharp."

"Do it," Jason says.

A rush of love for my teammates wells up in me, and before I know it, I'm yelling, "Go, go Power Rangers!" I guess Zack's ridiculous cheer is starting to grow on me.

And then we're plummeting down to the surface of the moon, and my stomach hurtles into the void.

CHAPTER THIRTY-THREE

We crash down onto the moon's surface with a thunderous boom, pulverizing countless Putties beneath Goldar's armored body and scattering even more with a resounding collision that craters the ground. The impact shudders through my bones, but the fierce power in my body does not fade.

"Woohoo!" Zack yells.

Beneath us, Goldar's eyes drift shut and blood dribbles down the side of his mouth. There are visible cracks in his golden armor now.

My triumph drains. "Is he dead?"

"I read life signs," Billy says, not bothering to hide his relief.

Faintly, Kimberly says, "Good."

"We can't . . ." Zack's words trail off, and he sounds sick as he drops the Megazord hand with the sharp tusks of the Mastodon to our side.

"We can leave Goldar here." Jason says. "I doubt he'll give us anymore trouble today."

We all breathe a collective sigh of relief as our Megazord rolls off Goldar and lumbers to its feet. None of us want to be killers. We're just teenagers assigned with the impossible task of saving our home from a space invasion. *Not so impossible now.*

I look out at the hundreds of remaining Putties that are gathered around the rim of the crater we made in our crash. Without their general or Rita commanding them, they don't seem to be as much of a threat. But then they start to swarm toward us, teeth bared and sharp fingers extended. *Never mind.*

At least the Putties can't do us any harm while we're in Megazord formation, but we can't exactly sneak up on Rita like this. "If Rita sees us coming, she'll teleport away," I say out loud.

"I think she'll see us coming," Zack says, "since we're the size of a building."

"We need to disassemble the Megazord," Jason says.

"Except for Trini's, our individual Zords are too damaged to fight," Billy points out.

"Then we fight without our Zords." Kimberly's fingers flex as if she's holding her bow.

"Kimberly is right," Jason says. "We've all been training to fight Putties in lunar conditions. Billy, Kimberly, and I just need to keep them occupied until Trini and Zack destroy Rita's scepter. We can do this."

"Works for me," Zack says.

"Me too." I don't need my Zord to fight. Like Nai Nai said, the tiger is part of Chinese myth and our own ancestry. The tiger is in me.

"Megazord, disassemble!" Jason calls out.

There's a flash of multicolored lights, and our individual Zords are lined up next to each other.

"Power Rangers, unmerge!" Jason says.

I feel an uncoupling with my Zord, and in another flash of light, I'm standing with my team on my own human legs, facing the advancing Putties.

Kimberly forms her bow while Jason and Billy shape their own weapons. "We've got this," Kimberly says as she begins shooting down oncoming Putties.

"I have a lock on Rita's scepter," Billy says, readying his lance. "Sending coordinates to you now." A little red light blinks in my vision.

"Got it," I say, trying to keep my voice steady. "We sneak into the Moon Palace, follow the red light to Rita, destroy her scepter, and capture her while we're at it so Zordon can lock her back up in a space dumpster." Gulp. Now that I'm saying that, I can imagine a *lot* going wrong with this plan.

"Piece of cake," Zack says, "if the cake were a space sorceress hell-bent on revenge, that is."

"Good luck, you two." Jason points his sword toward the Moon Palace and then brings it back to point toward the Putties. "Like Kimberly said, we'll cover you."

I take a deep breath and turn to Zack. "Ready for that date?"

⚡

"The red blinking dot is leading us down that hall on the left," Zack whispers from where we're crouched behind a wide, gray stone pillar. The inside of the Moon Palace is as stark and colorless as its exterior and seems to be made up of a labyrinth of stone walls and dim lighting. If we didn't have Billy's red dot, we wouldn't have a chance in hell of finding Rita and her scepter.

At least the interior of the Moon Palace *does* have Earth gravity, and according to our helmet readings, Earth atmospheric conditions as well, but we're keeping our helmets on anyway.

"Is it weird that we haven't run into any Putties yet?" I stand and peer around the pillar.

"Maybe the Putties are all outside fighting the others." He doesn't sound too sure about that.

I inhale. "It's okay. We're ready for anything." My hands tingle, but I don't form my daggers yet. It's enough to know they're there.

The red dot blinks in my peripheral vision, and like Zack says, it's leading us down the farthest hallway to the left. "Let's go."

He nods, and we make our way down the dark hallway. I'm about to see if my helmet has a flashlight, but then in a blink, I can see the passage between the stone walls, stretching ahead of us.

"Whoa," Zack says. "Night vision."

"Go slowly anyway," I say. "There might be booby traps, and we don't know if our suits have sensors for that kind of thing."

"Good point."

We fall silent and walk stealthily down the hall until we reach a metal-studded door. The red dot has stopped blinking, and my breath goes short.

Rita's scepter, and probably Rita herself, is behind the door.

Zack and I look at each other, and although we can't see each other's faces, I know we're thinking the same thing. His power axe appears in his hand, and my twin power daggers form in mine.

In one swift move, he chops through the hinges of the door with his axe, and I follow up with a kick. The door crashes down in a metallic thud to reveal a brightly lit room hung with colorful silks.

And sitting on the far end of the room in an ornate gold throne . . . is Rita. "I've been expecting you."

Shock thunders through me as my eyes lock on the scepter in her hand. *No. It's not possible.* The jewel on top is glowing red.

"Damn," Zack breathes. "It looks like her battery is recharged."

Panic flutters in my chest. I guess Billy's scientific calculations are no match for Rita's sorcery. But we've come too far to give up now. If we don't destroy the scepter, she'll create more Putties to attack Angel Grove.

I step over the fallen door and into the room, and Zack follows me. Rita rises from the golden depths of her carved throne and descends the stone steps of her dais with her scepter still in her hand. "That giant monstrosity you created was impressive. What was it that Zordon called it again?" Her mouth twists. "Oh yes, the Megazord. Zordon always had a flair for the mundane and obvious."

"Says an evil witch who calls herself Rita Repulsa," Zack says loudly.

"That," she says with an amused curve of her bright red mouth, "is fully intentional and not in the least bit mundane."

"Maybe we don't taunt the sorceress with the fully charged kill wand," I mutter to Zack.

"Right. Sorry," he replies. "Nervous habit."

"I admit that 'Rita Repulsa' is a little over the top," she says musingly, "but at least I don't pretend to be someone I'm not—unlike your mentor." Her voice turns bitter. "Was Zordon the one who said I was evil? I'm sure he never told you what *he* has done in our millennia-old war."

She means her daughter. My body ices over, and my steps slow to a stop. At my side, Zack halts too.

I could tell her the truth about Zordon, but Rita would never believe me. I swallow past my clogged throat. "He told us."

Her eyes harden. "Then I suppose you are here to kill me on Zordon's orders."

"No," Zack says. "We're here to capture, not kill."

She sweeps her contemptuous gaze over the weapons in our hands. "Really?" Then she shrugs. "It doesn't matter. I will not let Zordon imprison me again. He only succeeded before because he had my daughter." Her voice goes low in pained fury. "But there is nothing in the universe that I love anymore. Your mentor has seen to that."

Sympathy twinges in me. "I am sorry you lost your daughter," I say, groping for the words to get through to her. "I know you also fell in love on Earth and gave birth to your daughter there. You made your home in our world even if it was three thousand years ago, so you must understand what this place means to us. Please don't destroy our home. It was once your home too."

"You are wrong, Yellow Ranger," Rita says. "I was betrayed by everyone I ever loved on Earth except for the child I lost there. What kind of home is that?"

"I don't know," I say helplessly. If I lost my family to a home that never accepted me—I would feel the same way.

"Keep her talking," Zack whispers to me. I start. For a moment, I forgot our mission to destroy her scepter. "Distract and Destroy Routine, take two—except this time, you do the distracting and I'll do the destroying." His hand brushes my arm before he steps to the side, slowly moving out of Rita's direct line of sight.

He thinks I'm sympathizing with Rita to distract her, but that's not what I was doing. I was preoccupied by the ache spreading through my chest. I did not expect to feel this connection that pulls taut between Rita and me.

"We are not that different," Rita says, as if reading my mind. "You draw your power from the Morphin Grid with your coins." She raises her scepter, and I tense. Zack freezes, but she doesn't even glance at him. Her eyes are on me. "And I use my magic to siphon power from the same source."

My heart stutters in surprise. "What?" How can the source of her power to create Putties and grow giants be the same as mine? My power lets me tap into my inner strength and connection to my heritage and my team. Rita's is used for destruction and revenge.

"Another thing Zordon apparently never told you." Her smile is bitter. "Tell me, little Ranger, did your mentor warn you of how dangerous I am?"

Out of the corner of my eye, I see Zack sneaking ever closer to Rita but still nowhere near striking distance. I have to give him more time. "Yes." I'm careful to not look directly at Zack. "Zordon warned us that you'd destroy our home if we didn't stop you."

"Typical," she sneers. Abruptly, she says, "I told Goldar to bring me one of you alive. He failed in that, but you have been kind enough to come on your own."

Huh? I have no idea where she's going with this. And then, suddenly, with a flash of cold fear—I do understand. "You're going to use us as bait for Zordon."

"I am sorry for what comes next, but it has to be done. I want Zordon to feel some measure of the pain I felt at the loss of my child, so I will do to him what he did to me." Rita is looking at me with pity in her eyes. "But I only need one of you for bait. The other will be for revenge."

Horror explodes in me as she points her scepter at Zack.

CHAPTER THIRTY-FOUR

N o!" I scream, my throat raw with terror.

Red lightning shoots toward Zack, but he drops to the ground, narrowly avoiding her deadly attack. Relief floods me. He's always been fast on his feet.

Zack brings up his axe to block another blast from the scepter, but when the crackling energy hits it, the axe erupts into a shower of black shards.

That could have been Zack. Fear wraps around me, but I don't hesitate. Gripping my daggers, I run at Rita.

Throwing aside the axe, which disappears on contact with the floor, Zack zigzags away from the bursts of energy from Rita's scepter. "Strike two for the Distract and Destroy Routine," he says breathlessly as he ducks behind the monstrosity of her gold throne.

"Then we double-team her." I expect her to turn her scepter on me and give Zack a reprieve, but instead, she disappears in a swirl of yellow flames just as I leap toward her, one dagger extended and the other pulled back in preparation for a thrust. I land on the ground in a crouch, tingling from the heat of her magical flames but unhurt. *Where did she go?*

Rita reappears at the foot of the stone dais, and I'm springing to my feet, but before I reach her, she blasts her own throne with a flare of vivid red. The throne splits in half with a loud crack.

"Crap!" Zack leaps from the gold wreckage.

My heart thunders in fear. She has teleportation and a lightning strike that can split apart solid gold. I don't know how we can beat her, but we have to try. "Billy says that scepter has limited power before it needs to recharge," I yell as I sprint toward her again. "We just need to run down its battery again." I don't mention that it took growing a giant Goldar last time to deplete her scepter's power.

"Billy," Zack says grimly as he dodges red lightning, "may have been wrong about a couple of key things." My pulse leaps in panic when a bolt from Rita's scepter cracks open the stone floor at Zack's feet, forcing him to jump back.

Why the hell is Rita only targeting Zack? Abruptly, I swerve from my charge at her to intercept Zack instead.

As I come to his side, Rita lifts her scepter, and the lightning attack stops. "I'd prefer to keep you alive, Yellow Ranger. Stand aside."

"Move, Trini." Zack's voice is tense as he tries to pull away from me, but I stay by his side. I'll be damned if I let Rita kill him out of misguided revenge.

"So be it." Rita levels her scepter at us and blasts a streak of lightning that lands between us.

We leap apart, and she swings her scepter back at Zack. Anger rises in me, and I throw one of my daggers straight at the red jewel set on top of the scepter, but with a sideways swipe, she knocks it out of the air. The dagger skitters on the stone floor and then dissipates in a spark of light.

"Zordon never killed your baby!" I yell desperately, lunging toward her.

She gives no sign of hearing me, aiming another blast at Zack.

"I don't think she believes you," Zack says as he jumps back from her strike.

I attack her with a flying kick, but she sidesteps me, smoothly blocking my flurry of dagger strikes with her scepter and my jabs and kicks with her bare hand. *Damn her.* From the way she fights, it's clear that she's had thousands of years to practice her moves. The hooked hand of the Northern Praying Mantis style. The clawed grab of the Tiger style. She has the moves of a predator, but she's on defense. Why? The answer stops me cold. *Because I'm not the one she's hunting.*

In that moment, Zack, her chosen prey, is rushing toward us. With a burst of frantic energy, I windmill my arms in the circular motion of Tiger style. She blocks my dagger with her scepter, but the back of my other hand, fingers in the claw formation, strikes her on her shoulder. She staggers, but to my dismay, recovers her balance almost immediately.

"Very good." Her mouth curves up in a bright red smile—and then she disappears in yellow flames.

I spin toward Zack, sudden fear freezing my blood. *She's a predator like me.*

So I know what she will do.

Heart pounding, I leap at Zack and knock him to the ground. We go down in a tangle of limbs, and he shouts, "What the hell, Trini!" But I'm already throwing my dagger into the yellow flames just beginning to form behind where Zack was.

Rita takes shape with a gasp of pain. My dagger hilt is protruding out of her stomach, right below her metal breastplate. My gut twists. I did that—I stabbed her. My dagger disappears into sparks, and she clasps a hand to the ugly wound seeping blood over the rich fabric of her copper-colored gown. "That actually hurt," she hisses even as the red jewel on her scepter glows and the injury begins to close before my eyes. I'm strangely relieved, but

I suppose it's too much to hope that her self-healing magic will drain the scepter's powers. But it's an opening, at least.

"I'll go high," Zack says.

"I'll go low." Without another word to each other, we spring into action. He flies through the air, trying to kick the staff out of her hand while I go low and try to sweep her feet out from under her. She grimaces and makes a wide sweep of her scepter, blasting off lightning strikes that crack the floor and walls. She is *pissed*. Zack and I flip and jump out of the way, but when we land breathlessly side by side against a silk-hung wall, I see that the arm of his suit is singed. Fear catches at my breath. If that strike had hit him straight on—he'd be dead.

"One of you must die," Rita says flatly, "and frankly, I don't care which one of you it is anymore."

Panic closes my throat as I try to shove Zack behind me, but he's trying to do the same with me. Another red lightning strike shoots toward us. We duck and roll in opposite directions, but this time, heat flashes across the top of my skull, and there's a loud crack like bone splitting apart.

"Trini!" Zack's voice is more scared than I've ever heard it.

Shakily, I rise to my feet, and the two halves of my helmet fall to the floor with a thud. It was my helmet that's broken, not my skull. "I'm okay." I brace myself for more lightning, but then I see the yellow flames forming around Rita. *No!* "Zack, watch out!" He looks around frantically, arms up in a blocking position.

My legs tense to jump toward him, but then there's a swirl of yellow flames directly in front of me and the cool touch of a red jewel against my temple. I freeze.

"Surprise," Rita purrs. "I told you I don't care who dies anymore." The jewel of her scepter begins to glow red against my forehead, and my chest tightens as I try to step away only to find the silk-covered stone wall at my back.

"Kill me instead!" Zack screams, anguish ringing through his voice.

"No." His pain jolts me out of my fear. Then I look directly in Rita's eyes—although I might be prey, I will stare into my killer's face.

Rita's whole body suddenly stiffens, shock sweeping across her face. "Xiao Laohu," she whispers.

I gasp, my mind reeling. *Why the hell is Rita calling me 'Little Tiger'?*

The scepter she holds trembles. "You have her eyes." Then she lowers her scepter.

My body vibrates with a dawning realization. *Her daughter.* I have her daughter's eyes. The breath whooshes out of me. Xiao Laohu must have been Rita's nickname for her own daughter, just like what my nai nai calls me.

We have always been connected, Rita and I.

A tingle of energy thrums through me, and before I have time to form a conscious thought, I am striking out, the power racing down my arm to form a dagger right before I plunge its blade into the heart of the blood-red jewel. Bright light flares out as the jewel cracks open.

Rita stumbles back, keeping her hold on the scepter, but her face pales as she stares at the jagged wound in the jewel. Then she looks back at me, her face unreadable.

My heart thunders against my ribcage as I gaze back at her, unable to say anything at all. The dagger in my hand fades to nothingness as exhaustion washes over me. I know I should be trying to capture Rita, but I'm just trying to stay upright.

Zack races to my side and grabs me by the shoulders before I slump over. "Are you okay?"

I swallow hard, but any answer I could have given is interrupted by the patter of running footsteps.

As I turn toward the sound, I glimpse Rita slipping behind a silk hanging on the wall, her horned headdress the last thing I see before she disappears into a fall of red fabric. Is she trying to hide? Then Kimberly, Billy, and Jason burst into the room.

"Trini! Zack!" Billy charges in with his lance out like a jousting knight.

"Are you okay?" Kimberly swivels around, bow in hand.

"We came as fast as we could." Jason points his sword at the wreckage of the golden throne. "Was Rita here?"

Zack gives a start. "Where did she go? She was right there next to that silk hanging."

My gaze goes to the wall. Damn. She wasn't just hiding. "She must have escaped through a secret passage when she heard you all coming."

Zack goes over and pushes aside the silk. A network of dark tunnels with several branches stretches out to the distance. "Yup. Secret tunnel." He comes back and pulls me to him, holding me tight like he never wants to let me go.

Fine by me. Mindful of his hurt arm, I lay my cheek against the spot where his heart beats fast and strong, wrapping my arms around his waist and holding on just as tightly.

"Okay . . ." Billy lets his lance drop. "I'm a little new to this superheroing thing, so I'm not sure what the protocol is when a powerful sorceress escapes through a secret passageway in her Moon Palace. Do we go after her?"

"Yeah," Kimberly says. "We should."

But I'm thinking of the pale blankness of Rita's face when she realized I had destroyed her conduit to the power below her Moon Palace. She had been defeated by a moment of mercy—something she had once warned us against. I'm not sure what I saw on her face, and I have no idea what she would have done if the rest of the team hadn't shown up—but I have a feeling that whatever she harbors in her heart now is more complicated than anger or revenge.

Still, I need to be sure that she's no longer a threat to Angel Grove. I raise my head from the warm solidness of Zack's chest. "What happened to the Putties?"

"They kind of . . . melted." Jason sounds puzzled. "And Goldar shrank back to his original size."

"Then we don't need to go after Rita," I say firmly. The Putties must have lost their animating force when I stabbed the jewel. "The scepter is destroyed. She won't be making any more Putties or giant monsters."

"Because of you." Zack's helmet flows away from his face, and the warm expression in his eyes makes my whole body melt. He looks over at the others. "Trini was the one who destroyed Rita's scepter."

Everyone turns to me, and I smile sheepishly. "Actually, it was a team effort."

"Trini, your helmet!" Kimberly says abruptly, sounding aghast. She points at the broken yellow helmet on the stone floor.

"And you're hurt, Zack!" Billy raises his lance again as if ready to defend us against any and all enemies.

"What happened here?" Jason breathes.

Zack smiles down at me. "You want to explain, Trini?"

"I think we . . . won." A rush of tenderness comes over me as I gaze at my friends. "Yes, we definitely did." I take a deep breath. "We just had our first victory as Power Rangers."

CHAPTER THIRTY-FIVE

Don't you have a celebration to attend, Trini?" Zordon looks at me with a puzzled expression.

"I'll join them later." I shift my weight nervously. The rest of the team beamed back to Angel Grove after we debriefed Zordon and Alpha 5 about our fight on the moon, but I told them that I needed to go back to the Power Chamber. "There's something I want to talk to you about."

"What is it that you want to tell me?" Zordon's eyes become intent on me. "Or is it a question that you want to ask me?"

How did he know? *Interstellar warrior scholar*, I remind myself.

"As you Earth youngsters would say," Alpha 5 interjects, "that is my cue to skedaddle."

I laugh. "Literally nobody would *ever* say that."

Alpha 5 is already walking to the door of the Power Chamber. "Nonetheless, this seems like a private conversation."

He's not wrong about that.

I turn back to Zordon. "Rita had the chance to kill me but she didn't." I swallow hard at the memory. "My helmet came off in the battle, so she saw my face." Billy was the one who figured out that I could just morph again to create a new helmet, which is a pretty cool trick, actually.

"Go on," Zordon says.

"When Rita saw my face, she called me Xiao Laohu." My breath catches.

Zordon's expression stills. "Rita used to call her daughter that."

"My nai nai calls me Xiao Laohu too. She says it's a nickname passed down to the girls in our family for many generations." I moisten my lips. "Rita said I had *her* eyes. She didn't say whose, but I thought it had to be her daughter's."

"I see."

"Am I Rita's descendant?" I blurt out. That's not the main question on my mind, but the thought of asking *that* question sends a shiver down my spine. *Is that why I was chosen to be the Yellow Ranger?*

"Who knows after three thousand years?" Zordon says slowly. "But anything is possible."

I nod. I'm not sure I want to know for certain anyway. It's not exactly comfortable to be related to an evil extraterrestrial—even though she might not have been totally evil and our relationship is many generations removed. But I can't help but feel that connection in the way my heart twists when I remember her pain and fury.

"Rita is right, you know," Zordon says, staring at me. "You do have her daughter's eyes. It's been three thousand years, but I still remember how that baby would look at me with those curious black eyes. I couldn't hold her, of course, since I was already trapped in the time warp." He sounds wistful, and I ache for him.

"I couldn't hold the baby," Zordon continues, "but I could honor her father's wish. Her father was my friend, and when he begged me to hide his daughter from Rita, I could not refuse."

My chest constricts. "That's why you let Rita believe you killed the baby." Zordon told us he wanted to save the baby because he couldn't save Rita from the destructive path her own father set her upon. But who's to say that Rita would have done the same with her own child? Even now, she felt the ache of that ancient loss so keenly that she was willing to level a whole town in revenge. Her anger might have been misplaced—but her grief was real. "You wanted to keep Rita from her daughter."

His head tilts as if he hears the accusation in my voice. "Are you saying I was wrong to do what I did?"

"I'm saying the child could have been her redemption." *You have her eyes.* Somehow, I don't think Rita regretted her moment of mercy even though it cost her the power of her scepter. After all, she slipped away without any attempt to avenge her loss. I remember what Nai Nai told me about the story of Chang'e and Hou Yi. "And you could have been the heavenly rabbit."

"Excuse me?" Zordon sounds startled.

Right—context. I must be picking up Nai Nai's habit of dropping mythological references into conversations. "It's an old story my nai nai told me. She said the Lord Archer was mad at his wife for stealing the elixir of immortality meant for him, so he chased after her, but the heavenly rabbit stopped Hou Yi from following Chang'e until he agreed to reconcile with her."

I gaze steadily at Zordon. "Rita said Earth was a place where she was betrayed by everyone she loved. You said the human she fell in love with was your friend. You could have tried to help them understand each other."

"You may be right," he says regretfully, "but it's hard to say. Space and time are strange things. Even though I am here in an interstellar dimension, I cannot see into other universes of what could have been. In another universe, I might have been her friend instead of her enemy. Or she might have been redeemed by a child she had with an Earthling she loved. Or she might have raised her daughter to be a conqueror of worlds like herself." He pauses. "In another universe, she might have killed you instead of showing you mercy."

"But *this* Rita didn't kill me."

"No, she didn't," he says, his gaze level. "Trini Kwan, there is a question you are not asking me."

Damn his wise-mentor ways. I reach up to touch the Saber-tooth Tiger coin, warm against my skin. "You said I was chosen to be the Yellow Ranger." He said he chose me because of my abilities and that the coin chose me because of its affinity with me. But that doesn't answer the question I have now.

I take a deep breath. "Why me?" It is the question I've had from the beginning, but I'm asking for a different reason this time. Now I wonder if I was chosen because I am descended from Zordon's age-old enemy and the child he saved from her destructive legacy.

"I already told you why," he says gently. "I said this team was in need of your heart, and I was right. You showed Rita compassion, and I believe it was your generous heart, rather than a matter of distant ancestry, that stayed her hand against you."

I gnaw my lip. I didn't consider that, but it's true that Rita seemed reluctant to kill me—even before she saw my faint resemblance to her long-lost daughter. I remember then what else she told me. "She said we were connected." *I use my magic to siphon power from the same source.* "Rita told me she draws her power from the Morphin Grid too."

Zordon pales. "Oh."

"Is that . . . ?" I gulp. "Important?" But, of course, it's obvious from Zordon's face that it is.

"I suspected it," he says slowly, "but it's becoming more and more clear what the energy source under Rita's Moon Palace is."

A chill enters my body. "What is it?"

"The Zeo Crystal." He inhales. "It can access the Morphin Grid directly, and it is a very great and very dangerous power."

That does *not* sound good. I remember then that he mentioned it before. The Zeo Crystal killed his mentor.

"What Rita told you was not entirely accurate," he says, seeming to regain his calm. "Rita might have been able to use sorcery to steal energy from the Zeo Crystal, but she cannot wield its full power. A force field protects the Zeo Crystal from being used by anyone who is not purely good."

Okay, that rules out Rita.

"So," Zordon continues, "Rita is not actually connected to the Morphin Grid like you and the others are."

I breathe a small sigh of relief. I'm glad Rita's destructive power is not the same as mine. Then worry sneaks back in. "Do you think it's actually the Zeo Crystal underneath Rita's Moon Palace?" Because I'm not loving the idea of trying to mine the moon for an energy source that could kill us.

He must see what I'm thinking from my expression. "I have already considered this as a possibility. If it is truly the Zeo Crystal, we will find a way to deal with it," he says reassuringly. "Especially since you have formed an excellent team, Trini."

"Me?" I ask, startled.

"Yes. It was you who got the Rangers to understand each other. It was you who saw the connection you all needed to form the Megazord." His eyes crinkle in a smile. "I don't know what team debriefing you were at, but that's what *I* heard from your teammates."

"Oh." I flush. "If you put it like that, I guess I can see why I'm a Power Ranger."

"As I said," Zordon says, "I cannot see into every universe, but I do know that every team needs a ranger with your heart. I suspect that you, Trini Kwan, would be a Power Ranger in each and every universe."

"Not just a Power Ranger." Nai Nai said I needed to accept who I am, and she was right. A slow smile creeps over my face. "The Yellow Ranger."

CHAPTER THIRTY-SIX

Trini, over here!" Billy calls out as I enter Ernie's newly repaired juice bar and gym. Thanks to a large donation from a mysterious benefactor (Zordon, of course), all the buildings and businesses damaged in the Putty attack, including Jason's family hardware store, are being fixed or rebuilt. Soon, everything will be back to normal.

Jason waves, and Kimberly cheers, "Yay, Trini is here!"

Zack grins. "Now the party can start!"

Okay, maybe not *normal* exactly, since my normal isn't having a whole table of friends excited to see me, but I'm not mad about it.

A rush of pure happiness washes over me as I wave back and walk past tables filled with kids from school. Everyone cranes their necks and gapes at me as I make my way to the others. No one seems to know why the timid Asian girl is suddenly sitting with a group who seem to have nothing in common with each other. But I know why, and it's not just because we're a superhero team that just saved Angel Grove from destruction.

It's because we're all friends.

Zack leaps up when I reach them, and a giddy feeling tingles through me. Okay, one of them is actually more than just a friend.

He begins to lean forward but then stops. "Uh, we haven't had this conversation yet, but how do you feel about being all couple-y in public?"

"Depends." I hide a smile. "Are we a couple?"

"Right," he says awkwardly. "We haven't had *that* conversation either."

Jason groans. "Please put him out of his misery, Trini."

"You should have heard him talking about you while we were waiting," Kimberly says.

"Really?" I look at Zack and am thrilled by the blush that steals over his face.

"Yeah," Billy says. "He wouldn't even let us have our drinks until you got here." He glances longingly at his blue smoothie. Kimberly has a pink smoothie, Jason has a mixed red berry juice, and Zack has the juice bar special—a purple drink combining a bunch of different juices and decorated with fruit on toothpicks. Not surprisingly, there's a yellow smoothie sitting before the empty spot at the table.

"Zack got you mango." Kimberly slides it toward me and winks. "He said it was sweet like you."

"I did not." Zack glares at the others. "Trini, what do you say we ditch our so-called friends and go have a real first date?"

I laugh and close the gap between us. Giving him a quick kiss, I say, "To answer your first question, I'm fine with PDA and would love to go on a date with you later." Warmth creeps up my neck and into my face. "And also yes to being a couple. If you were asking."

Zack reaches for my hand. "Oh, I was definitely asking."

We interlace our fingers, and joy shoots through my body. *Zack Taylor is my boyfriend!*

"Glad that's settled," Jason says. "We saved you a seat, Trini." He removes his backpack from the chair and studiously avoids looking at the table next to us.

I glance over to see Aimee sitting with her friends. She has her arms folded and is glowering at me. "Why is Aimee looking at me like she'd like to stab me with a Power Dagger?"

"Because we wouldn't let her steal your seat," Zack explains cheerfully.

Billy drinks from his smoothie. "Oh, this is so good." Then he puts the glass down. "If we want to stay inconspicuous," he remarks, "maybe we should stay away from Power Ranger–themed similes. Maybe avoid weapons, blood, and violence in our figurative language choices too, just to be on the safe side."

"Noted." I say, sitting down. As they all laugh and start talking, I look around the table. It's hard to believe that I'm friends with Kimberly, formerly the snooty new girl; Jason, the popular football captain; Billy, the school genius—*and* dating Zack, my old childhood friend.

Kimberly eventually notices how quiet I am and peers at me. "Everything okay, Trini?"

The others turn to me, and I flush, embarrassed to have been caught in my sappy thoughts. "I'm just happy that we're all friends now." Zack smiles and squeezes my arm.

"Hang on," Jason says with sudden alarm. "Were you thinking about some new threat Zordon told you about?"

I shake my head before I remember the Zeo Crystal.

Jason breathes a sigh of relief, and I decide not to mention the Zeo Crystal for now, but then Billy comments, "Well, there is still the Zeo Crystal."

Oops, there goes my "Don't Freak Out Jason" plan. I should have guessed that Zordon would have discussed it with Billy.

Jason tenses up again. "Excuse me?"

"The what?" Kimberly asks.

Zack raises an eyebrow at me, and I say guiltily, "I guess I do know something about this." Turning to Billy, I ask, "When did Zordon tell you about the Zeo Crystal?"

"At the debrief."

Now that I think about it, I *do* vaguely remember Billy and Zordon muttering on their own while the rest of us formed a human pyramid to reenact our battle against giant Goldar for Alpha 5. We were probably too busy trying to balance and not drop Kimberly to pay attention to Billy's and Zordon's conversation.

Billy sighs. "Didn't anyone pay attention to the debrief?"

"I think I got the gist," Zack says. "Basically, we defeated a giant armored winged monkey, an army of Putties, and a sorceress bent on conquest and revenge."

"That's what I got too," Kimberly agrees, sipping from her smoothie again.

"There was a bit more to it," Billy says dryly, "but don't worry. Zordon said we're unlikely to ever encounter the Zeo Crystal."

Jason relaxes again, and I really hate to do this to him, but . . . "We might actually need to deal with it," I say reluctantly.

"This is not happening," Jason murmurs.

"Zordon says that the energy source underneath Rita's Moon Palace might be the Zeo Crystal."

Billy's eyes widen. "But the Zeo Crystal can connect directly to the Morphin Grid."

I nod uneasily. "Zordon says Rita isn't able to actually wield the Zeo Crystal, so she can't directly access the Morphin Grid." I think about the cracked jewel in her scepter. "She can't take energy from the crystal either, because we destroyed her scepter."

"Still, the Zeo Crystal is supposed to be extremely powerful," Billy says in awe. "This discovery has all kinds of multidimensional ramifications."

"That's just lovely," Zack says, and Kimberly nods in glum agreement.

Billy gazes at us over the rim of his smoothie glass. "Do you know what this means?"

"It means trouble." Jason blows out his breath. "We'll have to—"

"Train!" we all chorus.

"We know," Kimberly says, "and let's not forget that Rita is still out there."

"Can we track her through her scepter even though the jewel is destroyed?" Zack asks.

"That's an interesting possibility," Billy says thoughtfully.

A swell of pride rises in me as I watch my team figure out the problems before us as if we've been working together for years. "Zordon said we'll deal with it, and I think so too," I say confidently.

They turn to me, and one by one, I watch their faces ease into certainty.

"You're right, Trini." Zack puts his arm around me. "We've got this."

"Go, go Power Rangers," Kimberly says softly. "Just trying it out, but I think I like it."

"I do too," Jason says. "This team can handle this crystal-thingy."

"Zeo Crystal," Billy says with long-suffering patience. "And yeah, we *can* handle it."

"A toast," I say, raising my smoothie.

Everyone picks up their own colorful drinks. As we clink our glasses together, I want to yell, "To the Power Rangers," but we're still in a juice bar surrounded by our classmates. So instead I say, "To us!" And I don't whisper it.

Loudly, my friends repeat, "To us!"

Heads turn, but I don't care. We can't announce the fact that we're superheroes, but other than that, we're not worried about what anyone else thinks. We know who we are. We're a team.

I might not know what's next for the Power Rangers—but I know we'll face it together.

ACKNOWLEDGMENTS

Writing this book was a dream come true. I mean—it's the *Mighty Morphin Power Rangers*! I have so many people to thank, so let's get to it. I am so grateful to my editor, Claire Stetzer at Amulet Books, for her excellent editorial eye and collaborative spirit. Claire, you understood my vision for Trini and her story, and I felt so supported in our journey to bring this book into the world! Thank you also to Anne Hetzel, who believed in me and gave me this amazing opportunity (I still can't believe I got to write this book). Thank you to Hasbro as well, and of course, thank you to everyone at Amulet! You're all so wonderful!

Thank you to Boom! Studios for the incredible storytelling you have done with the *Power Rangers* comics. I fell in love with the Power Rangers all over again through your stories. In particular, thank you to Ryan Parrot. Your expertise was invaluable, and did I mention that I'm a big fan of your work?!

No acknowledgement would be complete without thanking my fantastic agents, Christa (Heschke) Cifelli and Daniele Hunter. Christa, I'm still waiting on that pic of you dressed up as the Pink Ranger! Thank you to my husband, Joel, and my children, Liam and Kieran, for all your support. Thank you also to Christina Scheuer for talking over my initial concept and road bumps along the way. You are all my superheroes!

Most importantly, I want to thank the Power Rangers fans. It is an absolute honor to write this book for such an incredible and passionate fan base. I hope you have as much fun reading this book as I did writing it!